THE WORLD'S BEST SERIES

The World's Best Short Stories

I. *Short Story Masters: Early 19th Century*
II. *Short Story Masters: Late 19th & Early 20th Centuries*

Forthcoming:
III. *Famous Stories*
IV. *Fables and Tales*
V, VI. *Genres*
VII. *Characters*
VIII. *Places*
IX. *Cultures*
X. *Research and Reference: Criticism and Indexes*

The World's Best Poetry

Foundation Volumes I-X

Supplements:
I. *Twentieth Century English and American Verse, 1900-1929*
II. *Twentieth Century English and American Verse, 1930-1950*
III. *Critical Companion*
IV. *Minority Poetry of America*
V. *Twentieth Century Women Poets*
VI. *Twentieth Century African and Latin American Verse*
VII. *Twentieth Century Asian Verse*

CoreFiche: *World's Best Drama*

Microfiche with companion reference

The World's Best Short Stories

Anthology & Criticism

Volume II

Short Story Masters
Late 19th & Early
20th Centuries

James, Maupassant, Chekhov, O. Henry,
Crane, Anderson, Joyce, Mansfield

Prepared by
The Editorial Board

Roth Publishing, Inc.
Great Neck, NY

Acknowledgements

Permission to reprint copyrighted stories is gratefully acknowledged to the following:

HAROLD OBER ASSOCIATES INC., for "The Sad Horn Blowers" by Sherwood Anderson. Copyright © 1923 by Harper and Brothers. Copyright renewed 1950 by Eleanor Copenhaver Anderson.

ALFRED A. KNOPF INC., for "The Daughters of the Late Colonel" by Katherine Mansfield, reprinted from *The Short Stories of Katherine Mansfield.* Copyright 1922 by Alfred A. Knopf Inc. and renewed 1950 by John Middleton Murry.

VIKING PENGUIN INC., a division of Penguin Books USA Inc., for "Hands" and "The Untold Lie" from *Winesburg, Ohio* by Sherwood Anderson. Copyright 1919 by B.W. Huebsch, Inc. Copyright renewed 1947 by Eleanor Copenhaver Anderson. All rights reserved. "The Dead" from *Dubliners* by James Joyce. Copyright 1916 by B.W. Huebsch, Inc. Definitive Text Copyright © 1967 by the Estate of James Joyce. All rights reserved.

ISBN 0-89609-304-2
ISBN for 10 Volume Set 0-89609-400-6
Library of Congress Catalog Card Number 89-60440

Manufactured in the U.S.A.

Contents

Preface

The World's Best Short Stories is designed to give both the serious student and the general reader a large selection and broad range of stories from around the world. Its ten volumes organize the stories into seven reader-friendly groupings:

Short Story Masters (Volumes I and II)
Famous Stories (Volume III)
Fables and Tales (Volume IV)
Genres (Volumes V and VI)
Characters (Volume VII)
Places (Volume VIII)
Cultures (Volume IX)

Volume X is a research and reference guide and includes a cumulative index to all the volumes.

The arrangement of the stories suggests the multiple approaches for using these volumes. *Short Story Masters* focuses on the author; it contains stories that demonstrate the development of the short story as a conscious art form. *Famous Stories* is the volume to go to for well-known stories by authors who may or may not themselves be well-known. *Fables and Tales* includes fairy tales and other short non-realistic literature, as well as tales that are ancestors of the short story form. *Genres* is a kind of counterpart to *Short Story Masters*. Whereas *Masters* places the short story in the tradition of an evolving art, *Genres* puts it at the disposal of the general reader and the popular imagination. Included are fixed forms: mysteries, supernatural and ghost stories, detective fiction, science fiction, and other "types" indicative of the wide appeal of short stories.

The later volumes contain stories that are remarkable for a salient feature. The stories in *Characters* are portrait studies: their primary function is to examine the character of the hero or heroine. *Places* compiles stories that evoke a setting in a way that is memorable and important to the being of the story. Finally, *Cultures* uses ethnicity as its backdrop. It carries stories that are informed by their cultural setting.

The organization, variety, and breadth of **The World's Best Short Stories** makes it a unique anthology collection that can be used for study or read for pleasure.

Introduction

Short Story Masters is a two-volume survey that focuses on authors who have significantly contributed to the development of the short story. This second volume, *Late 19th & Early 20th Centuries*, includes stories by eight authors: Henry James, Guy de Maupassant, Anton Chekhov, O. Henry, Stephen Crane, Sherwood Anderson, James Joyce, and Katherine Mansfield. Each author is introduced by a chronology and a critical appreciation; a cumulative index to Volume I (containing stories by E.T.A. Hoffmann, Honoré de Balzác, Prosper Mérimeé, Nathaniel Hawthorne, Edgar Allen Poe, and Nikolai Gogol) and Volume II will be found at the back of this book.

Since the short story as a conscious art form is a nineteenth-century invention, it is no accident that twelve of the fourteen masters in Volumes I and II were born in the nineteenth century (Balzac nearly makes it with a birthdate of 1799; Hoffman was born in 1776). The authors in Volume I (again with the exception of Hoffmann) were all born within a ten year period at the turn of the century. Those in Volume II were born a generation or more later (beginning with James in 1843). Nearly all the stories were written before World War I (only Anderson and Mansfield were actively writing short stories after that). Six of the authors are American, three are French, two British, two Russian, and one German.

What constitutes a "short story master"? For purposes of this anthology, neither abundance nor dedication solely to the short story form. Rather, authors were chosen who helped make the short story evolve from a string of incidents into a fiction having a unified effect. Hawthorne and Poe were the first to be conscious of the short story as a technique, but Hoffmann and Balzac were important predecessors both in their use of short fiction and for struggling with narrative problems associated with short stories. Mérimeé pioneered the story of detached, dispassionate observation and Mauppassant followed him. Indeed, Mauppassant and O. Henry together are names that are nearly synonymous with *short story*. Gogol and Joyce wrote stories that are among the greatest shorts ("The Overcoat" and "The Dead," respectively), while James continually returned to short fiction to stretch its boundaries. Both Chekhov and Mansfield wrote stories of tone and mood; Crane and Anderson brought the technique home and made their stories idiomatically American.

The survey ends before the short story burgeoned in the twentieth century and became for its practitioners as flexible and varied a vessel for thought and feeling as lyric poetry. It is simply outside the scope of *Short Story Masters* to include those authors here: some of them will be included in later volumes of **The World's Best Short Stories**. The authors that have been included in *Masters* belong on anyone's list of contributors to the short story form; and most would be included on anyone's brief list. The intention has been to present a mix of the familiar and unfamiliar, to please with the reacquaintance of old stories and to surprise with the discovery of new ones.

James

1843	April 15. Henry James is born in New York City.
1862	Enrolls in Harvard Law School only to drop out one year later to pursue a full-time literary career.
1864	First piece of published fiction, *A Tragedy of Error*, appears unsigned in *Continental Monthly*. A year later his stories begin to appear in *Atlantic Monthly*; this magazine would remain an important outlet for his writings throughout his career.
1877	After several trans-Atlantic trips and intermediary stops in Paris and Rome, James settles in London.
1878	*The Europeans* is published. This is followed by *Daisy Miller* in 1879, and *Portrait of a Lady* in 1881.
1889-95	After a decade of diminished success, James turns to drama to revive his fortunes and reputation. He writes seven plays during this period.
1898	Purchases a small estate in Sussex; this would remain his principal residency for the rest of his life.
1902	*Wings of the Dove* is published. This is followed by *The Ambassadors* in 1903, and the *Golden Bowl* in 1904.
1911	After the death of his brother William, two autobiographical volumes are issued—*A Small Boy and Others* and *Notes of a Son and Brother*.
1915	Becomes a legal British subject.
1916	February 28. Dies of a heart attack in London.

Henry James

An artist who is at once individual and complete attracts a type of praise which is a sort of disparagement; and even those who overrate him underrate him. For the tendency is always to insist on his art; and by art is often meant merely arrangement. Because a very few colors can be harmoniously arranged in a picture, it is implied that he has not many colors on his palette. And as a study by Henry James was often in its tones something of a nocturne in grey and silver, even his eulogists managed to imply something slight or even thin about his work. Before attempting to touch upon what was really peculiar in the tone of it, it is necessary to correct, and even to contradict, this tenuous impression by the reminder of what he had in common with other great writers. For Henry James must be considered as a great man of letters; and the greatness itself is something which existed in geniuses utterly unlike him. It might seem startling and even comic to compare him to Dickens or even to Shakespeare; but what makes him great is what makes them great, and what alone can make a literary man in the ultimate sense great. It is ideas; the power of generating and making vivid an incessant output of ideas. It is untrue to say that what matters is quality and not quantity. Most men have made one good joke in their lives; but to make jokes as Dickens made them is to be a great man. Many forgotten poets have let fall a lyric with one really perfect image; but when we open any play of Shakespeare, good or bad, at any page, important or unimportant, with the practical certainty of finding some imagery that at least arrests the eye and probably enriches the memory, we are putting our trust in a great man. We are taking at random from a whole store of what are truly to be called great inventions when we think of Mrs. Todgers' wooden leg, or Mr. Fledgby's nose, or Mr. Pecksniff's pinions, or Mr. Swiveller's double-bedded room.

And wide as the distance may seem, it is true, in exactly the same sense, that we are taking at random from a treasury of unique inventions when we think of any two or three of the numberless new ideas of Henry James; of the two people who grew afraid of the mystical coincidence of never meeting; of the man who ceased to exist when he was left alone; of the mysterious unity that ran through all a writer's books like "the figure in the carpet"; of the pearls that were counted false for purposes of respectability and real for purposes of sale; of the sudden supernatural calm created like a garden in the skies by the breakdown of the brain at its busiest; of the wife who would not justify herself to her husband because his whole life was in his chivalry; and so on through a thousand more. Such an idea, though it may be as delicate as an atmosphere, is nevertheless as precise as a pun. It cannot be a coincidence; it is always a creation. He has been attacked for making a great deal of small things; but most of those who attacked him were making a great deal of large nothings. The point that is important about him is not whether the things with which he dealt were as small as some think them, or as large as he could make them; whether it was a fine shade in vulgarity or an occult tenacity of vice; whether it was the restless ten minutes of a visitor coming too early, or the restless ten years of a lover moved too late. The point is that the things were things; that we should have lost them if he had not given them; that no mere perfections of prose would have been a substitute for them; in short, that he never wrote about nothing. Each small notion had the serious thing called value—like a jewel, or, like what is both smaller and more valuable than a jewel, a seed.

His greatness is the greatest thing about him, therefore, and it is of a kind with that of other creative men. But when this large and rather neglected aspect has first been allowed for, it is possible to consider him as a peculiar and fastidious writer. Certainly his work is of a sort to which it is difficult to do justice amid the pulsation of the direct public energies with which most of us who are at all public-spirited feel ourselves concerned today. We should need to be at leisure in those large and vague spaces of gardens and great neglected houses which are the background of so many of his spiritual dramas, to grow fond of the fine shades of a whole science of shadows; and slowly appreciate the multitudinous colors of what seems at first monochrome. Some of his finest stories were ghost stories; and one must be alone to meet a ghost. And yet even the phrase I use indicates its own limitations, for no one seized more swiftly than Henry James the greatness of this awful time, in which we have to think even of ghosts in crowds. He had always been in his innermost being a mystic, and the dead were near to him; and he rose more magnificently, perhaps, than any other to that hour in which the dead were so living and so near to us all. A unique purity and disinterestedness had always attended his pen, and he had the reward of it in realizing moral proportion. He had never failed to see small things; nor did he fall into the more modern and enlightened error of failing to see big ones. He had no difficulty in adjusting his subtlety to the stupendous simplicity of a war for justice; his brain, like a Nasmyth hammer, had not unlearnt in a long course of tapping how to fall and shatter.

That he should feel the prodigy of the Prussian insult to mankind will only surprise those who have read him superficially; or perhaps only read his more superficial sketches. He by no means exhibits manners as more than morals though he may exhibit manners as more than many would think them. In a story like *The Turn of the Screw* he has rather the character of a divine detective. The woman who probes the stagnant secret of the depraved boy and girl is resolved to forgive and, therefore, unable to forget. She is a kind of inquisitor; and her morality is altogether of the old thorough and theological sort. It is a summons to repent and die, rather than a vague capacity to die and repent. And when at the last the deliverance of the boy's soul seems to be delayed by the appearance at the window of his evil genius, "the white face of the damned," it is perhaps the one place in all modern literature where that monosyllable is not a joke. And it is strongly significant that men of any belief and no belief have universally fallen back on such phraseology to find terms for the sneering savagery of the present enemy of Christendom. Honest grey-haired atheists are found judging the Prussian upon the paradoxical principle that there may be heaven, there must be hell. And the nations can find nothing but the language of demonology to describe a certain poison of pride, which is nonetheless a tyranny because it is also a temptation.

Henry James always stood, if ever a man did, for civilization; for that ordered life in which it is possible to tolerate and to understand. His whole world is made out of sympathy; out of a whole network of sympathies. It is a world of wireless telegraphy for the soul; of a psychological brotherhood of men of which the communications could not be cut. Sometimes this sympathy is almost more terrible than antipathy; and his very delicacies produce a sort of promiscuity of minds. Silence becomes a rending revelation. Short spaces or short speeches become overweighted with the awful worth of human life. Minute unto minute uttereth speech, and instant unto instant showeth knowledge. It is only when we have realized how perfect is the poise of such great human art that we can also realize its peril, and know that any outer thing which cannot make it must of necessity destroy it.

It has been customary to talk of Henry James's American origin as something almost antagonistic to the grace and rarity of his art. I am far from sure that this is not to miss a fine and serious strain in it. There is an element of idealism in the American tradition, which is very well typified in the sincere and sometimes exaggerated external deference to women. This particular sort of purity in the perceptions, very marked in him, he had originally owed, I think, to something other than the more mellow and matured European life in which he came afterwards to take his deepest pleasures. The older civilization gave him the wonderful things he wanted; but the wonder was his own.

—from The Common Man *by G.K. Chesterton*

Brooksmith

We are scattered now, the friends of the late Mr. Oliver Offord; but whenever we chance to meet I think we are conscious of a certain esoteric respect for each other. "Yes, you too have been in Arcadia," we seem not too grumpily to allow. When I pass the house in Mansfield Street I remember that Arcadia was there. I don't know who has it now, and don't want to know; it's enough to be so sure that if I should ring the bell there would be no such luck for me as that Brooksmith should open the door. Mr. Offord, the most agreeable, the most attaching of bachelors, was a retired diplomatist, living on his pension and on something of his own over and above; a good deal confined, by his infirmities, to his fireside and delighted to be found there any afternoon in the year, from five o'clock on, by such visitors as Brooksmith allowed to come up. Brooksmith was his butler and his most intimate friend, to whom we all stood, or I should say sat, in the same relation in which the subject of the sovereign finds himself to the prime minister. By having been for years, in foreign lands, the most delightful Englishman any one had ever known, Mr. Offord had in my opinion rendered signal service to his country. But I suppose he had been too much liked—liked even by those who didn't like *it*—so that as people of that sort never get titles or dotations for the horrid things they've *not* done, his principal reward was simply that we went to see him.

Oh we went perpetually, and it was not our fault if he was not overwhelmed with this particular honor. Any visitor who came once came again; to come merely once was a slight nobody, I'm sure, had ever put upon him. His circle therefore was essentially composed of habitués, who were habitués for each other as well as for him, as those of a happy salon should be. I remember vividly every element of the place, down to the intensely Londonish look of the grey opposite houses, in the gap of the white curtains of the high windows, and the exact spot where, on a particular afternoon, I put down my teacup for Brooksmith, lingering an instant, to gather it up as if he were plucking a flower. Mr. Offord's drawing room was indeed Brooksmith's garden, his pruned and tended human parterre, and if we all flourished there and grew well in our places it was largely owing to his supervision.

Many persons have heard much, though most have doubtless seen little, of the famous institution of the salon, and many are born to the depression of knowing that this finest flower of social life refuses to bloom where the English tongue is spoken. The explanation is usually that our women have not the skill to cultivate it—the art to direct through a smiling land, between suggestive shores, a sinuous stream of talk. My affectionate, my pious memory of Mr. Offord contradicts this induction only, I fear, more insidiously to confirm it.

The sallow and slightly smoked drawing room in which he spent so large a portion of the last years of his life certainly deserved the distinguished name; but on the other hand it couldn't be said at all to owe its stamp to any intervention throwing into relief the fact that there was no Mrs. Offord. The dear man had indeed, at the most, been capable of one of those sacrifices to which women are deemed peculiarly apt: he had recognized—under the influence, in some degree, it is true, of physical infirmity—that if you wish people to find you at home you must manage not to be out. He had in short accepted the truth which many dabblers in the social art are slow to learn, that you must really, as they say, take a line, and that the only way as yet discovered of being at home is to stay at home. Finally his own fireside had become a summary of his habits. Why should he ever have left it?—since this would have been leaving what was notoriously pleasantest in London, the compact charmed cluster (thinning away indeed into casual couples) round the fine old last-century chimney-piece which, with the exception of the remarkable collection of miniatures, was the best thing the place contained. Mr. Offord wasn't rich, he had nothing but his pension and the use for life of the somewhat superannuated house.

When I'm reminded by some opposed discomfort of the present hour how perfectly we were all handled there, I ask myself once more what had been the secret of such perfection. One had taken it for granted at the time, for anything that is supremely good produces more acceptance than surprise. I felt we were all happy, but I didn't consider how our happiness was managed. And yet there were questions to be asked, questions that strike me as singularly obvious now that there's nobody to answer them. Mr. Offord had solved the insoluble; he had, without feminine help—save in the sense that ladies were dying to come to him and that he saved the lives of several—established a salon; but I might have guessed that there was a method in his madness, a law in his success. He hadn't hit it off by a mere fluke. There was an art in it all, and how was the art so hidden? Who indeed if it came to that was the occult artist? Launching this enquiry the other day I had already got hold of the tail of my reply. I was helped by the very wonder of some of the conditions that came back to me—those that used to seem as natural as sunshine in a fine climate.

How was it for instance that we never were a crowd, never either too many or too few, always the right people *with* the right people—there must really have been no wrong people at all—always coming and going, never sticking fast nor overstaying, yet never popping in or out with an indecorous familiarity? How was it that we all sat where we wanted and moved when we wanted and met whom we wanted and escaped whom we wanted; joining, according to the accident of inclination, the general circle or falling in with a single talker on a convenient sofa? Why were all the sofas so convenient, the accidents so happy, the talkers so ready, the listeners so willing, the subjects presented to you in a rotation as quickly foreordained as the courses at dinner? A dearth of topics would have been as unheard of as a lapse in the service. These speculations couldn't fail to lead me to the fundamental truth that Brooksmith had been somehow at the bottom of the mystery. If he hadn't established the salon at least he had carried it on. Brooksmith in short was the artist!

We felt this covertly at the time, without formulating it, and were conscious, as an ordered and prosperous community, of his even-handed justice, all untainted with flunkeyism. He had none of that vulgarity—his touch was infinitely fine. The delicacy of it was clear to me on the first occasion my eyes rested, as they were so often to rest again, on the domestic revealed, in the turbid light of the street, by the opening of the house-door. I saw on the spot that though he had plenty of school he carried it without arrogance—he had remained articulate and human. *L'Ecole Anglaise* Mr. Offord used laughingly to call him when, later on, it happened more than once that we had some conversation about him. But I remember accusing Mr. Offord of not doing him quite ideal justice. That he wasn't one of the giants of the school, however, was admitted by my old friend, who really understood him perfectly and was devoted to him, as I shall show; which doubtless poor Brooksmith had himself felt, to his cost, when his value in the market was originally determined. The utility of his class in general is estimated by the foot and the inch, and poor Brooksmith had only about five feet three to put into circulation. He acknowledged the inadequacy of this provision, and I'm sure was penetrated with the everlasting fitness of the relation between service and stature. If *he* had been Mr. Offord he certainly would have found Brooksmith wanting, and indeed the laxity of his employer on this score was one of many things he had had to condone and to which he had at last indulgently adapted himself.

I remember the old man's saying to me: "Oh my servants, if they can live with me a fortnight they can live with me for ever. But it's the first fortnight that tries 'em." It was in the first fortnight for instance that Brooksmith had had to learn that he was exposed to being addressed as "my dear fellow" and "my poor child." Strange and deep must such a probation have been to him, and he doubtless emerged from it tempered and purified. This was written to a certain extent in his appearance; in his spare brisk little person, in his cloistered white face and extraordinarily polished hair, which told of responsibility, looked as if it were kept up to the same high standard as the plate; in his small clear anxious eyes, even in the permitted, though not exactly encouraged, tuft on his chin. "He thinks me rather mad, but I've broken him in, and now he likes the place, he likes the company," said the old man. I embraced this fully after I had become aware that Brooksmith's main characteristic was a deep and shy refinement, though I remember I was rather puzzled when, on another occasion, Mr. Offord remarked: "What he likes is the talk—mingling in the conversation." I was conscious I had never seen Brooksmith permit himself this freedom, but I guessed in a moment that what Mr. Offord alluded to was a participation more intense than any speech could have represented—that of being perpetually present on a hundred legitimate pretexts, errands, necessities, and breathing the very atmosphere of criticism, the famous criticism of life. "Quite an education, sir, isn't it, sir?" he said to me one day at the foot of the stairs when he was letting me out; and I've always remembered the words and the tone as the first sign of the quickening drama of poor Brooksmith's fate. It was indeed an education, but to what was this sensitive young man of thirty-five, of the servile class, being educated?

Practically and inevitably, for the time, to companionship, to the perpetual, the even exaggerated reference and appeal of a person brought to dependence by his time of life and his infirmities and always addicted moreover—this was the exaggeration—to the art of giving you pleasure by letting you do things for him. There were certain things Mr. Offord was capable of pretending he liked you to do even when he didn't—this, I mean, if he thought *you* liked them. If it happened that you didn't either—which was rare, yet might be—of course there were cross-purposes; but Brooksmith was there to prevent their going very far. This was precisely the way he acted as moderator; he averted misunderstandings or cleared them up. He had been capable, strange as it may appear, of acquiring for this purpose an insight into the French tongue, which was often used at Mr. Offord's; for besides being habitual to most of the foreigners, and they were many, who haunted the place or arrived with letters—letters often requiring a little worried consideration, of which

Brooksmith always had cognizance—it had really become the primary language of the master of the house. I don't know if all the *malentendus* were in French, but aknost all the explanations were, and this didn't a bit prevent Brooksmith's following them. I know Mr. Offord used to read passages to him from Montaigne and Saint-Simon, for he read perpetually when alone—when they were alone, that is—and Brooksmith was always about. Perhaps you'll say no wonder Mr. Offord's butler regarded him as "rather mad." However, if I'm not sure what he thought about Montaigne I'm convinced he admired Saint-Simon. A certain feeling for letters must have rubbed off on him from the mere handling of his master's books, which he was always carrying to and fro and putting back in their places.

I often noticed that if an anecdote or a quotation, much more a lively discussion, was going forward, he would, if busy with the fire or the curtains, the lamp or the tea, find a pretext for remaining in the room till the point should be reached. If his purpose was to catch it you weren't discreet, you were in fact scarce human, to call him off, and I shall never forget a look, a hard stony stare—I caught it in its passage—which, one day when there were a good many people in the room, he fastened upon the footman who was helping him in the service and who, in an undertone, had asked him some irrelevant question. It was the only manifestation of harshness I ever observed on Brooksmith's part, and I at first wondered what was the matter. Then I became conscious that Mr. Offord was relating a very curious anecdote, never before perhaps made so public, and imparted to the narrator by an eyewitness of the fact, bearing on Lord Byron's life in Italy. Nothing would induce me to reproduce it here, but Brooksmith had been in danger of losing it. If I ever should venture to reproduce it I shall feel how much I lose in not having my fellow auditor to refer to.

The first day Mr. Offord's door was closed was therefore a dark date in contemporary history. It was raining hard and my umbrella was wet, but Brooksmith received it from me exactly as if this were a preliminary for going upstairs. I observed however that instead of putting it away he held it poised and trickling over the rug, and I then became aware that he was looking at me with deep acknowledging eyes—his air of universal responsibility. I immediately understood—there was scarce need of question and answer as they passed between us. When I took in that our good friend had given up as never before, though only for the occasion, I exclaimed dolefully: "What a difference it will make—and to how many people!"

"I shall be one of them, sir!" said Brooksmith; and that was the beginning of the end.

Mr. Offord came down again, but the spell was broken, the great sign being that the conversation was for the first time not directed. It wandered and stumbled, a little frightened, like a lost child—it had let go the nurse's hand. "The worst of it is that now we shall talk about my health—*c'est la fin de tout,*" Mr. Offord said when he reappeared; and then I recognized what a note of change that would be—for he had never tolerated anything so provincial. We "ran" to each other's health as little as to the daily weather. The talk became ours, in a word—not his; and as ours, even when *he* talked, it could only be inferior. In this form it was a distress to Brooksmith, whose attention now wandered from it altogether: he had so much closer a vision of his master's intimate conditions than our superficialities represented. There were better hours, and he was more in and out of the room, but I could see he was conscious of the decline, almost of the collapse, of our great institution. He seemed to wish to take counsel with me about it, to feel responsible for its going on in some form or other. When for the second period—the first had lasted several days—he had to tell me that his employer didn't receive, I half-expected to hear him say after a moment "Do you think I ought to, sir, in his place?"—as he might have asked me, with the return of autumn, if I thought he had better light the drawing room fire.

He had a resigned philosophic sense of what his guests—our guests, as I came to regard them in our colloquies—would expect. His feeling was that he wouldn't absolutely have approved of himself as a substitute for Mr. Offord; but he was so saturated with the religion of habit that he would have made, for our friends, the necessary sacrifice to the divinity. He would take them on a little further and till they could look about them. I think I saw him also mentally confronted with the opportunity to deal—for once in his life—with some of his own dumb preferences, his limitations of sympathy, *weeding* a little in prospect and returning to a purer tradition. It was not unknown to me that he considered that toward the end of our host's career a certain laxity of selection had crept in.

At last it came to be the case that we all found the closed door more often than the open one; but even when it was closed Brooksmith managed a crack for me to squeeze through; so that practically I never turned away without having paid a visit. The difference simply came to be that the visit was to Brooksmith. It took place in the hall, at the familiar foot of the stairs, and we didn't sit down, at least Brooksmith didn't; moreover it was devoted wholly to one topic and always had the air of being already over—beginning, so to say, at the end. But it was always interesting—it always gave me something to think about. It's true that the subject of my meditation was ever the same—ever "It's all very well but what *will* become of Brooksmith?" Even my private answer to this question left me still unsatisfied. No doubt Mr. Offord would provide for him, but *what* would he provide?—that was the great point. He couldn't provide society; and society had become a necessity of Brooksmith's nature. I must add that he never showed a symptom of what I may call sordid solicitude—anxiety on his own account. He was rather livid and intensely grave, as befitted a man before whose eyes the "shade of that which once was great" was passing away. He had the solemnity of a person winding up, under depressing circumstances, a long-established and celebrated business; he was a kind of social executor or liquidator. But his manner seemed to testify exclusively to the uncertainty of *our* future. I couldn't in those days have afforded it—I lived in two rooms in Jermyn Street and didn't "keep a man"; but even if my income had permitted I shouldn't have ventured to say to Brooksmith (emulating Mr. Offord) "My dear fellow, I'll take you on." The whole tone of our intercourse was so much more an implication that it was *I* who should now want a lift. Indeed there was a tacit assurance in Brooksmith's whole attitude that he should have me on his mind.

One of the most assiduous members of our circle had been Lady Kenyon, and I remember his telling me one day that her ladyship had in spite of her own infirmities, lately much aggravated, been in person to inquire. In answer to this I remarked that she would feel it more than any one. Brooksmith had a pause before saying in a certain tone—there's no reproducing some of his tones—"I'll go and see her." I went to see her myself and learned he had waited on her; but when I said to her, in the form of a joke but with a core of earnest, that when all was over some of us ought to combine, to club together, and set Brooksmith up on his own account, she replied a trifle disappointingly: "Do you mean in a public-house?" I looked at her in a way that I think Brooksmith himself would have approved, and then I answered: "Yes, the Offord Arms." What I had meant of course was that for the love of art itself we ought to look to it that such a peculiar faculty and so much acquired experience shouldn't be wasted. I really think that if we had caused a few black-edged cards to be struck off and circulated—"Mr. Brooksmith will continue to receive on the old premises from four to seven; business carried on as usual during the alterations"—the greater number of us would have rallied.

Several times he took me upstairs—always by his own proposal—and our dear old friend, in bed (in a curious flowered and brocaded casaque which made him, especially as his head was tied up in a handkerchief to match, look, to my imagination, like the dying Voltaire) held for ten minutes a sadly shrunken little salon. I felt indeed each time as if I were attending the last *coucher* of some social sovereign. He was royally whimsical about his sufferings and not at all concerned—quite as if the Constitution provided for the case—about his successor. He glided over *our* sufferings charmingly, and none of his jokes—it was a gallant abstention, some of them would have been so easy—were at our expense. Now and again, I confess, there was one at Brooksmith's, but so pathetically sociable as to make the excellent man look at me in a way that seemed to say: "Do exchange a glance with me, or I shan't be able to stand it." What he wasn't able to stand was not what Mr. Offord said about him, but what he wasn't able to say in return. His idea of conversation for himself was giving you the convenience of speaking to him; and when he went to "see" Lady Kenyon for instance it was to carry her the tribute of his receptive silence. Where would the speech of his betters have been if proper service had been a manifestation of sound? In that case the fundamental difference would have had to be shown by *their* dumbness, and many of them, poor things, were dumb enough without that provision. Brooksmith took an unfailing interest in the preservation of the fundamental difference; it was the thing he had most on his conscience.

What had become of it however when Mr. Offord passed away like any inferior person—was relegated to eternal stillness after the manner of a butler above-stairs. His aspect on the event—for the several successive days—may be imagined, and the multiplication by funereal observance of the things he didn't say. When everything was over—it was late the same day—I knocked at the door of the house of mourning as I so often had done before. I could never call on Mr. Offord again, but I had come literally to call on Brooksmith. I wanted to ask him if there was anything I could do for him, tainted with vagueness as this enquiry could only be. My presumptuous dream of taking him into my own service had died away: my service wasn't worth his being taken into. My offer could only be to help him to find another place, and yet there was an indelicacy, as it were, in taking for granted that his thoughts would immediately be fixed on another. I had a hope that he would be able to give his life a different form—though certainly not the form, the frequent result of such bereavements, of his setting up a little shop. That would have been dreadful; for I should have wished to forward any enterprise he might embark in, yet how could I have brought myself to go and pay him shillings and take back coppers over a counter? My visit then was simply an intended compliment. He took it as such, gratefully and with all the tact in the world. He knew I really couldn't help him and that I knew he knew I couldn't; but we discussed the situation—with a good deal of elegant generality—at the foot of the stairs, in the hall already dismantled, where I had so often discussed other situations with him. The executors were in possession, as was still more apparent when he made me pass for a few minutes into the dining room, where various objects were muffled up for removal.

Two definite facts, however, he had to communicate; one being that he was to leave the house forever that night (servants, for some mysterious reason, seem always to depart by night), and the other—he mentioned it only at the last and with hesitation—that he was already aware his late master had left him a legacy of eighty pounds. "I'm very glad," I said, and Brooksmith was of the same mind: "It was so like him to think of me." This was all that passed between us on the subject, and I know nothing of his judgement of Mr. Offord's memento. Eighty pounds are always eighty pounds, and no one has ever left *me* an equal sum; but, all the same, for Brooksmith, I was disappointed. I don't know what I had expected, but it was almost a shock. Eighty pounds might stock a small shop—a *very* small shop; but, I repeat, I couldn't bear to think of that. I asked my friend if he had been able to save a little, and he replied: "No, sir; I've had to do things." I didn't enquire what things they might have been; they were his own affair, and I took his word for them as assentingly as if he had had the greatness of an ancient house to keep up; especially as there was something in his manner that seemed to convey a prospect of further sacrifice.

"I shall have to turn round a bit, sir—I shall have to look about me," he said; and then he added indulgently, magnanimously: "If you should happen to hear of anything for me—"

I couldn't let him finish; this was, in its essence, too much in the really grand manner. It would be a help to my getting him off my mind to be able to pretend I *could* find the right place, and that help he wished to give me, for it was doubtless painful to him to see me in so false a position. I interposed with a few words to the effect of how well aware I was that wherever he should go, whatever he should do, he would miss our old friend terribly—miss him even more than I should, having been with him so much more. This led him to make the speech that has remained with me as the very text of the whole episode.

"Oh sir, it's sad for *you*, very sad indeed, and for a great many gentlemen and ladies; that it is, sir. But for me, sir, it is, if I may say so, still graver even than that: it's just the loss of something that was everything. For me, sir," he went on with rising tears, "he was just *all*, if you know what I mean, sir. You have others, sir, I dare say—not that I would have you understand me to speak of them as in any way tantamount. But you have the pleasures of society, sir; if it's only in talking about him, sir, as I dare say you do freely—for all his blest memory has to fear from it—with gentlemen and ladies who have had the same honor. That's not for me, sir, and I've to keep my associations to myself. Mr. Offord was *my* society, and now, you see, I just haven't any. You go back to conversation, sir, after all, and I go back to my place," Brooksmith stammered, without exaggerated irony or dramatic bitterness, but with a flat unstudied veracity and his hand on the knob of the street door. He turned it to let me out and then he added: "I just go downstairs, sir, again, and I stay there."

"My poor child," I replied in my emotion, quite as Mr. Offord used to speak, "my dear fellow, leave it to me: *we'll* look after you, we'll all do something for you."

"Ah if you could give me some one *like* him! But there ain't two such in the world," Brooksmith said as we parted.

He had given me his address—the place where he would be to be heard of. For a long time I had no occasion to make use of the information: he proved on trial so very difficult a case. The people who knew him and had known Mr. Offord didn't want to take him, and yet I couldn't bear to try to thrust him among strangers—strangers to his past when not to his present. I spoke to many of our old friends about him and found them all governed by the odd mixture of feelings of which I myself was conscious—as well as disposed, further, to entertain a suspicion that he was "spoiled," with which I then would have nothing to do. In plain terms a certain embarrassment, a sensible awkwardness when they thought of it, attached to the idea of using him as a menial: they had met him so often in society. Many of them would have asked him, and did ask him, or rather did ask me to ask him, to come and see them; but a mere visiting list was not what I wanted for him. He was too short for people who were very particular; nevertheless I heard of an opening in a diplomatic household which led me to write him a note, though I was looking much less for something grand than for something human. Five days later I heard from him. The secretary's wife had decided, after keeping him waiting till then, that she couldn't take a servant out of a house in which there hadn't been a lady. The note had a P.S.: "It's a good job there wasn't, sir, such a lady as some."

A week later he came to see me and told me he was "suited," committed to some highly respectable people—they were something quite immense in the City—who lived on the Bayswater side of the Park. "I dare say it will be rather poor, sir," he admitted; "but I've seen the fireworks, haven't I, sir?—it can't be fireworks *every* night. After Mansfield Street there ain't much choice." There was a certain amount, however, it seemed; for the following year, calling one day on a country cousin, a lady of a certain age who was spending a fortnight in town with some friends of her own, a family unknown to me and resident in Chester Square, the door of the house was opened, to my surprise and gratification, by Brooksmith in person. When I came out I had some conversation with him from which I gathered that he had found the large City people too dull for endurance, and I guessed, though he didn't say it, that he had found them vulgar as well. I don't know what judgement he would have passed on his actual patrons if my relative hadn't been their friend; but in view of that connection he abstained from comment.

None was necessary, however, for before the lady in question brought her visit to a close they honored me with an invitation to dinner, which I accepted. There was a largeish party on the occasion, but I confess I thought of Brooksmith rather more than of the seated company. They required no depth of attention—they were all referable to usual irredeemable inevitable types. It was the world of cheerful commonplace and conscious gentility and prosperous density, a fun-fed material insular world, a world of hideous florid plate and ponderous order and thin conversation. There wasn't a word said about Byron, or even about a minor bard then much in view. Nothing would have induced me to look at Brooksmith in the course of the repast, and I felt sure that not even my overturning the wine would have induced him to meet my eye. We were in intellectual sympathy—we felt, as regards each other, a degree of social responsibility. In short we had been in Arcadia together, and we had both come to *this!* No wonder we were ashamed to be confronted. When he had helped on my overcoat, as I was going away, we parted, for the first time since the earliest days of Mansfield Street, in silence. I thought he looked lean and wasted, and I guessed that his new place wasn't more "human" than his previous one. There was plenty of beef and beer, but there was no reciprocity. The question for him to have asked before accepting the position wouldn't have been "How many footmen are kept?" but "How much imagination?"

The next time I went to the house—I confess it wasn't very soon—I encountered his successor, a personage who evidently enjoyed the good fortune of never having quitted his natural level. Could any be higher? he seemed to ask—over the heads of three footmen and even of some visitors. He made me feel as if Brooksmith were dead; but I didn't dare to enquire—I couldn't have borne his "I haven't the least idea, sir." I dispatched a note to the address that worthy had given me after Mr. Offord's death, but I received no answer. Six months later however I was favored with a visit from an elderly dreary dingy person who introduced herself to me as Mr. Brooksmith's aunt and from whom I learned that he was out of place and out of health and had allowed her to come and say to me that if I could spare half an hour to look in at him he would take it as a rare honor.

I went the next day—his messenger had given me a new address—and found my friend lodged in a short sordid street in Marylebone, one of those corners of London that wear the last expression of sickly meanness. The room into which I was shown was above the small establishment of a dyer and cleaner who had inflated kid gloves and discolored shawls in his shop-front. There was a great deal of grimy infant life up and down the place, and there was a hot moist smell within, as of the "boiling" of dirty linen. Brooksmith sat with a blanket over his legs at a clean little window where, from behind stiff bluish-white curtains, he could look across at a huckster's and a tinsmith's and a small greasy public-house. He had passed through an illness and was convalescent, and his mother, as well as his aunt, was in attendance on him. I liked the nearer relative, who was bland and intensely humble, but I had my doubts of the remoter, whom I connected perhaps unjustly with the opposite public-house—she seemed somehow greasy with the same grease—and whose furtive eye followed every movement of my hand as if to see if it weren't going into my pocket. It didn't take this direction—I couldn't, unsolicited, put myself at that sort of ease with

Brooksmith. Several times the door of the room opened and mysterious old women peeped in and shuffled back again. I don't know who they were; poor Brooksmith seemed encompassed with vague prying beery females.

He was vague himself, and evidently weak, and much embarrassed, and not an allusion was made between us to Mansfield Street. The vision of the salon of which he had been an ornament hovered before me however, by contrast, sufficiently. He assured me he was really getting better, and his mother remarked that he would come round if he could only get his spirits up. The aunt echoed this opinion, and I became more sure that in her own case she knew where to go for such a purpose. I'm afraid I was rather weak with my old friend, for I neglected the opportunity, so exceptionally good, to rebuke the levity which had led him to throw up honorable positions—fine stiff steady berths in Bayswater and Belgravia, with morning prayers, as I knew, attached to one of them. Very likely his reasons had been profane and sentimental; he didn't want morning prayers, he wanted to be somebody's dear fellow; but I couldn't be the person to rebuke him. He shufffed these episodes out of sight—I saw he had no wish to discuss them. I noted further, strangely enough, that it would probably be a questionable pleasure for him to see me again: he doubted now even of my power to condone his aberrations. He didn't wish to have to explain; and his behavior was likely in future to need explanation. When I bade him farewell he looked at me a moment with eyes that said everything: "How can I talk about those exquisite years in this place, before these people, with the old women poking their heads in? It was very good of you to come to see me; it wasn't my idea—*she* brought you. We've said everything; it's over; you'll lose all patience with me, and I'd rather you shouldn't see the rest." I sent him some money in a letter the next day, but I saw the rest only in the light of a barren sequel.

A whole year after my visit to him I became aware once, in dining out, that Brooksmith was one of the several servants who hovered behind our chairs. He hadn't opened the door of the house to me, nor had I recognized him in the array of retainers in the hall. This time I tried to catch his eye, but he never gave me a chance, and when he handed me a dish I could only be careful to thank him audibly. Indeed I partook of two *entrées* of which I had my doubts, subsequently converted into certainties, in order not to snub him. He looked well enough in health, but much older, and wore in an exceptionally marked degree the glazed and expressionless mask of the

British domestic *de race.* I saw with dismay that if I hadn't known him I should have taken him, on the showing of his countenance, for an extravagant illustration of irresponsive servile gloom. I said to myself that he had become a reactionary, gone over to the Philistines, thrown himself into religion, the religion of his "place," like a foreign lady *sur le retour.* I divined moreover that he was only engaged for the evening—he had become a mere waiter, had joined the band of the white-waistcoated who "go out." There was something pathetic in this fact—it was a terrible vulgarization of Brooksmith. It was the mercenary prose of butlerhood; he had given up the struggle for the poetry. If reciprocity was what he had missed where was the reciprocity now? Only in the bottoms of the wine-glasses and the five shillings—or whatever they get—clapped into his hand by the permanent man. However, I supposed he had taken up a precarious branch of his profession because it after all sent him less downstairs. His relations with London society were more superficial, but they were of course more various. As I went away on this occasion I looked out for him eagerly among the four or five attendants whose perpendicular persons, fluting the walls of London passages, are supposed to lubricate the process of departure; but he was not on duty. I asked one of the others if he were not in the house, and received the prompt answer: "Just left, sir. Anything I can do for you, sir?" I wanted to say "Please give him my kind regards"; but I abstained—I didn't want to compromise him; and I never came across him again.

Often and often, in dining out, I looked for him, sometimes accepting invitations on purpose to multiply the chances of my meeting him. But always in vain; so that as I met many other members of the casual class over and over again I at last adopted the theory that he always procured a list of expected guests beforehand and kept away from the banquets which he thus learned I was to grace. At last I gave up hope, and one day at the end of three years I received another visit from his aunt. She was drearier and dingier, almost squalid, and she was in great tribulation and want. Her sister, Mrs. Brooksmith, had been dead a year, and three months later her nephew had disappeared. He had always looked after her a bit—since her troubles; I never knew what her troubles had been—and now she hadn't so much as a petticoat to pawn. She had also a niece, to whom she had been everything before her troubles, but the niece had treated her most shameful. These were details; the great and romantic fact was Brooksmith's final evasion of his fate. He had gone out to wait one evening as usual, in a white waistcoat she had done up for him with her own hands—being due at a large party up Kensington way. But he had never come home again and had never arrived at the large party, nor at any party that any one could make out. No trace of him had come to light—no gleam of the white waistcoat had pierced the obscurity of his doom. This news was a sharp shock to me, for I had my ideas about his real destination. His aged relative had promptly, as she said, guessed the worst. Somehow and somewhere he had got out of the way altogether, and now I trust that, with characteristic deliberation, he is changing the plates of the immortal gods. As my depressing visitant also said, he never *had* got his spirits up. I was fortunately able to dismiss her with her own somewhat improved. But the dim ghost of poor Brooksmith is one of those that I see. He had indeed been spoiled.

The Real Thing

I

When the porter's wife (she used to answer the house-bell), announced "A gentleman—with a lady, sir," I had, as I often had in those days, for the wish was father to the thought, an immediate vision of sitters. Sitters my visitors in this case proved to be; but not in the sense I should have preferred. However, there was nothing at first to indicate that they might not have come for a portrait. The gentleman, a man of fifty, very high and very straight, with a moustache slightly grizzled and a dark grey walking-coat admirably fitted, both of which I noted professionally—I don't mean as a barber or yet as a tailor—would have struck me as a celebrity if celebrities often were striking. It was a truth of which I had for some time been conscious that a figure with a good deal of frontage was, as one might say, almost never a public institution. A glance at the lady helped to remind me of this paradoxical law: she also looked too distinguished to be a "personality." Moreover one would scarcely come across two variations together.

Neither of the pair spoke immediately—they only prolonged the preliminary gaze which suggested that each wished to give the other a chance. They were visibly shy; they stood there letting me take them in—which, as I afterwards perceived, was the most practical thing they could have done. In this way their embarrassment served their cause. I had seen people painfully reluctant to mention that they desired anything so gross as to be represented on canvas; but the scruples of my new friends appeared almost insurmountable. Yet the gentleman might have said "I should like a portrait of my wife," and the lady might have said "I should like a portrait of my husband." Perhaps they were not husband and wife—this naturally would make the matter more delicate. Perhaps they wished to be done together—in which case they ought to have brought a third person to break the news.

"We come from Mr. Rivet," the lady said at last, with a dim smile which had the effect of a moist sponge passed over a "sunk" piece of painting, as well as of a vague allusion to vanished beauty. She was as tall and straight, in her degree, as her companion, and with ten years less to carry. She looked as sad as a woman could look whose face was not charged with expression; that is, her tinted oval mask showed friction as an exposed surface shows it. The hand of time had played over her freely, but only to simplify. She was slim and stiff, and so well dressed, in dark blue cloth, with lappets and pockets and buttons, that it was clear she employed the same tailor as her husband. The couple had an indefinable air of prosperous thrift—they evidently got a good deal of luxury for their money. If I was to be one of their luxuries it would behove me to consider my terms.

"Ah, Claude Rivet recommended me?" I inquired; and I added that it was very kind of him, though I could reflect that, as he only painted landscape, this was not a sacrifice.

The lady looked very hard at the gentleman, and the gentleman looked round the room. Then staring at the floor a moment and stroking his moustache, he rested his pleasant eyes on me with the remark: "He said you were the right one."

"I try to be, when people want to sit."

"Yes, we should like to," said the lady anxiously.

"Do you mean together?"

My visitors exchanged a glance. "If you could do anything with *me,* I suppose it would be double," the gentleman stammered.

"Oh yes, there's naturally a higher charge for two figures than for one."

"We would like to make it pay," the husband confessed.

"That's very good of you," I returned, appreciating so unwonted a sympathy—for I supposed he meant pay the artist.

A sense of strangeness seemed to dawn on the lady. "We mean for the illustrations—Mr. Rivet said you might put one in."

"Put one in—an illustration?" I was equally confused.

"Sketch her off, you know," said the gentleman, coloring.

It was only then that I understood the service Claude Rivet had rendered me; he had told them that I worked in black and white, for magazines, for storybooks, for sketches of contemporary life, and consequently had frequent employment for models. These things were true, but it was not less true (I may confess it now—whether because the aspiration was to lead to everything or to nothing I leave the reader to guess), that I couldn't get the honors, to say nothing of the emoluments, of a great painter of portraits out of my head. My "illustrations" were my potboilers; I looked to a different branch of art (far and away the most interesting it had always seemed to me), to perpetuate my fame. There was no shame in looking to it also to make my fortune; but that fortune was by so much further from being made from the moment my visitors wished to be "done" for nothing. I was disappointed, for in the pictorial sense I had immediately *seen* them. I had seized their type—I had already settled what I would do with it. Something that wouldn't absolutely have pleased them, I afterwards reflected.

"Ah, you're—you're—a—?" I began, as soon as I had mastered my surprise. I couldn't bring out the dingy word "models"; it seemed to fit the case so little.

"We haven't had much practice," said the lady.

"We've go to *do* something, and we've thought that an artist in your line might perhaps make something of us," her husband threw off. He further mentioned that they didn't know many artists and that they had gone first, on the off chance (he painted views of course, but sometimes put in figures—perhaps I remembered), to Mr. Rivet, whom they had met a few years before at a place in Norfolk where he was sketching.

"We used to sketch a little ourselves," the lady hinted.

"It's very awkward, but we absolutely *must* do something," her husband went on.

"Of course, we're not so *very* young," she admitted, with a wan smile.

With the remark that I might as well know something more about them, the husband had handed me a card extracted from a neat new pocket-book (their appurtenances were all of the freshest) and inscribed with the words "Major Monarch."

Impressive as these words were they didn't carry my knowledge much further; but my visitor presently added: "I've left the army, and we've had the misfortune to lose our money. In fact our means are dreadfully small."

"It's an awful bore," said Mrs. Monarch.

They evidently wished to be discreet—to take care not to swagger because they were gentlefolks. I perceived they would have been willing to recognize this as something of a drawback, at the same time that I guessed at an underlying sense—their consolation in adversity—that they *had* their points. They certainly had; but these advantages struck me as preponderantly social; such for instance as would help to make a drawing room look well. However, a drawing room was always, or ought to be, a picture.

In consequence of his wife's allusion to their age Major Monarch observed: "Naturally, it's more for the figure that we thought of going in. We can still hold ourselves up." On the instant I saw that the figure was indeed their strong point. His "naturally" didn't sound vain, but it lighted up the question. "*She* has got the best," he continued, nodding at his wife, with a pleasant after-dinner absence of circumlocution. I could only reply, as if we were in fact sitting over our wine, that this didn't prevent his own from being very good; which led him in turn to rejoin: "We thought that if you ever have to do people like us, we might be something like it. *She*, particularly—for a lady in a book, you know."

I was so amused by them that, to get more of it, I did my best to take their point of view; and though it was an embarrassment to find myself appraising physically, as if they were animals on hire or useful blacks, a pair of whom I should have expected to meet only in one of the relations in which criticism is tacit, I looked at Mrs. Monarch judicially enough to be able to exclaim, after a moment, with conviction: "Oh yes, a lady in a book!" She was singularly like a bad illustration.

"We'll stand up, if you like," said the Major; and he raised himself before me with a really grand air.

I could take his measure at a glance—he was six feet two and a perfect gentleman. It would have paid any club in process of formation and in want of a stamp to engage him at a salary to stand in the principal window. What struck me immediately was that in coming to me they had rather missed their vocation; they could surely have been turned to better account for advertising purposes. I couldn't of course see the thing in detail, but I could see them make someone's fortune—I don't mean their own. There was something in them for a waistcoat-maker, an hotel-keeper, or a soap-vendor. I could imagine "We always use it" pinned on their bosoms with the greatest effect; I had a vision of the promptitude with which they would launch a *table d'hôte.*

Mrs. Monarch sat still, not from pride but from shyness, and presently her husband said to her: "Get up my dear and show how smart you are." She obeyed, but she had no need to get up to show it. She walked to the end of the studio, and then she came back blushing, with her fluttered eyes on her husband. I was reminded of an incident I had accidentally had a glimpse of in Paris—being with a friend there, a dramatist about to produce a play—when an actress came to him to ask to be intrusted with a part. She went through the paces before him, walked up and down as Mrs. Monarch was doing. Mrs. Monarch did it quite as well, but I abstained from applauding. It was very odd to see such people apply for such poor pay. She looked as if she had ten thousand a year. Her husband had used the word that described her: she was, in the London current jargon, essentially and typically "smart." Her figure was, in the same order of ideas, conspicuously and irreproachably "good." For a woman of her age her waist was surprisingly small; her elbow moreover had the orthodox crook. She held her head at the conventional angle; but why did she come to *me*? She ought to have tried on jackets at a big shop. I feared my visitors were not only destitute, but "artistic"—which would be a great complication. When she sat down again I thanked her, observing that what a draughtsman most valued in his model was the faculty of keeping quiet.

"Oh, *she* can keep quiet," said Major Monarch. Then he added, jocosely: "I've always kept her quiet."

"I'm not a nasty fidget, am I?" Mrs. Monarch appealed to her husband.

He addressed his answer to me. "Perhaps it isn't out of place to mention—because we ought to be quite businesslike, oughtn't we?—that when I married her she was known as the Beautiful Statue."

"Oh dear!" said Mrs. Monarch, ruefully.

"Of course I should want a certain amount of expression," I rejoined.

"Of *course*!" they both exclaimed.

"And then I suppose you know that you'll get awfully tired."

"Oh, we *never* get tired!" they eagerly cried.

"Have you had any kind of practice?"

They hesitated—they looked at each other. "We've been photographed, *immensely*," said Mrs. Monarch.

"She means the fellows have asked us," added the Major.

"I see—because you're so good-looking."

"I don't know what they thought, but they were always after us."

"We always got our photographs for nothing," smiled Mrs. Monarch.

"We might have brought some, my dear," her husband remarked.

"I'm not sure we have any left. We've given quantities away," she explained to me.

"With our autographs and that sort of thing," said the Major.

"Are they to be got in the shops?" I inquired, as a harmless pleasantry.

"Oh, yes; *hers*—they used to be."

"Not now," said Mrs. Monarch, with her eyes on the floor.

II

I could fancy the "sort of thing" they put on the presentation copies of their photographs, and I was sure they wrote a beautiful hand. It was odd how quickly I was sure of everything that concerned them. If they were now so poor as to have to earn shillings and pence, they never had had much of a margin. Their good looks had been their capital, and they had good-humoredly made the most of the career that this resource marked out for them. It was in their faces, the blankness, the deep intellectual repose of the twenty years of country-house visiting which had given them pleasant intonations. I could see the sunny drawing rooms, sprinkled with periodicals she didn't read, in which Mrs. Monarch had continuously sat; I could see the wet shrubberies in which she had walked, equipped to admiration for either exercise. I could see the rich covers the Major had helped to shoot and the wonderful garments in which, late at night, he repaired to the smoking room to talk about them. I could imagine their leggings and waterproofs, their knowing tweeds and rugs, their rolls of sticks and cases of tackle and neat umbrellas; and I could evoke the exact appearance of their servants and the compact variety of their luggage on the platforms of country stations.

They gave small tips, but they were liked; they didn't do anything themselves, but they were welcome. They looked so well everywhere; they gratified the general relish for stature, complexion, and "form." They knew it without fatuity or vulgarity, and they respected themselves in consequence. They were not superficial; they were thorough and kept themselves up—it had been their line. People with such a taste for activity had to have some line. I could feel how, even in a dull house, they could have been counted upon for cheerfulness. At present something had happened—it didn't matter what, their little income had grown less, it had grown least—and they had to do something for pocket money. Their friends liked them, but didn't like to support them. There was something about them that represented credit—their clothes, their manners, their type; but if credit is a large empty pocket in which an occasional chink reverberates, the chink at least must be audible. What they wanted of me was to help to make it so. Fortunately they had no children—I soon divined that. They would also perhaps wish our relations to be kept secret: this was why it was "for the figure"—the reproduction of the face would betray them.

I liked them—they were so simple; and I had no objection to them if they would suit. But, somehow, with all their perfections I didn't easily believe in them. After all they were amateurs, and the ruling passion of my life was the detestation of the amateur. Combined with this was another perversity—an innate preference for the represented subject over the real one: the defect of the real one was so apt to be a lack of representation. I liked things that appeared; then one was sure. Whether they *were* or not was a subordinate and almost always a profitless question. There were other considerations, the first of which was that I already had two or three people in use, notably a young person with big feet, in alpaca, from Kilburn, who for a couple of years had come to me regularly for my illustrations and with whom I was still—perhaps ignobly—satisfied. I frankly explained to my visitors how the case stood; but they had taken more precautions than I supposed. They had reasoned out their opportunity, for Claude Rivet had told them of the projected *édition de luxe* of one of the writers of our day—the rarest of the novelists—who, long neglected by the multitudinous vulgar and dearly prized by the attentive (need I mention Philip Vincent?) had had the happy fortune of seeing, late in life, the dawn and then the full light of a higher criticism—an estimate in which, on the part of the public, there was something really of expiation. The edition in question, planned by a publisher of taste, was practically an act of high reparation; the woodcuts with which it was to be enriched were the homage of English art to one of the most independent representatives of English letters. Major and Mrs. Monarch confessed to me that they had hoped I might be able to work *them* into my share of the enterprise. They knew I was to do the first of the books, *Rutland Ramsay*, but I had to make clear to them that my participation in the rest of the affair—this first book was to be a test—was to depend on the satisfaction I should give. If this should be limited my employers would drop me without a scruple. It was therefore a crisis for me, and naturally I was making special preparation, looking about for new people, if they should be necessary, and securing the best types. I admitted however that I should like to settle down to two or three good models who would do for everything.

"Should we have often to—a—put on special clothes?" Mrs. Monarch timidly demanded.

"Dear, yes—that's half the business."

"And should we be expected to supply our own costumes?"

"Oh, no; I've got a lot of things. A painter's models put on—or put off—anything he likes."

"And do you mean—a—the same?"

"The same?"

Mrs. Monarch looked at her husband again.

"Oh, she was just wondering," he explained, "if the costumes are in *general* use." I had to confess that they were, and I mentioned further that some of them (I had a lot of genuine, greasy last-century things) had served their time, a hundred years ago, on living, world-stained men and women. "We'll put on anything that *fits*," said the Major.

"Oh, I arrange that—they fit in the pictures."

"I'm afraid I should do better for the modern books. I would come as you like," said Mrs. Monarch.

"She has got a lot of clothes at home: they might do for contemporary life," her husband continued.

"Oh, I can fancy scenes in which you'd be quite natural." And indeed I could see the slipshod rearrangements of stale properties—the stories I tried to produce pictures for without the exasperation of reading them—whose sandy tracts the good lady might help to people. But I had to return to the fact that for this sort of work—the daily mechanical grind—I was already equipped; the people I was working with were fully adequate.

"We only thought we might be more like *some* characters," said Mrs. Monarch mildly, getting up.

Her husband also rose; he stood looking at me with a dim wistfulness that was touching in so fine a man. "Wouldn't it be rather a pull sometimes to have—a—to have—?" He hung fire; he wanted me to help him by phrasing what he meant. But I couldn't—I didn't know. So he brought it out, awkwardly: "The *real* thing; a gentleman, you know, or a lady." I was quite ready to give a general assent—I admitted that there was a great deal in that. This encouraged Major Monarch to say, following up his appeal with an unacted gulp: "It's awfully hard—we've tried everything." The gulp was communicative; it proved too much for his wife. Before I knew it Mrs. Monarch had dropped again upon a divan and burst into tears. Her husband sat down beside her, holding one of her hands; whereupon she quickly dried her eyes with the other, while I felt embarrassed as she looked up at me. "There isn't a confounded job I haven't applied for—waited for—prayed for. You can fancy we'd be pretty bad at first. Secretaryships and that sort of thing? You might as well ask for a peerage. I'd be *anything*—I'm strong; a messenger or a coalheaver. I'd put on a gold-laced cap and open carriage doors in front of the haberdasher's; I'd hang about a station, to carry portmanteaux; I'd be a postman. But they won't *look* at you; there are thousands, as good as yourself, already on the ground. *Gentlemen*, poor beggars, who have drunk their wine, who have kept their hunters!"

I was as reassuring as I knew how to be, and my visitors were presently on their feet again while, for the experiment, we agreed on an hour. We were discussing it when the door opened and Miss Churm came in with a wet umbrella. Miss Churm had to take the omnibus to Maida Vale and then walk half a mile. She looked a trifle blowsy and slightly splashed. I scarcely ever saw her come in without thinking afresh how odd it was that, being so little in herself, she should yet be so much in others. She was a meagre little Miss Churm, but she was an ample heroine of romance. She was only a freckled cockney, but she could represent everything from a fine lady to a shepherdess; she had the faculty, as she might have had a fine voice or long hair. She couldn't spell, and she loved beer, but she had two or three "points," and practice, and a knack, and mother-wit, and a kind of whimsical sensibility, and a love of the theatre, and seven sisters, and not an ounce of respect, especially for the "h." The first thing my visitors saw was that her umbrella was wet, and in their spotless perfection they visibly winced at it. The rain had come on since their arrival.

"I'm all in a soak; there *was* a mess of people in the bus. I wish you lived near a station," said Miss Churm. I requested her to get ready as quickly as possible, and she passed into the room in which she always changed her dress. But before going out she asked me what she was to get into this time.

"It's the Russian princess, don't you know?" I answered; "the one with the 'golden eyes,' in black velvet, for the long thing in the *Cheapside*."

"Golden eyes? I *say*!" cried Miss Churm, while my companions watched her with intensity as she withdrew. She always arranged herself, when she was late, before I could turn round; and I kept my visitors a little, on purpose, so that they might get an idea, from seeing her, what would be expected of themselves. I mentioned that she was quite my notion of an excellent model—she was really very clever.

"Do you think she looks like a Russian princess?" Major Monarch asked, with lurking alarm.

"When I make her, yes."

"Oh, if you have to *make* her—!" He reasoned, acutely.

"That's the most you can ask. There are so many that are not makeable."

"Well now, *here's* a lady"—and with a persuasive smile he passed his arm into his wife's—"who's already made!"

"Oh, I'm not a Russian princess," Mrs. Monarch protested, a little coldly. I could see that she had known some and didn't like them. There, immediately, was a complication of a kind that I never had to fear with Miss Churm.

This young lady came back in black velvet—the gown was rather rusty and very low on her lean shoulders—and with a Japanese fan in her red hands. I reminded her that in the scene I was doing she had to look over someone's head. "I forget whose it is; but it doesn't matter. Just look over a head."

"I'd rather look over a stove," said Miss Churm; and she took her station near the fire. She fell into position, settled herself into a tall attitude, gave a certain backward inclination to her head and a certain forward drop to her fan, and looked, at least to my prejudiced sense, distinguished and charming, foreign and dangerous. We left her looking so, while I went downstairs with Major and Mrs. Monarch.

"I think I could come about as near it as that," said Mrs. Monarch.

"Oh, you think she's shabby, but you must allow for the alchemy of art."

However, they went off with an evident increase of comfort, founded on their demonstrable advantage in being the real thing. I could fancy them shuddering over Miss Churm. She was very droll about them when I went back, for I told her what they wanted.

"Well, if *she* can sit I'll tyke to bookkeeping," said my model.

"She's very ladylike," I replied, as an innocent form of aggravation.

"So much the worse for you. That means she can't turn round."

"She'll do for the fashionable novels."

"Oh yes, she'll *do* for them!" my model humorously declared. "Ain't they bad enough without her?" I had often sociably denounced them to Miss Churm.

III

It was for the elucidation of a mystery in one of these works that I first tried Mrs. Monarch. Her husband came with her, to be useful if necessary—it was sufficiently clear that as a general thing he would prefer to come with her. At first I wondered if this were for "propriety's" sake—if he were going to be jealous and meddling. The idea was too tiresome, and if it had been confirmed it would speedily have brought our acquaintance to a close. But I soon saw there was nothing in it and that if he accompanied Mrs. Monarch it was (in addition to the chance of being wanted) simply because he had nothing else to do. When she was away from him his occupation was gone—she never *had* been away from him. I judged, rightly, that in their awkward situation their close union was their main comfort and that this union had no weak spot. It was a real marriage, an encouragement for the hesitating, a nut for pessimists to crack. Their address was humble (I remember afterwards thinking it had been the only thing about them that was really professional), and I could fancy the lamentable lodgings in which the Major would have been left alone. He could bear them with his wife—he couldn't bear them without her.

He had too much tact to try and make himself agreeable when he couldn't be useful; so he simply sat and waited, when I was too absorbed in my work to talk. But I liked to make him talk—it made my work, when it didn't interrupt it, less sordid, less special. To listen to him was to combine the excitement of going out with the economy of staying at home. There was only one hindrance: that I seemed not to know any of the people he and his wife had known. I think he wondered extremely, during the term of our intercourse, whom the deuce I *did* know. He hadn't a stray sixpence of an idea to fumble for; so we didn't spin it very fine—we confined ourselves to questions of leather and even of liquor (saddlers and breeches-makers and how to get good claret cheap), and matters like "good trains" and the habits of small game. His lore on these last subjects was astonishing, he managed to interweave the stationmaster with the ornithologist. When he couldn't talk about greater things he could talk cheerfully about smaller, and since I couldn't accompany him into reminiscences of the fashionable world he could lower the conversation without a visible effort to my level.

So earnest a desire to please was touching in a man who could so easily have knocked one down. He looked after the fire and had an opinion on the draught of the stove, without my asking him, and I could see that he thought many of my arrangements not half clever enough. I remember telling him that if I were only rich I would offer him a salary to come and teach me how to live. Sometimes he gave a random sigh, of which the essence was: "Give me even such a bare old barrack as *this*, and I'd do something with it!" When I wanted to use him he came alone; which was an illustration of the superior courage of women. His wife could bear her solitary second floor, and she was in general more discreet; showing by various small reserves that she was alive to the propriety of keeping our relations markedly professional—not letting them slide into sociability. She wished it to remain clear that she and the Major were employed, not cultivated, and if she approved of me as a superior, who could be kept in his place, she never thought me quite good enough for an equal.

She sat with great intensity, giving the whole of her mind to it, and was capable of remaining for an hour almost as motionless as if she were before a photographer's lens. I could see she had been photographed often, but somehow the very habit that made her good for that purpose unfitted her for mine. At first I was extremely pleased with her ladylike air, and it was a satisfaction, on coming to follow her lines, to see how good they were and how far they could lead the pencil. But after a few times I began to find her too insurmountably stiff; do what I would with it my drawing looked like a photograph or a copy of a photograph. Her figure had no variety of expression—she herself had no sense of variety. You may say this was my business, was only a question of placing her. I placed her in every conceivable position, but she managed to obliterate their differences. She was always a lady certainly, and into the bargain was always the same lady. She was the real thing, but always the same thing. There were moments when I was oppressed by the serenity of her confidence that she *was* the real thing. All her dealings with me and all her husband's were an implication that this was lucky for *me*. Meanwhile I found myself trying to invent types that approached her own, instead of making her own transform itself—in the clever way that was not impossible, for instance, to poor Miss Churm. Arrange as I would and take the precautions I would, she always, in my pictures, came out too tall—landing me in the dilemma of having represented a fascinating woman as seven feet high, which, out of respect perhaps to my own very much scantier inches, was far from my idea of such a personage.

The case was worse with the Major—nothing I could do would keep *him* down, so that he became useful only for the representation of brawny giants. I adored variety and range, I cherished human accidents, the illustrative note; I wanted to characterize closely, and the thing in the world I most hated was the danger of being ridden by a type. I had quarrelled with some of my friends about it—I had parted company with them for maintaining that one *had* to be, and that if the type was beautiful (witness Raphael and Leonardo), the servitude was only a gain. I was neither Leonardo nor Raphael; I might only be a presumptuous young modern searcher, but I held that everything was to be sacrificed sooner than character. When they averred that the haunting type in question could easily *be* character, I retorted, perhaps superficially: "Whose?" It couldn't be everybody's—it might end in being nobody's.

After I had drawn Mrs. Monarch a dozen times I perceived more clearly than before that the value of such a model as Miss Churm resided precisely in the fact that she had no positive stamp, combined of course with the other fact that what she did have was a curious and inexplicable talent for imitation. Her usual appearance was like a curtain which she could draw up at a request for a capital performance. This performance was simply suggestive; but it was a word to the wise—it was vivid and pretty. Sometimes, even, I thought it, though she was plain herself, too insipidly pretty; I made it a reproach to her that the figures drawn from her were monotonously (*bêtement*, as we used to say) graceful. Nothing made her more angry: it was so much her pride to feel that she could sit for characters that had nothing in common with each other. She would accuse me at such moments of taking away her "reputytion."

It suffered a certain shrinkage, this queer quality, from the repeated visits of my new friends. Miss Churm was greatly in demand, never in want of employment, so I had no scruple in putting her off occasionally, to try them more at my ease. It was certainly amusing at first to do the real thing—it was amusing to do Major Monarch's trousers. They *were* the real thing, even if he did come out colossal. It was amusing to do his wife's back hair (it was so mathematically neat) and the particular "smart" tension of her tight stays. She lent herself especially to positions in which the face was somewhat averted or blurred; she abounded in ladylike back views and *profils perdus*. When she stood erect she took naturally one of the attitudes in which court painters represent queens and princesses; so that I found myself wondering whether, to draw out this accomplishment, I couldn't get the editor of the *Cheapside* to publish a really royal romance, "A Tale of Buckingham Palace." Sometimes, however, the real thing and the make-believe came into contact; by which I mean that Miss Churm, keeping an appointment or coming to make one on days when I had much work in hand, encountered her invidious rivals. The encounter was not on their part, for they noticed her no more than if she had been the housemaid; not from intentional loftiness, but simply because, as yet, professionally, they didn't know how to fraternize as I could guess that they would have liked—or at least that the Major would. They couldn't talk about the omnibus—they always walked; and they didn't know what else to try—she wasn't interested in good trains or cheap claret. Besides, they must have felt—in the air—that she was amused at them, secretly derisive of their ever knowing how. She was not a person to conceal her scepticism if she had had a chance to show it. On the other hand Mrs. Monarch didn't think her tidy; for why else did she take pains to say to me (it was going out of the way, for Mrs. Monarch) that she didn't like dirty women?

One day when my young lady happened to be present with my other sitters (she even dropped in, when it was convenient, for a chat), I asked her to be as good as to lend a hand in getting tea—a service with which she was familiar and which was one of a class that, living as I did in a small way, with slender domestic resources, I often appeal to my models to render. They liked to lay hands on my property, to break the sitting, and sometimes the china—I made them feel Bohemian. The next time I saw Miss Churm after this incident she surprised me greatly by making a scene about it—she accused me of having wished to humiliate her. She had not resented the outrage at the time, but had seemed obliging and amused, enjoying the comedy of asking Mrs. Monarch, who sat vague and silent, whether she would have cream and sugar, and putting an exaggerated simper into the question. She had tried intonations—as if she too wished to pass for the real thing; till I was afraid my other visitors would take offense.

Oh, *they* were determined not to do this; and their touching patience was the measure of their great need. They would sit by the hour, uncomplaining, till I was ready to use them; they would come back on the chance of being wanted and would walk away cheerfully if they were not. I used to go to the door with them to see in what magnificent order they retreated. I tried to find other employment for them—I introduced them to several artists. But they didn't "take," for reasons I could appreciate, and I became conscious, rather anxiously, that after such disappointments they fell back upon me with a heavier weight. They did me the honor to think that it was I who was most *their* form. They were not picturesque enough for the painters, and in those days there were not so many serious workers in black and white. Besides, they had an eye to the great job I had mentioned to them—they had secretly set their hearts on supplying the right essence for my pictorial vindication of our fine novelist. They knew that for this undertaking I should want no costume effects, none of the frippery of past ages—that it was a case in which everything would be contemporary and satirical and, presumably, genteel. If I could work them into it their future would be assured, for the labor would of course be long and the occupation steady.

One day Mrs. Monarch came without her husband—she explained his absence by his having had to go to the City. While she sat there in her usual anxious stiffness there came, at the door, a knock which I immediately recognized as the subdued appeal of a model out of work. It was followed by the entrance of a young man whom I easily perceived to be a foreigner and who proved in fact an Italian acquainted with no English word but my name, which he uttered in a way that made it seem to include all others. I had not then visited his country, nor was I proficient in his tongue; but as he was not so meanly constituted—what Italian is?—as to depend only on that member for expression he conveyed to me, in familiar but graceful mimicry, that he was in search of exactly the employment in which the lady before me was engaged. I was not struck with him at first, and while I continued to draw I emitted rough sounds of discouragement and dismissal. He stood his ground, however, not importunately, but with a dumb, doglike fidelity in his eyes which amounted to innocent impudence—the manner of a devoted servant (he might have been in the house for years) unjustly suspected. Suddenly I saw that this very attitude and expression made a picture, whereupon I told him to sit down and wait till I should be free. There was another picture in the way he obeyed me, and I observed as I worked that there were others still in the way he looked wonderingly, with his head thrown back, about the high studio. He might have been crossing himself in St. Peter's. Before I finished I said to myself: "The fellow's a bankrupt orange-monger, but he's a treasure."

When Mrs. Monarch withdrew he passed across the room like a flash to open the door for her, standing there with the rapt, pure gaze of the young Dante spellbound by the young Beatrice. As I never insisted, in such situations, on the blankness of the British domestic, I reflected that he had the making of a servant (and I needed one, but couldn't pay him to be only that), as well as of a model; in short I made up my mind to adopt my bright adventurer if he would agree to officiate in the double capacity. He jumped at my offer, and in the event my rashness (for I had known nothing about him) was not brought home to me. He proved a sympathetic though a desultory ministrant, and had in a wonderful degree the *sentiment de la pose*. It was uncultivated, instinctive; a part of the happy instinct which had guided him to my door and helped him to spell out my name on the card nailed to it. He had had no other introduction to me than a guess, from the shape of my high north window, seen outside, that my place was a studio and that as a studio it would contain an artist. He had wandered to England in search of fortune, like other itinerants, and had embarked, with a partner and a small green handcart, on the sale of penny ices. The ices had melted away and the partner had dissolved in their train. My young man wore tight yellow trousers with reddish stripes and his name was Oronte. He was sallow but fair, and when I put him into some old clothes of my own he looked like an Englishman. He was as good as Miss Churm, who could look, when required, like an Italian.

IV

I thought Mrs. Monarch's face slightly convulsed when, on her coming back with her husband, she found Oronte installed. It was strange to have to recognize in a scrap of a *lazzarone* a competitor to her magnificent Major. It was she who scented danger first, for the Major was anecdotically unconscious. But Oronte gave us tea, with a hundred eager confusions (he had never seen such a queer process), and I think she thought better of me for having at last an "establishment." They saw a couple of drawings that I had made of the establishment, and Mrs. Monarch hinted that it never would have struck her that he had sat for them. "Now the drawings you make from *us*, they look exactly like us," she reminded me, smiling in triumph; and I recognized that this was indeed just their defect. When I drew the Monarchs I couldn't, somehow, get away from them—get into the character I wanted to represent; and I had not the least desire my model should be discoverable in my picture. Miss Churm never was, and Mrs. Monarch thought I hid her, very properly because she was vulgar; whereas if she was lost it was only as the dead who go to heaven are lost—in the gain of an angel the more.

By this time I had got a certain start with *Rutland Ramsay*, the first novel in the great projected series; that is, I had produced a dozen drawings, several with the help of the Major and his wife, and I had sent them in for approval. My understanding with the publishers, as I have already hinted, had been that I was to be left to do my work, in this particular case, as I liked, with the whole book committed to me; but my connection with the rest of the series was only contingent. There were moments when, frankly, it *was* a comfort to have the real thing under one's hand; for there were characters in *Rutland Ramsay* that were very much like it. There were people presumably as straight as the Major and women of as good a fashion as Mrs. Monarch. There was a great deal of country-house life—treated, it is true, in a fine, fanciful, ironical, generalized way—and there was a considerable implication of knickerbockers and kilts. There were certain things I had to settle at the outset; such things for instance as the exact appearance of the hero, the particular bloom of the heroine. The author of course gave me a lead, but there was a margin for interpretation. I took the Monarchs into my confidence, I told them frankly what I was about, I mentioned my embarrassments and alternatives. "Oh, take *him*!" Mrs. Monarch murmured sweetly, looking at her husband; and "What could you want better than my wife?" the Major inquired, with the comfortable candor that now prevailed between us.

I was not obliged to answer these remarks—I was only obliged to place my sitters. I was not easy in mind, and I postponed, a little timidly perhaps, the solution of the question. The book was a large canvas, the other figures were numerous, and I worked off at first some of the episodes in which the hero and the heroine were not concerned. When once I had set *them* up I should have to stick to them—I couldn't make my young man seven feet high in one place and five feet nine in another. I inclined on the whole to the latter measurements, though the Major more than once reminded me that *he* looked about as young as anyone. It was indeed quite possible to arrange him, for the figure, so that it would have been difficult to detect his age. After the spontaneous Oronte had been with me a month, and after I had given him to understand several different times that his native exuberance would presently constitute an insurmountable barrier to our further intercourse, I waked to a sense of his heroic capacity. He was only five feet seven, but the remaining inches were latent. I tried him almost secretly at first, for I was really rather afraid of the judgement my other models would pass on such a choice. If they regarded Miss Churm as little better than a snare, what would they think of the representation by a person so little the real thing as an Italian street vendor of a protagonist formed by a public school?

If I went a little in fear of them it was not because they bullied me, because they had got an oppressive foothold, but because in their really pathetic decorum and mysteriously permanent newness they counted on me so intensely. I was therefore very glad when Jack Hawley came home: he was always of such good counsel. He painted badly himself, but there was no one like him—for putting his finger on the place. He had been absent from England for a year; he had been somewhere—I don't remember where—to get a fresh eye. I was in a good deal of dread of any such organ, but we were old friends; he had been away for months and a sense of emptiness was creeping into my life. I hadn't dodged a missile for a year.

He came back with a fresh eye, but with the same old black velvet blouse, and the first evening he spent in my studio we smoked cigarettes till the small hours. He had done no work himself, he had only got the eye; so the field was clear for the production of my little things. He wanted to see what I had done for the *Cheapside*, but he was disappointed in the exhibition. That at least seemed the meaning of two or three comprehensive groans which, as he lounged on my big divan, on a folded leg, looking at my latest drawings, issued from his lips with the smoke of the cigarette.

"What's the matter with you?" I asked.

"What's the matter with *you*?"

"Nothing save that I'm mystified."

"You are indeed. You're quite off the hinge. What's the meaning of this new fad?" And he tossed me, with visible irreverence, a drawing in which I happened to have depicted both my majestic models. I asked if he didn't think it good, and he replied that it struck him as execrable, given the sort of thing I had always represented myself to him as wishing to arrive at; but I let that pass, I was so anxious to see exactly what he meant. The two figures in the picture looked colossal, but I supposed this was *not* what he meant inasmuch as, for aught he knew to the contrary, I might have been trying for that. I maintained that I was working exactly in the same way as when he last had done me the honor to commend me. "Well, there's a big hole somewhere," he answered; "wait a bit and I'll discover it." I depended upon him to do so: where else was the fresh eye? But he produced at last nothing more luminous than "I don't know—I don't like your types." This was lame, for a critic who had never consented to discuss with me anything but the question of execution, the direction of strokes, and the mystery of values.

"In the drawings you've been looking at I think my types are very handsome."

"Oh, they won't do!"

"I've had a couple of new models."

"I see you have. *They* won't do."

"Are you very sure of that?"

"Absolutely—they're stupid."

"You mean *I* am—for I ought to get round that."

"You *can't*—with such people. Who are they?"

I told him, as far as was necessary, and he declared, heartlessly: "*Ce sont des gens qu'il faut mettre à la porte.*"

"You've never seen them; they're awfully good," I compassionately objected.

"Not seen them. Why, all this recent work of yours drops to pieces with them. It's all I want to see of them."

"No one else has said anything against it—the *Cheapside* people are pleased."

"Everyone else is an ass, and the *Cheapside* people the biggest asses of all. Come, don't pretend, at this time of day, to have pretty illusions about the public, especially about publishers and editors. It's not for *such* animals you work—it's for those who know, *coloro che sanno*; so keep straight for *me* if you can't keep straight for yourself. There's a certain sort of thing you tried for from the first—and a very good thing it is. But this twaddle isn't *in* it." When I talked with Hawley later about *Rutland Ramsay* and its possible successors he declared that I must get back into my boat again or I would go to the bottom. His voice in short was the voice of warning.

I noted the warning, but I didn't turn my friends out of doors. They bored me a good deal; but the very fact that they bored me admonished me not to sacrifice them—if there was anything to be done with them—simply to irritation. As I look back at this phase they seem to me to have pervaded my life not a little. I have a vision of them as most of the time in my studio, seated, against the wall, on an old velvet bench to be out of the way, and looking like a pair of patient courtiers in a royal antechamber. I am convinced that during the coldest weeks of the winter they held their ground because it saved them fire. Their newness was losing its gloss, and it was impossible not to feel that they were objects of charity. Whenever Miss Churm arrived they went away, and after I was fairly launched in *Rutland Ramsay*, Miss Churm arrived pretty often. They managed to express to me tacitly that they supposed I wanted her for the low life of the book, and I let them suppose it, since they had attempted to study the work—it was lying about the studio—without discovering that it dealt only with the highest circles. They had dipped into the most brilliant of our novelists without deciphering many passages. I still took an hour from them, now and again, in spite of Jack Hawley's warning: it would be time enough to dismiss them, if dismissal should be necessary, when the rigor of the season was over. Hawley had made their acquaintance—he met them at my fireside—and thought them a ridiculous pair. Learning that he was a painter they tried to approach him, to show him too that they were the real thing; but he looked at them, across the big room, as if they were miles away: they were a compendium of everything that he most objected to in the social system of his country. Such people as that, all convention and patent leather, with ejaculations that stopped conversation, had no business in a studio. A studio was a place to learn to see, and how could you see through a pair of feather beds?

The main inconvenience I suffered at their hands was that, at first, I was shy of letting them discover how my artful little servant had begun to sit for me for *Rutland Ramsay*. They knew that I had been odd enough (they were prepared by this time to allow oddity to artists) to pick a foreign vagabond out of the streets, when I might have had a person with whiskers and credentials; but it was some time before they learned how high I rated his accomplishments. They found him in an attitude more than once, but they never doubted I was doing him as an organ grinder. There were several things they never guessed, and one of them was that for a striking scene in the novel, in which a footman briefly figured, it occurred to me to make use of

Major Monarch as the menial. I kept putting this off, I didn't like to ask him to don the livery—besides the difficulty of finding a livery to fit him. At last, one day late in the winter, when I was at work on the despised Oronte (he caught one's idea in an instant), and was in the glow of feeling that I was going very straight, they came in, the Major and his wife, with their society laugh about nothing (there was less and less to laugh at), like country-callers—they always reminded me of that—who have walked across the park after church and are presently persuaded to stay to luncheon. Luncheon was over, but they could stay to tea—I knew they wanted it. The fit was on me, however, and I couldn't let my ardor cool and my work wait, with the fading daylight, while my model prepared it. So I asked Mrs. Monarch if she would mind laying it out—a request which, for an instant, brought all the blood to her face. Her eyes were on her husband's for a second, and some mute telegraphy passed between them. Their folly was over the next instant; his cheerful shrewdness put an end to it. So far from pitying their wounded pride, I must add, I was moved to give it as complete a lesson as I could. They bustled about together and got out the cups and saucers and made the kettle boil. I know they felt as if they were waiting on my servant, and when the tea was prepared I said: "He'll have a cup, please—he's tired." Mrs. Monarch brought him one where he stood, and he took it from her as if he had been a gentleman at a party, squeezing a crush-hat with an elbow.

Then it came over me that she had made a great effort for me—made it with a kind of nobleness—and that I owed her a compensation. Each time I saw her after this I wondered what the compensation could be. I couldn't go on doing the wrong thing to oblige them. Oh, it was the wrong thing, the stamp of the work for which they sat—Hawley was not the only person to say it now. I sent in a large number of the drawings I had made for *Rutland Ramsay*, and I received a warning that was more to the point than Hawley's. The artistic adviser of the house for which I was working was of opinion that many of my illustrations were not what had been looked for. Most of these illustrations were the subjects in which the Monarchs had figured. Without going into the question of what *had* been looked for, I saw at this rate I shouldn't get the other books to do. I hurled myself in despair upon Miss Churm, I put her through all her paces. I not only adopted Oronte publicly as my hero, but one morning when the Major looked in to see if I didn't require him to finish a figure for the *Cheapside*, for which he had begun to sit the week before, I told him that I had changed my mind—I would do the drawing from my man. At this my visitor turned pale and stood looking at me. "Is *he* your idea of an English gentleman?" he asked.

I was disappointed, I was nervous, I wanted to get on with my work; so I replied with irritation: "Oh, my dear Major—I can't be ruined for *you*!"

He stood another moment; then, without a word, he quitted the studio. I drew a long breath when he was gone, for I said to myself that I shouldn't see him again. I had not told him definitely that I was in danger of having my work rejected, but I was vexed at his not having felt the catastrophe in the air, read with me the moral of our fruitless collaboration, the lesson that, in the deceptive atmosphere of art, even the highest respectability may fail of being plastic.

I didn't owe my friends money, but I did see them again. They reappeared together, three days later, and under the circumstances there was something tragic in the fact. It was a proof to me that they could find nothing else in life to do. They had threshed the matter out in a dismal conference—they had digested the bad news that they were not in for the series. If they were not useful to me even for the *Cheapside* their function seemed difficult to determine, and I could only judge at first that they had come, forgivingly, decorously, to take a last leave. This made me rejoice in secret that I had little leisure for a scene; for I had placed both my other models in position together and I was pegging away at a drawing from which I hoped to derive glory. It had been suggested by the passage in which Rutland Ramsey, drawing up a chair to Artemisia's piano-stool, says extraordinary things to her while she ostensibly fingers out a difficult piece of music. I had done Miss Churm at the piano before—it was an attitude in which she knew how to take on an absolutely poetic grace. I wished the two figures to "compose" together, intensely, and my little Italian had entered perfectly into my conception. The pair were vividly before me, the piano had been pulled out; it was a charming picture of blended youth and murmured love, which I had only to catch and keep. My visitors stood and looked at it, and I was friendly to them over my shoulder.

They made no response, but I was used to silent company and went on with my work, only a little disconcerted (even though exhilarated by the sense that *this* was at last the ideal thing) at not having got rid of them after all. Presently I heard Mrs. Monarch's sweet voice beside, or rather above me: "I wish her hair was a little better done." I looked up and she was staring with a strange fixedness at

Miss Churm, whose back was turned to her. "Do you mind my just touching it?" she went on—a question which made me spring up for an instant, as with the instinctive fear that she might do the young lady a harm. But she quieted me with a glance I shall never forget—I confess I should like to have been able to paint *that*—and went for a moment to my model. She spoke to her softly, laying a hand upon her shoulder and bending over her; and as the girl, understanding, gratefully assented, she disposed her rough curls, with a few quick passes, in such a way as to make Miss Churm's head twice as charming. It was one of the most heroic personal services I have ever seen rendered. Then Mrs. Monarch turned away with a low sigh and, looking about her as if for something to do, stooped to the floor with a noble humility and picked up a dirty rag that had dropped out of my paint-box.

The Major meanwhile had also been looking for something to do and, wandering to the other end of the studio, saw before him my breakfast things, neglected, unremoved. "I say, can't I be useful *here*?" he called out to me with an irrepressible quaver. I assented with a laugh that I fear was awkward and for the next ten minutes, while I worked, I heard the light clatter of china and the tinkle of spoons and glass. Mrs. Monarch assisted her husband—they washed up my crockery, they put it away. They wandered off into my little scullery, and I afterwards found that they had cleaned my knives and that my slender stock of plate had an unprecedented surface. When it came over me, the latent eloquence of what they were doing, I confess that my drawing was blurred for a moment—the picture swam. They had accepted their failure, but they couldn't accept their fate. They had bowed their heads in bewilderment to the perverse and cruel law in virtue of which the real thing could be so much less precious than the unreal; but they didn't want to starve. If my servants were my models, my models might be my servants. They would reverse the parts—the others would sit for the ladies and gentlemen, and *they* would do the work. They would still be in the studio—it was an intense dumb appeal to me not to turn them out. "Take us on," they wanted to say—"we'll do *anything*."

When all this hung before me the *afflatus* vanished—my pencil dropped from my hand. My sitting was spoiled and I got rid of my sitters, who were also evidently rather mystified and awestruck. Then, alone with the Major and his wife, I had a most uncomfortable moment. He put their prayer into a single sentence: "I say, you know—just let *us* do for you, can't you?" I couldn't—it was dreadful to see them emptying my slops; but I pretended I could to oblige them for about a week. Then I gave them a sum of money to go away; and I never saw them again. I obtained the remaining books, but my friend Hawley repeats that Major and Mrs. Monarch did me a permanent harm, got me into a second-rate trick. If it be true I am content to have paid the price—for the memory.

Maupassant

1850	August 5. Henri Rene Albert Guy de Maupassant born in Chateau de Miromesail, France.
1870-71	Leaves school, enlists in French army, and serves in the Franco-Prussian War.
1872-77	Serves as a clerk in the civil service, first for the Ministry of the Navy and then for the Ministry of Public Instruction. These work experiences would provide the inspiration for many of his later stories. Serves a literary apprenticeship under Gustave Flaubert which ends in 1880.
1880	*Des Vers*, a volume of poetry, is released, but receives little attention. *Boule de suif*, a story about the Franco-Prussian War, appears in *Soirees de Medan*, a collection of tales featuring such noted authors as Zola and Huysmans. The story receives the most critical acclaim of any in the collection.
1881	*La Maison Tellier* becomes his first collection of stories to be published.
1883-85	Produces many volumes of fiction, including the collections *Clair de lune* and *Contes et nouvelles*, and the novels *Une vie* and *Bel-ami*.
1888	Despite showing early signs of mental illness, Maupassant takes a sea voyage which inspires the travel book *Sur l'eau*.
1991	Suffering from severe paralysis and mental illness, Maupassant goes to Cannes on the Mediterranean to spend the winter. But after an attempted sucide in January of 1992, he is taken back to Paris.
1893	July 6. Guy de Maupassant dies in Paris.

Guy de Maupassant

Henri-Rene-Albert-Guy de Maupassant was born on August 5th, 1850; perhaps (there is conflicting evidence) at the Château de Miromesnil, near Dieppe, in the chapel of which he was baptized. His family (not of the old *noblesse*) came from Lorraine, but had dwelt in Normandy since the middle of the eighteenth century: not, however, in that ornate and pleasing residence which his father hired shortly before Guy's birth and soon afterwards relinquished. The Maupassants were by no means well off. His boyhood was chiefly spent at Etretat and Fécamp, little places on the coast. He grew up a robust, muscular boy, taking his pleasures in out-of-door life, and in the company of peasants and fishermen whom he afterwards described so well, and of their children. Unlike the sons of the bourgeoisie, he was not class conscious as far as such companions were concerned; and his upbringing helped to make him afterwards the kind of man whose servants are his friends. Bernard and Raymond, who managed his yacht, the *Bel-Ami*, adored him; and next to his mother and sister those two men were probably more distressed than other people when he went mad. Other people were chiefly inquisitive and excited when that happened.

His valet, François Tassart, who wrote an honest yet loyal book about his ten years' service (1883 to 1893), got better talk out of him than all but a few friends. Maupassant would often share his impressions of men, women and places with François, but remain shut up like an oyster with most people. It is important to remember in drawing his character that he was the sort of virile man of whom those going with him for a day's shoot or a sail would be likely to say afterwards, "that is a gentleman I like to work for"; or with whom any shepherd, peasant, old crone, farmer, fisherman, prostitute, house-drudge, would feel in a way at ease. In society, on the other hand, he was apt to be vulgar, dull, and boisterous—common. Yes, that's it, common.

He was fond of practical jokes too elaborate to be funny, and of boasting of his "conquests" and priapean feats. In Paris, talking and behaving thus, he was naturally sometimes fooled himself: sent on spoof assignments to meet a countess or a famous actress who never turned up, or told to go in fancy dress to a party where all were in ordinary clothes. Whether during his last years of flaming notoriety he resented these tit-for-tats, I do not know. I think probably not. I suspect that he was then living in so bad a dream that even a humiliation was a welcome counterirritant; as welcome as an unjust row over money with his devoted publisher. And if you imagine the disconcerting contrast between his behavior, consonant only with rollicking youthful spirits, and the settled gloom in his eyes, and his sultry silences (Taine compared him to *un petit taureau triste*), you will probably conclude that it was not M. Guy de Maupassant's social gifts that led to his being pestered to death with invitations, but just society's snobbishness; and here and there, no doubt, the itch on the part of sophisticated women to experience the thrill of being under the scrutiny of a merciless writer.

Pestered to exasperation he certainly was, while his own contributions to social life consisted of entertainments designed to revive in himself the spirit of those bygone rowdy Sundays on the Seine, when he was a Civil Service clerk, with Mouche and "les cinq papas": "Petit Bleu," "Tomahawk," "Flat-cap," "One-eye," and "Plumtree" (Maupassant himself). He invited fast quasi-fashionable women to dinner with one other man, and the women would proceed to describe their husbands' tastes and behavior in bawdy houses; he taught the parrot in his boudoir to squawk "Petit Cochon" as a greeting to any woman who came to see him; or he made it a condition of getting a schoolmistress a situation that she should first dress up as a pretty boy and nudge his other women guests under the table. He was not quick at discriminating between denizens of the *monde* and *demi-monde*, if both were richly dressed. In writing to Marie Bashkirtseff, he says that he has found it practical to pinch women at the opera: if that is taken in good part, he knows where he is; if it gives offense, he knows likewise.

All this is vulgar enough, like his own study in Paris, an etching of which is reproduced in that poor little book, M. George Normand's *La Fin de Maupassant.* His study recalls a line from Kipling's *The Mary Gloater*, "And your rooms at College was beastly—more like a whore's than a man's." Yes all vulgar enough; but even more desolating, when one recalls the depth of his feelings, the powers of his mind.

I think, too, we must imagine Maupassant in his relation to women during this period as in that predicament in which huntsmen with a reputation for hard riding find themselves when their nerve has begun, secretly, to fail.

In that room, however, with its podgy sofas and chairs, knickknacks, perfumes, cushions, marquetry, and palms, he wrote with the regularity of a bank clerk and the desperation of one working against time in a fading light; wrote, though often he could hardly see the words with his inflamed eyes, and though racked with headaches, which inhalations of ether temporarily relieved; wrote, taking down what, on one or two occasions, had seemed dictated to him by a fetch of himself seated on the other side of the table—that "Lui" whom he so dreaded to find beside his fire when he returned alone to his rooms at night.

His output was enormous, earning unprecedented sums, though today they seem modest enough. (500 francs went a long way in France in the eighties.) His novels sold quickly by the sixty, seventy thousand. They went even better than the collections of stories and sketches which, always first paid for at record figures by editors, he garnered rapidly together in volumes, sometimes publishing three in one year. He was as much a king of railway bookstalls in his day as Edgar Wallace ever was, but his books were not time killers. True, much of Maupassant's later work shows haste, and especially elaboration of subject matter which, when the influence of Flaubert was stronger upon him, he would have rejected as trivial. Yet the shadow of his beloved master was by his side, and this astonishing facility was the reward of ten years' apprenticeship. Maupassant still held, too, his master's creed that to be what one may be, to master the instrument which is one's gift, to learn to play on it to perfection is duty, conduct, everything—the only success in life. It is a guiding principle with obvious limitations, though nobler and with subtler and safer implications than most—than patriotism, for example; but it cannot shore up a tumbling life. Though Maupassant clung to it, the exercise of his gift at last seemed also vanity.

There was a touch of *la folie de grandeur* in his behavior, which made the young Léon Daudet, for example, report after meeting him that he seemed a strange mixture of genius, sick man and ass. His disease made him extremely sensitive to cold; his nerves to noises and crowds. Crowds are apt always to be oppressive to those who have a low opinion to human nature, but Maupassant's horror at finding himself in an audience or a crush sometimes amounted to a phobia. He would chuck everything and fly; solitude in open spaces beckoned like a heavenly promise of peace. "Anywhere, anywhere out of the world." And then to get away from women! A floating solitude was best of all. He would, however, be careful, before starting, to fix up an extremely lucrative contract for weekly sketches and impressions, and it is to one of these flights that we owe *Sur l'eau*. To earn more and more money became an increasing necessity now. He had to keep up his little yacht; his flat in Paris, a house at Etretat, a small villa near Cannes, and then there were his mother and his brother's family to help. In the confusion of his haunted life, his loyalty to such obligations remained as fixed as his habit of industry and his Norman cupidity.

Sur l'eau is the book which brings the reader nearest to Maupassant himself. He never wrote better than under the first intoxication of being alone, or more significantly than when the boon of solitude turned slowly to despair. Then the elemental poet is released in him; and that feeling of identity with earth, animals, and the instinctive life of men, doomed like the beasts, then finds an expression which can lend, occasionally, even to a trivial anecdote a certain grandeur. It is his jet-black pessimism that disinfects his vulgarity, his monkey-house view of sex, and excuses a laugh sometimes too contemptuous. A happy Maupassant would be as intolerable as that crass vulgarian Georges Daroy himself, the hero of *Bel-Ami*, with whom, by the way, he has some unpleasant affinities; but Maupassant alone with nature, himself, and human fate, appears to me lovable. Indeed, he attracts me so much that I am rather puzzled at it; and in case an analysis of my feelings towards him may lead others to examine theirs, I will attempt one.

In the first place I respond to his instinctive crude, direct, uncritical love of Life, and what accompanies that passion when strong (as smoke does fire), his resentment at decay and death. I love an author in whom, say, the spectacle of a school of porpoises plunging and turning in the sea, or of a stallion neighing and stamping in a field, rouses a kind of joy which is also, in some odd way, a fellow feeling.

Again only an author who is aware of the ridiculous and merciless egotism of human beings inspires me with confidence when he does draw attention to the strange intermittent nobility of human nature. When Maupassant melts or admires, I trust him; I am melted and I, too, admire. Then he has as a writer the master quality of sincerity; that is to say, he hates and loves genuinely. His moral sympathies are not always to be relied on; and, though everyone would prefer him to be always both refined and sincere, I would rather he were vulgar and sincere than only pretending, like most novelists, to have better preferences. Lastly he has the great virtue of the pessimist pity. His sense of the cruelty of nature and of man is as deep as his despair. He felt his own tragedy as part of the world's, and that is a mark of greatness.

—from Memories *by Desmond MacCarthy*

Two Friends

Besieged Paris was in the throes of famine. Even the sparrows on the roofs and the rats in the sewers were growing scarce. People were eating anything they could get.

As Monsieur Morissot, watchmaker by profession and idler for the nonce, was strolling along the boulevard one bright January morning, his hands in his trousers pockets and his stomach empty, he suddenly came face to face with a friend—Monsieur Sauvage, a fishing companion.

Before the war broke out, Morissot had been in the habit, every Sunday morning, of setting forth with a bamboo rod in his hand and a tin box on his back. He took the Argenteuil train, got out at Colombes, and walked thence to the Ile Marante. The moment he arrived at this place of his dreams he began fishing and remained till nightfall.

Every Sunday he met at this spot Monsieur Sauvage, a stout, jolly, little man, a draper in the Rue Notre Dame de Lorette, and also an ardent fisherman. They often spent half the day side by side, rod in hand and feet dangling over the water, and a sincere friendship had sprung up between the two.

Some days they did not speak; at other times they chatted; but they understood each other perfectly without the aid of words, having similar tastes and feelings.

In the spring, about ten o'clock in the morning, when the early sun caused a light mist to float on the water and gently warmed the backs of the two enthusiastic anglers, Morissot ~~would~~ occasionally remark to his neighbor:

"Isn't it pleasant here?"

To which the other would reply:

"I can't imagine anything better!"

And these few words sufficed to make them understand and appreciate each other.

In the autumn, towards the close of day, when the setting sun shed a blood-red color over the western sky, and the reflection of the crimson clouds tinged the whole river, brought a glow to the faces of the two friends, and gilded the trees, whose leaves were already turning at thc first chill touch of winter, Monsieur Sauvage would sometimes smile at Morissot, and say:

"What a glorious spectacle!"

And Morissot would answer, without taking his eyes from his float:

"This is much better than the boulevard, isn't it?"

As soon as they recognized each other they shook hands cordially, affected at the thought of meeting in such changed circumstances.

Monsieur Sauvage, with a sigh, murmured:

"These are sad times!"

Morissot shook his head mournfully.

"And such weather! This is the first fine day of the year."

The sky was, in fact, of a bright, cloudless blue. They walked along, side by side, reflective and sad.

"And to think of the fishing!" said Morissot.

"What good times we used to have!"

"When shall we be able to fish again?" asked Monsieur Sauvage.

They entered a small café, took an absinthe together, and then resumed their walk along the pavement.

Morissot stopped suddenly.

"Shall we have another absinthe?" he said.

"If you like," agreed Monsieur Sauvage.

And they entered a wine shop.

They were quite unsteady when they came out, owing to the effect of the alcohol on their empty stomachs. It was a fine, mild day, and a gentle breeze fanned their faces.

The fresh air completed the effect of the alcohol on Monsieur Sauvage. He stopped suddenly, saying:

"Suppose we go there?"

"Where?"

"Fishing."

"But where?"

"Why, to the old place. The French outposts are close to Colombes. I know Colonel Dumoulin, and we shall easily get leave to pass."

Morissot trembled with desire.

"Very well. I agree."

And they separated, to fetch their rods and lines.

An hour later they were walking side by side on the highroad. Presently they reached the villa occupied by the colonel. He smiled at their request, and granted it. They resumed their walk, furnished with a password.

Soon they left the outposts behind them, made their way through deserted Colombes, and found themselves on the outskirts of the small vineyards which border the Seine. It was about eleven o'clock.

Before them lay the village of Argenteuil, apparently lifeless. The heights of Orgement and Sannois dominated the landscape. The great plain, extending as far as Nanterre, was empty, quite empty—a waste of dun-colored soil and bare cherry trees.

Monsieur Sauvage, pointing to the heights, murmured:

"The Prussians are up yonder!"

And the sight of the deserted country filled the two friends with vague misgivings.

The Prussians! They had never seen them as yet, but they had felt their presence in the neighborhood of Paris for months past—ruining France, pillaging, massacring, and starving the people. And a kind of superstitious terror was added to the hatred they already felt towards this unknown, victorious nation.

"Suppose we were to meet any of them?" said Morissot.

"We'd offer them some fish," replied Monsieur Sauvage, with that Parisian lightheartedness which nothing can wholly quench.

Still, they hesitated to show themselves in the open country, overawed by the utter silence which reigned around them.

At last Monsieur Sauvage said boldly:

"Come, we'll make a start; only let us be careful!"

And they made their way through one of the vineyards, bent double, creeping along beneath the cover afforded by the vines, with eye and ear alert.

A strip of bare ground remained to be crossed before they could gain the river bank. They ran across this, and, as soon as they were at the water's edge, concealed themselves among the dry reeds.

Morissot placed his ear to the ground, to ascertain, if possible, whether footsteps were coming their way. He heard nothing. They seemed to be utterly alone.

Their confidence was restored, and they began to fish.

Before them the deserted Ile Marante hid them from the farther shore. The little restaurant was closed, and looked as if it had been deserted for years.

Monsieur Sauvage caught the first gudgeon, Monsieur Morissot the second, and almost every moment one or other raised his line with a little, glittering, silvery fish wriggling at the end; they were having excellent sport.

They slipped their catch gently into a close-meshed bag lying at their feet; they were filled with joy—thc joy of once more indulging in a pastime of which they had long been deprived.

The sun poured its rays on their backs; they no longer heard anything or thought of anything. They ignored the rest of the world; they were fishing.

But suddenly a rumbling sound, which seemed to come from the bowels of the earth, shook the ground beneath them: the cannon were resuming their thunder.

Morissot turned his head and could see towards the left, beyond the banks of the river, the formidable outline of Mont-Valérien, from whose summit arose a white puff of smoke.

The next instant a second puff followed the first, and in a few moments a fresh detonation made the earth tremble.

Others followed, and minute by minute the mountain gave forth its deadly breath and a white puff of smoke, which rose slowly into the peaceful heaven and floated above the summit of the cliff.

Monsieur Sauvage shrugged his shoulders.

"They are at it again!" he said.

Morissot, who was anxiously watching his float bobbing up and down, was suddenly seized with the angry impatience of a peaceful man towards the madmen who were firing thus, and remarked indignantly:

"What fools they are to kill one another like that!"

"They're worse than animals," replied Monsieur Sauvage.

And Morissot, who had just caught a bleak, declared:

"And to think that it will be just the same so long as there are governments!"

"The Republic would not have declared war," interposed Monsieur Sauvage.

Morissot interrupted him:

"Under a king we have foreign wars; under a republic we have civil war."

And the two began placidly discussing political problems with the sound common sense of peaceful, matter-of-fact citizens—agreeing on one point: that they would never be free. And Mont-Valérien thundered ceaselessly, demolishing the houses of the French with its cannon balls, grinding lives of men to powder, destroying many a dream, many a cherished hope, many a prospective happiness; ruthlessly causing endless woe and suffering in the hearts of wives, of daughters, of mothers, in other regions.

"Such is life!" declared Monsieur Sauvage.

"Say, rather, such is death!" replied Morissot, laughing.

But they suddenly trembled with alarm at the sound of footsteps behind them, and, turning round, they perceived close at hand four tall, bearded men, dressed after the manner of liveried servants and wearing flat caps on their heads. They were covering the two anglers with their rifles.

The rods slipped from their owners' grasp and floated away down the river.

In the space of a few seconds they were seized, bound, thrown into a boat, and taken across to the Ile Marante.

And behind the house they had thought deserted were about a score of German soldiers.

A shaggy-looking giant, who was bestriding a chair and smoking a long clay pipe, addressed them in excellent French with the words:

"Well, gentlemen, have you had good luck with your fishing?"

Then a soldier deposited at the officer's feet the bag full of fish, which he had taken care to bring away. The Prussian smiled.

"Not bad, I see. But we have something else to talk about. Listen to me, and don't be alarmed:

"You must know that, in my eyes, you are two spies sent to report my movements. Naturally, I capture you and I shoot you. You pretend to be fishing, the better to disguise your real errand. You have fallen into my hands, and must take the consequences. Such is war.

"But as you came here through the outposts you must have a password for your return. Tell me that password and I will let you go."

The two friends, pale as death, stood silently side by side, a slight fluttering of the hands alone betraying their emotion.

"No one will ever know," continued the officer.

"You will return peacefully to your homes, and the secret will disappear with you. If you refuse, it means death—instant death. Choose!"

They stood motionless, and did not open their lips.

The Prussian, perfectly calm, went on, with hand outstretched towards the river:

"Just think that in five minutes you will be at the bottom of that water. In five minutes! You have relations, I presume?"

Mont-Valérien still thundered.

The two fishermen remained silent. The German turned and gave an order in his own language. Then he moved his chair a little way off, that he might not be so near the prisoners, while a dozen men stepped forward, rifle in hand, and took up a position twenty paces off.

"I give you one minute," said the officer; "not a second longer."

Then he rose quickly, went over to the two Frenchmen, took Morissot by the arm, led him a short distance off, and said in a low voice:

"Quick! the password! Your friend will know nothing. I will pretend to relent."

Morissot answered not a word.

Then the Prussian took Monsieur Sauvage aside in like manner, and made him the same proposal.

Monsieur Sauvage made no reply.

Again they stood side by side.

The officer issued his orders; the soldiers raised their rifles.

Then by chance Morissot's eyes fell on the bag full of gudgeon lying in the grass a few feet from him.

A ray of sunlight made the still quivering fish glisten like silver. And Morissot's heart sank. Despite his efforts at self-control his eyes filled with tears.

"Good-bye, Monsieur Sauvage," he faltered.

"Good-bye, Monsieur Morissot," replied Sauvage.

They shook hands, trembling from head to foot with a dread beyond their mastery.

The officer cried:

"Fire!"

The twelve shots were as one.

Monsieur Sauvage fell forward instantaneously. Morissot, being the taller, swayed slightly and fell across his friend with face turned skyward and blood oozing from a rent in the breast of his coat.

The German issued fresh orders.

His men dispersed, and presently returned with ropes and large stones, which they attached to the feet of the two friends; then they carried them to the river bank.

Mont-Valérien, its summit now enshrouded in smoke, continued to thunder.

Two soldiers took Morissot by the head and the feet; two others did the same with Sauvage. The bodies, swung vigorously by strong hands, were cast to a distance, and, describing a curve, fell feet foremost into the stream.

The water splashed high, foamed, eddied, and then was still again; tiny waves lapped the shore.

A few streaks of blood flecked the surface of the river.

The officer, calm throughout, remarked, with grim humor:

"It's the fishes' turn now!"

Then he retraced his way to the house.

Suddenly he caught sight of the net full of gudgeons, lying forgotten in the grass. He picked it up, examined it, smiled, and called:

"Wilhelm!"

A white-aproned soldier responded to the summons, and the Prussian, tossing him the catch of the two dead men, said:

"Have these fish fried for me at once, while they are still alive; they'll make an excellent dish."

Then he relit his pipe.

A Family

I was going to see my friend Simon Radevin once more, for I had not seen him for fifteen years. Formerly he was my most intimate friend, and I used to spend long, quiet, and happy evenings with him. He was one of those men to whom one tells the most intimate affairs of the heart, and in whom one finds, when quietly talking, rare, clever, ingenious, and refined thoughts—thoughts which stimulate and capture the mind.

For years we had scarcely been separated: we had lived, traveled, thought, and dreamed together; had liked the same things with the same liking, admired the same books, comprehended the same works, shivered with the same sensations, and very often laughed at the same individuals, whom we understood completely, by merely exchanging a glance.

Then he married—quite unexpectedly married a little girl from the provinces, who had come to Paris in search of a husband. How ever could that little, thin, insipidly fair girl, with her weak hands, her light, vacant eyes, and her clear, silly voice, who was exactly like a hundred thousand marriageable dolls, have picked up that intelligent, clever young fellow? Can anyone understand these things? No doubt he had hoped for happiness, simple, quiet, and long-enduring happiness, in the arms of a good, tender, and faithful woman; he had seen all that in the transparent looks of that schoolgirl with light hair.

He had not dreamed of the fact that an active, living, and vibrating man grows tired as soon as he has comprehended the stupid reality of a commonplace life, unless indeed, he becomes so brutalized as to be callous to externals.

What would he be like when I met him again? Still lively, witty, light-hearted, and enthusiastic, or in a state of mental torpor through provincial life? A man can change a great deal in the course of fifteen years!

The train stopped at a small station, and as I got out of the carriage, a stout, a very stout man with red cheeks and a big stomach rushed up to me with open arms, exclaiming: "George!"

I embraced him, but I had not recognized him, and then I said, in astonishment: "By Jove! You have not grown thin!"

And he replied with a laugh: "What did you expect? Good living, a good table, and good nights! Eating and sleeping, that is my existence!"

I looked at him closely, trying to find the features I held so dear in that broad face. His eyes alone had not altered, but I no longer saw the same looks in them, and I said to myself: "If looks be the reflection of the mind, the thoughts in that head are not what they used to be—those thoughts which I knew so well."

Yet his eyes were bright, full of pleasure and friendship, but they had not that clear, intelligent expression which tells better than do words the value of the mind. Suddenly he said to me:

"Here are my two eldest children." A girl of fourteen, who was almost a woman, and a boy of thirteen, in the dress of a pupil from a lycée, came forward in a hesitating and awkward manner, and I said in a low voice: "Are they yours?"

"Of course they are," he replied laughing.

"How many have you?"

"Five! There are three more indoors."

He said that in a proud, self-satisfied, almost triumphant manner, and I felt profound pity, mingled with a feeling of vague contempt for this vainglorious and simple reproducer of his species, who spent his nights in his country house in uxorious pleasures.

I got into a carriage, which he drove himself, and we set off through the town, a dull, sleepy, gloomy town where nothing was moving in the streets save a few dogs and two or three maidservants. Here and there a shopkeeper standing at his door took off his hat, and Simon returned the salute and told me the man's name—no doubt to show me that he knew all the inhabitants personally. The thought struck me that he was thinking of becoming a candidate for the Chamber of Deputies, that dream of all who have buried themselves in the provinces.

We were soon out of the town; the carriage turned into a garden which had some pretensions to a park, and stopped in front of a turreted house, which tried to pass for a château.

"That is my den," Simon said, so that he might be complimented on it, and I replied that it was delightful.

A lady appeared on the steps, dressed up for a visitor, her hair done for a visitor, and with phrases ready prepared for a visitor. She was no longer the light-haired, insipid girl I had seen in church fifteen years previously, but a stout lady in curls and flounces, one of those ladies of uncertain age, without intellect, without any of those things which constitute a woman. In short she was a mother, a stout, commonplace mother, a human layer and brood mare, a machine of flesh which procreates, without mental care save for her children and her housekeeping book.

She welcomed me, and I went into the hall, where three children, ranged according to their height, were ranked for review, like firemen before a mayor. "Ah! ah! so there are the others?" said I. And Simon, who was radiant with pleasure, named them: "Jean, Sophie, and Gontran."

The door of the drawing room was open. I went in, and in the depths of an easy chair I saw something trembling, a man, an old, paralyzed man. Madame Radevin came forward and said: "This is my grandfather, Monsieur; he is eighty-seven." And then she shouted into the shaking old man's ears: "This is a friend of Simon's, grandpapa."

The old gentleman tried to say "Good day" to me, and he muttered: "Oua, oua, oua," and waved his hand.

I took a seat saying: "You are very kind, Monsieur."

Simon had just come in, and he said with a laugh: "So! You have made grandpapa's acquaintance. He is priceless, is that old man. He is the delight of the children, and he is so greedy that he almost kills himself at every meal. You have no idea what he would eat if he were allowed to do as he pleased. But you will see, you will see. He looks all the sweets over as if they were so many girls. You have never seen anything funnier; you will see it presently."

I was then shown to my room to change my dress for dinner, and hearing a great clatter behind me on the stairs, I turned round and saw that all the children were following me behind their father—to do me honor, no doubt.

My windows looked out on to a plain, a bare, interminable plain, an ocean of grass, of wheat, and of oats, without a clump of trees or any rising ground, a striking and melancholy picture of the life which they must be leading in that house.

A bell rang; it was for dinner, and so I went downstairs. Madame Radevin took my arm in a ceremonious manner, and we went into the dining room. A footman wheeled in the old man's armchair, who gave a greedy and curious look at the dessert, as with difficulty he turned his shaking head from one dish to the other.

Simon rubbed his hands, saying: "You will be amused." All the children understood that I was going to be indulged with the sight of their greedy grandfather and they began to laugh accordingly, while their mother merely smiled and shrugged her shoulders. Simon, making a speaking trumpet of his hands, shouted at the old man: "This evening there is sweet rice-cream," and the wrinkled face of the grandfather brightened, he trembled violently all over, showing that he had understood and was very pleased. The dinner began.

"Just look!" Simon whispered. The grandfather did not like the soup, and refused to eat it; but he was made to, on account of his health. The footman forced the spoon into his mouth, while the old man blew energetically, so as not to swallow the soup, which was thus scattered like a stream of water on to the table and over his neighbors. The children shook with delight at the spectacle, while their father, who was also amused, said: " Isn't the old man funny?"

During the whole meal they were all taken up solely with him. With his eyes he devoured the dishes which were put on the table, and with trembling hands tried to seize them and pull them to him. They put them almost within his reach to see his useless efforts, his trembling clutches at them, the piteous appeal of his whole nature, of his eyes, of his mouth, and of his nose as he smelled them. He slobbered on to his table napkin with eagerness, while uttering inarticulate grunts, and the whole family was highly amused at this horrible and grotesque scene.

Then they put a tiny morsel on to his plate, which he ate with feverish gluttony, in order to get something more as soon as possible. When the rice-cream was brought in, he nearly had a fit, and groaned with greediness. Gontran called out to him: "You have eaten too much already; you will have no more." And they pretended not to give him any. Then he began to cry—cry and tremble more violently than ever, while all the children laughed. At last, however, they gave him his helping, a very small piece. As he ate the first mouthful of the pudding, he made a comical and greedy noise in his throat, and a movement with his neck like ducks do, when they swallow too large a morsel, and then, when he had done, he began to stamp his feet, so as to get more.

I was seized with pity for this pitiable and ridiculous Tantalus, and interposed on his behalf: "Please, will you not give him a little more rice?"

But Simon replied: "Oh! no my dear fellow, if he were to eat too much, it might harm him at his age."

I held my tongue, and thought over these words. Oh! ethics! Oh! logic! Oh! wisdom! At his age! So they deprived him of his only remaining pleasure out of regard for his health! His health! What would he do with it, inert and trembling wreck that he was? They were taking care of his life, so they said. His life? How many days? Ten, twenty, fifty, or a hundred? Why? For his own sake? Or to preserve for some time longer, the spectacle of his impotent greediness in the family.

There was nothing left for him to do in this life, nothing whatever. He had one single wish left, one sole pleasure; why not grant him that last solace constantly, until he died?

After playing cards for a long time, I went up to my room and to bed; I was low-spirited and sad, sad, sad! I sat at my window, but I heard nothing but the beautiful warbling of a bird in a tree, somewhere in the distance. No doubt the bird was singing thus in a low voice during the night, to lull his mate, who was sleeping on her eggs.

And I thought of my poor friend's five children, and to myself pictured him snoring by the side of his ugly wife.

The Piece of String

It was market day, and from all the country round Goderville the peasants and their wives were coming towards the town. The men walked slowly, throwing the whole body forward at every step of their long, crooked legs. They were deformed from pushing the plough which makes the left shoulder higher, and bends their figures sideways; from reaping the grain, when they have to spread their legs so as to keep on their feet. Their starched blue blouses, glossy as though varnished, ornamented at collar and cuffs with a little embroidered design and blown out round their bony bodies, looked very much like balloons, whence issued two arms and two feet.

Some of these fellows dragged a cow or a calf at the end of a rope. And just behind the animal followed their wives beating it over the back with a leaf-covered branch to hasten its pace, and carrying large baskets out of which protruded the heads of chickens or ducks. These women walked more quickly and energetically than the men, with their erect, dried-up figures, adorned with scanty little shawls pinned over their flat bosoms, and their heads wrapped round with a white cloth, enclosing the hair and surmounted by a cap.

Now a char-à-banc passed by, jogging along behind a horse and shaking up strangely the two men on the seat, and the woman at the bottom of the cart who held fast to its sides to lessen the hard jolting.

In the market place at Goderville was a great crowd, a mingled multitude of men and beasts. The horns of cattle, the high, long-napped hats of wealthy peasants, the headdresses of the women rose above the surface of the throng. And the sharp, shrill, barking voices made a continuous, wild din, while above it occasionally rose a huge burst of laughter from the sturdy lungs of a merry peasant or a prolonged bellow from a cow tied fast to the wall of a house.

It all smelt of the stable, of milk, of hay and of perspiration, giving off that half-human, half-animal odor which is peculiar to country folks.

Maître Hauchecorne, of Bréauté, had just arrived at Goderville and was making his way towards the square when he perceived on the ground a little piece of string. Maître Hauchecorne, economical as are all true Normans, reflected that everything was worth picking up which could be of any use, and he stooped down, painfully, because he suffered from rheumatism. He took the bit of thin string from the ground and was carefully preparing to roll it up when he saw Maître Malandain, the harness maker, on his doorstep staring at him. They had once had a quarrel about a halter, and they had borne each other malice ever since. Maître Hauchecorne was overcome with a sort of shame at being seen by his enemy picking up a bit of string on the road. He quickly hid it beneath his blouse and then slipped it into his breeches pocket, then pretended to be still looking for something on the ground which he did not discover and finally went off towards the market place, his head bent forward and his body almost doubled in two by rhuematic pains.

He was at once lost in the crowd, which kept moving about slowly and noisily as it chaffered and bargained. The peasants examined the cows, went off, came back, always in doubt for fear of being cheated, never quite daring to decide, looking the seller square in the eye in the effort to discover the tricks of the man and the defect in the beast.

The women, having place their great baskets at their feet, had taken out the poultry, which lay upon the ground, their legs tied together, with terrified eyes and scarlet combs.

They listened to propositions, maintaining their prices in a decided manner with an impassive face or prehaps deciding to accept the smaller price offered, suddenly calling out to the customer who was starting to go away:

"All right, I'll let you have them, Maît' Anthime."

Then, little by little, the square became empty, and when the Angelus struck midday those who lived at a distance poured into the inns.

At Jourdain's the great room was filled with diners, just as the vast court was filled with vehicles of every sort—wagons, gigs, char-à-bancs, tilburies, innumerable vehicles which have no name, yellow with mud, misshapen, pieced together, some raising their shafts to heaven like two arms, some with their noses on the ground and their tail in the air.

Just opposite to where the diners were at the table the huge fireplace, with its bright flame, gave out a burning heat on the backs of those who sat at the right.

Three spits were turning, loaded with chickens, with pigeons and with joints of mutton, and a delectable odor of roast meat and of gravy flowing over crisp brown skin arose from the hearth, kindled merriment, and caused mouths to water.

All the aristocracy of the plough were eating there at Maît' Jourdain's, innkeeper and horse dealer, a sharp fellow who had made a great deal of money in his day.

The dishes were passed round, were emptied, as were the jugs of yellow cider. Everyone told of his affairs, of his purchases and his sales. They exchanged news about the crops. The weather was good for green stuff, but too wet for grain.

Suddenly the drum began to beat in the courtyard before the house; and they all, except some of the most indifferent, were on their feet at once and ran to the door, to the windows, their mouths full and napkins in their hand.

When the public crier had finished his tattoo he called forth in a jerky voice, pausing in the wrong places:

"Be it known to the inhabitants of Goderville and in general to all persons present at the market that there has been lost this morning on the Beuzeville road, between nine and ten o'clock, a black leather pocketbook containing five hundred francs and business papers. You are requested to return it to the mayor's office at once or to Maître Fortuné Houlbrèque, of Manneville. There will be twenty francs reward."

Then the man went away. They heard once more at a distance the dull beating of the drum and the faint voice of the crier. Then they all began to talk of this incident, reckoning up the chances which Maître Houlbrèque had of finding or of not finding his pocketbook again.

The meal went on. They were finishing their coffee when the corporal of gendarmes appeared on the threshold.

He asked:

"Is Maître Hauchecorne, of Bréauté, here?"

Maître Hauchecorne, seated at the other end of the table, answered:

"Here I am, here I am."

And he followed the corporal.

The mayor was waiting for him, seated in an armchair. He was the notary of the place, a tall, grave man of pompous speech.

"Maître Hauchecorne," said he, "this morning on the Beuzeville road, you were seen to pick up the pocketbook lost by Maître Houlbrèque, of Manneville."

The countryman looked at the mayor in amazement, frightened already at this suspicion which rested on him, he knew not why.

"I—I picked up that pocketbook?"

"Yes, you."

"I swear I don't even know anything about it."

"You were seen."

"I was seen—I? Who saw me?"

"Monsieur Malandain, the harness maker."

Then the old man remembered, understood, and, reddening with anger, said:

"Ah! he saw me, did he, the rascal? He saw me picking up this string here, M'sieu le Maire."

And fumbling at the bottom of his pocket, he pulled out of it the little end of string.

But the mayor incredulously shook his head:

"You will not make me believe, Maître Hauchecorne, that Monsieur Malandain, who is a man whose word can be relied on, has mistaken this string for a pocketbook."

The peasant, furious, raised his hand and spat on the ground beside him as if to attest his good faith, repeating:

"For all that, it is God's truth, M'sieu le Maire. There! On my soul's salvation, I repeat it."

The mayor continued:

"After you picked up the object in question, you even looked about for some time in the mud to see if a piece of money had not dropped out of it."

The good man was choking with indignation and fear.

"How can they tell—how can they tell such lies as that to slander an honest man! How can they?"

His protestations were in vain; he was not believed.

He was confronted with Monsieur Malandain, who repeated and sustained his testimony. They railed at one another for an hour. At his own request Maître Hauchecorne was searched. Nothing was found on him.

At last the mayor, much perplexed, sent him away, warning him that he would inform the public prosecutor and ask for orders.

The news had spread. When he left the mayor's office the old man was surrounded, interrogated with a curiosity which was serious or mocking, as the case might be, but into which no indignation entered. And he began to tell the story of the string. They did not believe him. They laughed.

He passed on, buttonholed by everyone, himself buttonholing his acquaintances, beginning over and over again his tale and his protestations, showing his pockets turned inside out to prove that he had nothing in them.

They said to him:

"You old rogue!"

He grew more and more angry, feverish, in despair at not being believed, and kept on telling his story.

The night came. It was time to go home. He left with three of his neighbors, to whom he pointed out the place where he had picked up the string, and all the way he talked of his adventure.

That evening he made the round of the village of Bréauté for the purpose of telling everyone. He met only unbelievers.

He brooded over it all night long.

The next day, about one in the afternoon, Marius Paumelle, a farm hand of Maître Breton, the market gardener at Ymauville, returned the pocketbook and its contents to Maître Holbrèque, of Manneville.

This man said, indeed, that he had found it on the road, but not knowing how to read, he had carried it home and given it to his master.

The news spread to the environs. Maître Hauchecorne was informed. He started off at once and began to relate his story with the *dénouement*. He was triumphant.

"What grieved me," said he, "was not the thing itself, do you understand, but it was being accused of lying. Nothing does you so much harm as being in disgrace for lying."

All day he talked of his adventure. He told it on the roads to the people who passed, at the cabaret to the people who drank, and next Sunday when they came out of church. He even stopped strangers to tell them about it. He was easy now, and yet something worried him without his knowing exactly what it was. People had a joking manner while they listened. They did not seem convinced. He seemed to feel their remarks behind his back.

On Tuesday of the following week he went to market at Goderville, prompted solely by the need of telling his story.

Malandain, standing on his doorstep, began to laugh as he saw him pass. Why?

He accosted a farmer of Criquetot, who did not let him finish, and giving him a punch in the pit of the stomach, cried in his face: "Oh, you great rogue!" Then the farmer turned his heel upon him.

Maître Hauchecorne grew more and more uneasy. Why had they called him a "great rogue"?

When seated at table in Jourdain's tavern he began again to explain the whole affair.

A horse dealer of Montivilliers shouted at him:

"Get out, get out, you old scamp! I know all about your piece of string."

Hauchecorne stammered:

"But since they found it again, the pocketbook!"

But the other continued:

"Hold your tongue; there's one who finds it and there's another who returns it. And no one's the wiser."

The farmer was speechless. He understood at last. They accused him of having had the pocketbook brought back by an accomplice, by a confederate.

He tried to protest. The whole table began to laugh .

He could not finish his dinner, and went away amid a chorus of jeers.

He went home indignant, choking with rage, with confusion, the more cast down since with his Norman craftiness he was, perhaps, capable of having done what they accused him of and even of boasting of it as a good trick. He was dimly conscious that it was impossible to prove his innocence, his craftiness being so well known. He felt himself struck to the heart by the injustice of the suspicion.

He began anew to tell his tale, lengthening his recital every day, each day adding new proofs, more energetic declarations and more sacred oaths, which he thought of, which he prepared in his hours of solitude, for his mind was entirely occupied with the story of the string. The more he denied it, the more artful his arguments, the less he was believed.

"Those are liars' proofs," they said behind his back.

He felt this. It preyed upon him and he exhausted himself in useless efforts.

He was visibly wasting away.

Jokers would make him tell the story of "the piece of string" to amuse them, just as you make a soldier who has been on a campaign tell his story of the battle. His mind kept growing weaker, and about the end of December he took to his bed.

He passed away early in January, and, in the ravings of death agony, he protested his innocence, repeating:

"A little piece of string—a little piece of string. See, here it is, M'sieu le Maire."

The Rabbit

Old Lecacheur appeared at the door of his house at his usual hour, between five and a quarter past five in the morning, to look after his men who were going to work.

With a red face, only half awake, his right eye open and the left nearly closed, he was buttoning his braces over his fat stomach with some difficulty, all the time looking into every corner of the farmyard with a searching glance. The sun was darting his oblique rays through the beech trees by the side of the ditch and the apple trees outside, making the cocks crow on the dunghill, and the pigeons coo on the roof. The smell of the cow stalls came through the open door, mingling in the fresh morning air with the pungent odor of the stable where the horses were neighing, with their heads turned toward the light.

As soon as his trousers were properly fastened, Lecacheur came out, and went first of all toward the hen house to count the morning's eggs, for he had been suspecting thefts for some time. But the servant girl ran up to him with lifted arms and cried:

"Master! Master! they have stolen a rabbit during the night."

"A rabbit?"

"Yes, Master, the big gray rabbit, from the hutch on the left." Whereupon the farmer quite opened his left eye, and said, simply:

"I must see that."

And off he went to inspect it. The hutch had been broken open and the rabbit was gone. Then he became thoughtful, closed his left eye again, scratched his nose, and after a little consideration, said to the frightened girl, who was standing stupidly before him:

"Go and fetch the gendarmes; say I expect them as soon as possible."

Lecacheur was mayor of the village, Pairgry-le Gras, and ruled it like a tyrant, on account of his money and position. As soon as the servant had disappeared in the direction of the village, which was only about five hundred yards off, he went into the house to have his morning coffee and to discuss the matter with his wife. He found her on her knees in front of the fire, trying to get it to burn up quickly. As soon as he got to the door, he said:

"Somebody has stolen the gray rabbit."

She turned round so quickly that she found herself sitting on the floor, and looking at her husband with distressed eyes, she said:

"What is it, Cacheux! Somebody has stolen a rabbit?"

"The big gray one."

She sighed: "How sad! Who can have done it?"

She was a little, thin, active, neat woman, who knew all about farming. But Lecacheur had his own ideas about the matter.

"It must be that fellow Polyte."

His wife got up suddenly and said in a furious voice:

"He did it! he did it! You need not look for any one else. He did it! You have said it, Cacheux!"

All her peasant's fury, all her avarice, all the rage of a saving woman against the man of whom she had always been suspicious, and against the girl whom she had always suspected, could be seen in the contraction of her mouth, in the wrinkles in her cheeks, and in the forehead of her thin, exasperated face.

"And what have you done?" she asked.

"I have sent for the gendarmes."

This Polyte was a laborer, who had been employed on the farm for a few days, and had been dismissed by Lecacheur for an insolent answer. He was an old soldier, and was supposed to have retained his habits of marauding and debauchery from his campaigns in Africa. He did anything for a livelihood, but whether working as a mason, a navvy, a reaper, whether he broke stones or lopped trees, he was always lazy. So he remained in no position long, and had, at times, to change his neighborhood to obtain work.

From the first day that he came to the farm, Lecacheur's wife had detested him, and now she was sure that he had committed the robbery.

In about half an hour the two gendarmes arrived. Brigadier Sénateur was very tall and thin, and Gendarme Lenient, short and fat. Lecacheur made them sit down and told them the affair, and then they went and saw the scene of the theft, in order to verify the fact that the hutch had been broken open, and to collect all the proofs they could. When they got back to the kitchen, the mistress brought in some wine, filled their glasses and asked with a distrustful look:

"Shall you catch him?"

The brigadier, who had his sword between his legs, appeared thoughtful. Certainly, he was sure of taking him, if he was pointed out to him, but if not, he could not himself answer for being able to discover him. After reflecting for a long time, he put this simple question:

"Do you know the thief?"

And Lecacheur replied, with a look of Normandy slyness in his eyes:

"As for knowing him, I do not, as I did not see him commit the robbery. If I had seen him, I should have made him eat it raw, skin and flesh, without a drop of cider to wash it down. As for saying who it is, I cannot, although I believe it is that good-for-nothing Polyte."

Then he related at length his troubles with Polyte, his leaving his service, his bad reputation, things which had been told him, accumulating insignificant and minute proofs. Then the brigadier, who had been listening very attentively while he emptied his glass and filled it again, turned to his gendarme with an indifferent air, and said:

"We must go and look in the cottage of Severin's wife." At which the gendarme smiled and nodded three times.

Then Madame Lecacheur came to them, and very quietly, with all a peasant's cunning, questioned the brigadier in her turn. The shepherd Severin, a simpleton, a sort of brute who had been brought up from youth among his bleating flocks, and who knew of scarcely anything besides them in the world, had nevertheless preserved the peasant's instinct for saving, at the bottom of his heart. For years and years he had hidden in hollow trees and crevices in the rocks, all that he earned, either as shepherd, or by curing the fractures of animals (for the bonesetter's secret had been handed down to him by the old shepherd whose place he took), by touch or advice, for one day he bought a small property consisting of a cottage and a field, for three thousand francs.

A few months later it became known that he was going to marry a servant notorious for her bad morals, the innkeeper's servant. The young fellows said that the girl, knowing that he was pretty well off, had been to his cottage every night, and had taken him, bewitched him, led him on to matrimony, little by little, night by night.

And then, having been to the mayor's office and to church, she lived in the house which her man had bought, while he continued to tend his flocks, day and night, on the plains.

And the brigadier added:

"Polyte has been sleeping with her for three weeks, for the thief has no place of his own to go to!"

The gendarme made a little joke:

"He takes the shepherd's blankets."

Madame Lecacheur, seized by a fresh access of rage, of rage increased by a married woman's anger against debauchery, exclaimed:

"It is she, I am sure. Go there. Ah! the blackguard thieves!"

But the brigadier was quite unmoved.

"A minute," he said. "Let us wait until twelve o'clock; as Polyte goes and dines there every day, I shall catch them with it under their noses."

The gendarme smiled, pleased at his chief's idea, and Lecacheur also smiled now, for the affair of the shepherd struck him as very funny: deceived husbands are always amusing.

Twelve o'clock has just struck when the brigadier, followed by his man, knocked gently three times at the door of a small lonely house, situated at the corner of a wood, some five hundred yards from the village.

They stood close against the wall, so as not to be seen from within, and waited. As nobody answered, the brigadier knocked again in a minute or two. It was so quiet that the house seemed uninhabited; but Lenient, the gendarme, who had very quick ears, said that he heard somebody moving about inside. Sénateur got angry. He would not allow anyone to resist the authority of the law for a moment, and, knocking at the door with the hilt of his sword, he cried out:

"Open the door, in the name of the law."

As this order had no effect, he roared out:

"If you do not obey, I shall smash the lock. I am the brigadier of the gendarmerie, by G-d! Here, Lenient."

He had not finished speaking when the door opened and Sénateur saw before him a fat girl, with a very red color, blowsy, with pendent breasts, big stomach, and broad hips, a sort of sanguine and sensual female, the wife of the shepherd Severin. He entered the cottage.

"I have come to pay you a visit, as I want to make a little search," he said, and he looked about him. On the table there was a plate, a jug of cider and a glass half full, which proved that a meal had been going on. Two knives were lying side by side, and the shrewd gendarme winked at his superior officer.

"It smells good," the latter said.

"One might swear that it was stewed rabbit," Lenient added, much amused.

"Will you have a glass of brandy?" the peasant woman asked.

"No, thank you; I only want the skin of the rabbit that you are eating."

She pretended not to understand, but she was trembling.

"What rabbit?"

The brigadier had taken a seat, and was calmly wiping his forehead.

"Come, come, you are not going to try and make us believe that you live on couch grass. What were you eating there all by yourself for your dinner?"

"I? Nothing whatever, I swear to you. A mite of butter on my bread."

"You are a novice, my good woman—*a mite of butter on your bread.* You are mistaken; you ought to have said: a mite of butter on the rabbit. By G-d, your butter smells good! It is special butter, extra good butter, butter fit for a wedding; certainly not household butter!"

The gendarme was shaking with laughter, and repeated:

"Not household butter, certainly."

As Brigadier Sénateur was a joker, all the gendarmes had grown facetious, and the officer continued:

"Where is your butter?"

"My butter?"

"Yes, your butter."

"In the jar."

"Then where is the butter jar?"

"Here it is."

She brought out an old cup, at the bottom of which there was a layer of rancid, salt butter. The brigadier smelled it, and said, with a shake of his head:

"It is not the same. I want the butter that smells of the rabbit. Come, Lenient, open your eyes; look under the sideboard, my good fellow, and I will look under the bed."

Having shut the door, he went up to the bed and tried to move it; but it was fixed to the wall, and had not been moved for more than half a century, apparently. Then the brigadier stooped, and made his uniform crack. A button had flown off.

"Lenient," he said.

"Yes, brigadier?"

"Come here, my lad, and look under the bed; I am too tall. I will look after the sideboard."

He got up and waited while his man executed his orders.

Lenient, who was short and stout, took off his kepi, laid himself on his stomach, and putting his face on the floor looked at the black cavity under the bed. Then, suddenly, he exclaimed:

"All right, here we are!"

"What have you got? The rabbit?"

"No, the thief."

"The thief! Pull him out, pull him out!"

The gendarme had put his arms under the bed and laid hold of something. He pulled with all his might, and at last a foot, shod in a thick boot, appeared, which he was holding in his right hand. The brigadier grabbed it, crying:

"Pull! pull!"

And Lenient, who was on his knees by that time, was pulling at the other leg. But it was a hard job, for the prisoner kicked out hard, and arched up his back across the bed.

"Courage! courage! pull! pull!" Sénateur cried, and they pulled with all their strength—so hard that the wooden bar gave way, and the victim came out as far as his head. At last they got that out also, and saw the terrified and furious face of Polyte, whose arms remained stretched out under the bed.

"Pull away!" the brigadier kept on exclaiming. Then they heard a strange noise as the arms followed the shoulders and the hands the arms. In the hands was the handle of a saucepan, and at the end of the handle the pan itself, which contained stewed rabbit.

"Good Lord! good Lord!" the brigadier shouted in his delight, while Lenient took charge of the man. The rabbit's skin, an overwhelming proof, was discovered under the mattress, and the gendarmes returned in triumph to the village with their prisoner and their booty.

A week later, as the affair had made much stir, Lecacheur, on going into the *mairie* to consult the schoolmaster, was told that the shepherd Severin had been waiting for him for more than an hour. He found him sitting on a chair in a corner with his stick between his legs. When he saw the mayor, he got up, took off his cap, and said:

"Good morning, Maître Cacheux"; and then he remained standing, timid and embarrassed.

"What do you want?" the former said.

"This is it, Monsicur. Is it true that somebody stole one of your rabbits last week?"

"Yes, it is quite true, Severin."

"Who stole the rabbit?"

"Polyte Ancas, the laborer."

"Right! right! And is it also true that it was found under my bed?"

"What do you mean, the rabbit?"

"The rabbit and then Polyte."

"Yes, my poor Severin, quite true, but who told you?"

"Pretty well everybody. I understand! And I suppose you know all about marriages, as you marry people?"

"What about marriage?"

"With regard to one's rights."

"What rights?"

"The husband's rights and then the wife's rights."

"Of course I do."

"Oh! Then just tell me, M'sieu Cacheux, has my wife the right to go to bed with Polyte?"

"What do you mean by going to bed with Polyte?"

"Yes, has she any right before the law, and seeing that she is my wife, to go to bed with Polyte?"

"Why of course not, of course not."

"If I catch him there again, shall I have the right to thrash him and her also?"

"Why—why—why, yes."

"Very well, then; I will tell you why I want to know. One night last week, as I had my suspicions, I came in suddenly, and they were not behaving properly. I chucked Polyte out, to go and sleep somewhere else; but that was all, as I did not know what my rights were. This time I did not see them; I only heard of it from others. That is over, and we will not say any more about it; but if I catch them again, by G-d! if I catch them again, I will make them lose all taste for such nonsense, Maître Cacheux, as sure as my name is Severin."

Love

Three Pages from a Sportsman's Book

I have just read among the general news in one of the papers a drama of passion. He killed her and then he killed himself, so he must have loved her. What matters He or She? Their love alone matters to me; and it does not interest me because it moves me or astonishes me, or because it softens me or makes me think, but because it recalls to my mind a remembrance of my youth, a strange recollection of a hunting adventure where Love appeared to me, as the Cross appeared to the early Christians, in the midst of the heavens.

I was born with all the instincts and the senses of primitive man, tempered by the arguments and the restraints of a civilized being. I am passionately fond of shooting, yet the sight of the wounded animal, of the blood on its feathers and on my hands, affects my heart so as almost to make it stop.

That year the cold weather set in suddenly toward the end of autumn, and I was invited by one of my cousins, Karl de Rauville, to go with him and shoot ducks on the marshes, at daybreak.

My cousin was a jolly fellow of forty, with red hair, very stout and bearded, a country gentleman, an amiable semibrute, of a happy disposition and endowed with that Gallic wit which makes even mediocrity agreeable. He lived in a house, half farmhouse, half château, situated in a broad valley through which a river ran. The hills right and left were covered with woods, old manorial woods where magnificent trees still remained, and where the rarest feathered game in that part of France was to be found. Eagles were shot there occasionally, and birds of passage, such as rarely venture into our over-populated part of the country, invariably lighted amid these giant oaks, as if they knew or recognized some little corner of a primeval forest which had remained there to serve them as a shelter during their short nocturnal halt.

In the valley there were large meadows watered by trenches and separated by hedges; then, further on, the river, which up to that point had been kept between banks, expanded into a vast marsh. That marsh was the best shooting ground I ever saw. It was my cousin's chief care, and he kept it as a preserve. Through the rushes that covered it, and made it rustling and rough, narrow passages had been cut, through which the flat-bottomed boats, impelled and steered by poles, passed along silently over dead water, brushing up against the reeds and making the swift fish take refuge in the weeds, and the wild fowl, with their pointed, black heads, dive suddenly.

I am passionately fond of the water: of the sea, though it is too vast, too full of movement, impossible to hold; of the rivers which are so beautiful, but which pass on, and flee away; and above all of the marshes, where the whole unknown existence of aquatic animals palpitates. The marsh is an entire world in itself on the world of earth—a different world, which has its own life, its settled inhabitants and its passing travelers, its voices, its noises, and above all its mystery. Nothing is more impressive, nothing more disquieting, more terrifying occasionally, than a fen. Why should a vague terror hang over these low plains covered with water? Is it the low rustling of the rushes, the strange will-o'-the-wisp lights, the silence which prevails on calm nights, the still mists which hang over the surface like a shroud; or is it the almost inaudible splashing, so slight and so gentle, yet sometimes more terrifying than the cannons of men or the thunders of the skies, which make these marshes resemble countries one has dreamed of, terrible countries holding an unknown and dangerous secret?

No, something else belongs to it—another mystery, profounder and graver, floats amid these thick mists, perhaps the mystery of the creation itself! For was it not in stagnant and muddy water, amid the heavy humidity of moist land under the heat of the sun, that the first germ of life pulsated and expanded to the day?

I arrived at my cousin's in the evening. It was freezing hard enough to split the stones.

During dinner, in the large room whose sideboards, walls, and ceiling were covered with stuffed birds, with wings extended or perched on branches to which they were nailed,—hawks, herons, owls, nightjars, buzzards, tiercels, vultures, falcons,—my cousin who, dressed in a sealskin jacket, himself resembled some strange animal from a cold country, told me what preparations he had made for that same night.

We were to start at half past three in the morning, so as to arrive at the place which he had chosen for our watching-place at about half past four. On that spot a hut had been built of lumps of ice, so as to shelter us somewhat from the trying wind which precedes daybreak, a wind so cold as to tear the flesh like a saw, cut it like the blade of a knife, prick it like a poisoned sting, twist it like a pair of pincers, and burn it like fire.

My cousin rubbed his hands: "I have never known such a frost," he said; "it is already twelve degrees below zero at six o'clock in the evening."

I threw myself on to my bed immediately after we had finished our meal, and went to sleep by the light of a bright fire burning in the grate.

At three o'clock he woke me. In my turn, I put on a sheepskin, and found my cousin Karl covered with a bearskin. After having each swallowed two cups of scalding coffee, followed by glasses of liqueur brandy, we started, accompanied by a gamekeeper and our dogs, Plongeon and Pierrot.

From the first moment that I got outside, I felt chilled to the very marrow. It was one of those nights on which the earth seems dead with cold. The frozen air becomes resisting and palpable, such pain does it cause; no breath of wind moves it, it is fixed and motionless; it bites you, pierces through you, dries you, kills the trees, the plants, the insects, the small birds themselves, who fall from the branches on to the hard ground, and become stiff themselves under the grip of the cold.

The moon, which was in her last quarter and was inclining all to one side, seemed fainting in the midst of space, so weak that she was unable to wane, forced to stay up yonder, seized and paralyzed by the severity of the weather. She shed a cold, mournful light over the world, that dying and wan light which she gives us every month, at the end of her period.

Karl and I walked side by side, our backs bent, our hands in our pockets and our guns under our arms. Our boots, which were wrapped in wool so that we might be able to walk without slipping on the frozen river, made no sound, and I looked at the white vapor which our dogs' breath made.

We were soon on the edge of the marsh, and entered one of the lanes of dry rushes which ran through the low forest.

Our elbows, which touched the long, ribbonlike leaves, left a slight noise behind us, and I was seized, as I had never been before, by the powerful and singular emotion which marshes cause in me. This one was dead, dead from cold, since we were walking on it, in the middle of its population of dried rushes.

Suddenly, at the turn of one of the lanes, I perceived the ice hut which had been constructed to shelter us. I went in, and as we had nearly an hour to wait before the wandering birds would awake, I rolled myself up in my rug in order to try and get warm. Then, lying on my back, I began to look at the misshapen moon, which had four horns through the vaguely transparent walls of this polar house. But the frost of the frozen marshes, the cold of these walls, the cold from the firmament penetrated me so terribly that I began to cough. My cousin Karl became uneasy.

"No matter if we do not kill much today," he said: "I do not want you to catch cold; we will light a fire." And he told the gamekeeper to cut some rushes.

We made a pile in the middle of our hut which had a hole in the middle of the roof to let out the smoke, and when the red flames rose up to the clear, crystal blocks they began to melt, gently, imperceptibly, as if they were sweating. Karl, who had remained outside, called out to me: "Come and look here!" I went out of the hut and remained struck with astonishment. Our hut, in the shape of a cone, looked like an enormous diamond with a heart of fire, which had been suddenly planted there in the midst of the frozen water of the marsh. And inside, we saw two fantastic forms, those of our dogs, who were warming themselves at the fire.

But a peculiar cry, a lost, a wandering cry, passed over our heads, and the light from our hearth showed us the wild birds. Nothing moves one so much as the first clamor of a life which one does not see, which passes through the somber air so quickly and so far off, just before the first streak of a winter's day appears on the horizon. It seems to me, at this glacial hour of dawn, as if that passing cry which is carried away by the wings of a bird is the sigh of a soul from the world!

"Put out the fire," said Karl, "it is getting daylight."

The sky was, in fact, beginning to grow pale, and the flights of ducks made long, rapid streaks which were soon obliterated on the sky.

A stream of light burst out into the night; Karl had fired, and the two dogs ran forward.

And then, nearly every minute, now he, now I, aimed rapidly as soon as the shadow of a flying flock appeared above the rushes. And Pierrot and Plongeon, out of breath but happy, retrieved the bleeding birds, whose eyes still, occasionally, looked at us.

The sun had risen, and it was a bright day with a blue sky, and we were thinking of taking our departure, when two birds with extended necks and outstretched wings, glided rapidly over our heads. I fired, and one of them fell almost at my feet. It was a teal, with a silver breast, and then, in the blue space above me, I heard a voice, the voice of a bird. It was a short, repeated, heart-rending lament; and the bird, the little animal that had been spared began to turn round in the blue sky, over our heads, looking at its dead companion which I was holding in my hand.

Karl was on his knees, his gun to his shoulder watching it eagerly, until it should be within shot. "You have killed the duck," he said, "and the drake will not fly away."

He certainly did not fly away; he circled over our heads continually, and continued his cries. Never have any groans of suffering pained me so much as that desolate appeal, as that lamentable reproach of this poor bird which was lost in space.

Occasionally he took flight under the menace of the gun which followed his movements, and seemed ready to continue his flight alone, but as he could not make up his mind to this, he returned to find his mate.

"Leave her on the ground," Karl said to me, "he will come within shot by and by." And he did indeed come near us, careless of danger, infatuated by his animal love, by his affection for his mate, which I had just killed.

Karl fired, and it was as if somebody had cut the string which held the bird suspended. I saw something black descend, and I heard the noise of a fall among the rushes. And Pierrot brought it to me.

I put them—they were already cold—into the same game bag, and I returned to Paris the same evening.

Saved

The little Marquise de Rennedon came rushing in like a ball through the window. She began to laugh before she spoke, to laugh till she cried, like she had done a month previously, when she had told her friend that she had betrayed the Marquis in order to have her revenge, but only once, just because he was really too stupid and too jealous.

The little Baroness de Grangerie had thrown the book which she was reading on to the sofa, and looked at Annette, curiously. She was already laughing herself, and at last she asked:

"What have you been doing now?"

"Oh! my dear!—my dear! it is too funny—too funny. Just fancy—I am saved!—saved!—saved!"

"How do you mean, saved?"

"Yes, saved!"

"From what?"

"From my husband, my dear, saved! Delivered! free! free! free!"

"How free? In what?"

"In what? Divorce! yes a divorce! I have my divorce!"

"You are divorced?"

"No, not yet; how stupid you are! One does not get divorced in three hours! But I have my proofs that he has deceived me—caught in the very act—just think!—in the very act. I have got him tight."

"Oh! do tell me all about it! So he deceived you?"

"Yes, that is to say no—yes and no—I do not know. At any rate, I have proofs, and that is the chief thing."

"How did you manage it?"

"How did I manage it? This is how! I have been energetic, very energetic. For the last three months he has been odious, altogether odious, brutal, coarse, a despot—in one word, vile. So I said to myself: This cannot last, I must have a divorce! But how?—for it is not very easy. I tried to make him beat me, but he would not. He vexed me from morning till night, made me go out when I did not wish to, and to remain at home when I wanted to dine out; he made my life unbearable for me from one week's end to the other, but he never struck me.

"Then I tried to find out whether he had a mistress. Yes, he had one, but he took a thousand precautions in going to see her, and they could never be caught together. Guess what I did then?"

"I cannot guess."

"Oh! you could never guess. I asked my brother to procure me a photograph of the creature."

"Of your husband's mistress?"

"Yes. It cost Jacques fifteen louis, the price of an evening, from seven o'clock till midnight, including a dinner, at three louis an hour, and he obtained the photograph into the bargain."

"It appears to me that he might have obtained it anyhow by means of some artifice and without—without—without being obliged to take the original at the same time."

"Oh! she is pretty, and Jacques did not mind the least. And then, I wanted some details about her, physical details about her figure, her breast, her complexion, a thousand things, in fact."

"I do not understand you."

"You shall see. When I had learned all that I wanted to know, I went to a—how shall I put it—to a man of business—you know—one of those men who transact business of all sorts—agents of—of—of publicity and complicity—one of those men—well, you understand what I mean."

"Pretty nearly, I think. And what did you say to him?"

"I said to him, showing the photograph of Clarisse (her name is Clarisse): 'Monsieur, I want a lady's maid who resembles this photograph. I require one who is pretty, elegant, neat, and sharp. I will pay her whatever is necessary, and if it costs me ten thousand francs so much the worse. I shall not require her for more than three months.'

"The man looked extremely astonished, and said: 'Do you require a maid of an irreproachable character, Madame?' I blushed, and stammered: 'Yes of course, for honesty.' He continued: 'And—then—as regards morals?' I did not venture to reply, so I only made a sign with my head which signified *No*. Then suddenly, I comprehended that he had a horrible suspicion and losing my presence of mind, I exclaimed: 'Oh! Monsieur,—it is for my husband, in order that I may surprise him.'

"Then the man began to laugh, and from his looks I gathered that I had regained his esteem. He even thought I was brave, and I would willingly have made a bet that at that moment he was longing to shake hands with me. However, he said to me: 'In a week, Madame, I shall have what you require; I will answer for my success, and you shall not pay me until I have succeeded. So this is a photograph of your husband's mistress?'

"'Yes, Monsieur.'

"'A handsome woman, and not too stout. And what scent?'

"I did not understand, and repeated: 'What scent?'

"He smiled: 'Yes, Madame, perfume is essential in tempting a man, for it unconsciously brings to his mind certain reminiscences which dispose him to action; the perfume creates an obscure confusion in his mind, and disturbs and energizes him by recalling his pleasures to him. You must also try to find out what your husband is in the habit of eating when he dines with his lady, and you might give him the same dishes the day you catch him. Oh! we have got him, Madame, we have got him.'

"I went away delighted, for here I had lighted on a very intelligent man.

"Three days later, I saw a tall, dark girl arrive at my house; she was very handsome, and her looks were modest and bold at the same time, the peculiar look of a female rake. She behaved very properly toward me, and as I did not exactly know what she was, I called her Mademoiselle, but she said immediately: 'Oh! pray, Madame, only call me Rose.' And she began to talk.

"'Well, Rose, you know why you have come here?'

"'I can guess it, Madame.'

"'Very good, my girl—and that will not be too much bother for you?'

"'Oh! Madame, this will be the eighth divorce that I shall have caused; I am used to it.'

"'Why, that is capital. Will it take you long to succeed?'

"'Oh? Madame, that depends entirely on Monsieur's temperament. When I have seen Monsieur for five minutes alone, I shall be able to tell you exactly.'

"'You will see him soon, my child, but I must tell you that he is not handsome.'

"'That does not matter to me, Madame. I have already separated some very ugly ones. But I must ask you, Madame, whether you have discovered his favorite perfume?'

"'Yes, Rose—verbena.'

"'So much the better, Madame, for I am also very fond of that scent! Can you also tell me, Madame, whether Monsieur's mistress wears silk underclothing and nightdresses?'

"'No, my child, cambric and lace.'

"'Oh! then she is altogether of superior station, for silk underclothing is getting quite common.'

"'What you say is quite true!'

"'Well, Madame, I will enter your service.' And so as a matter of fact she did immediately, and as if she had done nothing else all her life.

"An hour later my husband came home. Rose did not even raise her eyes to him, but he raised his eyes to her. She already smelled strongly of verbena. In five minutes she left the room, and he immediately asked me: 'Who is that girl?'

"'Why—my new lady's maid.'

"'Where did you pick her up?'

"'Baroness de Grangerie got her for me with the best references.'

"'Ah! she is rather pretty!'

"'Do you think so?'

"'Why, yes—for a lady's maid.'

"I was delighted, for I felt that he was already biting, and that same evening Rose said to me: 'I can now promise you that it will not take more than a fortnight, Monsieur is very easily caught!'

"'Ah! you have tried already?'

"'No, Madame, he only asked what my name was, so that he might hear what my voice was like.'

"'Very well, my dear Rose. Get on as quick as you can.'

"'Do not be alarmed, Madame; I shall only resist long enough not to make myself depreciated.'

"At the end of a week, my husband scarcely ever went out; I saw him roaming about the house the whole alternoon, and what was most significant in the matter was that he no longer prevented me from going out. And I, I was out of doors nearly the whole day long—in order—in order to leave him at liberty.

"On the ninth day, while Rose was undressing me, she said to me with a timid air: 'It happened this morning, Madame.'

"I was rather surprised, or rather overcome even, not at the part itself, but at the way in which she told me, and I stammered out: 'And—and—it went off well?'

"'Oh! yes, very well, Madame. For the last three days he has been pressing me, but I did not wish matters to proceed too quickly. You will tell me when you want us to be caught, Madame.'

"'Yes, certainly. Here! let us say Thursday.'

"'Very well, Madame, I shall grant nothing more till then, so as to keep Monsieur on the alert.'

"'You are sure not to fail?'

"'Oh! quite sure, Madame. I will excite him, so as to make him be there at the very moment which you may appoint.'

"'Let us say five o'clock then.'

"'Very well, Madame, and where?'

"'Well—in my bedroom.'

"'Very good, Madame, in your bedroom.'

"'You will understand what I did then, my dear. I went and fetched mamma and papa first of all, and then my uncle d'Orvelin, the President, and Monsieur Raplet, the Judge, my husband's friend. I had not told them what I was going to show them, but I made them all go on tiptoe as far as the door of my room. I waited till five o'clock exactly, and oh! how my heart beat! I had made the porter come upstairs as well, so as to have an additional witness! And then—and then at the moment when the clock began to strike, I opened the door wide. Ah! ah! ah! Here he was evidently—it was quite evident, my dear. Oh! what a head! If you had only seen his head! And he turned round, the idiot! Oh! how funny he looked—I laughed, I laughed. And papa was angry and wanted to give my husband a beating. And the porter, a good servant helped him to dress himself before us—before us. He buttoned his braces for him—what a joke it was! As for Rose, she was perfect, absolutely perfect. She cried—oh! she cried very well. She is an invaluable girl. If you ever want her, don't forget!

"And here I am. I came immediately to tell you of the affair directly. I am free. Long live divorce!"

And she began to dance in the middle of the drawing room, while the little Baroness, who was thoughtful and put out, said:

"Why did you not invite me to see it?"

The Necklace

She was one of those pretty and charming young girls who sometimes are born, as if by a slip of fate, into a family of clerks. She had no dowry, no expectations, no way of being known, understood, loved, and wedded by any rich and distinguished man; so she let herself be married to a little clerk of the Ministry of Public Instruction.

She dressed plainly because she could not dress well, but she was as unhappy as if she had really fallen from a higher station; since with women there is neither caste nor rank, for beauty, grace and charm take the place of birth and breeding. Natural ingenuity, instinct for what is elegant, a supple mind are their sole hierarchy, and often make of women of the people the equals of the very greatest ladies.

Mathilde suffered ceaselessly, feeling herself born to enjoy all delicacies and all luxuries. She was distressed at the poverty of her dwelling, at the bareness of the walls, at the shabby chairs, the ugliness of the curtains. All those things, of which another woman of her rank would never even have been conscious, tortured her and made her angry. The sight of the little Breton peasant who did her humble housework aroused in her despairing regrets and bewildering dreams. She thought of silent antechambers hung with Oriental tapestry, illumined by tall bronze candelabra, and of two great footmen in knee breeches who sleep in the big armchairs, made drowsy by the oppressive heat of the stove. She thought of long reception halls hung with ancient silk, of the dainty cabinets containing priceless curiosities and of little coquettish perfumed reception rooms made for chatting at five o'clock with intimate friends, with men famous and sought after, whom all women envy and whose attention they all desire.

When she sat down to dinner, before the round table covered with a tablecloth in use three days, opposite her husband, who uncovered the soup tureen and declared with a delighted air, "Ah, the good soup! I don't know anything better than that," she thought of dainty dinners, of shining silverware, of tapestry that peopled the walls with ancient personages and with strange birds flying in the midst of a fairy forest; and she thought of delicious dishes served on marvellous plates and of the whispered gallantries to which you listen with a sphinxlike smile while you are eating the wings of a quail.

She had no gowns, no jewels, nothing. And she loved nothing but that. She felt made for that. She would have liked so much to please, to be envied, to be charming, to be sought after.

She had a friend, a former schoolmate at the convent, who was rich, and whom she did not like to go to see any more because she felt so sad when she came home.

But one evening her husband came home with a triumphant air and holding a large envelope in his hand.

"There," said he, "there is something for you."

She tore the paper quickly and drew out a printed card which bore these words:

> The Minister of Public Instruction and Madame Georges Ramponneau request the honor of M. and Madame Loisel's company at the palace of the Ministry on Monday evening, January 18th.

Instead of being delighted, as her husband had hoped, she threw the invitation on the table crossly, muttering:

"What do you wish me to do with that?"

"Why, my dear, I thought you would be glad. You never go out, and this is such a fine opportunity. I had great trouble to get it. Everyone wants to go; it is very select, and they are not giving many invitations to clerks. The whole official world will be there."

She looked at him with an irritated glance and said impatiently:

"And what do you wish me to put on my back?"

He had not thought of that. He stammered:

"Why, the gown you go to the theatre in. It looks very well to me."

He stopped, distracted, seeing that his wife was weeping. Two great tears ran slowly from the corners of her eyes towards the corners of her mouth.

"What's the matter? What's the matter?" he asked.

By a violent effort she conquered her grief and replied in a calm voice, while she wiped away her tears:

"Nothing. Only I have no gown, and, therefore, I can't go to this ball. Give your card to some colleague whose wife is better equipped than I am."

He was in despair. He resumed:

"Come, let us see, Mathilde. How much would it cost, a suitable gown, which you could use on other occasions—something very simple?"

She reflected several seconds, making her calculations and wondering also what sum she could ask without drawing on herself an immediate refusal and a frightened exclamation from the economical clerk.

Finally she replied hesitatingly:

"I don't know exactly, but I think I could manage it with four hundred francs."

He grew a little pale, because he was laying aside just that amount to buy a gun and treat himself to a little shooting next summer on the plain of Nanterre, with several friends who went to shoot larks there of a Sunday.

But he said:

"Very well. I will give you four hundred francs. And try to have a pretty gown."

The day of the ball drew near and Madame Loisel seemed sad, uneasy, anxious. Her frock was ready, however. Her husband said to her one evening:

"What is the matter? Come, you have seemed very queer these last three days."

And she answered:

"It annoys me not to have a single piece of jewelery, not a single ornament, nothing to put on. I shall look poverty stricken. I would almost rather not go at all."

"You might wear natural flowers," said her husband. "They're quite fashionable at this time of year. For ten francs you can get two or three magnificent roses."

She was not convinced.

"No; there's nothing more humiliating than to look poor among other women who are rich."

"How stupid you are!" her husband cried. "Go and look up your friend, Madame Forestier, and ask her to lend you some jewels. You're intimate enough with her to do that."

She uttered a cry of joy:

"True! I never thought of it."

The next day she went to her friend and told her of her distress.

Madame Forestier went to a wardrobe with a mirror, took out a large jewel box, brought it back, opened it and said to Madame Loisel:

"Choose, my dear."

She saw first some bracelets, then a pearl necklace, then a Venetian gold cross set with precious stones, of admirable workmanship. She tried on the ornaments before the mirror, hesitated and could not make up her mind to part with them, to give them back. She kept asking:

"Haven't you any more?"

"Why, yes. Look further; I don't know what you like."

Suddenly she discovered, in a black satin box, a superb diamond necklace, and her heart throbbed with an immoderate desire. Her hands trembled as she took it. She fastened it round her throat, and was lost in ecstasy at her reflection in the mirror.

Then she asked, hesitating, filled with anxious doubt:

"Will you lend me this, only this?"

"Why, yes, certainly."

She threw her arms round her friend's neck, kissed her passionately, and then fled with her treasure.

The night of the ball arrived. Madame Loisel was a great success. She was prettier than any other woman present, elegant, graceful, smiling and filled with joy. All the men looked at her, asked her name, sought to be introduced. All the attachés of the Cabinet wished to waltz with her. She was remarked by the minister himself.

She danced with rapture, with passion, intoxicated by pleasure, forgetting all in the triumph of her beauty, in the glory of her success, in a sort of cloud of happiness composed of all this homage and admiration, and of that sense of triumph which is so sweet to woman's heart.

She left the ball about four o'clock in the morning. Her husband had been sleeping since midnight in a little deserted anteroom with three other gentlemen whose wives were enjoying the ball.

He threw over her shoulders the wraps he had brought, the modest wraps of common life, the poverty of which contrasted with the elegance of the ball dress. She felt this and wished to escape so as not to be remarked by the other women, who were enveloping themselves in costly furs.

Loisel held her back, saying: "Wait a bit. You will catch cold outside. I will call a cab."

But she did not listen to him and rapidly descended the stairs. When they reached the street they could not find a carriage and began to look for one, shouting after the cabmen passing at a distance.

They went towards the Seine in despair, shivering with cold. At last they found on the quay one of those ancient night cabs which, as though they were ashamed to show their shabbiness during the day, are never seen round Paris until after dark.

It took them to their dwelling in the Rue des Martyrs, and sadly they mounted the stairs to their flat. All was ended for her. As to him, he reflected that he must be at the ministry at ten o'clock that morning.

She removed her wraps before the glass so as to see herself once more in all her glory. But suddenly she uttered a cry. She no longer had the necklace round her neck!

"What is the matter with you?" demanded her husband, already half undressed.

She turned distractedly towards him.

"I have—I have—I've lost Madame Forestier's necklace," she cried.

He stood up, bewildered.

"What!—how? Impossible!"

They looked among the folds of her skirt, of her cloak, in her pockets, everywhere, but did not find it.

"You're sure you had it on when you left the ball?" he asked.

"Yes, I felt it in the vestibule of the minister's house."

"But if you had lost it in the street we should have heard it fall. It must be in the cab."

"Yes, probably. Did you take his number?"

"No. And you—didn't you notice it?"

"No."

They looked, thunderstruck, at each other. At last Loisel put on his clothes.

"I shall go back on foot," said he, "over the whole route, to see whether I can find it."

He went out. She sat waiting on a chair in her ball dress, without strength to go to bed, overwhelmed, without any fire, without a thought.

Her husband returned about seven o'clock. He had found nothing.

He went to police headquarters, to the newspaper offices to offer a reward; he went to the cab companies—everywhere, in fact, whither he was urged by the least spark of hope.

She waited all day, in the same condition of mad fear before this terrible calamity.

Loisel returned at night with a hollow, pale face. He had discovered nothing.

"You must write to your friend," said he, "that you have broken the clasp of her necklace and that you are having it mended. That will give us time to turn round."

She wrote at his dictation.

At the end of a week they had lost all hope. Loisel, who had aged five years, declared:

"We must consider how to replace that ornament."

The next day they took the box that had contained it and went to the jeweller whose name was found within. He consulted his books.

"It was not I, madame, who sold that necklace; I must simply have furnished the case."

Then they went from jeweller to jeweller, searching for a necklace like the other, trying to recall it, both sick with chagrin and grief.

They found, in a shop at the Palais Royal, a string of diamonds that seemed to them exactly like the one they had lost. It was worth forty thousand francs. They could have it for thirty-six.

So they begged the jeweller not to sell it for three days yet. And they made a bargain that he should buy it back for thirty-four thousand francs, in case they should find the lost necklace before the end of February.

Loisel possessed eighteen thousand francs which his father had left him. He would borrow the rest.

He did borrow, asking a thousand francs of one, five hundred of another, five louis here, three louis there. He gave notes, took up ruinous obligations, dealt with usurers and all the race of lenders. He compromised all the rest of his life, risked signing a note without even knowing whether he could meet it; and, frightened by the trouble yet to come, by the black misery that was about to fail upon him, by the prospect of all the physical privations and moral tortures that he was to suffer, he went to get the new necklace, laying upon the jeweller's counter thirty-six thousand francs.

When Madame Loisel took back the necklace Madame Forestier said to her with a chilly manner:

"You should have returned it sooner; I might have needed it."

She did not open the case, as her friend had so much feared. If she had detected the substitution, what would she have thought, what would she have said? Would she not have taken Madame Loisel for a thief?

Thereafter Madame Loisel knew the horrible existence of the needy. She bore her part, however, with sudden heroism. That dreadful debt must be paid. She would pay it. They dismissed their servant; they changed their lodgings; they rented a garret under the roof.

She came to know what heavy housework meant and the odious cares of the kitchen. She washed the dishes, using her dainty fingers and rosy nails on greasy pots and pans. She washed the soiled linen, the shirts and the dishcloths, which she dried upon a line; she took the slops down to the street every morning and carried up the water, stopping for breath at every landing. And dressed like a woman of the people, she went to the fruiterer, the grocer, the butcher, a basket on her arm, bargaining, meeting with impertinence, defending her miserable money, sou by sou.

Every month they had to meet some notes, renew others, obtain more time.

Her husband worked in the evenings, making up a tradesman's accounts, and late at night he often copied manuscript for five sous a page.

This life lasted ten years.

At the end of ten years they had paid everything, everything with the rates of usury and the accumulations of the compound interest.

Madame Loisel looked old now. She had become the woman of impoverished households—strong and hard and rough. With frowsy hair, skirts askew and red hands, she talked loud while washing the floor with great swishes of water. But sometimes, when her husband was at the office, she sat down near the window and thought of that gay evening of long ago, of that ball where she had looked so beautiful and been so much admired.

What would have happened if she had not lost that necklace? Who knows? who knows? How strange and changeful is life! How small a thing is needed to make or ruin us!

But one Sunday, having gone to take a walk in the Champs Élysées to refresh herself after the labors of the week, she suddenly saw a woman who was leading a child. It was Madame Forestier, still young, still beautiful, still charming.

Madame Loisel felt moved. Should she speak to her? Yes, certainly. And now that she had paid, she would tell her all about it. Why not?

She went up.

"Good day, Jeanne."

The other, astonished to be familiarly addressed by this plain goodwife, did not recognize her at all and stammered:

"But—madame!—I do not know—You must be mistaken."

"No. I am Mathilde Loisel."

Her friend uttered a cry.

"Oh, my poor Mathilde! How you are changed!

"Yes, I have had a very hard life, since I last saw you, and great poverty—and that because of you!"

"Of me! How so?"

"Do you remember that diamond necklace you lent me to wear at the ministerial ball?"

"Yes. Well?"

"Well, I lost it."

"What do you mean? You brought it back."

"I brought you back another exactly like it. And it has taken us ten years to pay for it. You can understand that it was not easy for us, for us who had nothing. At last it is ended, and I am very glad."

Madame Forestier had stopped.

"You say that you bought a necklace of diamonds to replace mine?"

"Yes. You never noticed it, then! They were very similar."

And she smiled with a joy that was at once proud and ingenuous.

Madame Forestier, deeply moved, took her hands.

"Oh, my poor Mathilde! Why, my necklace was paste! It was worth at most only five hundred francs!"

Chekhov

1860	January 17. Anton Pavlovich Chekhov is born in Taganrog, Russia.
1884	Graduates from Moscow University and begins practicing medicine. Stories written in a popular humor magazine gain favorable attention.
1885	Stories contributed to the national newspaper, *New Times*, are enthusiastically received.
1886	The collection, *Motley Stories,* is released. A second collection, *In the Twilight*, is released two years later.
1887	The play, *Ivanoff,* is successfully produced.
1890	Makes trip to Sakhalin Island, a penal colony, to study its existing conditions.
1897	An attack of tuberculosis forces Chekhov to move to the morc temperate climate of Yalta. Although severely limited by this illness, he continues his work on dramas.
1898	*The Seagull* is presented by the Moscow Art Theater. The same group produces *Uncle Vanya* in 1889 and *The Three Sisters* in 1901.
1904	*The Cherry Orchard* is produced. Chekhov dies at the health resort in Badenweiler, Germany, on July 2.

Anton Chekhov

Anton Pavlovich Chekhov, like Pushkin, Lermontov, Bielinsky, and Garshin, died young, and although he wrote a goodly number of plays and stories which gave him a high reputation in Russia, he did not live to enjoy international fame. This is partly owing to the nature of his work, but more perhaps to the total eclipse of other contemporary writers by Gorky. There are signs now that his delicate and unpretentious art will outlast the sensational flare of the other's reputation. Gorky himself has generously tried to help in the perpetuation of Chekhov's name, by publishing a volume of personal reminiscences of his dead friend.

Like Gogol and Artsybashev, Chekhov was a man of the South, being born at Taganrog, a seaport on a gulf of the Black Sea, near the mouth of the river Don. The date of his birth is the 17 January 1860. His father was a clever serf, who, by good business foresight, bought his freedom early in life. Although the father never had much education himself, he gave his four children every possible advantage. Anton studied in the Greek school in his native city, and then entered the Faculty of Medicine at the University of Moscow. "I don't well remember why I chose the medical faculty," he remarked later, "but I never regretted that choice." He took his degree, but entered upon no regular practice. For a year he worked in a hospital in a small town near Moscow, and in 1892, he freely offered his medical services during an epidemic of cholera. His professional experiences were of immense service to him in analyzing the characters of various patients whom he treated, and his scientific training he always believed helped him greatly in the writing of his stories and plays, which are all psychological studies.

He knew he had not very long to live, for before he had really begun his literary career signs of tuberculosis had plainly become manifest. He died in Germany, the 2 July 1904, and his funeral at Moscow was a national event.

Chekhov was a fine conversationalist, and fond of society; despite the terrible gloom of his stories, he had distinct gifts as a wit, and was a great favorite at dinner parties and social gatherings. He joked freely on his deathbed. He was warm-hearted and generous, and gave money gladly to poor students and overworked schoolteachers. His innate modesty and lack of self-assertion made him very slow at personal advertisement, and his dislike of Tolstoy's views prevented at first an acquaintance with the old sage. Later, however, Tolstoy, being deeply interested in him, sought him out, and the two writers became friends. At this time many Russians believed that Chekhov was the legitimate heir to Tolstoy's fame.

In 1879, while still in the University of Moscow, Chekhov began to write short stories, of a more or less humorous nature, which were published in reviews. His first book appeared in 1887. Some critics sounded a note of warning, which he heeded. They said "it was too bad that such a talented young man should spend all his time making people laugh." This indirect advice, coupled with maturity of years and incipient disease, changed the writer's point of view, and his best known work is typically Russian in its tragic intensity.

Chekhov is *durch und durch echt russisch*: no one but a Russian would ever have conceived such characters, or reported such conversations. We often wonder that physical exercise and bodily recreation are so conspicuously absent from Russian books. But we should remember that a Russian conversation is one of the most violent forms of physical exercise, as it is among the French and Italians. Although Chekhov belongs to our day, and represents contemporary Russia, he stands in the middle of the highway of Russian fiction, and in his method of art harks back to the great masters. He perhaps resembles Turgenev more than any other of his predecessors, but he is only a faint echo. He is like Turgenev in the delicacy and in the aloofness of his art. He has at times that combination of the absolutely real with the absolutely fantastic that is so characteristic of Gogol: one of his best stories, *The Black Monk*, might have been written by the author of *The Cloak* and *The Portrait*. He is like Dostoevsky in his uncompromising depiction of utter degradation; but he has little of Dostoevsky's glowing sympathy and heartpower. He resembles Tolstoy least of all. The two chief features of Tolstoy's work—self-revelation and moral teaching—must have been abhorrent to Chekhov, for his stories tell us almost nothing about himself and his own opinions, and they teach nothing. His art is impersonal, and he is content with mere diagnosis. His only point of contact with Tolstoy is his grim fidelity to detail, the peculiar Russian realism common to every Russian novelist. Tolstoy said that Chekhov resembled Guy de Maupassant. This is entirely wide of the mark. He resembles Guy de Maupassant merely in the fact that, like the Frenchman, he wrote short stories.

Among recent writers Chekhov is at the farthest remove from his friend Gorky and most akin to Andreev. It is probable that Andreev learned something from him. Unlike Turgenev, both Chekhov and Andreev study mental disease. Their best charasters are abnormal; they have some fatal taint in the mind which turns this goodly frame, the earth, into a sterile promonotory; this majestical roof fretted with golden fire, into a foul and pestilent congregation of vapors. Neither Chekhov nor Andreev have attempted to lift that black pall of despair that hangs over Russian fiction.

Chekhov was a physician and an invalid; he saw sickness without and sickness within. Small wonder that his stories deal with the unhealthy and the doomed. For just as Artsybashev's tuberculosis has made him create the modern Tamburlaine as a mental enjoyment of physical activity, so the less turbulent nature of Chekhov has made him reproduce in his creatures of the imagination his own sufferings and fears. I think he was afraid of mental as well as physical decay, for he has studied insanity with the same assiduity as that displayed by Andreev in his nerve-wrecking story A *Dilemma*.

In *Ward No. 6*, which no one should read late at night, Chekhov has given us a picture of an insane asylum, which, if the conditions there depicted are true to life, would indicate that some parts of Russia have not advanced one step since Gogol wrote *The Inspector General*. The patients are beaten and hammered into insensibility by a brutal keeper; they live amidst intolerable filth. The attending physician is a typical Russian, who sees clearly the horror and abomination of the place, but has not sufficient will power to make a change. He is fascinated by one of the patients, with whom he talks for hours. His fondness for this man leads his friends to believe that he is insane, and they begin to treat him with that humoring condescension and pity which would be sufficient in itself to drive a man out of his mind. He is finally invited by his younger colleague to visit the asylum to examine a strange case; when he reaches the building, he himself is shoved into Ward No. 6, and realizes that the doors are shut upon him forever. In about twenty-four hours he dies, but in those hours he goes through a hell of physical and mental torment.

The fear of death, which to an intensely intellectual people like the Russians, is an obsession of terror, and shadows all their literature,—it appears all through Tolstoy's diary and novels,—is analyzed in many forms by Chekhov. In *Ward No. 6* Chekhov pays his respects to Tolstoy's creed of self-denial, through the lips of the doctor's favorite madman.

> A creed which teaches indifference to wealth, indifference to the conveniences of life, and contempt for suffering is quite incomprehensible to the great majority who never knew either wealth or the conveniences of life, and to whom contempt for suffering would mean contempt for their own lives, which are made up of feelings of hunger, cold, loss, insult, and a Hamlet-like terror of death. All life lies in these feelings, and life may be hated or wearied of, but never despised. Yes, I repeat it, the teachings of the Stoics can never have a future; from the beginning of time, life has consisted in sensibility to pain and response to irritation.

No better indictment has ever been made against those to whom self-denial and renunciation are merely a luxurious attitude of the mind.

Chekhov's sympathy with imagination and his hatred for commonplace folk who stupidly try to repress its manifestations are shown again and again in his tales. He loves especially the imagination of children; and he shows them as infinitely wiser than their practical parents. In the short sketch *An Event*, the children are wild with delight over the advent of three kittens, and cannot understand their father's disgust for the little beasts, and his cruel indifference to their welfare. The cat is their mother, that they know; but who is the father? The kittens must have a father, so the children drag out the wooden rocking-horse, and place him beside his wife and offspring.

In the story *At Home* the father's bewilderment at the creative imagination and the curious caprices of his little boy's mind is tenderly and beautifully described. The father knows he is not bringing him up wisely, but is utterly at a loss how to go at the problem, having none of the intuitive sympathy of a woman. The boy is busy with a pencil, and represents sounds by shapes, letters by colors. For example, "the sound of an orchestra he drew as a round smoky spot; whistling as a spiral thread." In making letters, he always painted L yellow, M red, and A black. He draws a picture of a horse with a soldier standing in front of it. The father rebukes him for bad perpsective, and tells him that the soldier in his picture is taller than the house. But the boy replies, "If you drew the soldier smaller, you wouldn't be able to see his eyes."

Chekhov is eternally at war with the practical, with the narrowminded, with the commonplace. Where there is no vision, the people perish.

Professor Brückner has well said that Chekhov was by profession a physician, but an artist by the grace of God. He was indeed an exquisite artist, and if his place in Russian literature is not large, it seems permanent. He does not rank among the greatest. He lacks the tremendous force of Tolstoy, the flawless perfection of Turgenev, and the mighty world-embracing sympathy of Great-heart Dostoevsky. But he is a faithful interpreter of Russian life, and although his art was objective, one cannot help feeling the essential goodness of the man behind his work, and loving him for it.

—*from* Essays on Russian Novelists *by William Lyon Phelps*

A Journey by Cart

They left the city at half past eight.

The highway was dry and a splendid April sun was beating fiercely down, but the snow still lay in the woods and wayside ditches. The long, dark, cruel winter was only just over, spring had come in a breath, but to Maria Vasilievna driving along the road in the cart there was nothing either new or attractive in the warmth, or the listless, misty woods flushed with the first heat of spring, or in the flocks of crows flying far away across the wide, flooded meadows, or in the marvellous, unfathomable sky into which one felt one could sail away with such infinite pleasure. Maria Vasilievna had been a schoolteacher for thirty years, and it would have been impossible for her to count the number of times she had driven to town for her salary, and returned home as she was doing now. It mattered not to her whether the season were spring, as now, or winter, or autumn with darkess and rain; she invariably longed for one thing and one thing only: a speedy end to her journey.

She felt as if she had lived in this part of the world for a long, long time, even a hundred years or more, and it seemed to her that she knew every stone and every tree along the roadside between her school and the city. Here lay her past and her present as well, and she could not conceive of a future beyond her school and the road and the city, and then the road and her school again, and then once more the road and the city.

Of her past before she had been a schoolteacher she had long since ceased to think—she had almost forgotten it. She had had a father and mother once, and had lived with them in a large apartment near the Red Gate in Moscow, but her recollection of that life was as vague and shadowy as a dream. Her father had died when she was ten years old, and her mother had soon followed him. She had had a brother, an officer, with whom she had corresponded at first, but he had lost the habit of writing to her after a while, and had stopped answering her letters. Of her former belongings her mother's photograph was now her only possession, and this had been so faded by the dampness of the school that her mother's features had all disappeared except the eyebrows and hair.

When they had gone three miles on their way old daddy Simon, who was driving the cart, turned round and said:

"They have caught one of the town officials and have shipped him away. They say he killed the mayor of Moscow with the help of some Germans."

"Who told you that?"

"Ivan Ionoff read it in the paper at the inn."

For a long time neither spoke. Maria Vasilievna was thinking of her school, and the coming examinations for which she was preparing four boys and one girl. And just as her mind is full of these examinations, a landholder named Khanoff drove up with a four-in-hand harnessed to an open carriage. It was he who had held the examination in her school the year before. As he drove up alongside her cart he recognized her, bowed, and exclaimed:

"Good morning! Are you on your way home, may I ask?"

Khanoff was a man of forty or thereabouts. His expression was listless and blasé, and he had already begun to age perceptibly, but he was handsome still and admired by women. He lived alone on a large estate; he had no business anywhere, and it was said of him that he never did anything at home but walk about and whistle, or else play chess with his old man servant. It was also rumoured that he was a hard drinker. Maria Vasilievna remembered that, as a matter of fact, at the last examination even the papers that he had brought with him had smelled of scent and wine. Everything he had had on that day had been new, and Maria Vasilievna had liked him very much, and had even felt shy sitting there beside him. She was used to receiving the visits of cold, critical examiners, but this one did not remember a single prayer, and did not know what questions he ought to ask. He had been extremely considerate and polite, and had given all the children full marks for everything.

"I am on my way to visit Bakvist," he now continued to Maria Vasilievna. "Is it true that he is away from home?"

They turned from the highway into a lane, Khanoff in the lead, Simon following him. The four horses proceeded at a footpace, straining to drag the heavy carriage through the mud. Simon tacked hither and thither across the road, first driving round a bump, then round a puddle, and jumping down from his seat every minute or so to give his horse a helpful push. Maria Vasilievna continued to think about the school, and whether the questions at the examinations would be difficult or easy. She felt annoyed with the board of the zemstvo, for she had been there yesterday, and had found no one in. How badly it was managed! Here it was two years since she had been asking to have the school watchman discharged for loafing and being rude to her and beating her scholars, and yet no one had paid any heed to her request. The president of the board was hardly ever in his office, and when he was, would vow with tears in his eyes that he hadn't time to attend to her now. The school inspector came only three times a year, and knew nothing about his business anyway, as he had formerly been an exciseman, and had obtained the office of inspector through favor. The school board seldom met, and no one ever knew where their meetings were held. The warden was an illiterate peasant who owned a tannery, a rough and stupid man and a close friend of the watchman's. In fact, the Lord only knew whom one could turn to to have complaints remedied and wrongs put right!

"He really is handsome!" thought the schoolteacher glancing at Khanoff.

The road grew worse and worse. They entered a wood. There was no possibility of turning out of the track here, the ruts were deep and full of gurgling, running water. Prickly twigs beat against their faces.

"What a road, eh?" cried Khanoff laughing.

The schoolteacher looked at him and marvelled that this queer fellow should be living here.

"What good do his wealth, his handsome face, and his fine culture do him in this Godforsaken mud and solitude?" she thought. "He has abandoned any advantage that fate may have given him, and is enduring the same hardships as Simon, tramping with him along this impossible road. Why does any one live here who could live in St. Petersburg or abroad?"

And it seemed to her that it would be worth this rich man's while to make a good road out of this bad one, so that he might not have to struggle with the mud, and be forced to see the despair written on the faces of Simon and his coachman. But he only laughed, and was obviously absolutely indifferent to it all, asking for no better life than this.

"He is kind and gentle and unsophisticated," Maria Vasilievna thought again. "He does not understand the hardships of life any more than he knew the suitable prayers to say at the examination. He gives globes to the school and sincerely thinks himself a useful man and a conspicuous benefactor of popular education. Much they need his globes in this wilderness!"

"Sit tight, Vasilievna!" shouted Simon.

The cart tipped violently to one side and seemed to be falling over. Something heavy rolled down on Maria Vasilievna's feet, it proved to be the purchases she had made in the city. They were crawling up a steep, clayey hill now. Torrents of water were rushing noisily down on either side of the track, and seemed to have eaten away the road bed. Surely it would be impossible to get by! The horses began to snort. Khanoff jumped out of his carriage and walked along the edge of the road in his long overcoat. He felt hot.

"What a road!" he laughed again. "My carriage will soon be smashed to bits at this rate!"

"And who asked you to go driving in weather like this?" asked Simon sternly. "Why don't you stay at home?"

"It is tiresome staying at home, daddy. I don't like it."

He looked gallant and tall walking beside old Simon, but in spite of his grace there was an almost imperceptible something about his walk that betrayed a being already rotten at the core, weak, and nearing his downfall. And the air in the woods suddenly seemed to carry an odor of wine. Maria Vasilievna shuddered, and began to feel sorry for this man who for some unknown reason was going to his ruin. She thought that if she were his wife or his sister she would gladly give up her whole life to rescuing him from disaster. His wife? Alas! He lived alone on his great estate, and she lived alone in a forlorn little village, and yet the very idea that they might one day become intimate and equal seemed to her impossible and absurd. Life was like that! And, at bottom, all human relationships and all life were so incomprehensible that if you thought about them at all dread would overwhelm you and your heart would stop beating.

"And how incomprehensible it is, too," she thought, "that God should give such beauty and charm, and such kind, melancholy eyes to weak, unhappy, useless people, and make every one like them so!"

"I turn off to the right here," Khanoff said, getting into his carriage. "Farewell! A pleasant journey to you!"

And once more Maria Vasilievna's thoughts turned to her scholars, and the coming examinations, and the watchman, and the school board, until a gust of wind from the right bringing her the rumbling of the departing carriage, other reveries mingled with these thoughts, and she longed to dream of handsome eyes and love and the happiness that would never be hers.

She, a wife! Alas, how cold her little room was early in the morning! No one ever lit her stove, because the watchman was always away somewhere. Her pupils came at daybreak, with a great noise, bringing in with them mud and snow, and everything was so bleak and so uncomfortable in her little quarters of one small bedroom which also served as a kitchen! Her head ached every day when school was over. She was obliged to collect money from her scholars to buy wood and pay the watchman, and then to give it to that fat, insolent peasant, the warden, and beg him for mercy's sake to send her a load of wood. And at night she would dream of examinations and peasants and snow drifts. This life had aged and hardened her, and she had grown plain and angular and awkward, as if lead had been emptied into her veins. She was afraid of everything, and never dared to sit down in the presence of the warden or a member of the school board. If she mentioned any one of them in his absence, she always spoke of him respectfully as "his Honor." No one found her attractive; her life was spent without love, without friendship, without acquaintances who interested her. What a terrible calamity it would be were she, in her situation, to fall in love!

"Sit tight, Vasilievna!"

Once more they were crawling up a steep hill.

She had felt no call to be a teacher; want had forced her to be one. She never thought about her mission in life or the value of education; the most important things to her were, not her scholars nor their instruction, but the examinations. And how could she think of a mission, and of the value of education? Schoolteachers, and poor doctors, and apothecaries, struggling with their heavy labors, have not even the consolation of thinking that they are advancing an ideal, and helping mankind. Their heads are too full of thoughts of their daily crust of bread, their wood, the bad roads, and their sicknesses for that. Their life is tedious and hard. Only those stand it for any length of time who are silent beasts of burden, like Maria Vasilievna. Those who are sensitive and impetuous and nervous, and who talk of their mission in life and of advancing a great ideal, soon become exhausted and give up the fight.

To find a dryer, shorter road, Simon sometimes struck across a meadow or drove through a backyard, but in some places the peasants would not let him pass, in others the land belonged to a priest; here the road was blocked, there Ivan Ionoff had bought a piece of land from his master and surrounded it with a ditch. In such cases they had to turn back.

They arrived at Nijni Gorodishe. In the snowy, grimy yard around the tavern stood rows of wagons laden with huge flasks of oil of vitriol. A great crowd of carriers had assembled in the tavern, and the air reeked of vodka, tobacco, and sheepskin coats. Loud talk filled the room, and the door with its weight and pulley banged incessantly. In the tap room behind a partition someone was playing on the concertina without a moment's pause. Maria Vasilievna sat down to her tea, while at a nearby table a group of peasants saturated with tea and the heat of the room were drinking vodka and beer.

A confused babel filled the room.

"Did you hear that, Kuzma? Ha! Ha! What's that? By God! Ivan Dementitch, you'll catch it for that! Look, brother!"

A small, blackbearded, pockmarked peasant, who had been drunk for a long time, gave an exclamation of surprise and swore an ugly oath.

"What do you mean by swearing, you!" shouted Simon angrily from where he sat, far away at the other end of the room. "Can't you see there's a lady here?"

"A lady!" mocked someone from another corner.

"You pig, you!"

"I didn't mean to do it—" faltered the little peasant with embarrassment. "Excuse me! My money is as good here as hers. How do you do?"

"How do you do?" answered the schoolteacher.

"Very well, thank you kindly."

Maria Vasilievna enjoyed her tea, and grew as flushed as the peasants. Her thoughts were once more running on the watchman and the wood.

"Look there, brother!" she heard a voice at the the table cry. "There's the schoolmarm from Viasovia! I know her! She's a nice lady."

"Yes, she's a nice lady."

The door banged, men came and went. Maria Vasilievna sat absorbed in the same thoughts that had occupied her before, and the concertina behind the partition never ceased making music for an instant. Patches of sunlight that had lain on the door when she had come in had moved up to the counter, then to the walls, and now had finally disappeared. So it was afternoon. The carriers at the table next to hers rose and prepared to leave. The little peasant went up to Maria Vasilievna swaying slightly, and held out his hand. The others followed him; all shook hands with the schoolteacher, and went out one by one. The door banged and whined nine times.

"Get ready, Vasilievna!" Simon cried.

They started again, still at a walk.

"A little school was built here in Nijni Gorodishe, not long ago," said Simon, looking back. "Some of the people sinned greatly."

"In what way?"

"It seems the president of the school board grabbed one thousand roubles, and the warden another thousand, and the teacher five hundred."

"A school always costs several thousand roubles. It is very wrong to repeat scandal, daddy. What you have just to told me is nonsense."

"I don't know anything about it. I only tell you what people say."

It was clear, however, that Simon did not believe the schoolteacher. None of the peasants believed her. They all thought that her salary was too large (she got twenty roubles a month, and they thought that five would have been plenty), and they also believed that most of the money which she collected from the children for wood she pocketed herself. The warden thought as all the other peasants did, and made a little out of the wood himself, besides receiving secret pay from the peasants unknown to the authorities.

But now, thank goodness, they had finally passed through the last of the woods, and from here on their road would lie through flat fields all the way to Viasovia. Only a few miles more to go, and then they would cross the river, and then the railway track, and then they would be at home.

"Where are you going, Simon?" asked Maria Vasilievna. "Take the right-hand road across the bridge!"

"What's that? We can cross here. It isn't very deep."

"Don't let the horse drown!"

"What's that?"

"There is Khanoff crossing the bridge!" cried Maria Vasilievna, catching sight of a carriage and four in the distance at their right. "Isn't that he?"

"That's him all right. He must have found Bakvist away. My goodness, what a donkey to drive all the way round when this road is two miles shorter!"

They plunged into the river. In summertime it was a tiny stream, in late spring it dwindled rapidly to a fordable river after the freshets, and by August it was generally dry, but during flood time it was a torrent of swift, cold, turbid water some fifty feet wide. Fresh wheel tracks were visible now on the bank leading down to the water's edge; someone, then, must have crossed here.

"Get up!" cried Simon, madly jerking the reins and flapping his arms like a pair of wings. "Get up!"

The horse waded into the stream up to his belly, stopped, and then plunged on again, throwing his whole weight into the collar. Maria Vasilievna felt a sharp wave of cold water lap her feet.

"Go on!" she cried, rising in her seat. "Go on!"

They drove out on the opposite bank.

"Well, of all things! My goodness!" muttered Simon. "What a worthless lot those zemstvo people are—"

Maria Vasilievna's goloshes and shoes were full of water, and the bottom of her dress and coat and one of her sleeves were soaked and dripping. Her sugar and flour were wet through, and this was harder to bear than all the rest. In her despair she could only wave her arms, and cry:

"Oh, Simon, Simon! How stupid you are, really—"

The gate was down when they reached the railway crossing, an express train was leaving the station. They stood and waited for the train to go by, and Maria Vasilievna shivered with cold from head to foot.

Viasovia was already in sight; there was the school with its green roof, and there stood the church with its blazing crosses reflecting the rays of the setting sun. The windows of the station were flashing, too, and a cloud of rosy steam was rising from the engine. Everything seemed to the schoolteacher to be shivering with cold.

At last the train appeared. Its windows were blazing like the crosses on the church, and their brilliance was dazzling. A lady was standing on the platform of one of the first-class carriages. One glance at her as she slipped past, and Maria Vasilievna thought: "My mother!" What a resemblance there was! There was her mother's thick and luxuriant hair; there were her forehead and the poise of her head. For the first time in all these thirty years Maria Vasilievna saw in imagination her mother, her father, and her brother in their apartment in Moscow, saw everything down to the least detail, even to the globe of goldfish in the sitting room. She heard the strains of a piano, and the sound of her father's voice, and saw herself young and pretty and gaily dressed, in a warm, brightly lighted room with her family about her. Great joy and happiness suddenly welled up in her heart, and she pressed her hands to her temples in rapture, crying softly with a note of deep entreaty in her voice:

"Mother!"

Then she wept, she could not have said why. At that moment Khanoff drove up with his four-in-hand, and when she saw him she smiled and nodded to him as if he and she were near and dear to each other, for she was conjuring up in her fancy a felicity that could never be hers. The sky, the trees, and the windows of the houses seemed to be reflecting her happiness nnd rejoicing with her. No! Her mother and father had not died; she had never been a school-teacher; all that had been a long, strange, painful dream, and now she was awake.

"Vasilievna! Sit down!"

And in a breath everything vanished. The gate slowly rose. Shivering and numb with cold Maria Vasilievna sat down in the cart again. The four-in-hand crossed the track and Simon followed. The watchman at the crossing took off his cap as they drove by.

"Here is Viasovia! The journey is over!"

At Home

"They sent over from Grigorievitch's for some book, but I said that you were not at home. The postman has brought the newspapers and two letters. And, Yevgénii Petróvitch, I really must ask you to do something in regard to Serózha. I caught him smoking the day before yesterday, and again today. When I began to scold him, in his usual way he put his hands over his ears, and shouted so as to drown my voice."

Yevgénii Petróvitch Buikovsky, Procuror of the District Court, who had only just returned from the Session House and was taking off his gloves in his study, looked for a moment at the complaining governess and laughed:

"Serózha smoking!" He shrugged his shoulders. "I can imagine that whipper-snapper with a cigarette! How old is he?"

"Seven. Of course you may not take it seriously, but at his age smoking is a bad and injurious habit, and bad habits should be rooted out in their beginning."

"Very true. But where does he get the tobacco?"

"On your table."

"On my table! Ask him to come here."

When the governess left the room, Buikovsky sat in his armchair in front of his desk, shut his eyes, and began to think. He pictured in imagination his Serózha with a gigantic cigarette a yard long, surrounded by clouds of tobacco smoke. The caricature made him laugh in spite of himself; but at the same time the serious, worried face of his governess reminded him of a time, now long passed by, a half-forgotten time, when smoking in the schoolroom or nursery inspired in teachers and parents a strange and not quite comprehensible horror. No other word but horror would describe it. The culprits were mercilessly flogged, expelled from school, their lives marred, and this, although not one of the schoolmasters or parents could say what precisely constitutes the danger and guilt of smoking. Even very intelligent men did not hesitate to fight a vice which they did not understand. Yevgénii Petróvitch remembered the director of his own school, a benevolent and highly educated old man, who was struck with such terror when he caught a boy with a cigarette that he became pale, immediately convoked an extraordinary council of masters, and condemned the offender to expulsion. Such indeed appears to be the law of life; the more intangible the evil the more fiercely and mercilessly is it combated.

The Procuror remembered two or three cases of expulsion, and recalling the subsequent lives of the victims, he could not but conclude that such punishment was often a much greater evil than the vice itself....But the animal organism is gifted with capacity to adapt itself rapidly, to accustom itself to changes, to different atmospheres, otherwise every man would feel that his rational actions were based upon an irrational foundation, and that there was little reasoned truth and conviction even in such responsibilities—responsibilities terrible in their results—as those of the schoolmaster, and lawyer, the writer....

And such thoughts, light and inconsequential, which enter only a tired and resting brain, wandered about in Yevgénii Petróvitch's head; they spring no one knows where or why, vanish soon, and, it would seem, wander only on the outskirts of the brain without penetrating far. For men who are obliged for whole hours, even for whole days, to think official thoughts all in the same direction, such free, domestic speculations are an agreeable comfort.

It was nine o'clock. Overhead from the second story came the footfalls of someone walking from corner to corner; and still higher, on the third story, someone was playing scales. The footsteps of the man who, judging by his walk, was thinking tensely or suffering from toothache, and the monotonous scales in the evening stillness, combined to create a drowsy atmosphere favorable to idle thoughts. From the nursery came the voices of Serózha and his governess.

"Papa has come?" cried the boy. "Papa has co-o-me! Papa! papa!"

"*Votre père vous appelle, allez vite,*" cried the governess, piping like a frightened bird...."Do you hear?"

"What shall I say to him?" thought Yevgénii Petróvitch.

And before he had decided what to say, in came his son Serózha, a boy of seven years old. He was one of those little boys whose sex can be distinguished only by their clothes—weakly, pale-faced, delicate....Everything about him seemed tender and soft; his movements, his curly hair, his looks, his velvet jacket.

"Good evening, papa," he began in a soft voice, climbing on his father's knee, and kissing his neck. "You wanted me?"

"Wait a minute, wait a minute, Sergéi Yevgénitch," answered the Procuror, pushing him off. "Before I allow you to kiss me I want to talk to you, and to talk seriously.... I am very angry with you, and do not love you any more...understand that, brother; I do not love you, and you are not my son....No!"

Serózha looked earnestly at his father, turned his eyes on to the chair, and shrugged his shoulders.

"What have I done?" he asked in doubt, twitching his eyes. "I have not been in your study all day and touched nothing."

"Natálya Semiónovna has just been complaining to me that she caught you smoking....Is it true? Do you smoke?"

"Yes, I smoked once, father....It is true."

"There, you see, you tell lies also," said the Procuror, frowning, and trying at the same time to smother a smile. "Natálya Semiónovna saw you smoking twice. That is to say, you are found out in three acts of misconduct—you smoke, you take another person's tobacco, and you lie. Three faults!"

"Akh, yes," remembered Serózha, with smiling eyes. "It is true. I smoked twice—today and once before."

"That is to say you smoked not once but twice. I am very, very displeased with you! You used to be a good boy, but now I see you are spoiled and have become naughty."

Yevgénii Petróvitch straightened Serózha's collar, and thought: "What else shall I say to him?"

"It is very bad," he continued. "I did not expect this from you. In the first place you have no right to go to another person's table and take tobacco which does not belong to you. A man has a right to enjoy only his own property, and if he takes another's then...he is a wicked man." (This is not the way to go about it, thought the Procuror.) "For instance, Natálya Semiónovna has a boxful of dresses. That is her box, and we have not, that is neither you nor I have, any right to touch it, as it is not ours.... Isn't that plain? You have your horses and pictures...I do not take them. Perhaps I have often felt that I wanted to take them...but they are yours, not mine!"

"Please, father, take them if you like," said Serózha, raising his eyebrows. "Always take anything of mine, father. This yellow dog which is on your table is mine, but I don't mind...."

"You don't understand me," said Buikovsky. "The dog you gave me, it is now mine, and I can do with it what I like; but the tobacco I did not give to you. The tobacco is mine." (How can I make him understand? thought the Procuror. Not in this way.) "If I feel that I want to smoke someone else's tobacco I first of all ask for permission...."

And idly joining phrase to phrase, and imitating the language of children, Buikovsky began to explain what is meant by property. Serózha looked at his chest, and listened attentively (he loved to talk to his father in the evenings), then set his elbows on the table edge and began to concentrate his shortsighted eyes upon the papers and inkstand. His glance wandered around the table, and paused on a bottle of gum-arabic.

"Papa, what is gum made of?" he asked, suddenly lifting the bottle to his eyes.

Buikovsky took the bottle, put it back on the table, and continued: "In the second place, you smoke....That is very bad! If I smoke, then...it does not follow that everyone may. I smoke, and know...that it is not clever, and I scold myself, and do not love myself on account of it...." (I am a nice teacher, thought the Procuror.) "Tobacco seriously injures the health, and people who smoke die sooner than they ought to. It is particularly injurious to little boys like you. You have a weak chest, you have not yet got strong, and in weak people tobacco smoke produces consumption and other complaints. Uncle Ignatius died of consumption. If he had not smoked perhaps he would have been alive today."

Serózha looked thoughtfully at the lamp, touched the shade with his fingers, and sighed.

"Uncle Ignatius played splendidly on the fiddle!" he said. "His fiddle is now at Grigorievitch's."

Serózha again set his elbows on the table and lost himself in thought. On his pale face was the expession of one who is listening intently or following the course of his own thoughts; sorrow and something like fright showed themselves in his big, staring eyes. Probably he was thinking of death, which had so lately carried away his mother and Uncle Ignatius. Death is a thing which carries away mothers and uncles and leaves on the earth only children and fiddles. Dead people live in the sky somewhere, near the stars, and thence look down upon the earth. How do they bear the separation?

"What shall I say to him?" asked the Procuror. "He is not listening. Apparently he thinks there is nothing serious either in his faults or in my arguments. How can I explain it to him?"

The Procuror rose and walked up and down the room.

"In my time these questions were decided very simply," he thought. "Every boy caught smoking was flogged. The cowards and babies, therefore, gave up smoking, but the brave and cunning bore their floggings, carried the tobacco in their boots and smoked in the stable. When they were caught in the stable and again flogged, they smoked on the riverbank...and so on until they were grown up. My own mother in order to keep me from smoking used to give me money and sweets. Nowadays all these methods are regarded as petty or immoral. Taking logic as his standpoint, the modern teacher tries to inspire in the child good principles not out of fear, not out of wish for distinction or reward, but consciously."

While he walked and talked, Serózha climbed on the chair next to the table and began to draw. To prevent the destruction of business papers and the splashing of ink, his father had provided a packet of paper, cut especially for him, and a blue pencil.

"Today the cook was chopping cabbage and cut her finger," he said, meantime sketching a house and twitching his eyebrows. "She cried so loud that we were all frightened and ran into the kitchen. Such a stupid! Natálya Semiónovna ordered her to bathe her finger in cold water, but she sucked it....How could she put her dirty finger in her mouth! Papa that is bad manners!"

He further told how during dinner time an organ grinder came into the yard with a little girl who sang and danced to his music.

"He has his own current of thoughts," thought the Procuror. "In his head he has a world of his own, and he knows better than anyone else what is serious and what is not. To gain his attention and conscience it is no use imitating his language...what is wanted is to understand and reason also in his manner. He would understand me perfectly if I really disliked tobacco, if I were angry, or cried....For that reason mothers are irreplaceable in bringing up children, for they alone can feel and cry and laugh like children....With logic and morals nothing can be done. What shall I say to him?"

And Yevgénii Petróvitch found it strange and absurd that he, an experienced jurist, half his life struggling with all kinds of interruptions, prejudices, and punishments, was absolutely at a loss for something to say to his son.

"Listen, give me your word of honor that you will not smoke!" he said.

"Word of honor!" drawled Serózha, pressing hard on his pencil and bending down to the sketch. "Word of honor!"

"But has he any idea what 'word of honor' means?" Buikovsky asked himself. "No, I am a bad teacher! If a schoolmaster or any of our lawyers were to see me now, he would call me a rag, and suspect me of super-subtlety....But in school and in court all these stupid problems are decided much more simply than at home when you are dealing with those whom you love. Love is exacting and complicates the business. If this boy were not my son, but a pupil or a prisoner at the bar, I should not be such a coward and scatterbrains...."

Yevgénii Petróvitch sat at the table and took up one of Serózha's sketches. It depicted a house with a crooked roof, and smoke which, like lightning, zigzagged from the chimney to the edge of the paper; beside the house stood a soldier with dots for eyes, and a bayonet shaped like the figure four.

"A man cannot be taller than a house," said the Procuror. "Look! the roof of your house only goes up to the soldier's shoulder."

Serózha climbed on his father's knee, and wriggled for a long time before he felt comfortable.

"No, papa," he said, looking at the drawing. "If you drew the soldier smaller you wouldn't be able to see his eyes."

Was it necessary to argue? From daily observation the Procuror had become convinced that children, like savages have their own artistic outlook, and their own requirements, inaccessible to the understanding of adults. Under close observation Serózha to an adult seemed abnormal. He found it possible and reasonable to draw men taller than houses, and to express with the pencil not only objects but also his own sentiments. Thus, the sound of an orchestra he drew as a round, smoky spot; whistling as a spiral thread....According to his ideas, sounds were closely allied with forms and color, and when painting letters he always colored L yellow, M red, A black, and so on.

Throwing away his sketch, Serózha again wriggled, settled himself more comfortably, and occupied himself with his father's beard. First he carefully smoothed it down, then divided it in two, and arranged it to look like whiskers.

"Now you are like Iván Stepánovitch," he muttered; "but wait, in a minute you will be like...like the porter. Papa, why do porters stand in doorways? Is it to keep out robbers?"

The Procuror felt on his face the child's breath, touched with his cheek the child's hair. In his heart rose a sudden feeling of warmth and softness, a softness that made it seem that not only his hands but all his soul lay upon the velvet of Serózha's coat. He looked into the great, dark eyes of his child, and it seemed to him that out of their big pupils looked at him his mother, and his wife, and all whom he had ever loved.

"What is the good of thrashing him?" he asked.

"Punishment is...and why turn myself into a schoolmaster?...Formerly men were simple; they thought less, and solved problems bravely....Now, we think too much; logic has eaten us up....The more cultivated a man, the more he thinks, the more he surrenders himself to subtleties, the less firm is his will, the greater his timidity in the face of affairs. And, indeed, if you look into it, what a lot of courage and faith in one's self does it need to teach a child, to judge a criminal, to write a big book...."

The clock struck ten.

"Now, child, time for bed," said the Procuror. "Say good night, and go."

"No, papa," frowned Serózha. "I may stay a little longer. Talk to me about something. Tell me a story."

"I will, only after the story you must go straight to bed."

Yevgénii Petróvitch sometimes spent his free evenings telling Serózha stories. Like most men of affairs he could not repeat by heart a single verse or remember a single fairy tale; and every time was obliged to improvise. As a rule he began with the jingle, "Once upon a time, and a very good time it was," and followed this up with all kinds of innocent nonsense, at the beginning having not the slightest idea of what would be the middle and the end. Scenery, characters, situations all came at hazard, and fable and moral flowed out by themselves without regard to the teller's will. Serózha dearly loved these improvisations, and the Procuror noticed that the simpler and less pretentious the plots, the more they affected the child.

"Listen," he began, raising his eyes to the ceiling. "Once upon a time, and a very good time it was, there lived an old, a very, very old tsar, with a long grey beard, and...this kind of moustaches. Well! He lived in a glass palace which shone and sparkled in the sun like a big lump of clean ice....The palace...brother mine...the palace stood in a great garden where, you know, grew oranges...pears, cherry trees...and blossomed tulips, roses, water lilies...and birds of different colors sang....Yes....On the trees hung glass bells which, when the breeze blew, sounded so musically that it was a joy to listen. Glass gives out a softer and more tender sound than metal.... Well? Where was I? In the garden were fountains....You remember you saw a fountain in the country, at Aunt Sonia's. Just the same kind of fountains stood in the king's garden, only they were much bigger, and the jets of water rose as high as the tops of the tallest poplars."

Yevgénii Petróvitch thought for a moment and continued:

"The old tsar had an only son, the heir to his throne—a little boy about your size. He was a good boy. He was never peevish, went to bed early, never touched anything on the table...and in all ways was a model. But he had one fault—he smoked."

Serózha listened intently, and without blinking looked straight in his father's eyes. The Procuror continued, and thought: "What next?" He hesitated for a moment, and ended his story thus:

"From too much smoking, the tsarevitch got ill with consumption, and died...when he was twenty years old. His sick and feeble old father was left without any help. There was no one to govern the kingdom and defend the palace. His enemies came and killed the old man, and destroyed the palace, and now in the garden are neither cherry trees nor birds nor bells....So it was, brother."

The end of the plot seemed to Yevgénii Petróvitch naïve and ridiculous. But on Serózha the whole story produced a strong impression. Again his eyes took on an expression of sorrow and something like fright; he looked thoughtfully at the dark window, shuddered, and said in a weak voice:

"I will not smoke any more."

"They will tell me that this parable acted by means of beauty and artistic form," he speculated. "That may be so, but that is no consolation....That does not make it an honest method....Why is it morals and truth cannot be presented in a raw form, but only with mixtures, always sugared and gilded like a pill. This is not normal....It is falsification, deception...a trick."

And he thought of those assessors who find it absolutely necessary to make a "speech"; of the public which understands history only through epics and historical novels; and of himself drawing a philosophy of life not from sermons and laws, but from fables, romances, poetry....

"Medicine must be sweetened, truth made beautiful....And this good fortune man has taken advantage of from the time of Adam....And after all maybe it is natural thus, and cannot be otherwise...there are in nature many useful and expedient deceits and illusions...."

He sat down to his work, but idle, domestic thoughts long wandered in his brain. From the third story no longer came the sound of the scales. But the occupant of the second story long continued to walk up and down....

The Scandal Monger

Akhineyev, the teacher of penmanship, was marrying off his daughter Natalia to Loshadinikh, the instructor on geography and history.

The wedding festivities were in full swing. The hall resounded with singing, playing and the scuffle of dancing feet. Hired servants in black frock coats and dirty white cravats were scurrying madly about the room. Tarantulov, the instructor in mathematics, the Frenchman Pasdequoi and Msda, the junior inspector were seated together upon the sofa telling the guests, amidst many interruptions and corrections of each other, all the cases known to them of persons having been buried alive, and were moreover airing their views upon spiritualism. None of the three believed in spiritualism, to be sure, but they were willing to admit that there was much in this world that could not be explained by human intelligence.

In another room Dodonski, teacher of literature, was explaining the circumstances under which a sentry might fire upon civilians. The conversation was, as you see, a trifle gruesome, yet highly animated.

Through the windows, from without, looked in a crowd of envious people whose social position did not grant them the privilege of entrance.

At exactly twelve o'clock the master of the house, Akhineyev, stepped into the kitchen to see whether all was ready for the wedding supper. From floor to ceiling the kitchen steamed with an aroma of geese, ducks and countless other appetizing dishes. Upon two tables were beheld, in artistic disorder, the ingredients of a truly Lucullian banquet. And Marfa the cook, a buxom woman with a two-story stomach, was busy about the table.

"My dear woman, just let me have a look at that fish," requested Akhineyev, chuckling and rubbing his palms together. "Mm! What a delicious odor! Enough to make you eat the whole kitchen up! Let's see that fish, do!"

Marfa went over to one of the chairs and carefully removed a greasy newspaper, underneath which there reposed upon a gigantic platter a huge whitefish, garnished with capers, olives and vegetables. Akhineyev looked at the fish and almost melted with rapture. His countenance beamed; his eyes almost popped out of their sockets. He leaned forward and with his lips made a sound resembling the squeal of an ungreased axle. For a moment he stood motionless, then snapped his fingers and smacked his lips again.

"Aha! The music of a passionate kiss...Whom are you kissing there?...Marfa?" came a voice from the adjoining room, and in the doorway there appeared the close-cropped head of Akhineyev's colleague Vanykin.

"Who is the lucky fellow? Aha....fine! Mr. Akhineyev himself! Bravo, grandpa! Excellent! A nice little tête-a-tête with a charming lady..."

"I'm not kissing anybody," retorted Akhineyev, embarrassed. "What an idea! You...I was merely smacking my lips...with delight...as I looked upon the fish here..."

Vanykin's features wrinkled with laughter and he disappeared. Akhineyev turned red.

"The deuce!" he thought. "Now this fellow is going around everywhere gossiping about me. A thing like this can easily spread through the whole city...The jackass!"

Akhineyev returned to the hall shyly, and glanced furtively in all directions for Vanykin. That worthy was standing by the piano telling something in his most cavalier-like manner to the inspector's mother-in-law, who smiled in evident pleasure.

"It's about me!" suspected Akhineyev. "About me, devil take the rascal! And she, she believes every word and laughs! Such a silly goose! Good God! No, I must not allow this. No...I must do something to discredit him in advance...I'll speak to everybody about the incident and unmask him as a stupid gossip-monger!"

Akhineyev scratched himself and then, still in embarrassment, walked over to Pasdequoi.

"I was just in the kitchen to settle some details about the supper," he said to the Frenchman. "I know that you're very fond of fish, and I've got one down there about two yards long! He-he-he!...Yes, and then,—I almost forgot it—In the kitchen just now, such a funny joke! You see, I come into the kitchen and want to take a look at the dishes...I see the fish and from sheer delight...such a splendid specimen...I smacked my lips, so...And at this very moment in pops that bad sheep Vanykin and says...ha-ha-ha!...and says, 'Aha! You're kissing somebody here?'...Such a fool, —imagining that I was kissing Marfa, the cook! Why, that woman looks as if... —Fie! To kiss a thing like her! There's a fool for you! Such an ass!"

"Who's that?" asked Tarantulov, coming in.

"Vanykin! You see, I come into the kitchen..."

The tale of Marfa and the fish was repeated.

"Think of it! Why, I'd just as soon kiss a mongrel as kiss Marfa..." And Akhineyev, turning around, noticed Mr. Msda.

"We were just speaking of Vanykin," said Akhineyev to Msda. "Such a simpleton! Pops into the kitchen, sees me near Marfa the cook and at once makes up a whole story. 'So, you're kissing Marfa?' says he to me. He was a little bit tipsy, upon my word! And I answered that I'd sooner kiss a turkey than kiss Marfa. And I reminded him, too, that I was a married man. Think of his silly idea! Ridiculous!"

"What's ridiculous?" asked the rector, happening to pass by.

"That chap Vanykin. I'm in the kitchen, you understand, looking at the fish..."

And so forth. In the course of a half hour nearly all the guests were fully informed of the story of the fish.

"Now let him tell as many people as he wishes!" thought Akhineyev, rubbing his palms. "Just let him! As soon as he begins I can say to him, 'Spare your breath, dear friend! We know all about it already!'"

And the thought so comforted Akhineyev that he drank four glasses more than were good for him. After the supper he led the newlywed couple to the bridal chamber, went to bed and slept like a log. By the next morning he had forgotten the tale of the fish completely. But woe! Man proposes and God disposes...The evil tongue accomplished its wicked work and Akhineyev's cunning was all in vain! Exactly a week later, on a Wednesday, just after the third lesson had begun and Akhineyev was standing in the classroom correcting the exaggerated slope of the pupil Vissekin's handwriting, the Director stepped over to him and called him to one side.

"My dear Mr. Akhineyev," said the Director.—"You will pardon me...It is really none of my business, but I must speak to you about it...It is my official duty...You must know that the rumor is running through the city that you have certain relations with...with your cook...Of course it's no affair of mine, as I have said, but...live with her, kiss her...to your heart's content. But I beg of you, not so publicly! I beg of you! Do not forget your high calling!"

A cold shiver ran down Akhineyev's spine and he lost his self-composure. As if he had been stung by a gigantic swarm of bees, or scalded with boiling water, he flew to his home. On the way it seemed to him that the whole city were staring at him as if he had been tarred and feathered...At home a new vexation was awaiting him.

"Why don't you eat?" asked his wife at dinner time. "What are you dreaming about? Your love?" Are you yearning for Marfa? You Mohammedan, you! I know everything! My eyes have been opened! You...barbarian!"

And slap! he received a blow over the cheek. He arose from the table and as if a trance, with neither hat nor coat, he went to Vanykin. He found Vanykin at home.

"You slanderer!" cried Akhineyev, turning upon him. "Why have you soiled my reputation before the whole world? How dare you have slandered me!"

"What do you mean, —'slandered?' Where did you ever get that notion?"

"Then who *did* invent the story that I had been kissing Marfa? I suppose it wasn't you, eh? Not you, eh?"

Vanykin began to blink, and his whole lively countenance was convulsed with twitching. Raising his eyes to the ikon in the corner, he cried out, "May God punish me! I swear by the salvation of my soul that I never repeated a word of the story! May I be cursed with eternal damnation! May I..."

There was no questioning Vanykin's sincerity. It was clear that he had not spread the gossip.

"But who then? Who?" muttered Akhineyev, beating his fists against his breasts and mentally going over the list of all his friends. "Who then?"

The Bishop

I

It was on the eve of Palm Sunday; vespers were being sung in the Staro-Petrovski Convent. The hour was nearly ten when the palm leaves were distributed, and the little shrine lamps were growing dim; their wicks had burnt low, and a soft haze hung in the chapel. As the worshippers surged forward in the twilight like the waves of the sea, it seemed to his Reverence Peter, who had been feeling ill for three days, that the people who came to him for palm leaves all looked alike, and, men or women, old or young, all had the same expression in their eyes. He could not see the doors through the haze; the endless procession rolled toward him, and seemed as if it must go on rolling forever. A choir of women's voices was singing and a nun was reading the canon.

How hot and close the air was, and how long the prayers! His Reverence was tired. His dry, parching breath was coming quickly and painfully, his shoulders were aching, and his legs were trembling. The occasional cries of an idiot in the gallery annoyed him. And now, as a climax, his Reverence saw, as in a delirium, his own mother whom he had not seen for nine years coming toward him in the crowd. She, or an old woman exactly like her, took a palm leaf from his hands, and moved away looking at him all the while with a glad, sweet smile, until she was lost in the crowd. And for some reason the tears began to course down his cheeks. His heart was happy and peaceful, but his eyes were fixed on a distant part of the chapel where the prayers were being read, and where no human being could be distinguished among the shadows. The tears glistened on his cheeks and beard. Then someone who was standing near him began to weep, too, and then another, and then another, until little by little the chapel was filled with a low sound of weeping. Then the convent choir began to sing, the weeping stopped, and everything went on as before.

Soon afterward the service ended. The fine, jubilant notes of the heavy chapel bells were throbbing through the moonlit garden as the bishop stepped into his coach and drove away. The white walls, the crosses on the graves, the silvery birches, and the far away moon hanging directly over the monastery, all seemed to be living a life of their own, incomprehensible, but very near to mankind. It was early in April, and a chilly night had succeeded a warm spring day. A light frost was falling, but the breath of spring could be felt in the soft, cool air. The road from the monastery was sandy, the horses were obliged to proceed at a walk, and, bathed in the bright, tranquil moonlight, a stream of pilgrims was crawling along on either side of the coach. All were thoughtful, no one spoke. Everything around them, the trees, the sky, and even the moon, looked so young and intimate and friendly that they were reluctant to break the spell which they hoped might last forever.

Finally the coach entered the city, and rolled down the main street. All the stores were closed but that of Erakin, the millionaire merchant. He was trying his electric lights for the first time, and they were flashing so violently that a crowd had collected in front of the store. Then came wide, dark streets in endless succession, and then the highway, and fields, and the smell of pines. Suddenly a white crenelated wall loomed before him, and beyond it rose a tall belfry flanked by five flashing golden cupolas, all bathed in moonlight. This was the Pankratievski Monastery where his Reverence Peter lived. Here, too, the calm, brooding moon was floating directly above the monastery. The coach drove through the gate, its wheels crunching on the sand. Here and there the dark forms of monks started out into the moonlight and footsteps rang along the flagstone paths.

"Your mother has been here while you were away, your Reverence," a lay brother told the bishop as he entered his room.

"My mother? When did she come?"

"Before vespers. She first found out where you were, and then drove to the convent."

"Then it was she whom I saw just now in the chapel! Oh, Father in heaven!"

And his Reverence laughed for joy.

"She told me to tell you, your Reverence," the lay brother continued, "that she would come back tomorrow. She had a little girl with her, a grandchild, I think. She is stopping at Ovsianikoff's inn."

"What time is it now?"

"It is after eleven."

"What a nuisance!"

His Reverence sat down irresolutely in his sitting room, unwilling to believe that it was already so late. His arms and legs were racked with pain, the back of his neck was aching, and he felt uncomfortable and hot. When he had rested a few moments he went into his bedroom and there, too, he sat down, and dreamed of his mother. He heard the lay brother walking away and Father Sisoi the priest coughing in the next room. The monastery clock struck the quarter.

His Reverence undressed and began his prayers. He spoke the old, familiar words with scrupulous attention, and at the same time he thought of his mother. She had nine children, and about forty grandchildren. She had lived from the age of seventeen to the age of sixty with her husband the deacon in a little village. His Reverence remembered her from the days of his earliest childhood, and, ah, how he had loved her! Oh, that dear, precious, unforgettable childhood of his! Why did those years that had vanished forever seem so much brighter and richer and gayer than they really had been? How tender and kind his mother had been when he was ill in his childhood and youth!

His prayers mingled with the memories that burned ever brighter and brighter in his heart like a flame, but they did not hinder his thoughts of his mother.

When he had prayed he lay down, and as soon as he found himself in the dark there rose before his eyes the vision of his dead father, his mother, and Lyesopolye, his native village. The creaking of wagon wheels, the bleating of sheep, the sound of church bells on a clear summer morning, ah, how pleasant it was to think of these things! He remembered Father Simeon, the old priest at Lyesopolye, a kind, gentle, goodnatured old man. He himself had been small, and the priest's son had been a huge strapping novice with a terrible bass voice. He remembered how this young priest had scolded the cook once, and had shouted: "Ah, you she-ass of Jehovah!" And Father Simeon had said nothing, and had only been mortified because he could not for the life of him remember reading of an ass of that name in the Bible!

Father Simeon had been succeeded by Father Demian, a hard drinker who sometimes even went so far as to see green snakes. He had actually borne the nickname of "Demian the Snake-Seer" in the village. Matvei Nikolaitch had been the schoolmaster, a kind, intelligent man, but a hard drinker, too. He never thrashed his scholars, but for some reason he kept a little bundle of birch twigs hanging on his wall, under which was a tablet bearing the absolutely unintelligible inscription: "Betula Kinderbalsamica Secuta."

He had had a woolly black dog whom he called "Syntax."

The bishop laughed. Eight miles from Lyesopolye lay the village of Obnino possessing a miraculous icon. A procession started from Obnino every summer bearing the wonder-working icon and making the round of all the neighboring villages. The churchbells would ring all day long first in one village, then in another, and to Little Paul (his Reverence was called Little Paul then) the air itself seemed tremulous with rapture. Barefoot, hatless, and infinitely happy, he followed the icon with a naïve smile on his lips and naïve faith in his heart.

Until the age of fifteen Little Paul had been so slow at his lessons that his parents had even thought of taking him out of the ecclesiastical school and putting him to work in the village store.

The bishop turned over so as to break the train of his thoughts, and tried to go to sleep.

"My mother has come!" he remembered, and laughed.

The moon was shining in through the window, and the floor was lit by its rays while he lay in shadow. A cricket was chirping. Father Sisoi was snoring in the next room, and there was a forlorn, friendless, even a vagrant note in the old man's cadences.

Sisoi had once been the steward of a diocesan bishop and was known as "Father Former Steward." He was seventy years old, and lived sometimes in a monastery sixteen miles away, sometimes in the city, sometimes wherever he happened to be. Three days ago he had turned up at the Pankratievski Monastery, and the bishop had kept him here in order to discuss with him at his leisure the affairs of the monastery.

The bell for matins rang at half past one. Father Sisoi coughed, growled something, and got up.

"Father Sisoi!" called the bishop.

Sisoi came in dressed in a white cassock, carrying a candle in his hand.

"I can't go to sleep," his Reverence said. "I must be ill. I don't know what the matter is; I have fever."

"You have caught cold, your Lordship. I must rub you with tallow."

Father Sisoi stood looking at him for a while and turned: "Ah-h—the Lord have mercy on us!"

"Erakin has electricity in his store now—I hate it!" he continued.

Father Sisoi was aged, and round-shouldered, and gaunt. He was always displeased with something or other, and his eyes, which protruded like those of a crab, always wore an angry expression.

"I don't like it at all," he repeated—"I hate it."

II

Next day, on Palm Sunday, his Reverence officiated at the cathedral in the city. Then he went to the diocesan bishop's, then to see a general's wife who was very ill, and at last he drove home. At two o'clock two beloved guests were having dinner with him, his aged mother, and his little niece Kitty, a child of eight. The spring sun was peeping cheerily in through the window as they sat at their meal, and was shining merrily on the white tablecloth, and on Kitty's red hair. Through the double panes they heard the rooks cawing, and the magpies chattering in the garden.

"It is nine years since I saw you last," said the old mother, "and yet when I caught sight of you in the convent chapel yesterday I thought to myself: God bless me, he has not changed a bit! Only perhaps you are a little thinner than you were, and your beard has grown longer. Oh, holy Mother, Queen of Heaven! Everybody was crying yesterday. As soon as I saw you, I began to cry myself, I don't know why. His holy will be done!"

In spite of the tenderness with which she said this, it was clear that she was not at her ease. It was as if she did not know whether to address the bishop by the familiar "thee" or the formal "you," and whether she ought to laugh or not. She seemed to feel herself more of a poor deacon's wife than a mother in his presence. Meanwhile Kitty was sitting with her eyes glued to the face of her uncle the bishop as if she were trying to make out what manner of man this was. Her hair had escaped from her comb and her bow of velvet ribbon, and was standing straight up around her head like a halo. Her eyes were foxy and bright.

She had broken a glass before sitting down, and now, as she talked, her grandmother kept moving first a glass, and then a wine glass out of her reach. As the bishop sat listening to his mother, he remembered how, many, many years ago, she had sometimes taken him and his brothers and sisters to visit relatives whom they considered rich. She had been busy with her own children in those days, and now she was busy with her grandchildren, and had come to visit him with Kitty here.

"Your sister Varenka has four children"—she was telling him—"Kitty is the oldest. God knows why, her father fell ill and died three days before Assumption. So my Varenka has been thrown out into the cold world."

"And how is my brother Nikanor?" the bishop asked.

"He is well, thank the Lord. He is pretty well, praise be to God. But his son Nikolasha wouldn't go into the church, and is at college instead learning to be a doctor. He thinks it is best, but who knows? However, God's will be done!"

"Nikolasha cuts up dead people!" said Kitty, spilling some water into her lap.

"Sit still child!" her grandmother said, quietly taking the glass out of her hands.

"How long it is since we have seen one another!" exclaimed his Reverence, tenderly stroking his mother's shoulder and hand. "I missed you when I was abroad, I missed you dreadfully."

"Thank you very much!"

"I used to sit by my window in the evening listening to the band playing, and feeling lonely and forlorn. Sometimes I would suddenly grow so homesick that I used to think I would gladly give everything I had in the world for a glimpse of you and home."

His mother smiled and beamed, and then immediately drew a long face and said stiffly:

"Thank you very much!"

The bishop's mood changed. He looked at his mother, and could not understand where she had acquired that deferential, humble expression of face and voice, what the meaning of it might be. He hardly recognized her, and felt sorrowful and vexed. Besides, his head was still aching, and his legs were racked with pain. The fish he was eating tasted insipid and he was very thirsty.

After dinner two wealthy lady landowners visited him, and sat for an hour and a half with faces a mile long, never uttering a word. Then an archimandrite, a gloomy, taciturn man, came on business. Then the bells rang for vespers, the sun set behind the woods, and the day was done. As soon as he got back from church the bishop said his prayers, and went to bed, drawing the covers up closely about his ears. The moonlight troubled him, and soon the sound of voices came to his ears. Father Sisoi was talking politics with his mother in the next room.

"There is a war in Japan now," he was saying.

"The Japanese belong to the same race as the Montenegrins. They fell under the Turkish yoke at the same time."

And then the bishop heard his mother's voice say:

"And so, you see, when we had said our prayers, and had our tea, we went to Father Yegor—"

She kept saying over and over again that they "had tea," as if all she knew of life was tea drinking.

The memory of his seminary and college life slowly and mistily took shape in the bishop's mind. He had been a teacher of Greek for three years, until he could no longer read without glasses, and then he had taken the vows, and had been made an inspector. When he was thirty-two he had been made the rector of a seminary, and then an archimandrite. At that time his life had been so easy and pleasant, and had seemed to stretch so far, far into the future that he could see absolutely no end to it. But his health had failed, and he had nearly lost his eyesight. His doctors had advised him to give up his work and go abroad.

"And what did you do next?" asked Father Sisoi in the adjoining room.

"And then we had tea," answered his mother.

"Why, Father, your beard is green!" exclaimed Kitty suddenly. And she burst out laughing.

The bishop remembered that the color of Father Sisoi's beard really did verge on green, and he, too, laughed.

"My goodness! What a plague that child is!" cried Father Sisoi in a loud voice, for he was growing angry. "You're a spoiled baby you are! Sit still!"

The bishop recalled the new white church in which he had officiated when he was abroad, and the sound of a warm sea. Eight years had slipped by while he was there; then he had been recalled to Russia, and now he was already a bishop, and the past had faded away into the mist as if it had been but a dream.

Father Sisoi came into his room with a candle in his hand.

"Well, well!" he exclaimed, surprised. "Asleep already, your Reverence?"

"Why not?"

"It's early yet, only ten o'clock! I bought a candle this evening and wanted to rub you with tallow."

"I have a fever," the bishop said, sitting up. "I suppose something ought to be done. My head feels so queer."

Sisoi began to rub the bishop's chest and back with tallow.

"There—there—" he said. "Oh, Lord God Almighty! There! I went to town today, and saw that—what do you call him?—that archpresbyter Sidonski. I had tea with him. I hate him! Oh Lord God Almighty! There! I hate him!"

III

The diocesan bishop was very old and very fat, and had been ill in bed with gout for a month. So his Reverence Peter had been visiting him almost every day, and had received his suppliants for him. And now that he was ill he was appalled to think of the futilities and trifles they asked for and wept over. He felt annoyed at their ignorance and cowardice. The very number of all those useless trivialities oppressed him, and he felt as if he could understand the diocesan bishop who had written "Lessons in Free Will" when he was young, and now seemed so absorbed in details that the memory of everything else, even of God, had forsaken him. Peter must have grown out of touch with Russian life while he was abroad, for it was hard for him to grow used to it now. The people seemed rough, the women stupid and tiresome, the novices and their teachers uneducated and often disorderly. And then the documents that passed through his hands by the hundreds of thousands! The provosts gave all the priests in the diocese, young and old, and their wives and children marks for good behavior, and he was obliged to talk about all this, and read about it, and write serious articles on it. His Reverence never had a moment which he could call his own; all day his nerves were on edge, and he only grew calm when he found himself in church.

He could not grow accustomed to the terror which he involuntarily inspired in every breast in spite of his quiet and modest ways. Everyone in the district seemed to shrivel and quake and apologize as soon as he looked at them. Everyone trembled in his presence; even the old archpresbyters fell down at his feet, and not long ago one suppliant, the old wife of a village priest, had been prevented by terror from uttering a word, and had gone away without asking for anything. And he, who had never been able to say a harsh word in his sermons, and who never blamed people because he pitied them so, would grow exasperated with these suppliants, and hurl their petitions to the ground. Not a soul had spoken sincerely and naturally to him since he had been here; even his old mother had changed, yes, she had changed very much! Why did she talk so freely to Sisoi when all the while she was so serious and ill at ease with him, her own son? It was not like her at all! The only person who behaved naturally in his presence, and who said whatever came into his head was old man Sisoi, who had lived with bishops all his life, and had outlasted eleven of them. And therefore his Reverence felt at ease with Sisoi, even though he was, without doubt, a rough and quarrelsome person.

After morning prayers on Tuesday the bishop received his suppliants, and lost his temper with them. He felt ill, as usual, and longed to go to bed, but he had hardly entered his room before he was told that the young merchant Erakin, a benefactor of the monastery, had called on very important business. The bishop was obliged to receive him. Erakin stayed about an hour talking in a very loud voice, and it was hard to understand what he was trying to say.

After he had gone there came an abbess from a distant convent, and by the time she had gone the bells were tolling for vespers; it was time for the bishop to go to church.

The monks sang melodiously and rapturously that evening; a young, black-bearded priest officiated. His Reverence listened as they sang of the Bridegroom and of the chamber swept and garnished, and felt neither repentance nor sorrow, but only a deep peace of mind. He sat by the altar where the shadows were deepest, and was swept in imagination back into the days of his childhood and youth, when he had first heard these words sung. The tears trickled down his cheeks, and he meditated on how he had attained everything in life that it was possible for a man in his position to attain; his faith was unsullied, and yet all was not clear to him; something was lacking, and he did not want to die. It still seemed to him that he was leaving unfound the most important thing of all. Something of which he had dimly dreamed in the past, hopes that had thrilled his heart as a child, a schoolboy, and a traveller in foreign lands, troubled him still.

"How beautifully they are singing today!" he thought, "Oh, how beautifully!"

IV

On Thursday he held a service in the cathedral. It was the festival of the Washing of Feet. When the service was over, and the people had gone to their several homes, the sun was shining brightly and cheerily, and the air was warm. The gutters were streaming with bubbling water, and the tender songs of larks came floating in from the fields beyond the city, bringing peace to his heart. The trees were already awake, and over them brooded the blue, unfathomable sky.

His Reverence went to bed as soon as he reached home, and told the lay brother to close his shutters. The room grew dark. Oh, how tired he was!

As on the day before, the sound of voices and the tinkling of glasses came to him from the next room. His mother was gaily recounting some tale to Father Sisoi, with many a quaint word and saying, and the old man was listening gloomily, and answering in a gruff voice:

"Well, I never! Did they, indeed? What do you think of that!"

And once more the bishop felt annoyed, and then hurt that the old lady should be so natural and simple with strangers, and so silent and awkward with her own son. It even seemed to him that she always tried to find some pretext for standing in his presence, as if she felt uneasy sitting down. And his father? If he had been alive, he would probably not have been able to utter a word when the bishop was there.

Something in the next room fell to the floor with a crash. Kitty had evidently broken a cup or a saucer, for Father Sisoi suddenly snorted, and cried angrily:

"What a terrible plague this child is! Merciful heavens! No one could keep her supplied with china!"

Then silence fell. When he opened his eyes again, the bishop saw Kitty standing by his bedside staring at him, her red hair standing up around her head like a halo, as usual.

"Is that you, Kitty?" he asked. "Who is that opening and shutting doors down there?"

"I don't hear anything."

He stroked her head.

"So your cousin Nikolasha cuts up dead people, does he?" he asked, after a pause.

"Yes, he is learning to."

"Is he nice?"

"Yes, very, only he drinks a lot."

"What did your father die of?"

"Papa grew weaker and weaker, and thinner and thinner, and then came his sore throat. And I was ill, too, and so was my brother Fedia. We all had sore throats. Papa died, Uncle, but we got well."

Her chin quivered, her eyes filled with tears. "Oh, your Reverence!" she cried in a shrill voice, beginning to weep bitterly. "Dear Uncle, mother and all of us are so unhappy! Do give us a little money! Help us, Uncle darling!"

He also shed tears, and for a moment could not speak for emotion. He stroked her hair, and touched her shoulder, and said:

"All right, all right, little child. Wait until Easter comes, then we will talk about it. I'll help you."

His mother came quietly and timidly into the room, and said a prayer before the icon. When she saw that he was awake, she asked:

"Would you like a little soup?"

"No, thanks," he answered. "I'm not hungry."

"I don't believe you are well—I can see that you are not well. You really mustn't fall ill! You have to be on your feet all day long. My goodness, it makes one tired to see you! Never mind, Easter is no longer over the hills and far away. When Easter comes you will rest. God will give us time for a little talk then, but now I'm not going to worry you any more with my silly chatter. Come, Kitty, let his Lordship have another forty winks—"

And the bishop remembered that, when he was a boy, she had used exactly the same half playful, half respectful tone to all high dignitaries of the church. Only by her strangely tender eyes, and by the anxious look which she gave him as she left the room could any one have guessed that she was his mother. He shut his eyes, and seemed to be asleep, but he heard the clock strike twice, and Father Sisoi coughing next door. His mother came in again, and looked shyly at him. Suddenly there came a bang, and a door slammed; a vehicle of some kind drove up to the front steps. The lay brother came into the bishop's room, and called:

"Your Reverence!"

"What is it?"

"Here is the coach! It is time to go to our Lord's Passion—"

"What time is it?"

"Quarter to eight."

The bishop dressed, and drove to the cathedral. He had to stand motionless in the center of the church while the twelve gospels were being read, and the first and longest and most beautiful of them all he read himself. A strong, valiant mood took hold of him. He knew this gospel, beginning "The Son of Man is risen today—," by heart, and as he repeated it, he raised his eyes, and saw a sea of little lights about him. He heard the sputtering of candles, but the people had disappeared. He felt surrounded by those whom he had known in his youth; he felt that they would always be here until—God knew when!

His father had been a deacon, his grandfather had been a priest, and his great grandfather a deacon. He sprang from a race that had belonged to the church since Christianity first came to Russia, and his love for the ritual of the church, the clergy, and the sound of church bells was inborn in him, deeply, irradicably implanted in his heart. When he was in church, especially when he was taking part in the service himself, he felt active and valorous and happy. And so it was with him now. Only, after the eighth gospel had been read, he felt that his voice was becoming so feeble that, even his cough was inaudible; his head was aching, and he began to fear that he might collapse. His legs were growing numb; in a little while he ceased to have any sensation in them at all, and could not imagine what he was standing on, and why he did not fall down.

It was quarter to twelve when the service ended. The bishop went to bed as soon as he reached home, without even saying his prayers. As he pulled his blanket up over him, he suddenly wished that he were abroad; he passionately wished it. He would give his life, he thought, to cease from seeing these cheap, wooden walls and that low ceiling, to cease from smelling the stale scent of the monastery.

If there were only someone with whom he could talk, someone to whom he could unburden his heart!

He heard steps in the adjoining room, and tried to recall who it might be. At last the door opened, and Father Sisoi came in with a candle in one hand, and a teacup in the other.

"In bed already, your Reverence?" he asked. "I have come to rub your chest with vinegar and vodka. It is a fine thing, if rubbed in good and hard. Oh, Lord God Almighty! There—there—I have just come from our monastery. I hate it. I am going away from here tomorrow, my Lord. Oh, Lord, God Almighty—there—"

Sisoi never could stay long in one place, and he now felt as if he had been in this monastery for a year. It was hard to tell from what he said where his home was, whether there was anyone or anything in the world that he loved, and whether he believed in God or not. He himself never could make out why he had become a monk, but then, he never gave it any thought, and the time when he had taken the vows had long since faded from his memory. He thought he must have been born a monk.

"Yes, I am going away tomorrow. Bother this place!"

"I want to have a talk with you—I never seem to have the time—" whispered the bishop, making a great effort to speak. "You see, I don't know anyone—or anything—here—"

"Very well then, I shall stay until Sunday, but no longer! Bother this place!"

"What sort of a bishop am I?" his Reverence went on, in a faint voice. "I ought to have been a village priest, or a deacon, or a plain monk. All this is choking me—it is choking me—"

"What's that? Oh, Lord God Almighty! There—go to sleep now, your Reverence. What do you mean? What's all this you are saying? Good night!"

All night long the bishop lay awake, and in the morning he grew very ill. The lay brother took fright and ran first to the archimandrite, and then for the monastery doctor who lived in the city. The doctor, a stout, elderly man, with a long, grey beard, looked intently at his Reverence, shook his head, knit his brows, and finally said:

"I'll tell you what, your Reverence; you have typhoid."

The bishop grew very thin and pale in the next hour, his eyes grew larger, his face became covered with wrinkles, and he looked quite small and old. He felt as if he were the thinnest, weakest, puniest man in the whole world, and as if everything that had occurred before this had been left far, far behind, and would never happen again.

"How glad I am of that!" he thought. "Oh, how glad!"

His aged mother came into the room. When she saw his wrinkled face and his great eyes, she was seized with fear, and, falling down on her knees by his bedside, she began kissing his face, his shoulders, and his hands. He seemed to her to be the thinnest, weakest, puniest man in the world, and she forgot that he was a bishop, and kissed him as if he had been a little child whom she dearly, dearly loved.

"Little Paul, my dearie!" she cried. "My little son, why do you look like this? Little Paul, oh, answer me!"

Kitty, pale and severe, stood near them, and could not understand what was the matter with her uncle, and why granny wore such a look of suffering on her face, and spoke such heartrending words. And he, he was speechless, and knew nothing of what was going on around him. He was dreaming that he was an ordinary man once more, striding swiftly and merrily through the open country, a staff in his hand, bathed in sunshine, with the wide sky above him, as free as a bird to go wherever his fancy led him.

"My little son! My little Paul! Answer me!" begged his mother.

"Don't bother his Lordship," said Sisoi. "Let him sleep. What's the matter?"

Three doctors came, consulted together, and drove away. The day seemed long, incredibly long, and then came the long, long night. Just before dawn on Saturday morning the lay brother went to the old mother who was lying on a sofa in the sitting room, and asked her to come into the bedroom; his Reverence had gone to eternal peace.

Next day was Easter. There were forty-two churches in the city, and two monasteries, and the deep, joyous notes of their bells pealed out over the town from morning until night. The birds were caroling, the bright sun was shining. The big market place was full of noise; barrel organs were droning, concertinas were squealing, and drunken voices were ringing through the air. Trotting races were held in the main street that afternoon; in a word, all was merry and gay, as had been the year before and as, doubtless, it would be the year to come.

A month later a new bishop was appointed, and everyone forgot his Reverence Peter. Only the dead man's mother, who is living now in a little country town with her son the deacon, when she goes out at sunset to meet her cow, and joins the other women on the way, tells them about her children and grandchildren, and her boy who became a bishop.

And when she mentions him she looks at them shyly, for she is afraid they will not believe her.

And, as a matter of fact, not all of them do.

O. Henry

1862	September 11. William Sydney Porter born in Greensboro, North Carolina.
1884	After spending two years on a Texas ranch, he moves to Austin, where he spends the next twelve years holding various jobs—as a clerk, draftsman, bank teller, and newspaper reporter. In 1887, he marries Athol Este Roach, the stepdaughter of a prominent Austin merchant.
1894	Launches humorous weekly, *The Rolling Stone*. The paper dies after just one year. Leaves Austin to become a columnist for the *Houston Daily Post*.
1896-97	Indicted for misappropriating funds while an employee of the First National Bank of Austin, Porter flees to Honduras, and travels throughout Latin America as a fugitive until his wife's terminal illness forces him to return to Austin. Soon after, she dies.
1898-1901	Stands trial and is convicted for embezzlement. Serves three and a half years of a five year sentence at the Federal Division of the Ohio State Penitentiary. While incarcerated, he writes numerous stories drawing upon past experiences in the Southwest. He takes the pen name "O. Henry" while in prison.
1902-10	Moves to New York, where he quickly becomes the nation's most popular short fiction writer. He writes prolifically until his death on June 5, 1910. Despite his eminent success, Porter dies a pauper. Royalties from subsequent editions of his stories are used to pay his debts.

O. Henry

O. Henry's last words spoken with a smile, were, "I don't want to go home in the dark." Could he return to us he would find that he did not go home in the dark, but that an increasing radiance shines about his name and fame. He is read today not only in English but also in French, Spanish, German, Swedish, Dano-Norwegian and Japanese. "I'm not a critic," a woman said to me in Brooklyn recently, "and know nothing about the technique of the short story. But I do know that, whenever I feel low-spirited, O. Henry is my best restorative." She is typical, I think, of O. Henry's large and increasing clientele of readers. They not only read him but come more and more under the spell of his genial and companionable nature. The entertainer has become both friend and comrade.

Certain phases of O. Henry's work are salient and distinctive. He is, for example, the only writer in English or American literature who won his place solely by the writing of short stories. Irving soon passed from the story to history and biography; Hawthorne "found himself famous" only after he began his wider career as a novelist; Poe was a critic, short story writer, and poet; Bret Harte is our greatest parodist, but it is impossible—thinks his latest biographer—to say whether he will make "his appeal to posterity mainly as a poet or prose writer"; Henry James attained his most characteristic expression in the novel; Stevenson and Kipling would be secure in their immortality if they had never written a short story. In singleness of impression, therefore, as well as in bulk, 0. Henry's two hundred and fifty short stories represent the most significant effort yet made by an English-speaking writer to win and hold a place in letters not by that loose thing known as the story that is short, but by that artistic triumph known as the "short story."

O. Henry is also the only short story writer known to us whose workshop contained no rejected manuscripts. Some of his stories were widely traveled, he tells us, but they all landed at last. "My first story," he said, "was paid for, but I never saw it in print." This was "The Miracle of Lava Cañon," which was accepted by the McClure Company on December 2, 1897, and marked for "publication September 18, 1898." From this date to the appearance of his last story, "Let Me Feel Your Pulse," published shortly after his death, *every story* submitted to a publisher was sooner or later accepted. This unique record is a testimonial to the faith that O. Henry kept with his art. "Write to please yourself," he once gave as the only rule, and from this high standard he never swerved. The story must be as good as he could make it before he was willing for the public to see it.

It will help us to appraise O. Henry's art if we remember that he did not find himself in the short story at once. Even after he had won national recognition by the publication of "The Four Million" in 1906, he felt the call of other types and of other talents. In the last conversation that I had with him, in New York, in February, 1908, he talked glowingly of a drama upon which he was engaged, and spoke weariedly about the demands made upon him by the publishers to whom he had promised short stories before they were completely written. "Sometimes there will come a telephone message about two o'clock in the morning," he remarked, "saying, 'We must have the rest of that story today.' I ask them to read me the last paragraph of the first instalment so that I can know just where to start." I told him that I didn't believe a word of this, that his stories were so notable for their unity as to prove a continuousness in the creative process, even if the story were not all written at once. But he continued to proclaim the superiority of the drama. The drama that he had in mind, however, was not a new creation. It was a reshaping of his short story "The World and the Door," in which he believed that he had hit upon a great truth, viz., "that every human soul has this tendency toward respectability, that it is greater than love"; nobody, thought O. Henry, should be classed as permanently down and out. In boyhood days it was not the drama or the short story that drew him; it was the cartoonist's art. To our way of thinking, no such youthful genius in pen or pencil sketch had yet appeared. Later on, he tried his hand as editor of *The Rolling Stone* in Austin, Texas, and as reporter on *The Houston Post*. After his establishment in New York he felt the lure not only of the drama but also of poetry, the musical comedy, and the autobiographical novel. But all these diversions, though they lessened the number of short stories that he might have written, contributed indirectly to the excellence of those that he did write; they flowed *from* his art at first, but returned later in deepened volume *to* it. Nothing helps a man more to do what he can do than to know what he can't do.

The first impression that the reader of O. Henry gets is one of originality. O. Henry was a voice, not an echo. He has been compared with many writers, American and foreign, but no one has called him an imitator of anyone else. The O. Henry touch is altogether distinctive in narrative art. He had read much, thought much, and suffered much before he became famous. But every discipline had developed him centrally rather than marginally. If you were thrown with him often you would have observed in him a great equality rather than a steep superiority. I have never known a nature so widely receptive as his, but at the same time so eagerly but quietly reactive. His reactions, however, were not those of criticism or rejection. They partook more of the nature of an instinctive human interest, of a wide and liberal understanding, of a keen but sympathetic determination to see life just as you saw it. The critical judgment must wait. Talk with him five minutes and he could reproduce you to a button in a pencil sketch, and probably reveal some central trait in you unknown even to yourself. There would certainly be something amusing about you, though no one else may ever have discovered it before.

His originality, therefore, is not the originality of novel things but of old things probed a little more deeply. He took old themes—love, habit, the voiceless part of our population, the humor and pathos of daily life, the West versus the East, the South versus the North, the romance and unexpectedness of the commonplace, the things that you and I have in common—and gave them a new meaning, a new interest, a new appeal. Even his literary allusions are of the old-fashioned sort. Though he was saturated with magazine literature and newspaper happenings, the books that had left the deepest impress upon him were the Bible, Shakespeare, Tennyson, and the Arabian Nights. To the Bible he makes his largest number of references, sixty-three; to Shakespeare, thirty-four; to Tennyson, twenty-one; to the Arabian Nights, fourteen. These were familiar to him from childhood, and his use of them indicates anew the quality of his originality. Instead of exploiting the new, he reinterpreted the old.

Much has been written about O. Henry's humor as shown in his calculated misquotations, his inverted phrasing, his verbal coruscations. But O. Henry's humor is only incidentally a thing of words and phrases. You may omit these and O. Henry would still be a great humorist. Had these been essential, his stories could never have survived translation, for translation shears away remorselessly all that is merely verbal. No, O. Henry's characters are not humorous because they say funny things. They *say funny things because they are humorous.* O. Henry's humor has been acclaimed by a world of grateful readers because, like the humor of Shakespeare and Molière and Cervantes, it rises naturally and spontaneously from the situations in which his characters are placed. The situations become themselves creative; they belong to the elemental nature of comedy. They are matrix rather than copy, and the humor is born rather than made.

A special distinction of O. Henry's humor is that it is not harsh, or cynical, or derisive. It is humane because it is fundamentally human. It is associative rather than separative in its effect. As soon as you read one of his stories you want to read it aloud to others. But you do not have to pick your audience for fear that feelings will be hurt. Rich or poor, educated or illiterate, employer or employee, black or white, man or woman—all will find their common heritage of humanity reached and enriched. Much of the stage humor of today, certainly that of the school of Wilde and Shaw, derives most of its sparkle from what has been called "the neat reversal of middle-class conceptions." There is no such reversal in O. Henry. Instead of pitting class against class, he reveals class to class and section to section. He seems to say: "You think the other fellow is funny. Well, you are just as funny as he is."

With his originality and humor must be considered his Americanism. He never visited England or the Continent. But he knew his own country; and his journeyings in Central America, South America, and Mexico gave him just the angle of contrast that was needed to enable him to run the boundary line sharply between what was American and what was not. If we omit the stories of New York and Texas, which include one hundred and seventy titles, there are left twenty additional states represented by O. Henry's backgrounds. If he had not visited all of these and studied their regional differentials at first hand, he had at least heard intimately about them. He knew them accurately enough to make both plot and characters fit naturally and revealingly into each setting that he chose.

But Americanism is not a matter of geography. It is a spirit, a mood, a temperament, an attitude toward men and things, a way of looking at life, of expressing life, and of achieving life. Foreigners detect it more readily than we do. Thus Hugh Walpole, writing in the *London Daily Mail,* declares that American literature has at last become "independent"; and he hails O. Henry as "the true father of this new American literature."

It is impossible to corral Americanism in the confines of a scientific definition, but one element of O. Henry's Americanism emerges in a report that came from the battlefields of France. "As a trench companion," so ran a soldier's comment, "O. Henry cannot be surpassed. He is brief, he is witty, he is deliciously human. Without meaning to, apparently, he teaches a philosophy of cheerful acceptance of 'The Things That Are To Be.'"Add to this his instinctive aversion to indecency in every form; recall, too, his exacting idealism which made him say almost with his latest breath, "I want to get at something bigger. What I have done is child's play to what I can do, to what I know it is in me to do"—and you have the American, the artist, and the man in one.

—*from* Southern Literary Studies *by C. Alphonso Smith*

While the Auto Waits

Promptly at the beginning of twilight, came again to that quiet corner of that quiet, small park the girl in gray. She sat upon a bench and read a book, for there was yet to come a half hour in which print could be accomplished.

To repeat: Her dress was gray, and plain enough to mask its impeccancy of style and fit. A large-meshed veil imprisoned her turban hat and a face that shone through it with a calm and unconscious beauty. She had come there at the same hour on the day previous, and on the day before that; and there was one who knew it.

The young man who knew it hovered near, relying upon burnt sacrifices to the great joss, Luck. His piety was rewarded, for, in turning a page, her book slipped from her fingers and bounded from the bench a full yard away.

The young man pounced upon it with instant avidity, returning it to its owner with that air that seems to flourish in parks and public places—a compound of gallantry and hope, tempered with respect for the policeman on the beat. In a pleasant voice, he risked an inconsequent remark upon the weather—that introductory topic responsible for so much of the world's unhappiness—and stood poised for a moment, awaiting his fate.

The girl looked him over leisurely; at his ordinary, neat dress and his features distinguished by nothing particular in the way of expression.

"You may sit down, if you like," she said in a full, deliberate contralto. "Really, I would like to have you do so. The light is too bad for reading. I would prefer to talk."

The vassal of Luck slid upon the seat by her side with compliasance.

"Do you know," he said, speaking the formula with which park chairmen open their meetings, "that you are quite the stunningest girl I have seen in a long time? I had my eye on you yesterday. Didn't know somebody was bowled over by those pretty lamps of yours, did you, honeysuckle?"

"Whoever you are," said the girl, in icy tones, "you must remember that I am a lady. I will excuse the remark you have just made because the mistake was, doubtless, not an unnatural one—in your circle. I asked you to sit down; if the invitation must constitute me your honeysuckle, consider it withdrawn."

"I earnestly beg your pardon," pleaded the young man. His expression of satisfaction had changed to one of penitence and humility. "It was my fault, you know—I mean, there are girls in parks, you know—that is, of course, you don't know, but—"

"Abandon the subject, if you please. Of course I know. Now, tell me about these people passing and crowding, each way, along these paths. Where are they going? Why do they hurry so? Are they happy?"

The young man had promptly abandoned his air of coquetry. His cue was now for a waiting part; he could not guess the rôle he would be expected to play.

"It *is* interesting to watch them," he replied, postulating her mood. "It is the wonderful drama of life. Some are going to supper and some to—er—other places. One wonders what their histories are."

"I do not," said the girl; "I am not so inquisitive. I come here to sit beause here, only, can I be near the great, common, throbbing heart of humanity. My part in life is cast where its beats are never felt. Can you surmise why I spoke to you, Mr.—?"

"Parkenstacker," supplied the young man. Then he looked eager and hopeful.

"No," said the girl, holding up a slender finger, and smiling slightly. "You would recognize it immediately. It is impossible to keep one's name out of print. Or even one's portrait. This veil and this hat of my maid furnish me with an *incog.* You should have seen the chauffeur stare at it when he thought I did not see. Candidly, there are five or six names that belong in the holy of holies, and mine, by the accident of birth, is one of them. I spoke to you, Mr. Stackenpot—"

"Parkenstacker," corrected the young man, modestly.

"—Mr. Parkenstacker, because I wanted to talk, for once, with a natural man—one unspoiled by the despicable gloss of wealth and supposed social superiority. Oh! you do not know how weary I am of it—money, money, money! And of the men who surround me, dancing like little marionettes all cut by the same pattern. I am sick of pleasure, of jewels, of travel, of society, of luxuries of all kinds."

"I always had an idea," ventured the young man, hesitatingly, "that money must be a pretty good thing."

"A competence is to be desired. But when you have so many millions that—!" She concluded the sentence with a gesture of despair. "It is the monotony of it," she continued, "that palls. Drives, dinners, theatres, balls, suppers, with the gilding of superfluous wealth over it all. Sometimes the very tinkle of the ice in my champagne glass nearly drives me mad."

Mr. Parkenstacker looked ingenuously interested.

"I have always liked," he said, "to read and hear about the ways of wealthy and fashionable folks. I suppose I am a bit of a snob. But I like to have my information accurate. Now, I had formed the opinion that champagne is cooled in the bottle and not by placing ice in the glass."

The girl gave a musical laugh of genuine amusement.

"You should know," she explained, in an indulgent tone, "that we of the non-useful class depend for our amusement upon departure from precedent. Just now it is a fad to put ice in champagne. The idea was originated by a visiting Prince of Tartary while dining at the Waldorf. It will soon give some other whim. Just as at a dinner party this week on Madison Avenue a green kid glove was laid by the plate of each guest to be put on and used while eating olives."

"I see," admitted the young man, humbly. "These special diversions of the inner circle do not become familiar to the common public."

"Sometimes," continued the girl, acknowledging his confession of error by a slight bow, "I have thought that if I ever should love a man it would be one of lowly station. One who is a worker and not a drone. But, doubtless, the claims of caste and wealth will prove stronger than my inclination. Just now I am besieged by two. One is a Grand Duke of a German principality. I think he has, or has had, a wife, somewhere, driven mad by his intemperance and cruelty. The other is an English Marquis, so cold and mercenary that I even prefer the diabolism of the Duke. What is it that impels me to tell you these things, Mr. Packenstacker?"

"Parkenstacker," breathed the young man. "Indeed, you cannot know how much I appreciate your confidences."

The girl contemplated him with a calm, impersonal regard that befitted the difference in their stations.

"What is your line of business, Mr. Parkenstacker?" she asked.

"A very humble one. But I hope to rise in the world. Were you really in earnest when you said that you could love a man of lowly position?"

"Indeed I was. But I said 'might.' There is the Grand Duke and the Marquis, you know. Yes; no calling could be too humble were the man what I would wish him to be."

"I work," declared Mr. Parkenstacker, "in a restaurant."

The girl shrank slightly.

"Not as a waiter?" she said, a little imploringly. "Labor is noble, but—personal attendance, you know—valets and—"

"I am not a waiter. I am cashier in"—on the street they faced that bounded the opposite side of the park was the brilliant electric sign "RESTAURANT"—"I am cashier in that restaurant you see there."

The girl consulted a tiny watch set in a bracelet of rich design upon her left wrist, and rose, hurriedly. She thrust her book into a glittering reticule suspended from her waist, for which, however, the book was too large.

"Why are you not at work?" she asked.

"I am on the night turn," said the young man; "it is yet an hour before my period begins. May I not hope to see you again?"

"I do not know. Perhaps—but the whim may not seize me again. I must go quickly now. There is a dinner, and a box at the play—and, oh! the same old round. Perhaps you noticed an automobile at the upper corner of the park as you came. One with a white body."

"And red running gear?" asked the young man, knitting his brows reflectively.

"Yes. I always come in that. Pierre waits for me there. He supposes me to be shopping in the department store across the square. Conceive of the bondage of the life wherein we must deceive even our chauffeurs. Goodnight."

"But it is dark now," said Mr. Parkenstacker, "and the park is full of rude men. May I not walk—?"

"If you have the slightest regard for my wishes," said the girl, firmly, "you will remain at this bench for ten minutes after I have left. I do not mean to accuse you, but you are probably aware that autos generally bear the monogram of their owner. Again, goodnight."

Swift and stately she moved away through the dusk. The young man watched her graceful form as she reached the pavement at the park's edge, and turned up along it toward the corner where stood the automobile. Then he treacherously and unhesitatingly began to dodge and skim among the park trees and shrubbery in a course parallel to her route, keeping her well in sight.

When she reached the corner she turned her head to glance at the motor car, and then passed it, continuing on across the street. Sheltered behind a convenient standing cab, the young man followed her movements closely with his eyes. Passing down the sidewalk of the street opposite the park, she entered the restaurant with the blazing sign. The place was one of those frankly glaring establishments, all white paint and glass, where one may dine cheaply and conspicuously. The girl penetrated the restaurant to some retreat at its rear, whence she quickly emerged without her hat and veil.

The cashier's desk was well to the front. A red-haired girl on the stool climbed down, glancing pointedly at the clock as she did so. The girl in gray mounted in her place.

The young man thrust his hands into his pockets and walked slowly back along the sidewalk. At the corner his foot struck a small, papercovered volume lying there, sending it sliding to the edge of the turf. By its picturesque cover he recognized it as the book the girl had been reading. He picked it up carelessly, and saw that its title was "New Arabian Nights," the author being of the name of Stevenson. He dropped it again upon the grass, and lounged, irresolute, for a minute. Then he stepped into the automobile, reclined upon the cushions, and said two words to the chauffeur:

"Club, Henri."

An Unfinished Story

We no longer groan and heap ashes upon our heads when the flames of Tophet are mentioned. For, even the preachers have begun to tell us that God is radium, or ether or some scientific compound, and that the worst we wicked ones may expect is a chemical reaction. This is a pleasing hypothesis; but there lingers yet some of the old, goodly terror of orthodoxy.

There are but two subjects upon which one may discourse with a free imagination, and without the possibility of being controverted. You may talk of your dreams; and you may tell what you heard a parrot say. Both Morpheus and the bird are incompetent witnesses; and your listener dare not attack your recital. The baseless fabric of a vision, then, shall furnish my theme—chosen with apologies and regrets instead of the more limited field of pretty Polly's small talk.

I had a dream that was so far removed from the higher criticism that it had to do with the ancient, respectable, and lamented bar-of-judgment theory.

Gabriel had played his trump; and those of us who could not follow suit were arraigned for examination. I noticed at one side a gathering of professional bondsmen in solemn black and collars that buttoned behind; but it seemed there was some trouble about their real estate titles; and they did not appear to be getting any of us out.

A fly cop—an angel policeman—flew over to me and took me by the left wing. Near at hand was a group of very prosperous-looking spirits arraigned for judgement.

"Do you belong with that bunch?" the policeman asked.

"Who are they?" was my answer.

"Why," said he, "they are —"

But this irrelevant stuff is taking up space that the story should occupy.

Dulcie worked in a department store. She sold Hamburg edging, or stuffed peppers, or automobiles, or other little trinkets such as they keep in department stores. Of what she earned, Dulcie received six dollars per week. The remainder was credited to her and debited to somebody else's account in the ledger kept by G—Oh, primal energy, you say, Reverend Doctor—Well, then, in the Ledger of Primal Energy.

During her first year in the store, Dulcie was paid five dollars per week. It would be instructive to know how she lived on that amount. Don't care? Very well; probably you are interested in larger amounts. Six dollars is a larger amount. I will tell you how she lived on six dollars per week.

One afternoon at six, when Dulcie was sticking her hat pin within an eighth of an inch of her *medulla oblongata,* she said to her chum, Sadie—the girl that waits on you with her left side:

"Say, Sade, I made a date for dinner this evening with Piggy."

"You never did!" exclaimed Sadie, admiringly. "Well, ain't you the lucky one? Piggy's an awful swell; and he always takes a girl to swell places. He took Blanche up to the Hoffman House one evening, where they have swell music, and you see a lot of swells. You'll have a swell time, Dulce."

Dulcie hurried homeward. Her eyes were shining, and her cheeks showed the delicate pink of life's—real life's—approaching dawn. It was Friday; and she had fifty cents left of her week's wages.

The streets were filled with the rush-hour floods of people. The electric lights of Broadway were glowing—calling moths from miles, from leagues, from hundreds of leagues out of darkness around to come in and attend the singeing school. Men in accurate clothes, with faces like those carved on cherry stones by the old salts in sailors' homes, turned and stared at Dulcie as she sped, unheeding, past them. Manhattan, the night-blooming cereus, was beginning to unfold its dead-white, heavy-odored petals.

Dulcie stopped in a store where goods were cheap and bought an imitation lace collar with her fifty cents. That money was to have been spent otherwise—fifteen cents for supper, ten cents for breakfast, ten cents for lunch. Another dime was to be added to her small store of savings; and five cents was to be squandered for licorice drops—the kind that made your cheek look like the toothache, and last as long. The licorice was an extravagance—almost a carouse—but what is life without pleasures?

Dulcie lived in a furnished room. There is this difference between a furnished room and a boardinghouse. In a furnished room, other people do not know it when you go hungry.

Dulcie went up to her room—the third-floor-back in a West Side brownstone-front. She lit the gas. Scientists tell us that the diamond is the hardest substance known. Their mistake. Landladies know of a compound beside which the diamond is as putty. They pack it in the tips of gasburners; and one may stand on a chair and dig at it in vain until one's fingers are pink and bruised. A hairpin will not remove it; therefore let us call it immovable.

So Dulcie lit the gas. In its one-fourth-candle-power glow we will observe the room.

Couch-bed, dresser, table, washstand, chair—of this much the landlady was guilty. The rest was Dulcie's. On the dresser were her treasures—a gilt china vase presented to her by Sadie, a calendar issued by a pickle works, a book on the divination of dreams, some rice powder in a glass dish, and a cluster of artificial cherries tied with a pink ribbon.

Against the wrinkly mirror stood pictures of General Kitchener, William Muldoon, the Duchess of Marlborough, and Benvenuto Cellini.

Against one wall was a plaster of Paris plaque of an O'Callahan in a Roman helmet. Near it was a violent oleograph of a lemon-colored child assaulting an inflammatory butterfly. This was Dulcie's final judgment in art; but it had never been upset. Her rest had never been disturbed by whispers of stolen copes; no critic had elevated his eyebrows at her infantile entomologist.

Piggy was to call for her at seven. While she swiftly makes ready, let us discreetly face the other way and gossip.

For the room, Dulcie paid two dollars per week. On weekdays her breakfast cost ten cents; she made coffee and cooked an egg over the gaslight while she was dressing. On Sunday mornings she feasted royally on veal chops and pineapple fritters at "Billy's" restaurant, at a cost of twenty-five cents—and tipped the waitress ten cents. New York presents so many temptations for one to run into extravagance. She had her lunches in the department store restaurant at a cost of sixty cents for the week; dinners were $1.05. The evening papers—show me a New Yorker going without his daily paper!—came to six cents; and two Sunday papers—one for the personal column and the other to read—were ten cents. The total amounts to $4.76. Now, one has to buy clothes, and—

I give it up. I hear of wonderful bargains in fabrics, and of miracles performed with needle and thread; but I am in doubt. I hold my pen poised in vain when I would add to Dulcie's life some of those joys that belong to woman by virtue of all the unwritten, sacred, natural, inactive ordinances of the equity of heaven. Twice she had been to Coney Island and had ridden the hobby-horses. 'Tis a weary thing to count your pleasures by summers instead of by hours.

Piggy needs but a word. When the girls named him, an undeserving stigma was cast upon the noble family of swine. The words-of-three-letters lesson in the old blue spelling book begins with Piggy's biography. He was fat; he had the soul of a rat, the habits of a bat, and the magnanimity of a cat.... He wore expensive clothes; and was a connoisseur in starvation. He could look at a shop-girl and tell you to an hour how long it had been since she had eaten anything more nourishing than marshmallows and tea. He hung about the shopping districts, and prowled around in department stores with his invitations to dinner. Men who escort dogs upon the streets at the end of a string look down upon him. He is a type; I can dwell upon him no longer; my pen is not the kind intended for him; I am no carpenter.

At ten minutes to seven Dulcie was ready. She looked at herself in the wrinkly mirror. The reflection was satisfactory. The dark blue dress, fitting without a wrinkle, the hat with its jaunty black feather, the butslightly-soiled gloves—all representing self-denial, even of food itself—were vastly becoming.

Dulcie forgot everything else for a moment except that she was beautiful, and that life was about to lift a corner of its mysterious veil for her to observe its wonders. No gentleman had ever asked her out before. Now she was going for a brief moment into the glitter and exalted show.

The girls said that Piggy was a "spender." There would be a grand dinner, and music, and splendidly dressed ladies to look at and things to eat that strangely twisted the girls' jaws when they tried to tell about them. No doubt she would be asked out again.

There was a blue pongee suit in a window that she knew—by saving twenty cents a week instead of ten in—let's see—Oh, it would run into years! But there was a second-hand store in Seventh Avenue where—

Somebody knocked at the door. Dulcie opened it. The landlady stood there with a spurious smile, sniffing for cooking by stolen gas.

"A gentleman's downstairs to see you," she said. "Name is Mr. Wiggins."

By such epithet was Piggy known to unfortunate ones who had to take him seriously.

Dulcie turned to the dresser to get her handkerchief; and then she stopped still, and bit her underlip hard. While looking in her mirror she had seen fairyland and herself, a princess, just awakening from a long slumber. She had forgotten one that was watching her with sad, beautiful, stern eyes—the only one there was to approve or condemn what she did. Straight and slender and tall, with a look of sorrowful reproach on his handsome, melancholy face, General Kitchener fixed his wonderful eyes on her out of his gilt photograph frame on the dresser.

Dulcie turned like an automatic doll to the landlady.

"Tell him I can't go," she said, dully. "Tell him I'm sick, or something. Tell him I'm not going out."

After the door was closed and locked, Dulcie fell upon her bed, crushing her black tip, and cried for ten minutes. General Kitchener was her only friend. He was Dulcie's ideal of a gallant knight. He looked as if he might have a secret sorrow, and his wonderful moustache was a dream, and she was a little afraid of that stern yet tender look in his eyes. She used to have little fancies that he would call at the house sometime, and ask for her, with his sword clanking against his high boots. Once, when a boy was rattling a piece of chain against a lamp post she had opened the window and looked out. But there was no use. She knew that General Kitchener was away over in Japan, leading his army against the savage Turks; and he would never step out of his gilt frarne for her. Yet one look from him had vanquished Piggy that night. Yes, for that night.

When her cry was over Dulcie got up and took off her best dress, and put on her old blue kimono. She wanted no dinner. She sang two verses of "Sammy." Then she became intensely interested in a little red speck on the side of her nose. And after that was attended to, she drew up a chair to the rickety table, and told her fortune with an old deck of cards.

"The horrid, impudent thing!" she said aloud. "And I never gave him a word or a look to make him think it!"

At nine o'clock Dulcie took a tin box of crackers and a little pot of raspberry jam out of her trunk and had a feast. She offered General Kitchener some jam on a cracker; but he only looked at her as the sphinx would have looked at a butterfly—if there are butterflies in the desert.

"Don't eat if you don't want to," said Dulcie. "And don't put on so many airs and scold so with your eyes. I wonder if you'd be so superior and snippy if you had to live on six dollars a week."

It was not a good sign for Dulcie to be rude to General Kitchener. And then she turned Benvenuto Cellini face downward with a severe gesture. But that was not inexcusable; for she had always thought he was Henry VIII, and she did not approve of him.

At half-past nine Dulcie took a last look at the pictures on the dresser, turned out the light and skipped into bed. It's an awful thing to go to bed with a goodnight look at General Kitchener, William Muldoon, the Duchess of Marlborough, and Benvenuto Cellini.

This story doesn't really get anywhere at all. The rest of it comes later—sometime when Piggy asks Dulcie again to dine with him, and she is feeling lonelier than usual, and General Kitchener happens to be looking the other way; and then—

As I said before, I dreamed that I was standing near a crowd of prosperous-looking angels, and a policeman took me by the wing and asked if I belonged with them.

"Who are they?" I asked.

"Why," said he, "they are the men who hired working-girls, and paid 'em five or six dollars a week to live on. Are you one of the bunch?"

"Not on your immortality," said I. "I'm only a fellow that set hire to an orphan asylum, and murdered a blind man for his pennies."

The Furnished Room

Restless, shifting, fugacious as time itself is a certain vast bulk of the population of the red brick district of the lower West Side. Homeless they have a hundred homes. They flit from furnished room to furnished room, transients forever—transients in abode, transients in heart and mind. They sing "Home, Sweet Home" in ragtime; they carry their *lares et panates* in a bandbox; their vine is entwined about a picture hat; a rubber plant is their fig tree.

Hence the houses of this district, having had a thousand dwellers, should have a thousand tales to tell, mostly dull ones, no doubt; but it would be strange if there could not be found a ghost or two in the wake of all these vagrant guests.

One evening after dark a young man prowled among these crumbling red mansions, ringing their bells. At the twelfth he rested his lean hand-baggage upon the step and wiped the dust from his hatband and forehead. The bell sounded faint and far away in some remote, hollow depths.

To the door of this, the twelfth house whose bell he had rung, came a housekeeper who made him think of an unwholesome, surfeited worm that had eaten its nut to a hollow shell and now sought to fill the vacancy with edible lodgers.

He asked if there was a room to let.

"Come in," said the housekeeper. Her voice came from her throat; her throat seemed lined with fur. "I have the third-floor back, vacant since a week back. Should you wish to look at it?"

The young man followed her up the stairs. A faint light from no particular source mitigated the shadows of the halls. They trod noiselessly upon a stair carpet that its own loom would have forsworn. It seemed to have become vegetable; to have degenerated in that rank, sunless air to lush lichen or spreading moss that grew in patches to the staircase and was viscid under the foot like organic matter. At each turn of the stairs were vacant niches in the wall. Perhaps plants had once been set within them. If so they had died in that foul and tainted air. It may be that statues of the saints had stood there, but it was not difficult to conceive that imps and devils had dragged them forth in the darkness and down the unholy depths of some furnished pit below.

"This is the room," said the housekeeper, from her furry throat. "It's a nice room. It ain't often vacant. I had some most elegant people in it last summer—no trouble at all, and paid in advance to the minute. The water's at the end of the hall. Sprowls and Mooney kept it three months. They done a vaudeville sketch. Miss B'retta Sprowls—you may have heard of her—Oh that was just the stage names—right there over the dresser is where the marriage certificate hung, framed. The gas is here, and you see there is plenty of closet room. It's a room everybody likes. It never stays idle long."

"Do you have many theatrical people rooming here?" asked the young man.

"They comes and goes. A good proportion of my lodgers is connected, with the theatres. Yes, sir, this is the theatrical district. Actor people never stays long anywhere. I get my share. Yes, they comes and they goes."

He engaged the room, paying for a week in advance. He was tired, he said, and would take possession at once. He counted out the money. The room had been made ready, she said, even to towels and water. As the housekeeper moved away he put, for the thousandth time, the question that he carried at the end of his tongue.

"A young girl—Miss Vashner—Miss Eloise Vashner—do you remember such a one among your lodgers? She would be singing on the stage, most likely. A fair girl, of medium height and slender, with reddish, gold hair and dark mole near her left eyebrow."

"No, I don't remember the name. Them stage people has names they change as often as their rooms. They comes and they goes. No, I don't call that one to mind."

No. Always no. Five months of ceaseless interrogation and the inevitable negative. So much time spent by day in questioning managers, agents, schools and choruses; by night among the audiences of theatres from all-star casts down to music halls so low that he dreaded to find what he most hoped for. He who had loved her best had tried to find her. He was sure that since her disappearance from home this great, water-girt city held her somewhere, but it was like a monstrous quicksand, shifting its particles constantly, with no foundation, its upper granules of today; buried tomorrow in ooze and slime.

The furnished room received its latest guest with a first glow of pseudohospitality, a hectic, haggard, perfunctory welcome like the specious smile of a demirep. The sophistical comfort came in reflected gleams from the decayed furniture, the ragged brocade upholstery of a couch and two chairs, a foot-wide cheap pier glass between the two windows, from one or two gilt picture frames and a brass bedstead in a corner.

The guest reclined, inert, upon a chair, while the room, confused in speech as though it were an apartment in Babel, tried to discourse to him of its divers tenantry.

A polychromatic rug like some brilliant-flowered, rectangular, tropical islet lay surrounded by a billowy sea of soiled matting. Upon the gaypapered wall were those pictures that pursue the homeless one from house to house—The Huguenot Lovers, The First Quarrel, The Wedding Breakfast, Psyche at the Fountain. The mantel's chastely severe outline was ingloriously veiled behind some pert drapery drawn rakishly askew like the sashes of the Amazonian ballet. Upon it was some desolate flotsam cast aside by the room's marooned when a lucky sail had borne them to a fresh port—a trifling vase or two, pictures of actresses, a medicine bottle, some stray cards out of a deck.

One by one, as the characters of a cryptograph became explicit, the little signs left by the furnished rooms' procession of guests developed a significance. The threadbare space in the rug in front of the dresser told that lovely women had marched in the throng. The tiny fingerprints on the wall spoke of little prisoners trying to feel their way to sun and air. A splattered stain, raying like the shadow of a bursting bomb, witnessed where a hurled glass or bottle had splintered with its contents against the wall. Across the pier glass had been scrawled with a diamond in staggering letters the name "Marie." It seemed that the succession of dwellers in the furnished room had turned in fury—perhaps tempted beyond forbearance by its garish coldness—and wreaked upon it their passions. The furniture was chipped and bruised; the couch, distorted by bursting springs, seemed a horrible monster that had been slain during the stress of some grotesque convulsion. Some more potent unheaval had cloven a great slice from the marble mantel. Each plank in the floor owned its particular cant and shriek as from a separate and individual agony. It seemed incredible that all this malice and injury had been wrought upon the room by those who had called it for a time their home; and yet it may have been the cheated home instinct suriving blindly, the resentful rage at false household gods that had kindled their wrath. A hut that is our own we can sweep and adorn and cherish.

The young tenant in the chair allowed these thoughts to file, softshod, through his mind, while there drifted into the room furnished sounds and furnished scents. He heard in one room a tittering and incontinent, slack laughter; in others the monologue of a scold, the rattling of dice, a lullaby, and one crying dully; above him a banjo tinkled with spirit. Doors banged somewhere; the elevated trains roared intermittently; a cat yowled miserably upon a back fence. And he breathed the breath of the house—a dank savor rather than a smell—cold, musty effluvium as from underground vaults mingled with the reeking exhalations of linoleum and mildewed and rotten woodwork.

Then suddenly, as he rested there, the room was filled with the strong, sweet odor of mignonette. It came as upon a single buffet of wind with such sureness and fragrance and emphasis that it almost seemed a living visitant. And the man cried aloud: "What, dear?" as if he had been called, and sprang up and faced about. The rich odor clung to him and wrapped him around. He reached out his arms for it, all his senses for the time confused and commingled. How could one be peremptorily called by an odor? Surely it must have been a sound. But, was it not the sound that had touched, that had caressed him?

"She has been in this room," he cried, and he sprang to wrest from it a token, for he knew he would recognize the smallest thing that had belonged to her or that she had touched. This enveloping scent of mignonette, the odor that she had loved and made her own—whence came it?

The room had been but carelessly set in order. Scattered upon the flimsy dresser scarf were half a dozen hairpins—those discreet, indistinguishable friends of womankind, feminine of gender, infinite mood and uncommunicative of tense. These he ignored, conscious of their triumphant lack of identity. Ransacking the drawers of the dresser he came upon a discarded, tiny, ragged handkerchief. He pressed it to his face. It was racy and insolent with heliotrope; he hurled it to the floor. In another drawer he found odd buttons, a theatre programme, a pawnbroker's card, two lost marshmallows, a book on the divination of dreams. In the last was a woman's black satin hair bow, which halted him, poised between ice and fire. But the black satin hair bow also is femininity's demure, impersonal common ornament and tells no tales.

And then he traversed the room like a hound on the scent, skimming the walls, considering the corners of the bulging matting on his hands and knees, rummaging mantel and tables, the curtains and hangings, the drunken cabinet in the corner, for a visible sign, unable to perceive that she was there beside, around, against, within, above him, clinging to him, wooing him, calling him so poignantly through the finer senses that even his grosser ones became cognizant of the call. Once again he answered loudly: "Yes, dear!" and turned, wild-eyed, to gaze on vacancy, for he could not yet discern form and color and love and outstretched arms in the odor of mignonette. Oh, God! whence that odor, and since when have odors had a voice to call? Thus he groped.

He burrowed in crevices and corners, and found corks and cigarettes. These he passed in passive contempt. But once he found in a fold of the matting a half-smoked cigar, and this he ground beneath his heel with a green and trenchant oath. He sifted the room from end to end. He found dreary and ignoble small records of many a peripatetic tenant; but of her whom he sought, and who may have lodged there, and whose spirit seemed to hover there, he found no trace.

And then he thought of the housekeeper.

He ran from the haunted room downstairs and to a door that showed a crack of light. She came out to his knock. He smothered his excitement as best he could.

"Will you tell me, madam," he besought her, "who occupied the room I have before I came?"

"Yes, sir. I can tell you again. 'Twas Sprowls and Mooney, as I said. Miss B'retta Sprowls it was in the theatres, but Missis Mooney she was. My house is well known for respectability. The marriage certificate hung, framed, on a nail over—"

"What kind of a lady was Miss Sprowls—in looks, I mean?"

"Why, black-haired, sir, short, and stout, with a comical face. They left a week ago Tuesday."

"And before they occupied it?"

"Why, there was a single gentleman connected with the draying business. He left owing me a week. Before him was Missis Crowder and two children that stayed four months; and back of them was old Mr. Doyle, whose sons paid for him. He kept the room six months. That goes back a year, sir, and further I do not remember."

He thanked her and crept back to his room. The room was dead. The essence that had vivified it was gone. The perfume of mignonette had departed. In its place was the old, stale odor of moldy house furniture, of atmosphere in storage.

The ebbing of his hope drained his faith. He sat staring at the yellow, singing gaslight. Soon he walked to the bed and began to tear the sheets into strips. With the blade of his knife he drove them tightly into every crevice around windows and door. When all was snug and taut he turned out the light, turned the gas full on again and laid himself gratefully upon the bed.

It was Mrs. McCool's night to go with the can for beer. So she fetched it and sat with Mrs. Purdy in one of those subterranean retreats where housekeepers foregather and the worm dieth seldom.

"I rented out my third-floor this evening," said Mrs. Purdy, across a fine circle of foam. "A young man took it. He went up to bed two hours ago."

"Now, did ye, Mrs. Purdy, ma'am?" said Mrs. McCool, with intense admiration. "You do be a wonder for rentin' rooms of that kind. And did ye tell him, then?" she concluded in a husky whisper laden with mystery.

"Rooms," said Mrs. Purdy, in her furriest tones, "are furnished for to rent. I did not tell him, Mrs. McCool."

"Tis right ye are ma'am; 'tis by renting rooms we kape alive. Ye have the rale sense for business, ma'am. There be many people will rayjict the rentin' of a room if they be tould a suicide has been after dyin' in the bed of it."

"As you say, we has our living to be making," remarked Mrs. Purdy.

"Yis, ma'am; 'tis true. 'Tis just one wake ago this day I helped ye lay out the third-floor-back. A pretty slip of a colleen she was to be killin' herself wid the gas—a swate little face she had, Mrs. Purdy, ma'am."

"She'd a-been called handsome, as you say," said Mrs. Purdy, assenting but critical, "but for that mole she had a-growin' by her left eyebrow. Do fill up your glass again, Mrs. McCool."

The Gift of the Magi

One dollar and eighty-seven cents. That was all. And sixty cents of it was in pennies. Pennies saved one and two at a time by bulldozing the grocer and the vegetable man and the butcher until one's cheeks burned with the silent imputation of parsimony that such close dealing implied. Three times Della counted it. One dollar and eighty-seven cents. And the next day would be Christmas.

There was clearly nothing to do but flop down on the shabby little couch and howl. So Della did it. Which instigates the moral reflection that life is made up of sobs, sniffles, and smiles, with sniffles predominating.

While the mistress of the home is gradually subsiding from the first stage to the second, take a look at the home. A furnished flat at $8 per week. It did not exactly beggar description, but it certainly had that word on the lookout for the mendicancy squad.

In the vestibule below was a letterbox into which no letter would go, and an electric button from which no mortal finger could coax a ring. Also appertaining thereunto was a card bearing the name "Mr. James Dillingham Young."

The "Dillingham" had been flung to the breeze during a former period of prosperity when its possessor was being paid $30 per week. Now, when the income was shrunk to $20, the letters of "Dillingham" looked blurred, as though they were thinking seriously of contracting to a modest and unassuming D. But whenever Mr. James Dillingham Young came home and reached his flat above he was called "Jim" and greatly hugged by Mrs. James Dillingham Young, already introduced to you as Della. Which is all very good.

Della finished her cry and attended to her cheeks with the powder rag. She stood by the window and looked out dully at a gray cat walking a gray fence in a gray backyard. Tomorrow would be Christmas Day, and she had only $1.87 with which to buy Jim a present. She had been saving every penny she could for months, with this result. Twenty dollars a week doesn't go far. Expenses had been greater than she had calculated. They always are. Only $1.87 to buy a present for Jim. Her Jim. Many a happy hour she had spent planning for something nice for him. Something fine and rare and sterling—something just a little bit near to being worthy of the honor of being owned by Jim.

There was a pier-glass between the windows of the room. Perhaps you have seen a pier-glass in an $8 flat. A very thin and very agile person may, by observing his reaction in a rapid sequence of longitudinal strips, obtain a fairly accurate conception of his looks. Della, being slender, had mastered the art.

Suddenly she whirled from the window and stood before the glass. Her eyes were shining brilliantly, but her face had lost its color within twenty seconds. Rapidly she pulled down her hair and let it fall to its full length.

Now, there were two possessions of the James Dillingham Youngs in which they both took a mighty pride. One was Jim's gold watch that had been his father's and his grandfather's. The other was Della's hair. Had the Queen of Sheba lived in the flat across the airshaft, Della would have let her hair hang out the window some day to dry just to depreciate Her Majesty's jewels and gifts. Had King Solomon been the janitor, with all his treasures piled up in the basement, Jim would have pulled out his watch every time he passed, just to see him pluck at his beard from envy.

So now Della's beautiful hair fell about her rippling and shining like a cascade of brown waters. It reached below her knee and made itself almost a garment for her. And then she did it up again nervously and quickly. Once she faltered for a minute and stood still while a tear or two splashed on the worn red carpet.

On went her old brown jacket; on went her old brown hat. With a whirl of skirts and with the brilliant sparkle still in her eyes, she fluttered out the door and down the stairs to the street.

Where she stopped the sign read: "Mme. Sofronie. Hair Goods of All Kinds." One flight up Della ran, and collected herself, panting. Madame, large, too white, chilly, hardly looked the "Sofronie."

"Will you buy my hair?" asked Della.

"I buy hair," said Madame. "Take yer hat off and let's have a sight at the looks of it."

Down rippled the brown cascade.

"Twenty dollars," said Madame, lifting the mass with a practiced hand.

"Give it to me quick," said Della.

Oh, and the next two hours tripped by on rosy wings. Forget the hashed metaphor. She was ransacking the stores for Jim's present.

She found it at last. It surely had been made for Jim and no one else. There was no other like it in any of the stores, and she had turned all of them inside out. It was a platinum fob chain simple and chaste in design, properly proclaiming its value by substance alone and not by meretricious ornamentation—as all good things should do. It was even worthy of The Watch. As soon as she saw it she knew that it must be Jim's. It was like him. Quietness and value—the description applied to both. Twenty-one dollars they took from her for it, and she hurried home with the 87 cents. With that chain on his watch Jim might be properly anxious about the time in any company. Grand as the watch was, he sometimes looked at it on the sly on account of the old leather strap that he used in place of a chain.

When Della reached home her intoxication gave way a little to prudence and reason. She got out her curling irons and lighted the gas and went to work repairing the ravages made by generosity added to love. Which is always a tremendous task, dear friends—a mammoth task.

Within forty minutes her head was covered with tiny, close-lying curls that made her look wonderfully like a truant schoolboy. She looked at her reflection in the mirror long, carefully, and critically.

"If Jim doesn't kill me," she said to herself, "before he takes a second look at me, he'll say I look like a Coney Island chorus girl. But what could I do—oh! what could I do with a dollar and eighty-seven cents?"

At 7 o'clock the coffee was made and the frying pan was on the back of the stove hot and ready to cook the chops.

Jim was never late. Della doubled the fob chain in her hand and sat on the corner of the table near the door that he always entered. Then she heard his step on the stair away down on the first flight, and she turned white for just a moment. She had a habit of saying little silent prayers about the simplest everyday things, and now she whispered: "Please God, make him think I am still pretty."

The door opened and Jim stepped in and closed it. He looked thin and very serious. Poor fellow, he was only twenty-two—and to be burdened with a family! He needed a new overcoat and he was without gloves.

Jim stopped inside the door, as immovable as a setter at the scent of quail. His eyes were fixed upon Della, and there was an expression in them that she could not read, and it terrified her. It was not anger, nor surprise, nor disapproval, nor horror, nor any of the sentiments that she had been prepared for. He simply stared at her fixedly with that peculiar expression on his face.

Della wriggled off the table and went for him.

"Jim, darling," she cried, "don't look at me that way. I had my hair cut off and sold it because I couldn't have lived through Christmas without giving you a present. It'll grow out again—you won't mind, will you? I just had to do it. My hair grows awfully fast. 'Merry Christmas!' Jim, and let's be happy. You don't know what a nice—what a beautiful, nice gift I've got for you."

"You've cut off your hair?" asked Jim, laboriously, as if he had not arrived at that patent fact yet even after the hardest mental labor.

"Cut it off and sold it," said Della. "Don't you like me just as well, anyhow? I'm me without my hair, ain't I?"

Jim looked about the room curiously.

"You say your hair is gone?" he said, with an air almost of idiocy.

"You needn't look for it," said Della. "It's sold, I tell you—sold and gone, too. It's Christmas Eve, boy. Be good to me, for it went for you. Maybe the hairs on my head were numbered," she went on with a sudden serious sweetness, "but nobody could ever count my love for you. Shall I put the chops on, Jim?"

Out of his trance Jim seemed quickly to wake. He enfolded his Della. For ten seconds let us regard with discreet scrutiny some inconsequential object in the other direction. Eight dollars a week or a million a year—what is the difference? A mathematician or a wit would give you the wrong answer. The magi brought valuable gifts, but that was not among them. This dark assertion will be illuminated later on.

Jim drew a package from his overcoat pocket and threw it upon the table.

"Don't make any mistake, Dell," he said, "about me. I don't think there's anything in the way of a haircut or a shave or a shampoo that could make me like my girl any less. But if you'll unwrap that package you may see why you had me going a while at first."

White fingers and nimble tore at the string and paper. And then an ecstatic scream of joy; and then, alas! a quick feminine charge to hysterical tears and wails, necessitating the immediate employment of all the comforting powers of the lord of the flat.

For there lay The Combs—the set of combs, side and back, that Della had worshipped for long in a Broadway window. Beautiful combs, pure tortoise shell, with jewelled rims—just the shade to wear in the beautiful vanished hair. They were expensive combs, she knew, and her heart had simply craved and yearned over them without the least hope of possession. And now, they were hers, but the tresses that should have adorned the coveted adornments were gone.

But she hugged them to her bosom, and at length she was able to look up with dim eyes and a smile and say: "My hair grows so fast, Jim!"

And then Della leaped up like a little singed cat and cried, "Oh, oh!"

Jim had not yet seen his beautiful present. She held it out to him eagerly upon her open palm. The dull precious metal seemed to flash with a reflection of her bright and ardent spirit.

"Isn't it a dandy, Jim? I hunted all over town to find it. You'll have to look at the time a hundred times a day now. Give me your watch. I want to see how it looks on it."

Instead of obeying, Jim tumbled down on the couch and put his hands under the back of his head and smiled.

"Dell," said he, "let's put our Christmas presents away and keep 'em a while. They're too nice to use just at present. I sold the watch to get the money to buy your combs. And now suppose you put the chops on."

The magi, as you know, were wise men—wonderfully wise men—who brought gifts to the Babe in the manger. They invented the art of giving Christmas presents. Being wise, their gifts were no doubt wise ones, possibly bearing the privilege of exchange in case of duplication. And here I have lamely related to you the uneventful chronicle of two foolish children in a flat who most unwisely sacrificed for each other the greatest treasures of their house. But in a last word to the wise of these days let it be said that of all who give gifts these two were the wisest. Of all who give and receive gifts, such as they are the wisest. Everywhere they are wisest. They are the magi.

The Robe of Peace

Mysteries follow one another so closely in a great city that the reading public and the friends of Johnny Bellchambers have ceased to marvel at his sudden and unexplained disappearance nearly a year ago. This particular mystery has now been cleared up, but the solution is so strange and incredible to the mind of the average man that only a select few who were in close touch with Bellchambers will give it full credence.

Johnny Bellchambers, as is well known, belonged to the intrinsically inner circle of the *élite.* Without any of the ostentation of the fashionable ones who endeavor to attract notice by eccentric display of wealth and show he still was *au fait* in everything that gave deserved luster to his high position in the ranks of society.

Especially did he shine in the matter of dress. In this he was the despair of imitators. Always correct, exquisitely groomed, and possessed of an unlimited wardrobe, he was conceded to be the best-dressed man in New York, and, therefore, in America. There was not a tailor in Gotham who would not have deemed it a precious boon to have been granted the privilege of making Bellchambers' clothes without a cent of pay. As he wore them, they would have been a priceless advertisement. Trousers were his especial passion. Here nothing but perfection would be noticed. He would have worn a patch as quickly as he would have overlooked a wrinkle. He kept a man in his apartments always busy pressing his ample supply. His friends said that three hours was the limit of time that he would wear these garments without exchanging.

Bellchambers disappeared very suddenly. For three days his absence brought no alarm to his friends, and then they began to operate the usual methods of inquiry. All of them failed. He had left absolutely no trace behind. Then the search for a motive was instituted, but none was found. He had no enemies, he had no debts, there was no woman. There were several thousand dollars in his bank to his credit. He had never showed any tendency toward mental eccentricity; in fact, he was of a particularly calm and well-balanced temperament. Every means of tracing the vanished man was made use of, but without avail. It was one of those cases—more numerous in late years—where men seem to have gone out like the flame of a candle, leaving not even a trail of smoke as a witness.

In May, Tom Eyres and Lancelot Gilliam, two of Bellchambers' old friends, went for a little run on the other side. While pottering around in Italy and Switzerland, they happened, one day, to hear of a monastery in the Swiss Alps that promised something outside of the ordinary tourist-beguiling attractions. The monastery was almost inaccessible to the average sight-seer, being on an extremely rugged and precipitous spur of the mountains. The attractions it possessed but did not advertise were, first, an exclusive and divine cordial made by the monks that was said to far surpass benedictine and chartreuse. Next a huge brass bell so purely and accurately cast that it had not ceased sounding since it was first rung three hundred years ago. Finally, it was asserted that no Englishman had ever set foot within its walls. Eyres and Gilliam decided that these three reports called for investigation.

It took them two days with the aid of two guides to reach the monastery of St. Gondrau. It stood upon a frozen, wind-swept crag with the snow piled about it in treacherous, drifting masses. They were hospitably received by the brothers whose duty it was to entertain the infrequent guest. They drank of the precious cordial, finding it rarely potent and reviving. They listened to the great, ever-echoing bell and learned that they were pioneer travelers, in those gray stone walls, over the Englishman whose restless feet have trodden nearly every corner of the earth.

At three o'clock on the afternoon they arrived, the two young Gothamites stood with good Brother Cristofer in the great, cold hallway of the monastery to watch the monks march past on their way to the refectory. They came slowly, pacing by twos, with their heads bowed, treading noiselessly with sandaled feet upon the rough stone flags. As the procession slowly filed past, Eyres suddenly gripped Gilliam by the arm. "Look," he whispered, eagerly, "at the one just opposite you now—the one on this side, with his hand at his waist—if that isn't Johnny Bellchambers then I never saw him!"

Gilliam saw and recognized the lost glass of fashion.

"What the deuce," said he, wonderingly, "is old Bell doing here? Tommy, it surely can't be he! Never heard of Bell having a turn for the religious. Fact is, I've heard him say things when a four-in-hand didn't seem to tie up just right that would bring him up for court-martial before any church."

"It's Bell, without a doubt," said Eyres, firmly, "or I'm pretty badly in need of an oculist. But think of Johnny Bellchambers, the Royal High Chancellor of swell togs and the Mahatma of pink teas, up here in cold storage doing penance in a snuff-colored bathrobe! I can't get it straight in my mind. Let's ask the jolly old boy that's doing the honors."

Brother Cristofer was appealed to for information. By that time the monks had passed into the refectory. He could not tell to which one they referred. Bellchambers? Ah, the brothers of St. Gondrau abandoned their worldly names when they took the vows. Did the gentlemen wish to speak with one of the brothers? If they would come to the refectory and indicate the one they wished to see, the reverend abbot in authority would, doubtless, permit it.

Eyres and Gilliam went into the dining hall and pointed out to Brother Cristofer the man they had seen. Yes, it was Johnny Bellchambers. They saw his face plainly now, as he sat among the dingy brothers, never looking up, eating broth from a coarse, brown bowl.

Permission to speak to one of the brothers was granted to the two travelers by the abbot, and they waited in a reception room for him to come. When he did come, treading softly in his sandals, both Eyres and Gilliam looked at him in perplexity and astonishment. It was Johnny Bellchambers, but he had a different look. Upon his smooth-shaven face was an expression of ineffable peace, of rapturous attainment, of perfect and complete happiness. His form was proudly erect, his eyes shone with a serene and gracious light. He was as neat and well-groomed as in the old New York days, but how differently was he clad! Now he seemed clothed in but a single garment—a long robe of rough brown cloth, gathered by a cord at the waist, and falling in straight, loose folds nearly to his feet. He shook hands with his visitors with his old ease and grace of manner. If there was any embarrassment in that meeting it was not manifested by Johnny Bellchambers. The room had no seats; they stood to converse.

"Glad to see you, old man," said Eyres, somewhat awkwardly. "Wasn't expecting to find you up here. Not a bad idea, though, after all. Society's an awful sham. Must be a relief to shake the giddy whirl and retire to—er—contemplation and—er—prayer and hymns, and those things."

"Oh, cut that, Tommy," said Bellchambers, cheerfully. "Don't be afraid that I'll pass around the plate. I go through these thing-umbobs with the rest of these old boys because they are the rules. I'm Brother Ambrose here, you know. I'm given just ten minutes to talk to you fellows. That's rather a new design in waistcoats you have on, isn't it, Gilliam? Are they wearing those things on Broadway now?"

"It's the same old Johnny," said Gilliam, joyfully. "What the devil—I mean why—Oh, confound it! what did you do it for, old man?"

"Peel the bathrobe," pleaded Eyres, almost tearfully, "and go back with us. The old crowd'll go wild to see you. This isn't in your line, Bell. I know half a dozen girls that wore the willow on the quiet when you shook us in that unaccountable way. Hand in your resignation, or get a dispensation, or whatever you have to do get a release from this ice factory. You'll get catarrh here, Johnny—and—My God! you haven't any socks on!"

Bellchambers looked down at his sandaled feet and smiled.

"You fellows don't understand," he said, soothingly. "It's nice of you to want me to go back, but the old life will never know me again. I have reached here the goal of all my ambitions. I am entirely happy and contented. Here I shall remain for the remainder of my days. You see this robe that I wear?" Bellchambers caressingly touched the straight-hanging garment: "At last I have found something that will not bag at the knees. I have attained—"

At that moment the deep boom of the great brass bell reverberated through the monastery. It must have been a summons to immediate devotions, for Brother Ambrose bowed his head, turned and left the chamber without another word. A slight wave of his hand as he passed through the stone doorway seemed to say a farewell to his old friends. They left the monastery without seeing him again.

And this is the story that Tommy Eyres and Lancelot Gilliam brought back with them from their latest European tour.

Friends in San Rosario

The westbound stopped at San Rosario on time at 8:20 A.M. A man with a thick black-leather wallet under his arm left the train and walked rapidly up the main street of the town. There were other passengers who also got off at San Rosario, but they either slouched limberly over to the railroad eating-house or the Silver Dollar saloon, or joined the groups of idlers about the station.

Indecision had no part in the movements of the man with the wallet. He was short in stature, but strongly built, with very light, closely trimmed hair, smooth, determined face, and aggressive, gold-rimmed nose glasses. He was well dressed in the prevailing Eastern style. His air denoted a quiet but conscious reserve force, if not actual authority.

After walking a distance of three squares he came to the center of the town's business area. Here another street of importance crossed the main one, forming the hub of San Rosario's life and commerce. Upon one corner stood the post office. Upon another Rubensky's

Clothing Emporium. The other two diagonally opposing corners were occupied by the town's two banks, the First National and the Stockmen's National. Into the First National Bank of San Rosario the newcomer walked, never slowing his brisk step until he stood at the cashier's window. The bank opened for business at nine, and the working force was already assembled, each member preparing his department for the day's business. The cashier was examining the mail when he noticed the stranger standing at his window.

"Bank doesn't open 'til nine," he remarked, curtly, but without feeling. He had had to make that statement so often to early birds since San Rosario adopted city banking hours.

"I am well aware of that," said the other man, in cool, brittle tones. "Will you kindly receive my card?"

The cashier drew the small, spotless parallelogram inside the bars of his wicket, and read:

J.F.C. NETTLEWICK
National Bank Examiner

"Oh—er—will you walk around inside, Mr.—er—Nettlewick. Your first visit—didn't know your business, of course. Walk right around, please."

The examiner was quickly inside the sacred precincts of the bank, where he was ponderously introduced to each employee in turn by Mr. Edlinger, the cashier—a middle-aged gentleman of deliberation, discretion, and method.

"I was kind of expecting Sam Turner round again, pretty soon," said Mr. Edlinger. "Sam's been examining us now for about four years. I guess you'll find us all right, though considering the tightness in business. Not overly much money on hand, but able to stand the storms, sir, stand the storms."

"Mr. Turner and I have been ordered by the Comptroller to exchange districts," said the examiner, in his decisive, formal tones. "He is covering my old territory in southern Illinois and Indiana. I will take the cash first, please."

Perry Dorsey, the teller, was already arranging his cash on the counter for the examiner's inspection. He knew it was right to a cent, and he had nothing to fear, but he was nervous and flustered. So was every man in the bank. There was something so icy and swift, so impersonal and uncompromising about this man that his very presence seemed an accusation. He looked to be a man who would never make nor overlook an error.

Mr. Nettlewick first seized the currency, and with a rapid, almost juggling motion, counted it by packages. Then he spun the sponge cup toward him and verified the count by bills. His thin, white fingers flew like some expert musician's upon the keys of a piano. He dumped the gold upon the counter with a crash, and the coins whined and sang as they skimmed across the marble slab from the tips of his nimble digits. The air was full of fractional currency when he came to the halves and quarters. He counted the last nickel and dime. He had the scales brought, and he weighed every sack of silver in the vault. He questioned Dorsey concerning each of the cash memoranda—certain checks, charge slips, etc., carried over from the previous day's work—with unimpeachable courtesy, yet with something so mysteriously momentous in his frigid manner, that the teller was reduced to pink cheeks and a stammering tongue.

This newly imported examiner was so different from Sam Turner. It had been Sam's way to enter the bank with a shout, pass the cigars, and tell the latest stories he had picked up on his rounds. His customary greeting to Dorsey had been, "Hello, Perry! Haven't skipped out with the boodle yet, I see." Turner's way of counting the cash had been different too. He would finger the packages of bills in a tired kind of way, and then go into the vault and kick over a few sacks of silver, and the thing was done. Halves and quarters and dimes? Not for Sam Turner. "No chicken feed for me," he would say when they were set before him. "I'm not in the agricultural department." But, then, Turner was a Texan, an old friend of the bank's president, and had known Dorsey since he was a baby.

While the examiner was counting the cash, Major Thomas B. Kingman—known to everyone as "Major Tom"—the president of the First National, drove up to the side door with his old dun horse and buggy, and came inside. He saw the examiner busy with the money, and, going into the little "pony corral," as he called it, in which his desk was railed off, he began to look over his letters.

Earlier, a little incident had occurred that even the sharp eyes of the examiner had failed to notice. When he had begun his work at the cash counter, Mr. Edlinger had winked significantly at Roy Wilson, the youthful bank messenger, and nodded his head slightly toward the front door. Roy understood, got his hat and walked leisurely out, with his collector's book under his arm. Once outside, he made a beeline for the Stockmen's National. That bank was also getting ready to open. No customers had, as yet, presented themselves.

"Say, you people!" cried Roy, with the familiarity of youth and long acquaintance, "you want to get a move on you. There's a new bank examiner over at the First, and he's a stem-winder. He's counting nickels on Perry, and he's got the whole outfit bluffed. Mr. Edlinger gave me the tip to let you know."

Mr. Buckley, president of the Stockmen's National—a stout, elderly man, looking like a farmer dressed for Sunday—heard Roy from his private office at the rear and called him.

"Has Major Kingman come down to the bank yet?" he asked of the boy.

"Yes, sir, he was just driving up as I left," said Roy.

"I want you to take him a note. Put it into his own hands as soon as you get back."

Mr. Buckley sat down and began to write.

Roy returned and handed to Major Kingman the envelope containing the note. The major read it, folded it, and slipped it into his vest pocket. He leaned back in his chair for a few moments as if he were meditating deeply, and then rose and went into the vault. He came out with the bulky, old-fashioned leather note case stamped on the back in gilt letters, "Bills Discounted." In this were the notes due the bank with their attached securities, and the major, in his rough way, dumped the lot upon his desk and began to sort them over.

By this time Nettlewick had finished his count of the cash. His pencil fluttered like a swallow over the sheet of paper on which he had set his figures. He opened his black wallet, which seemed to be also a kind of secret memorandum book, made a few rapid figures in it, wheeled and transfixed Dorsey with the glare of his spectacles. That look seemed to say: "You're safe this time, but—"

"Cash all correct," snapped the examiner. He made a dash for the individual bookkeeper, and, for a few minutes there was a fluttering of ledger leaves and a sailing of balance sheets through the air.

"How often do you balance your passbooks?" he demanded, suddenly.

"Er—once a month," faltered the individual bookkeeper, wondering how many years they would give him.

"All right," said the examiner, turning and charging upon the general bookkeeper, who had the statements of his foreign banks and their reconcilement memoranda ready. Everything there was found to be all right. Then the stub book of the certificates of deposit. Flutter—flutter—zip—zip—check! All right, list of overdrafts, please. Thanks. H'm-m. Unsigned bills of the bank next. All right.

Then came the cashier's turn, and easy-going Mr. Edlinger rubbed his nose and polished his glasses nervously under the quick fire of questions concerning the circulation, undivided profits, bank real estate, and stock ownership.

Presently Nettlewick was aware of a big man towering above him at his elbow—a man sixty years of age, rugged and hale, with a rough, grizzled beard, a mass of gray hair, and a pair of penetrating blue eyes that confronted the formidable glasses of the examiner without a flicker.

"Er—Major Kingman, our president—er—Mr. Nettlewick," said the cashier.

Two men of very different types shook hands. One was a finished product of the world of straight lines, conventional methods, and formal affairs. The other was something freer, wider, and nearer to nature. Tom Kingman had not been cut to any pattern. He had been mule-driver, cowboy, ranger, soldier, sheriff, prospector and cattleman. Now, when he was bank president, his old comrades from the prairies, of the saddle, tent, and trail, found no change in him. He had made his fortune when Texas cattle were at the high tide of value, and had organized the First National Bank of San Rosario. In spite of his largeness of heart and sometimes unwise generosity toward his old friends, the bank had prospered, for Major Tom Kingman knew men as well as he knew cattle. Of late years the cattle business had known a depression, and the major's bank was one of the few whose losses had not been great.

"And now," said the examiner, briskly, pulling out his watch, "the last thing is the loans. We will take them up now, if you please."

He had gone through the First National at almost record-breaking speed—but thoroughly, as he did everything. The running order of the bank was smooth and clean, and that had facilitated his work. There was but one other bank in the town. He received from the Government a fee of twenty-five dollars for each bank that he examined. He should be able to go over those loans and discounts in half an hour. If so, he could examine the other bank immediately afterward, and catch the 11:45, the only other train that day in the direction he was working. Otherwise, he would have to spend the night and Sunday in this uninteresting Western town. That was why Mr. Nettlewick was rushing matters.

"Come with me, sir," said Major Kingman, in his deep voice, that united the Southern drawl with the rhythmic twang of the West. "We will go over them together. Nobody in the bank knows those notes as I do. Some of 'em are a little wobbly on their legs, and some are mavericks without extra many brands on their backs, but they'll 'most all pay out at the round-up."

The two sat down at the president's desk. First, the examiner went through the notes at lightning speed, and added up their total, finding it to agree with the amount of loans carried on the book of daily balances. Next, he took up the larger loans, inquiring scrupulously into the condition of their endorsers or securities. The new examiner's mind seemed to course and turn and make unexpected dashes hither and thither like a bloodhound seeking a trail. Finally he pushed aside all the notes except a few, which he arranged in a neat pile before him, and began a dry, normal little speech.

"I find, sir, the condition of your bank to be very good, considering the poor crops and the depression in the cattle interests of your state. The clerical work seems to be done accurately and punctually. Your past-due paper is moderate in amount, and promises only a small loss. I would recommend the calling in of your large loans, and the making of only sixty and ninety day or call loans until general business revives. And now, there is one thing more, and I will have finished with the bank. Here are six notes aggregating something like $40,000. They are secured, according to their faces, by various stocks, bonds, shares, etc., to the value of $70,000. Those securities are missing from the notes to which they should be attached. I suppose you have them in the safe or vault. You will permit me to examine them."

Major Tom's light blue eyes turned unflinchingly toward the examiner.

"No, sir," he said, in a low but steady tone; "those securities are neither in the safe nor the vault. I have taken them. You may hold me personally responsible for their absence."

Nettlewick felt a slight thrill. He had not expected this. He had struck a momentous trail when the hunt was drawing to a close.

"Ah!" said the examiner. He waited a moment, and then continued: "May I ask you to explain more definitely?"

"The securities were taken by me," repeated the major. "It was not for my own use, but to save an old friend in trouble. Come in here, sir, and we'll talk it over."

He led the examiner into the bank's private office at the rear, and closed the door. There was a desk, and a table, and half-a-dozen leather-covered chairs. On the wall was the mounted head of a Texas steer with horns five feet from tip to tip. Opposite hung the major's old cavalry saber that he had carried at Shiloh and Fort Pillow.

Placing a chair for Nettlewick, the major seated himself by the window, from which he could see the post office and the carved limestone front of the Stockmen's National. He did not speak at once, and Nettlewick felt, perhaps, that the ice should be broken by something so near its own temperature as the voice of official warning.

"Your statement," he began, "since you have failed to modify it, amounts, as you must know, to a very serious thing. You are aware, also, of what my duty must compel me to do. I shall have to go before the United States Commissioner and make—"

"I know, I know," said Major Tom, with a wave of his hand. "You don't suppose I'd run a bank without being posted on national banking laws and the revised statutes! Do your duty. I'm not asking any favors. But I spoke of my friend. I did want you to hear me tell about Bob."

Nettlewick settled himself in his chair. There would be no leaving San Rosario for him that day. He would have to telegraph to the Comptroller of the Currency; he would have to swear out a warrant before the United States Commissioner for the arrest of Major Kingman; perhaps he would be ordered to close the bank on account of the loss of the securities. It was not the first crime the examiner had unearthed. Once or twice the terrible upheaval of human emotions that his investigations had loosed had almost caused a ripple in his official calm. He had seen bank men kneel and plead and cry like women for a chance—an hour's time—the overlooking of a single error. One cashier had shot himself at his desk before him. None of them had taken it with the dignity and coolness of this stern old Westerner. Nettlewick felt that he owed it to him at least to listen if he wished to talk. With his elbow on the arm of his chair, and his square chin resting upon the fingers of his right hand, the bank examiner waited to hear the confession of the president of the First National Bank of San Rosario.

"When a man's your friend," began Major Tom, somewhat didactically, "for forty years, and tried by water, fire, earth, and cyclones, when you can do him a little favor you feel like doing it."

("Embezzle for him $70,000 worth of securities," thought the examiner.)

"We were cowboys together, Bob and I," continued the major, speaking slowly, and deliberately, and musingly, as if his thoughts were rather with the past than the critical present, "and we prospected together for gold and silver over Arizona, New Mexico, and a good part of California. We were both in the war of sixty-one, but in different commands. We've fought Indians and horse thieves side by side; we've starved for weeks in a cabin in the Arizona mountains, buried twenty feet deep in snow; we've ridden herd together when the wind blew so hard the lightning couldn't strike—well, Bob and I have been through some rough spells since the first time we met in the branding camp of the old Anchor-Bar ranch. And during that time we've found it necessary more than once to help each other out of tight places. In those days it was expected of a man to stick to his friend, and he didn't ask any credit for it. Probably next day you'd need him to get at your back and help stand off a band of Apaches, or put a tourniquet on your leg above a rattlesnake bite and ride for whisky. So, after all, it was give and take, and if you didn't stand square with your pardner, why, you might be shy one when you needed him. But Bob was a man who was willing to go further than that. He never played a limit.

"Twenty years ago I was sheriff of this county and I made Bob my chief deputy. That was before the boom in cattle when we both made our stake. I was sheriff and collector, and it was a big thing for me then. I was married, and we had a boy and a girl—a four and a six year old. There was a comfortable house next to the courthouse, furnished by the county, rent free, and I was saving some money. Bob did most of the office work. Both of us had seen rough times and plenty of rustling and danger, and I tell you it was great to hear the rain and the sleet dashing against the windows of nights, and be warm and safe and comfortable, and know you could get up in the morning and be shaved and have folks call you 'mister.' And then, I had the finest wife and kids that ever struck the range, and my old friend with me enjoying the first fruits of prosperity and white shirts, and I guess I was happy. Yes, I was happy about that time."

The major sighed and glanced casually out of the window. The bank examiner changed his position, and leaned his chin upon his other hand.

"One winter," continued the major, "the money for the county taxes came pouring in so fast that I didn't have time to take the stuff to the bank for a week. I just shoved the checks into a cigar box and the money into a sack, and locked them in the big safe that belonged in the sheriff's office.

"I had been overworked that week, and was about sick, anyway. My nerves were out of order, and my sleep at night didn't seem to rest me. The doctor had some scientific name for it, and I was taking medicine. And so, added to the rest, I went to bed at night with that money on my mind. Not that there was much need of being worried, for the safe was a good one, and nobody but Bob and I knew the combination. On Friday night there was about $6,500 in cash in the bag. On Saturday morning I went to the office as usual. The safe was locked, and Bob was writing at his desk. I opened the safe, and the money was gone. I called Bob, and roused everybody in the courthouse to announce the robbery. It struck me that Bob took it pretty quiet, considering how much it reflected upon both him and me.

"Two days went by and we never got a clew. It couldn't have been burglars, for the safe had been opened by the combination in the proper way. People must have begun to talk, for one afternoon in comes Alice—that's my wife—and the boy and girl, and Alice stamps her foot, and her eyes flash, and she cries out, 'The lying wretches—Tom, Tom!' and I catch her in a faint, and bring her 'round little by little, and she lays her head down and cries and cries for the first time since she took Tom Kingman's name and fortunes. And Jack and Zilla—the youngsters—they were always wild as tiger's cubs to rush at Bob and climb all over him whenever they were allowed to come to the courthouse—they stood and kicked their little shoes, and herded together like scared partridges. They were having their first trip down into the shadows of life. Bob was working at his desk, and he got up and went out without a word. The grand jury was in session then, and the next morning Bob went before them and confessed that he stole the money. He said he lost it in a poker game. In fifteen minutes they had found a true bill and sent me the warrant to arrest the man with whom I'd been closer than a thousand brothers for many a year.

"I did it, and then I said to Bob, pointing: 'There's my house, and here's my office, and up there's Maine, and out that way is California, and over there is Florida—and that's your range 'til court meets. You're in my charge, and I take the responsibility. You be here when you're wanted.'

"'Thanks, Tom,' he said, kind of carelessly; 'I was sort of hoping you wouldn't lock me up. Court meets next Monday, so, if you don't object, I'll just loaf around the office until then. I've got one favor to ask, if it isn't too much. If you'd let the kids come out in the yard once in a while and have a romp I'd like it.'

"'Why not?' I answered him. 'They're welcome, and so are you. And come to my house the same as ever.' You see, Mr. Nettlewick, you can't make a friend of a thief, but neither can you make a thief of a friend, all at once."

The examiner made no answer. At that moment was heard the shrill whistle of a locomotive pulling into the depot. That was the train on the little, narrow-gauge road that struck into San Rosario from the south. The major cocked his ear and listened for a moment, and looked at his watch. The narrow gauge was in on time—10:35. The major continued.

"So Bob hung around the office, reading the papers and smoking. I put another deputy to work in his place, and, after a while, the first excitement of the case wore off.

"One day when we were alone in the office Bob came over to where I was sitting. He was looking sort of grim and blue—the same look he used to get when he'd been up watching for Indians all night or herd-riding.

"'Tom,' says he, 'it's harder than standing off redskins; it's harder than lying in the lava desert forty miles from water; but I'm going to stick it out to the end. You know that's been my style. But if you'd tip me the smallest kind of a sign—if you'd just say, "Bob I understand," why, it would make it lots easier.'

"I was surprised. 'I don't know what you mean, Bob,' I said. 'Of course, you know that I'd do anything under the sun to help you that I could. But you've got me guessing.'

"'All right, Tom,' was all he said, and he went back to his newspaper and lit another cigar.

"It was the night before the court met when I found out what he meant. I went to bed that night with the same old, light-headed, nervous feeling coming back upon me. I dropped off to sleep about midnight. When I woke I was standing half dressed in one of the courthouse corridors. Bob was holding one of my arms, our family doctor the other and Alice was shaking me and half crying. She had sent for the doctor without my knowing it, and when he came they had found me out of bed and missing, and had begun a search.

"'Sleep-walking,' said the doctor.

"All of us went back to the house, and the doctor told us some remarkable stories about the strange things people had done while in that condition. I was feeling rather chilly after my trip out, and, as my wife was out of the room at the time, I pulled open the door of an old wardrobe that stood in the room and dragged out a big quilt I had seen in there. With it tumbled out the bag of money for stealing which Bob was to be tried—and convicted—in the morning.

"'How the jumping rattlesnakes did that get there?' I yelled, and all hands must have seen how surprised I was. Bob knew in a flash.

"'You darned old snoozer,' he said, with the old-time look on his face, 'I saw you put it there. I watched you open the safe and take it out, and I followed you. I looked through the window and saw you hide it in that wardrobe.'

"'Then, you blankety-blank, flop-eared, sheep-headed coyote, what did you say you took it for?'

"'Because,' said Bob, simply, I didn't know you were asleep.'

"I saw him glance toward the door of the room where Jack and Zilla were, and I know then what it meant to be a man's friend from Bob's point of view."

Major Tom paused, and again directed his glance out of the window. He saw someone in the Stockmen's National Bank reach and draw a yellow shade down the whole length of its plate-glass, big front window, although the position of the sun did not seem to warrant such a defensive movement against its rays.

Nettlewick sat up straight in his chair. He had listened patiently, but without consuming interest, to the major's story. It had impressed him as irrelevant to the situation, and it could certainly have no effect upon the consequences. Those Western people, he thought, had an exaggerated sentimentality. They were not businesslike. They needed to be protected from their friends. Evidently the major had concluded. And what he had said amounted to nothing.

"May I ask," said the examiner, "if you have anything further to say that bears directly upon the question of those abstracted securities?"

"Abstracted securities, sir!" Major Tom turned suddenly in his chair, his blue eyes flashing upon the examiner. "What do you mean, sir?"

He drew from his coat pocket a batch of folded papers held together by a rubber band, tossed them into Nettlewick's hands, and rose to his feet.

"You'll find those securities there, sir, every stock, bond, and share of 'em. I took them from the notes while you were counting the cash. Examine and compare them for yourself."

The major led the way back into the banking room. The examiner, astounded, perplexed, nettled, at sea, followed. He felt that he had been made the victim of something that was not exactly a hoax, but that left him in the shoes of one who had been played upon, used, and then discarded, without even an inkling of the game. Perhaps, also, his official position had been irreverently juggled with. But there was nothing he could take hold of. An official report of the matter would be an absurdity. And, somehow, he felt that he would never know anything more about the matter than he did then.

Frigidly, mechanically, Nettlewick examined the securities, found them to tally with the notes, gathered his black wallet, and rose to depart.

"I will say," he protested, turning the indignant glare of his glasses upon Major Kingman, "that your statements—your misleading statements, which you have not condescended to explain—do not appear to be quite the thing, regarded either as business or humor. I do not understand such motives or actions."

Major Tom looked down at him serenely and not unkindly.

"Son," he said, "there are plenty of things in the chaparral, and on the prairies, and up the cañons that you don't understand. But I want to thank you for listening to a garrulous old man's prosy story. We old Texans love to talk about our adventures and our old comrades, and the home folks have long ago learned to run when we begin with 'Once upon a time,' so we have to spin our yarns to the stranger within our gates."

The major smiled, but the examiner only bowed coldly, and abruptly quitted the bank. They saw him travel diagonally across the street in a straight line and enter the Stockmen's National Bank.

Major Tom sat down at his desk and drew from his vest pocket the note Roy had given him. He had read it once, but hurriedly, and now, with something like a twinkle in his eyes, he read it again. These were the words he read:

Dear Tom:

I hear there's one of Uncle Sam's greyhounds going through you, and that means that we'll catch him inside of a couple of hours, maybe. Now, I want you to do something for me. We've got just

$2,200 in the bank, and the law requires that we have $20,000. I let Ross and Fisher have $18,000 late yesterday afternoon to buy up that Gibson bunch of cattle. They'll realize $40,000 in less than thirty days on the transaction, but that won't make my cash on hand look any prettier to that bank examiner. Now, I can't show him those notes, for they're just plain notes of hand without any security in sight, but you know very well that Pink Ross and Jim Fisher are two of the finest white men God ever made, and they'll do the square thing. You remember Jim Fisher—he was the one who shot that faro dealer in El Paso. I wired Sam Bradshaw's bank to send me $20,000, and it will get in on the narrow-gauge at 10:35. You can't let a bank examiner in to count $2,200 and close your doors. Tom, you hold that examiner. Hold him. Hold him if you have to rope him and sit on his head. Watch our front window after the narrow-gauge gets in, and when we've got the cash inside we'll pull down the shade for a signal. Don't turn him loose till then. I'm counting on you, Tom.

Your Old Pard,
Bob Buckley,
Prest. Stockmen's National

The major began to tear the note into small pieces and throw them into his waste basket. He gave a satisfied little chuckle as he did so.

"Confounded old reckless cowpuncher!" he growled, contentedly, "that pays him some on account for what he tried to do for me in the sheriff's office twenty years ago."

A Retrieved Reformation

A guard came to the prison shoe shop, where Jimmy Valentine was assiduously stiching uppers, and escorted him to the front office. There the warden handed Jimmy his pardon, which had been signed that morning by the governor. Jimmy took it in a tired kind of way. He had served nearly ten months of a four-year sentence. He had expected to stay only about three months, at the longest. When a man with as many friends on the outside as Jimmy Valentine had is received in the "stir" it is hardly worthwhile to cut his hair.

"Now, Valentine," said the warden, "you'll go out in the morning. Brace up, and make a man of yourself. You're not a bad fellow at heart. Stop cracking safes, and live straight."

"Me?" said Jimmy, in surprise. "Why, I never cracked a safe in my life."

"Oh, no," laughed the warden. "Of course not. Let's see, now. How was it you happened to get sent up on that Springfield job? Was it because you wouldn't prove an alibi for fear of compromising somebody in extremely high-toned society? Or was it simply a case of a mean old jury that had it in for you? It's always one or the other with you innocent victims."

"Me?" said Jimmy, still blankly virtuous. "Why, warden, I never was in Springfield in my life!"

"Take him back, Cronin," smiled the warden, "and fix him up with outgoing clothes. Unlock him at seven in the morning, and let him come to the bullpen. Better think over my advice, Valentine."

At a quarter past seven on the next morning Jimmy stood in the warden's outer office. He had on a suit of the villainously fitting, ready-made clothes and a pair of the stiff, squeaky shoes that the state furnishes to its discharged compulsory guests.

The clerk handed him a railroad ticket and the five-dollar bill with which the law expected him to rehabilitate himself into good citizenship and prosperity. The warden gave him a cigar, and shook hands. Valentine, 9762, was chronicled on the books "Pardoned by Governor," and Mr. James Valentine walked out into the sunshine.

Disregarding the song of the birds, the waving green trees, and the smell of the flowers, Jimmy headed straight for a restaurant. There he tasted the first sweet joys of liberty in the shape of a broiled chicken and a bottle of white wine—followed by a cigar a grade better than the one the warden had given him. From there he proceeded leisurely to the depot. He tossed a quarter into the hat of a blind man sitting by the door, and boarded his train. Three hours set him down in a little town near the state line. He went to the café of one Mike Dolan and shook hands with Mike, who was alone behind the bar.

"Sorry we couldn't make it sooner, Jimmy, me boy," said Mike. "But we had that protest from Springfleld to buck against, and the governor nearly balked. Feeling all right?"

"Fine," said Jimmy. "Got my key?"

He got his key and went upstairs, unlocking the door of a room at the rear. Everything was just as he had left it. There on the floor was still Ben Price's collar button that had been torn from that eminent detective's shirt-band when they had overpowered Jimmy to arrest him.

Pulling out from the wall a folding bed, Jimmy slid back a panel in the wall and dragged out a dust-covered suitcase. He opened this and gazed fondly at the finest set of burglar's tools in the East. It was a complete set, made of specially tempered steel, the latest designs in drills, punches, braces and bits, jimmies, clamps, and augers, with two or three novelties invented by Jimmy himself, in which he took pride. Over nine hundred dollars they had cost him to have made at—, a place where they make such things for the profession.

In half an hour Jimmy went downstairs and through the café. He was now dressed in tasteful and well-fitting clothes, and carried his dusted and cleaned suitcase in his hand.

"Got anything on?" asked Mike Dolan, genially.

"Me?" said Jimmy, in a puzzled tone. "I don't understand. I'm representing the New York Amalgamated Short Snap Biscuit Cracker and Frazzled Wheat Company."

This statement delighted Mike to such an extent that Jimmy had to take a seltzer-and-milk on the spot. He never touched "hard" drinks.

A week after thc release of Valentine, 9762, there was a neat job of safe-burglary done in Richmond, Indiana, with no clue to the author. A scant eight hundred dollars was all that was secured. Two weeks after that a patented, improved, burglar-proof safe in Logansport was opened like a cheese to the tune of fifteen hundred dollars, currency; securities and silver untouched. That began to interest the rogue-catchers. Then an old-fashioned bank safe in Jefferson City became active and threw out of its crater an eruption of bank notes amounting to five thousand dollars. The loses were now high enough to bring the matter up into Ben Price's class of work. By comparing notes, a remarkable similarity in the methods of the burglaries was noticed. Ben Price investigated the scenes of the robberies, and was heard to remark:

"That's Dandy Jim Valentine's autograph. He's resumed business. Look at that combination knob—jerked out as easy as pulling up a radish in wet weather. He's got the only clamps that can do it. And look how clean those tumblers were punched out! Jimmy never has to drill but one hole. Yes, I guess I want Mr. Valentine. He'll do his bit next time without any short-time or clemency foolishness."

Ben Price knew Jimmy's habits. He had learned them while working up the Springfield case. Long jumps, quick get-aways, no confederates, and a taste for good society—these ways had helped Mr. Valentine to become noted as a successful dodger of retribution. It was given out that Ben Price had taken up the trail of the elusive cracksman, and other people with burglar-proof safes felt more at ease.

One afternoon Jimmy Valentine and his suitcase climbed out of the mail-hack in Elmore, a little town five miles off the railroad down in the blackjack country of Arkansas. Jimmy, looking like an athletic young senior just home from college, went down the board sidewalk toward the hotel.

A young lady crossed the street, passed him at the corner and entered a door over which was the sign "The Elmore Bank." Jimmy Valentine looked into her eyes, forgot what he was, and became another man. She lowered her eyes and colored slightly. Young men of Jimmy's style and looks were scarce in Elmore.

Jimmy collared a boy that was loafing on the steps of the bank as if he were one of the stockholders, and began to ask him questions about the town, feeding him dimes at intervals. By and by the young lady came out, looking royally unconscious of the young man with the suitcase, and went her way.

"Isn't that young lady Miss Polly Simpson?" asked Jimmy, with specious guile.

"Naw," said the boy. "She's Annabel Adams. Her pa owns this bank. What'd you come to Elmore for? Is that a gold watch chain? I'm going to get a bulldog. Got any more dimes?"

Jimmy went to the Planter' Hotel, registered as Ralph D. Spencer, and engaged a room. He leaned on the desk and declared his platform to the clerk. He said he had come to Elmore to look for a location to go into business. How was the shoe business, now, in the town? He had thought of the shoe business. Was there an opening?

The clerk was impressed by the clothes and manner of Jimmy. He, himself, was something of a pattern of fashion to the thinly gilded youth of Elmore, but he now perceived his shortcomings. While trying to figure out Jimmy's manner of tying his four-in-hand he cordially gave information.

Yes, there ought to be a good opening in the shoe line. There wasn't an exclusive shoe store in the place. The dry-goods and general stores handled them. Business in all lines was fairly good.

Hoped Mr. Spencer would decide to locate in Elmore. He would find it a pleasant town to live in, and the people very sociable.

Mr. Spencer thought he would stop over in the town a few days and look over the situation. No, the clerk needn't call the boy. He would carry up his suitcase, himself; it was rather heavy.

Mr. Ralph Spencer, the phœnix that arose from Jimmy Valentine's ashes—ashes left by the flame of a sudden and alternative attack of love—remained in Elmore, and prospered. He opened a shoe store and secured a good run of trade.

Socially he was also a success, and made many friends. And he accomplished the wish of his heart. He met Miss Annabel Adams, and became more and more captivated by her charms.

At the end of a year the situation of Mr. Ralph Spencer was this: he had won the respect of the community, his shoe store was flourishing, and he and Annabel were engaged to be married in two weeks. Mr. Adams, the typical, plodding, country banker, approved of Spencer. Annabel's pride in him almost equalled her affection. He was as much at home in the family of Mr. Adams and that of Annabel's married sister as if he were already a member.

One day Jimmy sat down in his room and wrote this letter, which he mailed to the safe address of one of his old friends in St. Louis:

Dear Old Pal:

I want you to be at Sullivan's place, in Little Rock, next Wednesday night at nine o'clock. I want you to wind up some little matters for me. And, also, I want to make you a present of my kit of tools. I know you'll be glad to get them—you couldn't duplicate the lot for a thousand dollars. Say, Billy, I've quit the old business—a year ago. I've got a nice store. I'm making an honest living, and I'm going to marry the finest girl on earth two weeks from now. It's the only life, Billy—the straight one. I wouldn't touch a dollar of another man's money now for a million. After I get married I'm going to sell out and go West, where there won't be so much danger of having old scores brought up against me. I tell you, Billy, she's an angel. She believes in me; and I wouldn't do another crooked thing for the whole world. Be sure to be at Sully's, for I must see you. I'll bring along the tools with me.

Your old friend,
Jimmy

On the Monday night after Jimmy wrote this letter, Ben Price jogged unobtrusively into Elmore in a livery buggy. He lounged about town in his quiet way until he found out what he wanted to know. From the drugstore across the street from Spencer's shoestore he got a good look at Ralph D. Spencer.

"Going to marry the banker's daughter are you, Jimmy?" said Ben to himself, softly. "Well, I don't know!"

The next morning Jimmy took breakfast at the Adamses. He was going to Little Rock that day to order his wedding suit and buy something nice for Annabel. That would be the first time he had left town since he came to Elmore. It had been more than a year now since those last professional "jobs," and he thought he could safely venture out.

After breakfast quite a family party went down town together—Mr. Adams, Annabel, Jimmy, and Annabel's married sister with her two little girls, aged five and nine. They came by the hotel where Jimmy still boarded, and he ran up to his room and brought along his suitcase. Then they went on to the bank. There stood Jimmy's horse and buggy and Dolph Gibson, who was going to drive him over to the railroad station.

All went inside the high, carved oak railings into the banking-room—Jimmy included, for Mr. Adams's future son-in-law was welcome anywhere. The clerks were pleased to be greeted by the good-looking, agreeable young man who was going to marry Miss Annabel. Jimmy set his suitcase down. Annabel, whose heart was bubbling with happiness and lively youth, put on Jimmy's hat and picked up the suitcase. "Wouldn't I make a nice drummer" said Annabel. "My! Ralph, how heavy it is. Feels like it was full of gold bricks."

"Lot of nickel-plated shoehorns in there," said Jimmy, cooly, "that I'm going to return. Thought I'd save express charges by taking them up. I'm getting awfully economical."

The Elmore Bank had just put in a new safe and vault. Mr. Adams was very proud of it, and insisted on an inspection by everyone. The vault was a small one, but it had a new patented door. It fastened with three solid steel bolts thrown simultaneously with a single handle, and had a time lock. Mr. Adams beamingly explained its workings to Mr. Spencer, who showed a courteous but not too intelligent interest. The two children, May and Agatha, were delighted by the shining metal and funny clock and knobs.

While they were thus engaged Ben Price sauntered in and leaned on his elbow, looking casually inside between the railings. He told the teller that he didn't want anything; he was just waiting for a man he knew.

Suddenly there was a scream or two from the women, and a commotion. Unperceived by the elders, May, the nine-year-old girl, in a spirit of play, had shut Agatha in the vault. She had then shot the bolts and turned the knob of the combination as she had seen Mr. Adams do.

The old banker sprang to the handle and tugged at it for a moment. "The door can't be opened," he groaned. "The clock hasn't been wound nor the combination set."

Agatha's mother screamed again, hysterically.

"Hush!" said Mr. Adams, raising his trembling hand. "All be quiet tor a moment, Agatha!" he called as loudly as he could: "Listen to me." During the following silence they could just hear the faint sound of the child wildly shrieking in the dark vault in a panic of terror.

"My precious darling!" wailed the mother. "She will die of fright! Open the door! Oh, break it open! Can't you men do something?"

"There isn't a man nearer than Little Rock who can open that door," said Mr. Adams, in a shaky voice. "My God! Spencer, what shall we do? That child—she can't stand it long in there. There isn't enough air, and, besides, she'll go into convulsions from fright."

Agatha's mother, frantic now, beat the door of the vault with her hands. Somebody wildly suggested dynamite. Annabel turned to Jimmy, her large eyes full of anguish, but not yet despairing. To a woman nothing seems quite impossible to the powers of the man she worships.

"Can't you do something, Ralph—*try,* won't you?"

He looked at her with a queer, soft smile on his lips and in his keen eyes.

"Annabel," he said, "give me that rose you are wearing, will you?"

Hardly believing that she heard him aright, she unpinned the bud from the bosom of her dress, and placed it in his hand. Jimmy stuffed it into his vest pocket, threw off his coat and pulled up his shirt-sleeves. With that act Ralph D. Spencer passed away and Jimmy Valentine took his place.

"Get away from the door, all of you," he commanded, shortly.

He set his suitcase on the table, and opened it out flat. From that time on he seemed to be unconscious of the presence of anyone else.

He laid out the shining, queer implements swiftly and orderly, whistling softly to himself as he always did when at work. In a deep silence and immovable, the others watched him as if under a spell.

In a minute Jimmy's pet drill was biting smoothly into the steel door. In ten minutes—breaking his own burglarious record—he threw back the bolts and opened the door.

Agatha, almost collapsed, but safe, was gathered into her mother's arm. Jimmy Valentine put on his coat, and walked outside the railings toward the front door. As he went he thought he heard a faraway voice that he once knew call "Ralph!" But he never hesitated.

At the door a big man stood somewhat in his way.

"Hello, Ben!" said Jimmy, still with his strange smile. "Got around at last, have you? Well, let's go. I don't know that it makes much difference, now."

And then Ben Price acted rather strangely.

"Guess you're mistaken, Mr. Spencer," he said. "Don't believe I recognize you. Your buggy's waiting for you, ain't it?"

And Ben Price turned and strolled down the street.

Crane

1871	November 1. Stephen Crane is born in Newark, New Jersey.
1891	Leaves Syracuse University to pursue a journalism career in New York City. Spends the two days prior to Christmas writing his first novel, *Maggie: A Girl in the Streets*, inspired by his experiences living on New York's Bowery. His mother, Mary Crane, dies on December 7 .
1893	Borrows $1,000 from his brother, William, to finance the publication of *Maggie*. The book, published under the pseudonym Johnston Smith, receives little public attention.
1894	*The Red Badge of Courage* is published in installments in the *Philadelphia Free Press*; does not appear in book form until 1895.
1897	January 2. Crane is shipwrecked off the coast of Florida en route to Cuba to cover insurgents fighting Spanish Rule. This incident provides the inspiration for *The Open Boat*, which is published the following year. Moves to England with companion Cora Taylor, cultivates relationships with other expatriots, such as Joseph Conrad and Henry James.
1898	Returns to the United States and then to Cuba to cover the Spanish-American War for New York's *World*.
1900	Stricken with tuberculosis, Crane travels to Germany's Black Forest in search of a cure. He dies on June 5 in Badenweiler, Germany.

Stephen Crane

"I understand," wrote Crane, "that a man is born into the world with his own pair of eyes, and he is not at all responsible for his vision—he is merely responsible for his quality of personal honesty. To keep close to this personal honesty is my supreme ambition." Stephen Crane's virtues as a writer come from the honesty and the clarity with which he recorded what he saw; his weaknesses are the result of his failure to discover why he saw as he did.

In his most personal utterances, his poems, we see his intense and precocious bitterness. In *The Black Riders* he is the naked, bestial creature who eats his own heart. His revolt, directed against the God of his father and against the moral code of his generation, is the revolt of a man who has found life far less desirable than it had been represented as being, and who scarcely knows whether to blame the putative creator or his fellow men. In *War Is Kind* he is less concerned with the Deity and more with human stupidity and corruption. He no longer protests for he recognizes the blank indifference of the cosmos, and his sense of human frustration is so strong that he has little room even for pity.

Though we know too little of Crane's early life to be able to determine the genesis of his bitterness, we have seen enough of conditions in the period of his youth to have some understanding of such states of mind as his. He once said to a friend, "You can never do anything good esthetically—and you can never do anything with anything that's any good except esthetically—unless it has at one time meant something important to you." In the work by which we best know him Crane remembered this: it was not mere objectivity that guided his pen, but a bitter awareness of the importance—to him—of the materials with which he dealt.

Crane's first book, *Maggie*, expressed not merely his hatred and fear of the slums and their inhabitants but also his irritation with the treatment those phenomena received at the hands of his fellow writers. When Gilder questioned the book's grammar, which is certainly not beyond question, Crane cut him short: "You mean that the story's too honest?" That men could regard the slums condescendingly, ignoring their hideous squalor and sentimentalizing the vile men and women who lived in them, was an offense he could not forgive. He did not hestitate to make Maggie the stupid victim of stupid brutality, nor to make her brother a braggart and her mother a drunkard. He set down precisely what he saw, and he saw what he did because he was driven by a violent hatred, an almost physical loathing, for poverty and suffering. "In a story of mine called 'An Experiment in Misery,'" he wrote, "I have tried to make plain that the root of Bowery life is a sort of cowardice. Perhaps I mean a lack of ambition or to willingly be knocked flat and accept the licking." He hated the poor because they could consent to the ugliness of their surroundings, the brutality of their lives, the defeat of their hopes, because they continued to live on such terms. He saw in them the depths to which a human being might fall, and trembled at the abyss thus opened before him.

Hatred is a healthier emotion for the artist than pity. The hideousness anbd cowardice were there, and Crane's sensitiveness to color and sound and smell permitted him to describe them and to arouse the reader as he was himself aroused. Yet though we know what sort of person Maggie seems to Crane to be, we never know what sort of person she appeared to herself. As in "George's Mother," the author stands on the outside. He could not enter into his characters' lives because he did not understand them, and he did not understand them because he did not understand how they had come into existence. We see them merely as they present themselves to Crane, a symbol of everything he feared. As a result there is something dry and harsh in all Crane's work, even in *The Red Badge of Courage*. Here the description is peculiarly effective, and the irony is intense. Well might Crane feel, when he had actually seen war, that he had been surprisingly right. But not only is the bitterness misdirected; as in *Maggie*, the events of the story never quite touch us. Crane felt horror of such events, and that was his strength; he could not understand their significance, and that was his weakness.

The Red Badge of Courage made Crane famous at the age of twenty-four; it did not help him to find himself as an author. The magazines were open to him now, and he wrote voluminously, sometimes of the slums, sometimes of war, in his Whilomville stories about boys. With no clear purpose of his own, he was unusually open to suggestions from others, and he tried his hand at many themes. His wandering life paralleled the course of his literary tastes. In the end he turned, as did so many of his contemporaries, to England, where, at the age of twenty-nine, he died. Much of his later work is slight and ineffective. Perhaps it was because disease already crippled him; perhaps it was because it was increasingly difficult for him to find anything of real importance to him. He had never tried to orientate himself; the expression of his bitterness, which was almost miraculously possible for him in his early twenties, had seemed enough. To the end of his short life the world remained to him a blank mystery, full of hateful objects, and, unless he had transcended that attitude, unless he had learned to understand as well as to record, he would never have surpassed his earlier work. Yet we must not forget that in that early work he had broken some of the intolerable bonds that restrained the American novelist. For the sake of artistic integrity he had challenged some of the most sacred taboos. If it remained just as difficult for the artist to understand the world in which he lived, it was easier for him to record whatever he saw.

—*from* The Great Tradition: An Interpretation of American Literature Since the Civil War *by Granville Hicks*

The Upturned Face

"What will we do now?" said the adjutant, troubled and excited.

"Bury him," said Timothy Lean.

The two officers looked down close to their toes where lay the body of their comrade. The face was chalk blue; gleaming eyes stared at the sky. Over the two upright figures was a windy sound of bullets, and on the top of the hill Lean's prostrate company of Spitzbergen infantry was firing measured volleys.

"Don't you think it would be better—" began the adjutant. "We might leave him until tomorrow."

"No," said Lean. "I can't hold that post an hour longer. I've got to fall back, and we've got to bury old Bill."

"Of course," said the adjutant, at once. "Your men got entrenching tools?"

Lean shouted back to his little line, and two men came slowly, one with a pick, one with a shovel. They started in the direction of the Rostina sharpshooters. Bullets cracked near their ears. "Dig here," said Lean gruffly. The men, thus caused to lower their glances to the turf, became hurried and frightened, merely because they could not look to see whence the bullets came. The dull beat of the pick striking the earth sounded amid the swift snap of close bullets. Presently the other private began to shovel.

"I suppose," said the adjutant, slowly, "we'd better search his clothes for—things."

Lean nodded. Together in curious abstraction they looked at the body. Then Lean stirred his shoulders suddenly, arousing himself.

"Yes," he said, "we'd better see what he's got." He dropped to his knees, and his hands approached the body of the dead officer. But his hands wavered over the buttons of the tunic. The first button was brick red with drying blood, and he did not seem to dare touch it.

"Go on," said the adjutant, hoarsely.

Lean stretched his wooden hand, and his fingers fumbled the bloodstained buttons. At last he rose with ghastly face. He had gathered a watch, a whistle, a pipe, a tobacco pouch, a handkerchief, a little case of cards and papers. He looked at the adjutant. There was a silence. The adjutant was feeling that he had been a coward to make Lean do all the grisly business.

"Well," said Lean, "that's all, I think. You have his sword and revolver?"

"Yes," said the adjutant, his face working, and then he burst out in a sudden strange fury at the two privates. "Why don't you hurry up with that grave? What are you doing, anyhow? Hurry, do you hear? I never saw such stupid—"

Even as he cried out in his passion the two men were laboring for their lives. Ever overhead the bullets were spitting.

The grave was finished. It was not a masterpiece—a poor little shallow thing. Lean and the adjutant again looked at each other in a curious silent communication.

Suddenly the adjutant croaked out a weird laugh. It was a terrible laugh, which had its origin in that part of the mind which is first moved by the singing of the nerves. "Well," he said humorously to Lean, "I suppose we had best tumble him in."

"Yes," said Lean. The two privates stood waiting, bent over their implements. "I suppose," said Lean, "it would be better if we laid him in ourselves."

"Yes," said the adjutant. Then, apparently remembering that he had made Lean search the body, he stooped with great fortitude and took hold of the dead officer's clothing. Lean joined him. Both were particular that their fingers should not feel the corpse. They tugged away; the corpse lifted, heaved, toppled, flopped into the grave, and the two officers, straightening, looked again at each other—they were always looking at each other. They sighed with relief.

The adjutant said, "I suppose we should—we should say something. Do you know the service, Tim?"

"They don't read the service until the grave is filled in," said Lean, pressing his lips to an academic expression.

"Don't they?" said the adjutant, shocked that he had made the mistake. "Oh, well," he cried, suddenly, "let us—let us say something—while he can hear us."

"All right," said Lean. "Do you know the service?"

"I can't remember a line of it," said the adjutant.

Lean was extremely dubious. "I can repeat two lines, but—"

"Well, do it," said the adjutant. "Go as far as you can. That's better than nothing. And the beasts have got our range exactly."

Lean looked at his two men. "Attention," he barked. The privates came to attention with a click, looking much aggrieved. The adjutant lowered his helmet to his knee. Lean, bareheaded, he stood over the grave. The Rostina sharpshooters fired briskly.

"O Father, our friend has sunk in the deep waters of death, but his spirit has leaped toward Thee as the bubble arises from the lips of the drowning. Perceive, we beseech, O Father, the little flying bubble, and—"

Lean, although husky and ashamed, had suffered no hesitation up to this point, but he stopped with a hopeless feeling and looked at the corpse.

The adjutant moved uneasily. "And from Thy superb heights—" he began, and then he too came to an end.

"And from Thy superb heights," said Lean.

The adjutant suddenly remembered a phrase in the back of the Spitzbergen burial service, and he exploited it with the triumphant manner of a man who has recalled everything, and can go on.

"O God, have mercy—"

"O God, have mercy—" said Lean.

"Mercy," repeated the adjutant, in quick failure.

"Mercy," said Lean. And then he was moved by some violence of feeling, for he turned upon his two men and tigerishly said, "Throw the dirt in."

The fire of the Rostina sharpshooters was accurate and continuous.

One of the aggrieved privates came forward with his shovel. He lifted his first shovel-load of earth, and for a moment of inexplicable hesitation it was held poised above this corpse, which from its chalk-blue face looked keenly out from the grave. Then the soldier emptied his shovel on—on the feet.

Timothy Lean felt as if tons had been swiftly lifted from off his forehead. He had felt that perhaps the private might empty the shovel on—on the face. It had been emptied on the feet. There was a great point gained there—ha, ha!—the first shovelful had been emptied on the feet. How satisfactory!

The adjutant began to babble. "Well, of course—a man we've messed with all these years—impossible—you can't, you know, leave your intimate friends rotting on the field. Go on, for God's sake, and shovel, you."

The man with the shovel suddenly ducked, grabbed his left arm with his right hand, and looked at his officer for orders. Lean picked the shovel from the ground. "Go to the rear," he said to the wounded man. He also addressed the other private. "You get under cover, too; I'll finish this business."

The wounded man scrambled hard still for the top of the ridge without devoting any glances to the direction from whence the bullets came, and the other man followed at an equal pace; but he was different, in that he looked back anxiously three times.

This is merely the way—often—of the hit and unhit.

Timothy Lean filled the shovel, hesitated, and then, in a movement which was like a gesture of abhorrence, he flung the dirt into the grave, and as it landed it made a sound—plop. Lean suddenly stopped and mopped his brow—a tired laborer.

"Perhaps we have been wrong," said the adjutant. His glance wavered stupidly. "It might have been better if we hadn't buried him just at this time. Of course, if we advance tomorrow the body would have been—"

"Damn you," said Lean, "shut your mouth." He was not the senior officer.

He again filled the shovel and flung the earth. Always the earth made that sound—plop. For a space Lean worked frantically, like a man digging himself out of danger.

Soon there was nothing to be seen but the chalk-blue face. Lean filled the shovel. "Good God," he cried to the adjutant. "Why didn't you turn him somehow when you put him in? This—" Then Lean began to stutter.

The adjutant understood. He was pale to the lips. "Go on, man, he cried, beseechingly, almost in a shout.

Lean swung back the shovel. It went forward in a pendulum curve. When the earth landed it made a sound—plop.

The Open Boat

A Tale Intended to Be After the Fact:
Being the Experience of Four Men
From the Sunk Steamer *Commodore*

I

None of them knew the color of the sky. Their eyes glanced level, and were fastened upon the waves that swept toward them. These waves were of the hue of slate, save for the tops, which were of foaming white, and all of the men knew the colors of the sea. The horizon narrowed and widened, and dipped and rose, and at all times its edge was jagged with waves that seemed to thrust up in points like rocks.

Many a man ought to have a bathtub larger than the boat which here rode upon the sea. These waves were most wrongfully and barbarously abrupt and tall, and each froth-top was a problem in small-boat navigation.

The cook squatted in the bottom, and looked with both eyes at the six inches of gunwale which separated him from the ocean. His sleeves were rolled over his fat forearms, and the two flaps of his unbuttoned vest dangled as he bent to bail out the boat. Often he said, "Gawd! that was a narrow clip." As he remarked it he invariably gazed eastward over the broken sea.

The oiler, steering with one of the two oars in the boat, sometimes raised himself suddenly to keep clear of water that swirled in over the stern. It was a thin little oar, and it seemed often ready to snap.

The correspondent, pulling at the other oar, watched the waves and wondered why he was there.

The injured captain, lying in the bow, was at this time buried in that profound dejection and indifference which comes, temporarily at least, to even the bravest and most enduring when, willy-nilly, the firm fails, the army loses, the ship goes down. The mind of the master of a vessel is rooted deep in the timbers of her, though he command for a day or a decade; and this captain had on him the stern impression of a scene in the greys of dawn of seven turned faces, and later a stump of a topmast with a white ball on it, that slashed to and fro at the waves, went low and lower, and down. Thereafter there was something strange in his voice. Although steady, it was deep with mourning, and of a quality beyond oration or tears.

"Keep 'er a little more south, Billie," said he.

"A little more south, sir," said the oiler in the stern.

A seat in his boat was not unlike a seat upon a bucking broncho, and by the same token a broncho is not much smaller. The craft pranced and reared and plunged like an animal. As each wave came, and she rose for it, she seemed like a horse making at a fence outrageously high. The manner of her scramble over these walls of water is a mystic thing, and, moreover, at the top of them were ordinarily these problems in white water, the foam racing down from the summit of each wave requiring a new leap, and a leap from the air. Then, after scornfully bumping a crest, she would slide and race and splash down a long incline, and arrive bobbing and nodding in front of the next menace.

A singular disadvantage of the sea lies in the fact that after successfully surmounting one wave you discover that there is another behind it just as important and just as nervously anxious to do something effective in the way of swamping boats. In a ten-foot dinghy one can get an idea of the resources of the sea in the line of waves that is not probable to the average experience which is never at sea in a dinghy. As each slaty wall of water approached, it shut all else from the view of the men in the boat, and it was not difficult to imagine that this particular wave was the final outburst of the ocean, the last effort of the grim water. There was a terrible grace in the move of the waves, and they came in silence, save for the snarling of the crests.

In the wan light the faces of the men must have been grey. Their eyes must have glinted in strange ways as they gazed steadily astern. Viewed from a balcony, the whole thing would doubtless have been weirdly picturesque. But the men in the boat had no time to see it, and if they had had leisure, there were other things to occupy their minds. The sun swung steadily up the sky, and they knew it was broad day because the color of the sea changed from slate to emerald green streaked with amber lights, and the foam was like tumbling snow. The process of the breaking day was unknown to them. They were aware only of this effect upon the color of the waves that rolled toward them.

In disjointed sentences the cook and the correspondent argued as to the difference between a lifesaving station and a house of refuge. The cook had said: "There's a house of refuge just north of the Mosquito Inlet Light, and as soon as they see us they'll come off in their boat and pick us up."

"As soon as who see us?" said the correspondent.

"The crew," said the cook.

"Houses of refuge don't have crews," said the correspondent. "As I understand them, they are only places where clothes and grub are stored for the benefit of shipwrecked people. They don't carry crews."

"Oh, yes, they do," said the cook.

"No, they don't," said the correspondent.

"Well, we're not there yet, anyhow," said the oiler, in the stern.

"Well," said the cook, "perhaps it's not a house of refuge that I'm thinking of as being near Mosquito Inlet Light; perhaps it's a life-saving station."

"We're not there yet," said the oiler in the stern.

II

As the boat bounced from the top of each wave the wind tore through the hair of the hatless men, and as the craft plopped her stern down again the spray slashed past them. The crest of each of these waves was a hill, from the top of which the men surveyed for a moment a broad tumultuous expanse, shining and wind-riven. It was probably splendid, it was probably glorious, this play of the free sea, wild with lights of emerald and white and amber.

"Bully good thing it's an on-shore wind," said the cook. "If not, where would we be? Wouldn't have a show."

"That's right," said the correspondent.

The busy oiler nodded his assent.

Then the captain, in the bow, chuckled in a way that expressed humor, contempt, tragedy, all in one. "Do you think we've got much of a show now, boys?" said he.

Whereupon the three were silent, save for a trifle of hemming and hawing. To express any particular optimism at this time they felt to be childish and stupid, but they all doubtless possessed this sense of the situation in their minds. A young man thinks doggedly at such times. On the other hand, the ethics of their condition was decidedly against any open suggestion of hopelessness. So they were silent.

"Oh, well," said the captain, soothing his children, "we'll get ashore all right."

But there was that in his tone which made them think; so the oiler quoth, "Yes! if this wind holds."

The cook was bailing. "Yes! if we don't catch hell in the surf."

Canton-flannel gulls flew near and far. Sometimes they sat down on the sea, near patches of brown seaweed that rolled over the waves with a movement like carpets on a line in a gale. The birds sat comfortably in groups, and they were envied by some in the dinghy, for the wrath of the sea was no more to them than it was to a covey of prairie chickens a thousand miles inland. Often they came very close and stared at the men with black bead-like eyes. At these times they were uncanny and sinister in their unblinking scrutiny, and the men hooted angrily at them, telling them to be gone. One came, and evidently decided to alight on the top of the captain's head. The bird flew parallel to the boat and did not circle, but made short sidelong jumps in the air in chicken-fashion. His black eyes were wistfully fixed upon the captain's head. "Ugly brute," said the oiler to the bird. "You look as if you were made with a jackknife." The cook and the correspondent swore darkly at the creature. The captain naturally wished to knock it away with the end of a heavy painter, but he did not dare do it, because anything resembling an emphatic gesture would have capsized this freighted boat; and so, with his open hand, the captain gently and carefully waved the gull away. After it had been discouraged from the pursuit the captain breathed easier on account of his hair, and others breathed easier because the bird struck their minds at this time as being somehow gruesome and ominous.

In the meantime the oiler and the correspondent rowed. And also they rowed. They sat together in the same seat, and each rowed an oar. Then the oiler took both oars; then the correspondent took both oars; then the oiler; then the correspondent. They rowed and they rowed. The very ticklish part of the business was when the time came for the reclining one in the stern to take his turn at the oars. By the very last star of truth, it is easier to steal eggs from under a hen than it was to change seats in the dinghy. First the man in the stern slid his hand along the thwart and moved with care, as if he were of Sèvres. Then the man in the rowing-seat slid his hand along the other thwart. It was all done with the most extraordinary care. As the two sidled past each other, the whole party kept watchful eyes on the coming wave and the captain cried: "Look out, now! Steady, there!"

The brown mats of seaweed that appeared from time to time were like islands, bits of earth. They were travelling, apparently, neither one way nor the other. They were, to all intents, stationary. They informed the men in the boat that it was making progress slowly toward the land.

The captain, rearing cautiously in the bow after the dinghy soared on a great swell, said that he had seen the lighthouse at Mosquito Inlet. Presently the cook remarked that he had seen it. The correspondent was at the oars then, and for some reason he too wished to look at the lighthouse; but his back was toward the far shore, and the waves were important, and for some time he could not seize an opportunity to turn his head. But at last there came a wave more gentle than the others, and when at the crest of it he swiftly scoured the western horizon.

"See it?" said the captain.

"No," said the correspondent, slowly; "I didn't see anything."

"Look again," said the captain. He pointed. "It's exactly in that direction."

At the top of another wave the correspondent did as he was bid, and this time his eyes chanced on a small, still thing on the edge of the swaying horizon. It was precisely like the point of a pin. It took an anxious eye to find a lighthouse so tiny.

"Think we'll make it, Captain?"

"If this wind holds and the boat don't swamp, we can't do much else," said the captain.

The little boat, lifted by each towering sea and splashed viciously by the crests, made progress that in the absence of seaweed was not apparent to those in her. She seemed just a wee thing wallowing, miraculously top up, at the mercy of five oceans. Occasionally a great spread of water, like white flames, swarmed into her.

"Bail her, cook," said the captain, serenely.

"All right, Captain," said the cheerful cook.

III

It would be difficult to describe the subtle brotherhood of men that was here established on the seas. No one said that it was so. No one mentioned it. But it dwelt in the boat, and each amn felt it warm him. They were a captain, an oiler, a cook, and a correspondent, and they were friends—friends in a more curiously iron-bound degree then may be common. The hurt captain, lying against the water-jar in the bow, spoke always in a low voice and calmly; but he could never command a more ready and swiftly obedient crew than the motley three of the dinghy. It was more than a mere recognition of what was best for the common safety. There was surely in it a quality that was personal and heartfelt. And after this devotion to the commander of the boat, there was this comradeship, that the correspondent, for instance, who had been taught to be cynical of men, knew even at the time was the best experience of his life. But no one said that it was so. No one mentioned it.

"I wish we had a sail," remarked the captain. "We might try my overcoat on the end of an oar, and give you two boys a chance to rest." So the cook and the correspondent held the mast and spread wide the overcoat; the oiler steered; and the little boat made good way with her new rig. Sometimes the oiler had to scull sharply to keep a sea from breaking into the boat, but otherwise sailing was a success.

Meanwhile the lighthouse had been growing slowly larger. It had now almost assumed color, and appeared like a little grey shadow on the sky. The man at the oars could not be prevented from turning his head rather often to try for a glimpse of this little grey shadow.

At last, from the top of each wave, the men in the tossing boat could see land. Even as the lighthouse was an upright shadow on the sky, this land seemed but a long black shadow on the sea. It certainly was thinner than paper. "We must be about opposite New Smyrna," said the cook, who had coasted this shore often in schooner. "Captain, by the way, I believe they abandoned that lifesaving station there about a year ago."

"Did they?" said the captain.

The wind slowly died away. The cook and the correspondent were not now obliged to slave in order to hold high the oar. But the waves continued their own impetuous swooping at the dinghy, and the little craft, no longer under way, struggled woundily over them. The oiler or the correspondent took the oars again.

Shipwrecks are apropos of nothing. If men could only train for them and have them occur when the men had reached pink condition, there would be less drowning at sea. Of the four in the dinghy none had slept anytime worth mentioning for two days and two nights previous to embarking in the dinghy, and in the excitement of clambering about the deck of a foundering ship they had also forgotten to eat heartily.

For these reasons, and for others, neither the oiler nor the correspondent was fond of rowing at this time. The correspondent wondered ingenuously how in the name of all that was sane could there be people who thought it amusing to row a boat. It was not amusement; it was a diabolical punishment, and even a genius of mental aberrations could never conclude that it was anything but a horror to the muscles and a crime against the back. He mentioned to the boat in general how the amusement of rowing struck him, and the weary-faced oiler smiled in full sympathy. Previously to the foundering, by the way, the oiler had worked a double watch in the engine room of the ship.

"Take her easy now, boys," said the captain. "Don't spend yourselves. If we have to run a surf you'll need all your strength, because we'll sure have to swim for it. Take your time."

Slowly the land arose from the sea. From a black line it became a line of black and a line of white—trees and sand. Finally the captain said that he could make out a house on the shore. "That's the house of refuge, sure," said the cook. "They'll see us before long, and come out after us."

The distant lighthouse reared high.

"The keeper ought to be able to make us out now, if he's looking through a glass," said the captain. "He'll notify the life saving people."

"None of those other boats could have got ashore to give word of this wreck," said the oiler, in a low voice, "else the lifeboat would be out hunting us."

Slowly and beautifully the land loomed out of the sea. The wind came again. It had veered from the northeast to the southeast. Finally a new sound struck the ears of the men in the boat. It was the low thunder of the surf on the shore. "We'll never be able to make the lighthouse now," said the captain. "Swing her head a little more north, Billie."

"A little more north, sir," said the oiler.

Whereupon the little boat turned her nose once more down the wind, and all but the oarsmen watched the shore grow. Under the influence of this expansion doubt and direful apprehension were leaving the minds of the men. The management of the boat was still most absorbing, but it could not prevent a quiet cheerfulness. In an hour, perhaps, they would be ashore.

Their backbones had become thoroughly used to balancing in the boat, and they now rode this wild colt of a dinghy like circus men. The correspondent thought that he had been drenched to the skin, but happening to feel in the top pocket of his coat, he found therein eight cigars. Four of them were soaked with sea-water; four were perfectly scatheless. After a search, somebody produced three dry matches; and thereupon the four waifs rode impudently in their little boat and, with an assurance of all impending rescue shining in their eyes, puffed at the big cigars, and judged well and ill of all men. Everybody took a drink of water.

IV

"Cook," remarked the captain, "there don't seem to be any signs of life about your house of refuge."

"No," replied the cook. "Funny they don't see us!"

A broad stretch of lowly coast lay before the eyes of the men. It was of low dunes topped with dark vegetation. The roar of the surf was plain, and sometimes they could see the white lip of a wave as it spun up the beach. A tiny house was blocked out black upon the sky. Southward, the slim lighthouse lifted its little grey length.

Tide, wind, and waves were swinging the dinghy northward. "Funny they don't see us," said the men.

The surf's soar was here dulled, but its tone was nevertheless thunderous and mighty. As the boat swam over the great rollers the men sat listening to this roar. "We'll swamp sure," said everybody.

It is fair to say here that there was not a lifesaving station within twenty miles in either direction; but the men did not know this fact, and in consequence they made dark and opprobrious remarks concerning the eyesight of the nation's lifesavers. Four scowling men sat in the dinghy and surpassed records in the invention of epithets.

"Funny they don't see us."

The lightheartedness of a former time had completely faded. To their sharpened minds it was easy to conjure pictures of all kinds of incompetency and blindness and, indeed, cowardice. There was the shore of the populous land, and it was bitter and bitter to them that from it came no sign.

"Well," said the captain, ultimately, "I suppose we'll have to make a try for ourselves. If we stay out here too long, we'll none of us have strength left to swim after the boat swamps."

And so the oiler, who was at the oars, turned the boat straight for the shore. There was a sudden tightening of muscles. There was some thinking.

"If we don't all get ashore," said the captain—"if we don't all get ashore, I suppose you fellows know where to send news of my finish?"

They then briefly exchanged some addresses and admonitions. As for the reflections of the men, there was a great deal of rage in them. Perchance they might be formulated thus: "If I am going to be drowned—if I am going to be drowned—if I am going to be drowned, why, in the name of the seven mad gods who rule the sea, was I allowed to come thus far and contemplate sand and trees? Was I brought here merely to have my nose dragged away as I was about to nibble the sacred cheese of life? It is preposterous. If this old ninny-woman, Fate, cannot do better than this, she should be deprived of the management of men's fortunes. She is an old hen who knows not her intention. If she has decided to drown me, why did she not do it in the beginning and save me all this trouble? The whole affair is absurd.—But no; she cannot mean to drown me. She dare not drown me. She cannot drown me. Not after all this work." Afterward the man might have had an impulse to shake his fist at the clouds. "Just you drown me, now, and then hear what I call you!"

The billows that came at this time were more formidable. They seemed always just about to break and roll over the little boat in a turmoil of foam. There was a preparatory and long growl in the speech of them. No mind unused to the sea would have concluded that the dinghy could ascend these sheer heights in time. The shore was still afar. The oiler was a wily surfman. "Boys," he said swiftly, "she won't live three minutes more, and we're too far out to swim. Shall I take her to sea again, Captain?"

"Yes; go ahead!" said the captain.

This oiler, by a series of quick miracles and fast and steady oarsmanship, turned the boat in the middle of the surf and took her safely to sea again.

There was a considerable silence as the boat bumped over the furrowed sea to deeper water. Then somebody in gloom spoke: "Well, anyhow, they must have seen us from the shore by now."

The gulls went in slanting flight up the wind toward the grey, desolate east. A squall, marked by dingy clouds and clouds brick-red like smoke from a burning building, appeared from the southeast.

"What do you think of those lifesaving people? Ain't they peaches?"

"Funny they haven't seen us."

"Maybe they think we're out here for sport! Maybe they think we're fishin'. Maybe they think we're damned fools."

It was a long afternoon. A changed tide tried to force them southward, but wind and wave said northward. Far ahead, where coastline, sea, and sky formed their mighty angle, there were little dots which seemed to indicate a city on the shore.

"St. Augustine?"

The captain shook his head. "Too near Mosquito Inlet."

And the oiler rowed, and then the correspondent rowed; then the oiler rowed. It was a weary business. The human back become the seat of more aches and pains than are registered in books for the composite anatomy of a regiment. It is a limited area, but it can become the theatre of innumerable muscular conflicts, tangles, wrenches, knots, and other comforts.

"Did you ever like to row, Billie?" asked the correspondent.

"No," said the oiler; "hang, it!"

When one exchanged the rowing-seat for a place in the bottom of the boat, he suffered a bodily depression that caused him to be careless of everything save an obligation to wriggle one finger. There was cold seawater swashing to and fro in the boat, and he lay in it. His head, pillowed on a thwart, was within an inch of the swirl of a wave-crest, and sometimes a particularly obstreperous sea came inboard and drenched him once more. But these matters did not annoy him. It is almost certain that if the boat had capsized he would have tumbled comfortably out upon the ocean as if he felt sure that it was a great soft mattress.

"Look! There's a man on the shore!"

"Where?"

"There! See 'im? See 'im?"

"Yes, sure! He's walking along."

"Now he's stopped. Look! He's facing us!"

"He's waving at us!"

"So he is! By thunder!"

"Ah, now we're all right! Now we're all right! There'll be a boat out here for us in half an hour."

"He's going on. He's running. He's going up to that house there."

The remote beach seemed lower than the sea, and it required a searching glance to discern the little black figure. The captain saw a floating stick, and they rowed to it. A bath towel was by some weird chance in the boat, and, tying this on the stick, the captain waved it. The oarsman did not dare turn his head, so he was obliged to ask questions.

"What's he doing now?"

"He's standing still again. He's looking, I think.— There he goes again—toward the house.—Now's he's stopped again."

"Is he waving at us?"

"No, not now; he was, though."

"Look! There comes another man!"

"He's running."

"Look at him go, would you!"

"Why, he's on a bicycle. Now he's met the other man. They're both waving at us. Look!"

"There comes something up the beach."

"What the devil is that thing?"

"Why, it looks like a boat."

"Why, certainly, it's a boat."

"No; it's on wheels."

"Yes, so it is. Well, that must be the lifeboat. They drag them along shore on a wagon."

"That's the lifeboat, sure."

"No, by God, it's—it's an omnibus."

"I tell you it's a lifeboat."

"It is not! It's an omnibus. I can see it plain. See? One of these big hotel omnibuses."

"By thunder, you're right. It's an omnibus, sure as fate. What do you suppose they are doing with an omnibus? Maybe they are going around collecting the life-crew, hey?"

"That's it, likely. Look! There's a fellow waving a little black flag. He's standing on the steps of the omnibus. There come those other two fellows. Now they're all talking together. Look at the fellow with the flag. Maybe he ain't waving it!"

"That ain't a flag, is it? That's his coat. Why, certainly, that's his coat."

"So it is; it's his coat. He's taken it off and is waving it around his head. But would you look at him swing it!"

"Oh, say, there isn't any lifesaving station there. That's just a winter resort hotel omnibus that has brought over some of the boarders to see us drown."

"What's that idiot with the coat mean? What's he signalling, anyhow?"

"It looks as if he were trying to tell us to go north. There must be a lifesaving station up there."

"No; he think we're fishing. Just giving us a merry hand. See? Ah, there, Willie!"

"Well, I wish I could make something out of those signals. What do you suppose he means?"

"He don't mean anything; he's just playing."

"Well, if he's just signal us to try the surf again, or to go to sea and wait, or go north, or go south, or go to hell, there would be some reason in it. But look at him! He just stands there and keeps his coat revolving like a wheel. The ass!"

"There come more people."

"Now there's quite a mob. Look! Isn't that a boat?"

"Where? Oh, I see where you mean. No, that's no boat."

"That fellow is still waving his coat."

"He must think we like to see him do that. Why don't he quit it? It don't mean anything."

"I don't know. I think he is trying to make us go north. It must be that there's a lifesaving station there somewhere."

"Say, he ain't tired yet. Look at 'im wave!"

"Wonder how long he can keep that up. He's been revolving his coat ever since he caught sight of us. He's an idiot. Why aren't they getting men to bring a boat out? A fishing boat—one of those big yawls—could come out here all right. Why don't he do something?"

"Oh, it's all right now."

"They'll have a boat out here for us in less than no time, now that they've seen us."

A faint yellow tone came into the sky over the low land. The shadows on the sea slowly deepened. The wind bore coldness with it, and the men began to shiver.

"Holy smoke!" said one, allowing his voice to express his impious mood, "if we keep on monkeying out here! If we've got to flounder out here all night!"

"Oh, we'll never have to stay here all night! Don't you worry. They've seen us now, and it won't be long before they'll come chasing out after us."

The shore grew dusky. The man waving a coat blended gradually into this gloom, and it swallowed in the same manner the omnibus and the group of people. The spray, when it dashed uproariously over the side, made the voyagers shrink and swear like men who were being branded.

"I'd like to catch the chump who waved the coat. I feel like socking him one, just for luck."

"Why? What did he do?"

"Oh, nothing, but then he seemed so damned cheerful."

In the meantime the oiler rowed, and then the correspondent rowed, and then the oiler rowed. Grey-faced and bowed forward, they mechanically, turn by turn, plied the leaden oars. The form of the lighthouse had vanished from the southern horizon, but finally a pale star appeared, just lifting from the sea. The streaked saffron in the west passed before the all-merging darkness, and the sea to the east was black. The land had vanished, and was expressed only by the low and drear thunder of the surf.

"If I am going to be drowned—if I am going to be drowned—if I I am going to be drowned, why, in the name of the seven mad gods who rule the sea, was I allowed to come thus far and contemplate sand and trees? Was I brought here merely to have my nose dragged away as I was about to nibble the sacred cheese of life?"

The patient captain, drooped over the water-jar, was sometimes obliged to speak to the oarsman.

"Keep her head up! Keep her head up!"

"Keep her head up, sir." The voices were weary and low.

This was surely a quiet evening. All save the oarsman lay heavily and listlessly in the boat's bottom. As for him, his eyes were just capable of noting the tall black waves that swept forward in a most sinister silence, save for an occasional subdued growl of a crest.

The cook's head was on a thwart, and he looked without interest at the water under his nose. He was deep in other scenes. Finally he spoke. "Billie," he murmured, dreamfully, "what kind of pie do you like best?"

V

"Pie!" said the oiler and the correspondent, agitatedly. "Don't talk about those things, blast you!"

"Well," said the cook, "I was just thinking about ham sandwiches and—"

A night on the sea in an open boat is a long night. As darkness settled finally, the shine of the light, lifting from the sea in the south, changed to full gold. On the northern horizon a new light appeared, a small bluish gleam on the edge of the waters. These two lights were the furniture of the world. Otherwise there was nothing but waves.

Two men huddled in the stern, and distances were so magnificent in the dinghy that the rower was enabled to keep his feet partly warm by thrusting them under his companions. Their legs indeed extended far under the rowing seat until they touched the feet of the captain forward. Sometimes, despite the efforts of the tired oarsman, a wave came piling into the boat, an icy wave of the night, and the chilling water soaked them anew. They would twist their bodies for a moment and groan, and sleep the dead sleep once more, while the water in the boat gurgled about them as the craft rocked.

The plan of the oiler and the correspondent was for one to row until he lost the ability, and then arouse the other from his sea water couch in the bottom of the boat.

The oiler plied the oars until his head drooped forward and the overpowering sleep blinded him; and he rowed yet afterward. Then he touched a man in the bottom of the boat, and called his name. "Will you spell me for a little while?" he said, meekly.

"Sure, Billie," said the correspondent, awaking and dragging himself to a sitting position. They exchanged places carefully, and the oiler, cuddling down in the seawater at the cook's side, seemed to go to sleep instantly.

The particular violence of the sea had ceased. The waves came without snarling. The obligation of the man at the oars was to keep the boat headed so that the tilt of the rollers would not capsize her, and to preserve her from filling when the crests rushed past. The black waves were silent and hard to be seen in the darkness. Often one was almost upon the boat before the oarsman was aware.

In a low voice the correspondent addressed the captain. He was not sure that the captain was awake, although this iron man seemed to be always awake. "Captain, shall I keep her making for that light north, sir?"

The same steady voice answered him. "Yes. Keep it about two points off the port bow."

The cook had tied a life belt around himself in order to get even the warmth which this clumsy cork contrivance could donate, and he seemed almost stove-like when a rower, whose teeth invariably chattered wildly as soon as he ceased his labor, dropped down to sleep.

The correspondent, as he rowed, looked down at the two men sleeping underfoot. The cook's arm was around the oiler's shoulders, and, with their fragmentary clothing and haggard faces, they were the babes of the sea—a grotesque rendering of the old babes in the wood.

Later he must have grown stupid at his work, for suddenly there was a growling of water, and a crest came with a roar and a swash into the boat, and it was a wonder that it did not set the cook afloat in his life belt. The cook continued to sleep, but the oiler sat up, blinking his eyes and shaking with the new cold.

"Oh, I'm awful sorry, Billie," said the correspondent contritely.

"That's all right, old boy," said the oiler, and lay down again and was asleep.

Presently it seemed that even the captain dozed, and the correspondent thought that he was the one man afloat on all the oceans. The wind had a voice as it came over the waves, and it was sadder than the end.

There was a long, loud swishing astern of the boat, and a gleaming trail of phosphorescence, like blue flame, was furrowed on the black waters. It might have been made been made by a monstrous knife.

Then there came a stillness, while the correspondent breathed with open mouth and looked at the sea.

Suddenly there was another swish and another long flash of bluish light, and this time it was alongside the boat, and might almost have been reached with an oar. The correspondent saw an enormous fin speed like a shadow through the water, hurling the crystalline spray and leaving the long glowing trail.

The correspondent looked over his shoulder at the captain. His face was hidden, and he seemed to be asleep. He looked at the babes of the sea. They certainly were asleep. So, being bereft of sympathy, he leaned a little way to one side and swore softly into the sea.

But the thing did not then leave the vicinity of the boat. Ahead or astern, on one side or the other, at intervals long or short, fled the long sparkling streak, and there was to be heard the *whirroo* of the dark fin. The speed and power of the thing was greatly to be admired. It cut the water like a gigantic and keen projectile.

The presence if this biding thing did not affect the man with the same horror that it would if he had been a picnicker. He simply looked at the sea dully and swore in an undertone.

Nevertheless, it is true that he did not wish to be alone with the thing. He wished one of his companions to awake by chance and keep him company with it. But the captain hung motionless over the water-jar, and the oiler and the cook in the bottom of the boat were plunged in slumber.

VI

"If I am going to be drowned—if I am going to be drowned—if I am going to be drowned, why, in the name of the seven mad gods who rule the sea, was I allowed to come thus far and contemplate sand and trees?"

During this dismal night, it may be remarked that a man would conclude that it was really the intention of the seven mad gods to drown him, despite the abominable injustice of it. For it was certainly an abominable injustice to drown a man who had worked so hard, so hard. The man felt it would be a crime most unnatural.

Other people had drowned at sea since galleys swarmed with painted sails, but still—

When it occurs to a man that nature does not regard him as important, and that she feels she would not maim the universe by disposing of him, he at first wishes to throw bricks at the temple, and he hates deeply the fact that there are no bricks and no temples. Any visible expression of nature would surely be pelleted with his jeers.

Then if there be no tangible thing to hoot, he feels, perhaps, the desire to confront a personification and indulge in pleas, bowed to one knee, and with hands supplicant, saying, "Yes, but I love myself."

A high cold star on a winter's night is the word he feels that she says to him. Thereafter he knows the pathos of his situation.

The men in the dinghy had not discussed these matters, but each had, no doubt, reflected upon them in silence and according to his mind. There was seldom any expression upon their faces save the general one of complete weariness. Speech was devoted to the business of the boat.

To chime the notes of his emotion, a verse mysteriously entered the correspondent's head. He had even forgotten that he had forgotten this verse, but it suddenly was in his mind.

A soldier of the Legion lay dying in Algiers;
There was lack of woman's nursing, there was dearth of woman's tears;
But a comrade stood beside him, and he took that comrade's hand,
And he said, "I never shall see my own, my native land."

In his childhood the correspondent had been made acquainted with the fact that a soldier of the Legion lay dying in Algiers, but he had never regarded the fact as important. Myriads of his school fellows had informed him of the soldier's plight, but the dinning had naturally ended by making him perfectly indifferent. He had never considered it his affair that a soldier of the Legion lay dying in Algiers, nor had it appeared to him as a matter for sorrow. It was less to him than the breaking of a pencil's point.

Now, however, it quaintly came to him as a human, living thing. It was no longer merely a picture of a few throes in the breast of a poet, meanwhile drinking tea and warming his feet at the grate; it was an actuality—stern, mournful, and fine.

The correspondent plainly saw the soldier. He lay on the sand with his feet out straight and still. While his pale left hand was upon his chest in an attempt to thwart the going of his life, the blood came between his fingers. In the far Algerian distance, a city of low square forms was set against a sky that was faint with the last sunset hues. The correspondent, plying the oars and dreaming of the slow and slower movements of the lips of the soldier, was moved by a profound and perfectly impersonal comprehension. He was sorry for the soldier of the Legion who lay dying in Algiers.

The thing which had followed the boat and waited had evidently grown bored at the delay. There was no longer to be heard the slash of the cutwater, and there was no longer the flame of the long trail. The light in the north still glimmered, but it was apparently no nearer to the boat. Sometimes the boom of the surf rang in the correspondent's ears, and he turned the craft seaward then and rowed harder. Southward, someone had evidently built a watch fire on the beach. It was too low and too far to be seen, but it made a shimmering, roseate reflection upon the bluff in back of it, and this could be discerned from the boat. The wind came stronger, and sometimes a wave suddenly raged out like a mountain cat, and there was to be seen the sheen and sparkle of a broken crest.

The captain, in the bow, moved on his water jar and sat erect. "Pretty long night," he observed to the correspondent. He looked at the shore. "Those lifesaving people take their time."

"Did you see that shark playing around?"

"Yes, I saw him. He was a big fellow, all right."

"Wish I had known you were awake."

Later the correspondent spoke into the bottom of the boat. "Billie!" There was a slow and gradual disentanglement. "Billie, will you spell me?"

"Sure," said the oiler.

As soon as the correspondent touched the cold, comfortable sea water in the bottom of the boat and had huddled close to the cook's life belt he was deep in sleep, despite the fact that his teeth played all the popular airs. This sleep was so good to him that it was but a moment before he heard a voice call his name in a tone that demonstrated the last stages of exhaustion.

"Will you spell me?"

"Sure, Billie."

The light in the north had mysteriously vanished, but the correspondent took his course from the wide-awake captain.

Later in the night they took the boat farther out to sea, and the captain directed the cook to take one oar at the stern and keep the boat facing the seas. He was to call out if he should hear the thunder of the surf. This plan enabled the oiler and the correspondent to get respite together. "We'll give those boys a chance to get into shape again," said the captain. They curled down and, after a few preliminary chatterings and trembles, slept once more the dead sleep. Neither knew they had bequeathed to the cook the company of another shark, or perhaps the same shark.

As the boat caroused on the waves, spray occasionally bumped over the side and gave them a fresh soaking, but this had no power to break their repose. The ominous slash of the wind and the water affected them as it would have affected mummies.

"Boys," said the cook, with the notes of every reluctance in his voice, "she's drifted in pretty close. I guess one of you had better take her to sea again." The correspondent, aroused, heard the crash of the toppled crests.

As he was rowing, the captain gave him some whiskey-and-water, and this steadied the chills out of him. "If I ever get ashore and anybody shows me even a photograph of an oar—"

At last there was a short conversation.

"Billie!—Billie, will you spell me?"

"Sure," said the oiler.

VII

When the correspondent again opened his eyes, the sea and the sky were each of the grey hue of the dawning. Later, carmine and gold was painted upon the waters. The morning appeared finally, in its splendor, with a sky of pure blue, and the sunlight flamed on the tips of the waves.

On the distant dunes were set many little black cottages, and a tall white windmill reared above them. No man, nor dog, nor bicycle appeared on the beach. The cottages might have formed a deserted village.

The voyagers scanned the shore. A conference was held in the boat. "Well," said the captain, "if no help is coming, we might better try a run through the surf right away. If we stay out here much longer we will be too weak to do anything for ourselves at all." The others silently acquiesced in this reasoning. The boat was headed for the beach. The correspondent wondered if none ever ascended the tall wind tower, and if then they never looked seaward. This tower was a giant, standing with its back to the plight of the ants. It represented in a degree, to the correspondent, the serenity of nature amid the struggles of the individual—nature in the wind, and nature in the vision of men. She did not seem cruel to him then, nor beneficient, nor treacherous, nor wise. But she was indifferent, flatly indifferent. It is, perhaps, plausible, that a man in this situation, impressed with the unconcern of the universe, should see the innumerable flaws of his life, and have them taste wickedly in his mind, and wish for another chance. A distinction between right and wrong seems absurdly clear to him, then, in this new ignorance of the grave-edge, and he understands that if he were given another opportunity he would mend his conduct and his words, and be better and brighter during an introduction or at a tea.

"Now, boys," said the captain, "she is going to swamp sure. All we can do is to work her in as far as possible, and then when she swamps, pile out and scramble for the beach. Keep cool now, and don't jump until she swamps sure."

The oiler took the oars. Over his shoulders he scanned the surf. "Captain," he said, "I think I'd better bring her about and keep her head-on to the seas and back her in."

"All right, Billie," said the captain. "Back her in." The oiler swung the boat then, and, seated in the stern, the cook and the correspondent were obliged to look over their shoulders to contemplate the lonely and indifferent shore.

The monstrous inshore rollers heaved the boat high until the men were again enabled to see the white sheets of water scudding up the slanted beach. "We won't get in very close," said the captain. Each time a man could wrest his attention from the rollers, he turned his glance toward the shore, and in the expression of the eyes during this contemplation there was a singular quality. The correspondent, observing the others, knew that they were not afraid, but the full meaning of their glances was shrouded.

As for himself, he was too tired to grapple fundamentally with the fact. He tried to coerce his mind into thinking of it, but the mind was dominated at this time by the muscles, and the muscles said they did not care. It merely occurred to him that if he should drown it would be a shame.

There were no hurried words, no pallor, no plain agitation. "Now, remember to get well clear of the boat when you jump," said the captain.

Seaward the crest of a roller suddenly fell with a thunderous crash, and the long white comber came roaring down upon the boat.

"Steady now," said the captain. The men were silent. They turned their eyes from the shore to the comber and waited. The boat slid up the incline, leaped at the furious top, bounced over it, and swung down the long back of the wave. Some water had been shipped, and the cook bailed it out.

But the next crest crashed also. The tumbling, boiling flood of white water caught the boat and whirled it almost perpendicular. Water swarmed in from all sides. The correspondent had his hands on the gunwale at this time, and when the water entered at that place he swiftly withdrew his fingers, as if he objected to wetting them.

The little boat, drunken with this weight of water, reeled and snuggled deeper into the sea.

"Bail her out, cook! Bail her out!" said the captain.

"All right, Captain," said the cook.

"Now, boys, the next one will do for us sure," said the oiler. "Mind to jump clear of the boat."

The third wave moved forward, huge, furious, implacable. It fairly swallowed the dinghy, and almost simultaneously the men tumbled into the sea. A piece of lifebelt had lain in the bottom of the boat, and as the correspondent went overboard he held this to his chest with his left hand.

The January water was icy, and he reflected immediately that it was colder than he had expected to find it off the coast of Florida. This appeared to his dazed mind as a fact important enough to be noted at the time. The coldness of the water was sad; it was tragic. This fact was somehow mixed and confused with his opinion of his own situation, so that it seemed almost a proper reason for tears. The water was cold.

When he came to the surface he was conscious of little but the noisy water. Afterward he saw his companions in the sea. The oiler was ahead in the race. He was swimming strongly and rapidly. Off to the correspondent's left, the cook's great white and corked back bulged out of the water; and in the rear the captain was hanging with his one good hand to the keel of the overturned dinghy.

There is a certain immovable quality to a shore, and the correspondent wondered at it amid the confusion of the sea.

It seemed also very attractive; but the correspondent knew that it was a long journey, and he paddled leisurely. The piece of life preserver lay under him, and sometimes he whirled down the incline of a wave as if he were on a hand sled.

But finally he arrived at a place in the sea where travel was beset with difficulty. He did not pause swimming to inquire what manner of current had caught him, but there his progress ceased. The shore was set before him like a bit of scenery on a stage, and he looked at it and understood with his eyes each detail of it.

As the cook passed, much farther to the left, the captain was calling to him, "Turn over on your back, cook! Turn over on your back and use the oar."

"All right, sir." The cook turned on his back, and, paddling with an oar, went ahead as if he were a canoe.

Presently the boat also passed to the left of the correspondent, with the captain clinging with one hand to the keel. He would have appeared like a man raising himself to look over a board fence if it were not for the extraordinary gymnastics of the boat. The correspondent marvelled that the captain could still hold to it.

They passed on nearer to shore—the oiler, the cook, the captain—and following them went the water jar, bouncing gaily over the seas.

The correspondent remained in the grip of this strange new enemy—a current. The shore, with its white slope of sand and its green bluff topped with little silent cottages, was spread like a picture before him. It was very near to him then, but he was impressed as one who, in a gallery, looks at a scene from Brittany or Algiers.

He thought: "I am going to drown? Can it be possible? Can it be possible? Can it be possible?" Perhaps an individual must consider his own death to be the final phenomenon of nature.

But later a wave perhaps whirled him out of this small deadly current, for he found suddenly that he could again make progress toward the shore. Later still he was aware that the captain, clinging with one hand to the keel of the dinghy, had his face turned away from the shore and toward him, and was calling his name. "Come to the boat! Come to the boat!"

In his struggle to reach the captain and the boat, he reflected that when one gets properly wearied drowning must really be a comfortable arrangement—a cessation of hostilities accompanied by a large degree of relief; and he was glad of it, for the main thing in his mind for some moments had been horror of the temporary agony. He did not wish to be hurt.

Presently he saw a man running along the shore. He was undressing with most remarkable speed. Coat, trousers, shirt, everything flew magically off him.

"Come to the boat!" called the captain.

"All right, Captain." As the correspondent paddled, he saw the captain let himself down to bottom and leave the boat. Then the correspondent performed his one little marvel of the voyage. A large wave caught him and flung him with ease and supreme speed completely over the boat and far beyond it. It struck him even then as an event in gymnastics and a true miracle of the sea. An overturned boat in the surf is not a plaything to a swimming man.

The correspondent arrived in water that reached only to his waist, but his condition did not enable him to stand for more than a moment. Each wave knocked him into a heap, and the undertow pulled at him.

Then he saw the man who had been running and undressing, and undressing and running, come bounding into the water. He dragged ashore the cook, and then waded toward the captain; but the captain waved him away and sent him to the correspondent. He was naked—naked as a tree in winter; but a halo was about his head, and he shone like a saint. He gave a strong pull, and a long drag, and a bully heave at the correspondent's hand. The correspondent, schooled in the minor formulae, said, "Thanks, old man." But suddenly the man cried, "What's that?" He pointed a swift finger. The correspondent said, "Go."

In the shallows, face downward, lay the oiler. His forehead touched sand that was periodically, between each wave, clear of the sea.

The correspondent did not know all that transpired afterward. When he achieved safe ground he fell, striking the sand with each particular part of his body. It was as if he had dropped from a roof, but the thud was grateful to him.

It seemed that instantly the beach was populated with men with blankets, clothes, and flasks, and women with coffee pots and all the remedies sacred to their minds. The welcome of the land to the men from the sea was warm and generous; but a still and dripping shape was carried slowly up the beach, and the land's welcome for it could only be the different and sinister hospitality of the grave.

When it came night, the white waves paced to and fro in the moonlight, and the wind brought the sound of the great sea's voice to the men on the shore, and they felt that they could then be interpreters.

The Blue Hotel

I

The Palace Hotel at Fort Romper was painted a light blue, a shade that is on the legs of a kind of heron, causing the bird to declare its position against any background. The Palace Hotel, then, was always screaming and howling in a way that made the dazzling winter landscape of Nebraska seem only a grey swampish hush. It stood alone on the prairie, and when the snow was falling the town two hundred yards away was not visible. But when the traveller alighted at the railway station he was obliged to pass the Palace Hotel before he could come upon the company of low clapboard houses which composed Fort Romper, and it was not to be thought that any traveller could pass the Palace Hotel without looking at it. Pat Scully, the proprietor, had proved himself a master of strategy when he chose his paints. It is true that on clear days, when the great transcontinental expresses, long lines of swaying pullmans, swept through Fort Romper, passengers were overcome at the sight, and the cult that knows the brown-reds and the subdivisions of the dark greens of the East expressed shame, pity, horror, in a laugh. But to the citizens of this prairie town and to the people who would naturally stop there, Pat Scully had performed a feat. With this opulence and splendor, these creeds, classes, egotisms, that streamed through Romper on the rails day after day, they had no color in common.

As if the displayed delights of such a blue hotel were not sufficiently enticing, it was Scully's habit to go every morning and evening to meet the leisurely trains that stopped at Romper and work his seductions upon any man that he might see wavering, gripsack in hand.

One morning, when a snow-crusted engine dragged its long string of freight cars and its one passenger coach to the station, Scully performed the marvel of catching three men. One was a shaky and quick-eyed Swede, with a great shining cheap valise; one was a tall bronzed cowboy, who was on his way to a ranch near the Dakota line; one was a little silent man from the East, who didn't look it, and didn't announce it. Scully practically made them prisoners. He was so nimble and merry and kindly that each probably felt it would be the height of brutality to try to escape. They trudged off over the creaking board sidewalks in the wake of the eager little Irishman. He wore a heavy fur cap squeezed tightly down on his head. It caused his two red ears to stick out stiffly, as if they were made of tin.

At last, Scully, elaborately, with boisterous hospitality, conducted them through the portals of the blue hotel. The room which they entered was small. It seemed to be merely a proper temple for an enormous stove, which, in the center, was humming with godlike violence. At various points on its surface the iron had become luminous and glowed yellow from the heat. Beside the stove Scully's son Johnnie was playing High-Five with an old farmer who had whiskers both grey and sandy. They were quarrelling. Frequently the old farmer turned his face toward a box of sawdust—colored brown from tobacco juice—that was behind the stove, and spat with an air of great impatience and irritation. With a loud flourish of words Scully destroyed the game of cards, and bustled his son upstairs with part of the baggage of the new guests. He himself conducted them to three basins of the coldest water in the world. The cowboy and the Easterner burnished themselves fiery red with this water, until it seemed to be some kind of metal polish. The Swede, however, merely dipped his fingers gingerly and with trepidation. It was notable that throughout this series of small ceremonies the three travellers were made to feel that Scully was very benevolent. He was conferring great favors upon them. He handed the towel from one to another with an air of philanthropic impulse.

Afterward they went to the first room, and, sitting about the stove, listened to Scully's officious clamor at his daughters, who were preparing the midday meal.They reflected in the silence of experienced men who tread carefully amid new people. Nevertheless, the old farmer, stationary, invincible in his chair near the warmest part of the stove, turned his face from the sawdust box frequently and addressed a glowing commonplace to the strangers. Usually he was answered in short but adequate sentences by either the cowboy or the Easterner. The Swede said nothing. He seemed to be occupied in making furtive estimates of each man in the room. One might have thought that he had the sense of silly suspicion which comes to guilt. He resembled a badly frightened man.

Later, at dinner, he spoke a little, addressing his conversation entirely to Scully. He volunteered that he had come from New York, where for ten years he had worked as a tailor. These facts seemed to strike Scully as fascinating, and afterward he volunteered that he had lived at Romper for fourteen years. The Swede asked about the crops and the price of labor. He seemed barely to listen to Scully's extended replies. His eyes continued to rove from man to man.

Finally, with a laugh and a wink, he said that some of these Western communities were very dangerous; and after his statement he straightened his legs under the table, tilted his head, and laughed again, loudly. It was plain that the demonstration had no meaning to the others. They looked at him wondering and in silence.

II

As the men trooped heavily back into the front room, the two little windows presented views of a turmoiling sea of snow. The huge arms of the wind were making attempts—mighty, circular, futile—to embrace the flakes as they sped. A gatepost like a still man with a blanched face stood aghast amid this profligate fury. In a hearty voice Scully announced the presence of a blizzard. The guests of the blue hotel, lighting their pipes, assented with grunts of lazy masculine contentment. No island of the sea could be exempt in the degree of this little room with its humming stove. Johnnie, son of Scully, in a tone which defined his opinion of his ability as a card player, challenged the old farmer of both grey and sandy whiskers to a game of High-Five. The farmer agreed with a contemptuous and bitter scoff. They sat close to the stove, and squared their knees under a wide board. The cowboy and the Easterner watched the game with interest. The Swede remained near the window, aloof, but with a countenance that showed signs of an inexplicable excitement.

The play of Johnnie and the grey-beard was suddenly ended by another quarrel. The old man arose while casting a look of heated scorn at his adversary. He slowly buttoned his coat, and then stalked with fabulous dignity from the room. In the discreet silence of all the other men the Swede laughed. His laughter rang somehow childish. Men by this time had begun to look at him askance, as if they wished to inquire what ailed him.

A new game was formed jocosely. The cowboy volunteered to become the partner of Johnnie, and they all then turned to ask the Swede to throw in his lot with the little Easterner. He asked some questions about the game, and, learning that it wore many names, and that he had played it when it was under an alias, he accepted the invitation. He strode toward the men nervously, as if he expected to be assaulted. Finally, seated, he gazed from face to face and laughed shrilly. This laugh was so strange that the Easterner looked up quickly, the cowboy sat intent and with his mouth open, and Johnnie paused, holding the cards with still fingers.

Afterward there was a short silence. Then Johnnie said, "Well, let's get at it. Come on now!" They pulled their chairs forward until their knees were bunched under the board. They began to play, and their interest in the game caused the others to forget the manner of the Swede.

The cowboy was a board whacker. Each time that he held superior cards he whanged them, one by one, with exceeding force, down upon the improvised table, and took the tricks with a glowing air of prowess and pride that sent thrills of indignation into the hearts of his opponents. A game with a board whacker in it is sure to become intense. The countenances of the Easterner and the Swede were miserable whenever the cowboy thundered down his aces and kings, while Johnnie, his eyes gleaming with joy, chuckled and chuckled.

Because of the absorbing play none considered the strange ways of the Swede. They paid strict heed to the game. Finally, during a lull caused by a new deal, the Swede suddenly addressed Johnnie: "I suppose there have been a good many men killed in this room." The jaws of the others dropped and they looked at him.

"What in hell are you talking about?" said Johnnie.

The Swede laughed again his blatant laugh, full of a kind of false courage and defiance. "Oh, you know what I mean all right," he answered.

"I'm a liar if I do!" Johnnie protested. The card was halted, and the men stared at the Swede. Johnnie evidently felt that as the son of the proprietor he should make a direct inquiry. "Now, what might you be drivin' at, mister?" he asked. The Swede winked at him. It was a wink full of cunning. His fingers shook on the edge of the board. "Oh, maybe you think I have been to nowheres. Maybe you think I'm a tenderfoot?"

"I don't know nothin' about you," answered Johnnie, "and I don't give a damn where you've been. All I got to say is that I don't know what you're driving at. There hain't never been nobody killed in this room."

The cowboy, who had been steadily gazing at the Swede, then spoke: "What's wrong with you, mister?"

Apparently it seemed to the Swede that he was formidably menaced. He shivered and turned white near the corners of his mouth. He sent an appealing glance in the direction of the little Easterner. During these moments he did not forget to wear his air of advanced pot-valor. "They say they don't know what I mean," he remarked mockingly to the Easterner.

The latter answered after prolonged and cautious reflection. "I don't understand you," he said, impassively.

The Swede made a movement then which announced that he thought he had encountered treachery from the only quarter where he had expected sympathy, if not help. "Oh, I see you are all against me. I see—"

The cowboy was in a state of deep stupefaction. "Say," he cried, as he tumbled the deck violently down upon the board, "say, what are you gittin' at, hey?"

The Swede sprang up with the celerity of a man escaping from a snake on the floor. "I don't want to fight!" he shouted. "I don't want to fight!"

The cowboy stretched his long legs indolently and deliberately. His hands were in his pockets. He spat into the sawdust box. "Well, who the hell thought you did?" he inquired.

The Swede backed rapidly toward a corner of the room. His hands were out protectingly in front of his chest, but he was making an obvious struggle to control his fright. "Gentlemen," he quavered, "I suppose I am going to be killed before I can leave this house! I suppose I am going to be killed before I can leave this house!" In his eyes was the dying swan look. Through the windows could be seen the snow turning blue in the shadow of dusk. The wind tore at the house, and some loose thing beat regularly against the clapboards like a spirit tapping.

A door opened, and Scully himself entered. He paused in surprise as he noted the tragic attitude of the Swede. Then he said, "What's the matter here?"

The Swede answered him swiftly and eagerly: "These men are going to kill me."

"Kill you!" ejaculated Scully. "Kill you! What are you talkin'?"

The Swede made the gesture of a martyr.

Scully wheeled sternly upon his son. "What is this, Johnnie?"

The lad had grown sullen. "Damned if I know," he answered. "I can't make no sense to it." He began to shuffle the cards, fluttering them together with an angry snap. "He says a good many men have been killed in this room, or something like that. And he says he's goin' to be killed here too. I don't know what ails him. He's crazy, I shouldn't wonder."

Scully then looked for explanation to the cowboy, but the cowboy simply shrugged his shoulders.

"Kill you?" said Scully again to the Swede. "Kill you? Man, you're off your nut."

"Oh, I know," burst out the Swede. "I know what will happen. Yes, I'm crazy—yes. Yes, of course, I'm crazy—yes. But I know one thing—" There was a sort of sweat of misery and terror upon his face. "I know I won't get out of here alive."

The cowboy drew a deep breath, as if his mind was passing into the last stages of dissolution. "Well, I'm doggoned," he whispered to himself.

Scully wheeled suddenly and faced his son. "You've been troublin' this man!"

Johnnie s voice was loud with its burden of grievance. "Why, good Gawd, I ain't done nothin' to 'im."

The Swede broke in. "Gentleman, do not disturb yourselves. I will leave this house. I will go away, because"—he accused them dramatically with his glance—"because I do not want to be killed."

Scully was furious with his son. "Will you tell me what is the matter, you young divil? What's the matter, anyhow? Speak out!"

"Blame, it!" cried Johnnie in despair, "don't I tell you I don't know? He—he says we want to kill him, and that's all I know. I can't tell what ails him."

The Swede continued to repeat: "Never mind, Mr. Scully; never mind. I will leave this house. I will go away, because I do not wish to he killed. Yes, of course, I am crazy—yes. But I know one thing! I will go away. I will leave this house. Never mind, Mr. Scully; never mind. I will go away."

"You will not go 'way," said Scully. "You will not go 'way until I hear the reason of this business. If anybody has troubled you I will take care of him. This is my house. You are under my roof, and I will not allow any peaceable man to be troubled here." He cast a terrible eye upon Johnnie, the cowboy, and the Easterner.

"Never mind, Mr. Scully; never mind. I will go away. I do not wish to be killed." The Swede moved toward the door which opened upon the stairs. It was evidently his intention to go at once for his baggage.

"No, no," shouted Scully peremptorily; but the white-faced man slid by him and disappeared. "Now," said Scully severely, "what does this mane?"

Johnnie and the cowboy cried together: "Why, we didn't do nothin' to 'im!"

Scully's eyes were cold. "No," he said, "you didn't?"

Johnnie swore a deep oath. "Why, this is the wildest loon I ever see. We didn't do nothin' at all. We were jest sittin' here playin' cards, and he—"

The father suddenly spoke to the Easterner. "Mr. Blanc," he asked, "what has these boys been doin'?"

The Easterner reflected again. "I didn't see anything wrong at all," he said at last, slowly.

Scully began to howl. "But what does it mane?" He stared ferociously at his son. "I have a mind to lather you for this, me boy."

Johnnie was frantic. "Well, what have I done?" he bawled at his father.

III

"I think you are tongue-tied," said Scully finally to his son, the cowboy, and the Easterner; and at the end of this scornful sentence he left the room.

Upstairs the Swede was swiftly fastening the straps of his great valise. Once his back happened to be half turned toward the door, and, hearing a noise there, he wheeled and sprang up, uttering a loud cry. Scully's wrinkled visage showed grimly in the light of the small lamp he carried. This yellow effulgence, streaming upward, colored only his prominent features, and left his eyes, for instance, in mysterious shadow. He resembled a murderer.

"Man! man!" he exclaimed, "have you gone daffy?"

"Oh, no! Oh, no!" rejoined the other. "There are people in this world who know pretty nearly as much as you do—understand?"

"For a moment they stood gazing at each other. Upon the Swede's deathly pale cheeks were two spots brightly crimson and sharply edged, as if they had been carefully painted. Scully placed the light on the table and sat himself on the edge of the bed. He spoke ruminatively. "By cracky, I never heard of such a thing in my life. It's a complete muddle. I can't, for the soul of me, think how you ever got this idea into your head." Presently he lifted his eyes and asked: "And did you sure think they were going to kill you?"

The Swede scanned the old man as if he wished to see into his mind. "I did," he said at last. He obviously suspected that this answer might precipitate an outbreak. As he pulled on a strap his whole arm shook, the elbow wavering like a bit of paper.

Scully banged his hand impressively on the footboard of the bed. "Why, man, we're goin' to have a line of ilictric streetcars in this town next spring."

"'A line of electric streetcars,'" repeated the Swede, stupidly.

"And," said Scully, "there's a new railroad goin' to be built down from Broken Arm to here. Not to mintion the four churches and the smashin' big brick schoolhouse. Then there's the big factory, too. Why, in two years Romper'll be a met-tro-*pol*-is."

Having finished the preparation of his baggage, the Swede straightened himself. "Mr. Scully," he said, with sudden hardihood, "how much do I owe you?"

"You don't owe me anythin'," said the old man, angrily.

"Yes, I do," retorted the Swede. He took seventy-five cents from his pocket and tendered it to Scully; but the latter snapped his fingers in disdainful refusal. However, it happened that they both stood gazing in a strange fashion at three silver pieces on the Swede's open palm.

"I'll not take your money," said Scully at last. "Not after what's been goin' on here." Then a plan seemed to strike him. "Here," he cried, picking up his lamp and moving toward the door. "Here! Come with me a minute."

"No," said the Swede, in overwhelming alarm.

"Yes," urged the old man. "Come on! I want you to come and see a picter—just across the hall—in my room."

The Swede must have concluded that his hour was come. His jaw dropped and his teeth showed like a dead man's. He ultimately followed Scully across the corridor, but he had the step of one hung in chains.

Scully flashed the light high on the wall of his own chamber. There was revealed a ridiculous photograph of a little girl. She was leaning against a balustrade of gorgeous decoration, and the formidable bang to her hair was prominent. The figure was as graceful as an upright sled-stake, and, withal, it was of the hue of lead. "There," said Scully, tenderly, "that's the picter of my little girl that died. Her name was Carrie. She had the purtiest hair you ever saw! I was that fond of her, she—"

Turning then, he saw that the Swede was not contemplating the picture at all, but, instead, was keeping keen watch on the gloom in the rear.

"Look, man!" cried Scully, heartily. "That's the picter of my little gal that died. Her name was Carrie.

And then here's the picter of my oldest boy, Michael. He's a lawyer in Lincoln, an' doin' well. I gave that boy a grand eddication, and I'm glad for it now. He's a fine boy. Look at 'im now. Ain't he bold as blazes, him there in Lincoln, an honored an respicted gintleman! An honored and respicted gintleman," concluded Scully with a flourish. And, so saying, he smote the Swede jovially on the back.

The Swede faintly smiled.

"Now," said the old man, "there's only one more thing." He dropped suddenly to the floor and thrust his head beneath the bed. The Swede could hear his muffled voice. "I'd keep it under me piller if it wasn't for that boy Johnnie. Then there's the old woman— Where is it now? I never put it twice in the same place. Ah, now come out with you!"

Presently he backed clumsily from under the bed dragging with him an old coat rolled into a bundle. "I've fetched him," he muttered. Kneeling on the floor, he unrolled the coat and extracted from its heart a large yellow-brown whisky bottle.

His first maneuver was to hold the bottle up to the light. Reassured, apparently, that nobody had been tampering with it, he thrust it with a generous movement toward the Swede.

The weak-kneed Swede was about to eagerly clutch this element of strength, but he suddenly jerked his hand away and cast a look of horror upon Scully.

"Drink," said the old man affectionately. He had risen to his feet, and now stood facing the Swede.

There was a silence. Then again Scully said: "Drink!"

The Swede laughed wildly. He grabbed the bottle, put it to his mouth; and as his lips curled absurdly around the opening and his throat worked, he kept his glance, burning with hatred, upon the old man's face.

IV

After the departure of Scully the three men with the card board still upon their knees, preserved for a long time an astounded silence. Then Johnnie said: "That's the dod-dangedest Swede I ever see."

"He ain't no Swede," said the cowboy, scornfully.

"Well, what is he then?" cried Johnnie. "What is he then?"

"It's my opinion," replied the cowboy deliberately, "he's some kind of a Dutchman." It was a venerable custom of the country to entitle as Swedes all lighthaired men who spoke with a heavy tongue. In consequence the idea of the cowboy was not without its daring. "Yes, sir," he repeated. "It's my opinion this feller is some kind of a Dutchman."

"Well, he says he's a Swede, anyhow," muttered Johnnie, sulkily. He turned to the Easterner: "What do you think, Mr. Blanc?"

"Oh, I don't know," replied the Easterner.

"Well, what do you think makes him act that way?" asked the cowboy.

"Why, he's frightened." The Easterner knocked his pipe against a rim of the stove. "He's clear frightened out of his boots."

"What at?" cried Johnnie and the cowboy together.

The Easterner reflected over his answer.

"What at?" cried the others again.

"Oh, I don't know, but it seems to me this man has been reading dime novels, and he thinks he's right out in the middle of it—the shootin' and stabbin' and all."

"But," said the cowboy, deeply scandalized, "this ain't Wyoming, ner none of them places. This is Nebrasker."

"Yes," added Johnnie, "an' why don't he wait till he gits *out West?*"

The travelled Easterner laughed. "It isn't different there even—not in these days. But he thinks he's right in the middle of hell."

Johnnie and the cowboy mused long.

"It's awful funny," remarked Johnnie at last.

"Yes," said the cowboy. "This is a queer game. I hope we don't git snowed in, because then we'd have to stand this here man bein' around with us all the time. That woudn't be no good."

"I wish pop would throw him out," said Johnnie.

Presently they heard a loud stamping on the stairs, accompanied by ringing jokes in the voice of old Scully, and laughter, evidently from the Swede. The men around the stove stared vacantly at each other. "Gosh!" said the cowboy. The door flew open, and old Scully, flushed and anecdotal, came into the room. He was jabbering at the

Swede, who followed him, laughing bravely. It was the entry of two roisterers from a banquet hall.

"Come now," said Scully sharply to the three seated men, "move up and give us a chance at the stove." The cowboy and the Easterner obediently sidled their chairs to make room for the newcomers. Johnnie, however, simply arranged himself in a more indolent attitude, and then remained motionless.

"Come! Git over, there," said Scully.

"Plenty of room on the other side of the stove," said Johnnie.

"Do you think we want to sit in the draught?" roared the father.

But the Swede here interposed with a grandeur of confidence. "No, no. Let the boy sit where he likes," he cried in a bullying voice to the father.

"All right! All right!" said Scully, deferentially. The cowboy and the Easterner exchanged glances of wonder.

The five chairs were formed in a crescent about one side of the stove. The Swede began to talk; he talked arrogantly, profanely, angrily. Johnnie, the cowboy, and the Easterner maintained a morose silence, while old Scully appeared to be receptive and eager, breaking in constantly with sympathetic ejaculations.

Finally the Swede announced that he was thirsty. He moved in his chair, and said that he would go for a drink of water.

"I'll git it for you," cried Scully at once.

"No," said the Swede, contemptuously. "I'll get it for myself." He arose and stalked with the air of an owner off into the executive parts of the hotel.

As soon as the Swede was out of hearing Scully sprang to his feet and whispered intensely to the others: "Upstairs he thought I was tryin' to poison 'im."

"Say," said Johnnie, "this makes me sick. Why don't you throw 'im out in the snow?"

"Why, he's all right now," declared Scully. "It was only that he was from the East, and he thought this was a tough place. That's all. He's all right now."

The cowboy looked with admiration upon the Easterner. "You were straight," he said. "You were on to that there Dutchman."

"Well," said Johnnie to his father, "he may be all right now, but I don't see it. Other times he was scared, but now he's too fresh."

Scully's speech was always a combination of Irish brogue and idiom, Western twang and idiom, and scraps of curiously formal diction taken from the storybooks and newspapers. He now hurled a strange mass of language at the head of his son. "What do I keep? What do I keep? What do I keep?" he demanded, in a voice of thunder. He slapped his knee impressively, to indicate that he himself was going to make reply, and that all should heed. "I keep a hotel," he shouted. "A hotel, do you mind? A guest under my roof has sacred privileges. He is to be intimidated by none. Not one word shall he hear that would prijudice him in favor of goin' away. I'll not have it. There's no place in this here town where they can say they iver took in a guest of mine because he was afraid to stay here." He wheeled suddenly upon the cowboy and the Easterner. "Am I right?"

"Yes, Mr. Scully," said the cowboy, "I think you're right."

"Yes, Mr. Scully," said the Easterner, "I think you're right."

V

At six-o'clock supper, the Swede fizzed like a fire wheel. He sometimes seemed on the point of bursting into riotous song, and in all his madness he was encouraged by old Scully. The Easterner was encased in reserve; the cowboy sat in wide-mouthed amazement, forgetting to eat, while Johnnie wrathily demolished great plates of food. The daughters of the house, when they were obliged to replenish the biscuits, approached as warily as Indians, and, having succeeded in their purpose, fled with ill-concealed trepidation. The Swede domineered the whole feast, and he gave it the appearance of a cruel bacchanal. He seemed to have grown suddenly taller; he gazed, brutally disdainful, into every face. His voice rang through the room. Once when he jabbed out harpoon-fashion with his fork to pinion a biscuit, the weapon nearly impaled the hand of the Easterner, which had been stretched quietly out for the same biscuit.

After supper, as the men filed toward the other room, the Swede smote Scully ruthlessly on the shoulder. "Well, old boy, that was a good, square meal." Johnnie looked hopefully at his father; he knew that shoulder was tender from an old fall; and, indeed, it appeared for a moment as if Scully was going to flame out over the matter, but in the end he smiled a sickly smile and remained silent. The others understood from his manner that he was admitting his responsibility for the Swede's new viewpoint.

Johnnie, however, addressed his parent in an aside. "Why don't you license somebody to kick you downstairs?" Scully scowled darkly by way of reply.

When they were gathered about the stove, the Swede insisted on another game of High-Five. Scully gently deprecated the plan at first, but the Swede turned a wolfish glare upon him. The old man subsided, and the Swede canvassed the others. In his tone there was always a great threat. The cowboy and the Easterner both remarked indifferently that they would play. Scully said that he would presently have to go to meet the 6:58 train, and so the Swede turned menacingly upon Johnnie. For a moment their glances crossed like blades, and then Johnnie smiled and said, "Yes, I'll play."

They formed a square, with the little board on their knees. The Easterner and the Swede were again partners. As the play went on, it was noticeable that the cowboy was not board-whacking as usual. Meanwhile, Scully, near the lamp, had put on his spectacles and, with an appearance curiously like an old priest, was reading a newspaper. In time he went out to meet the 6:58 train, and, despite his precautions, a gust of polar wind whirled into the room as he opened the door. Besides scattering the cards, it chilled the players to the marrow. The Swede cursed frightfully. When Scully returned, his entrance disturbed a cosy and friendly scene. The Swede again cursed. But presently they were once more intent, their heads bent forward and their hands moving swiftly. The Swede had adopted the fashion of board-whacking.

Scully took up his paper and for a long time remained immersed in matters which were extraordinarily remote from him. The lamp burned badly, and once he stopped to adjust the wick. The newspaper, as he turned from page to page, rustled with a slow and comfortable sound. Then suddenly he heard three terrible words: "You are cheatin'!"

Such scenes often prove that there can be little of dramatic import in environment. Any room can present a tragic front; any room can be comic. This little den was now hideous as a torture chamber. The new faces of the men themselves had changed it upon the instant. The Swede held a huge fist in front of Johnnie's face, while the latter looked steadily over it into the blazing orbs of his accuser. The Easterner had grown pallid; the cowboy's jaw had dropped in that expression of bovine amazement which was one of his important mannerisms. After the three words, the first sound in the room was made by Scully's paper as it floated forgotten to his feet. His spectacles had also fallen from his nose, but by a clutch he had saved them in air. His hand, grasping the spectacles, now remained poised awkwardly and near his shoulder. He stared at the card players.

Probably the silence was while a second elapsed. Then, if the floor had been suddenly twitched out from under the men they could not have moved quicker. The five had projected themselves headlong toward a common point. It happened that Johnnie, in rising to hurl himself upon the Swede, had stumbled slightly because of his curiously instinctive care for the cards and the board. The loss of the moment allowed time for the arrival of Scully, and also allowed the cowboy time to give the Swede a great push which sent him staggering back. The men found tongue together, and hoarse shouts of rage, appeal, or fear burst from every throat. The cowboy pushed and jostled feverishly at the Swede, and the Easterner and Scully clung wildly to Johnnie; but through the smoky air, above the swaying bodies of the peace compellers, the eyes of the two warriors ever sought each other in glances of challenge that were at once hot and steely.

Of course the board had been overturned, and now the whole company of cards was scattered over the floor, where the boots of the men trampled the fat and painted kings and queens as they gazed with their silly eyes at the war that was waging above them.

Scully's voice was dominating the yells. "Stop now! Stop, I say! Stop, now—"

Johnnie, as he struggled to burst through the rank formed by Scully and the Easternerer, was crying, "Well, he says I cheated! He says I cheated! I won't allow no man to say I cheated! If he says I cheated, he's a— —!"

The cowboy was telling the Swede, "Quit, now! Quit, d'ye hear—"

The screams of the Swede never ceased: "He did cheat! I saw him! I saw him—"

As for the Easterner, he was importuning in a voice that was not heeded: "Wait a moment, can't you? Oh, wait a moment. What's the good of a fight over a game of cards? Wait a moment—"

In this tumult no complete sentences were clear. "Cheat"—"Quit"—"He says"—these fragments pierced the uproar and rang out sharply. It was remarkable that, whereas Scully undoubtedly made the most noise, he was the least heard of any of the riotous band.

Then suddenly, there was a great cessation. It was as if each man had paused for a breath; and although the room was still lighted with the anger of men, it could be seen that there was no danger of immediate conflict, and at once Johnnie, shouldering his way forward, almost succeeded in confronting the Swede. "What did you say I cheated for? What did you say I cheated for? I don't cheat, and I won't let no man say I do!"

The Swede said, "I saw you! I saw you!"

"Well," cried Johnnie, "I'll fight any man what says I cheat!"

"No, you won't," said the cowboy. "Not here."

"Ah, be still, can't you?" said Scully, coming between them.

The quiet was sufficient to allow the Easterner's voice to be heard. He was repeating, "Oh, wait a moment, can't you? What's the good of a fight over a game of cards? Wait a moment!"

Johnnie, his red face appearing above his father's shoulder, hailed the Swede again. "Did you say I cheated?"

The Swede showed his teeth. "Yes."

"Then," said Johnnie, "we must fight."

"Yes, fight," roared the Swede. He was like a demoniac. "Yes, fight! I'll show you what kind of a man I am! I'll show you who you want to fight! Maybe you think I can't fight! Maybe you think I can't! I'll show you, you skin, you card sharp! Yes, you cheated! You cheated! You cheated!"

"Well, let's go at it, then, mister," said Johnnie, coolly.

The cowboy's brow was beaded with sweat from his efforts in intercepting all sorts of raids. He turned in despair to Scully. "What are you goin' to do now?"

A change had come over the Celtic visage of the old man. He now seemed all eagerness; his eyes glowed.

"We'll let them fight," he answered, stalwartly. "I can't put up with it any longer. I've stood this damned Swede till I'm sick. We'll let them fight."

VI

The men prepared to go out of doors. The Easterner was so nervous that he had great difficulty in getting his arms into the sleeves of his new leather coat. As the cowboy drew his fur cap down over his ears his hands trembled. In fact, Johnnie and old Scully were the only ones who displayed no agitation. These preliminaries were conducted without words.

Scully threw open the door. "Well, come on," he said. Instantly a terrific wind caused the flame of the lamp to struggle at its wick, while a puff of black smoke sprang from the chimney top. The stove was in mid-current of the blast, and its voice swelled to equal the roar of the storm. Some of the scarred and bedabbled cards were caught up from the floor and dashed helplessly against the farther wall. The men lowered their heads and plunged into the tempest as into a sea.

No snow was falling, but great whirls and clouds of flakes, swept up from the ground by the frantic winds, were screaming southward with the speed of bullets. The covered land was blue with the sheen of an unearthly satin, and there was no other hue save where, at the low, black railway station—which seemed incredibly distant—one light gleamed like a tiny jewel. As the men floundered into a thigh-deep drift, it was known that the Swede was bawling out something. Scully went to him, put a hand on his shoulder, and projected an ear. "What's that you say?" he shouted.

"I say," bawled the Swede again, "I won't stand much show against this gang. I know you'll all pitch on me."

Scully smote him reproachfully on the arm. "Tut, man!" he yelled. The wind tore the words from Scully's lips and scattered them far alee.

"You are all a gang of—" boomed the Swede, but the storm also seized the remainder of this sentence.

Immediately turning their backs upon the wind, the men had swung around a corner to the sheltered side of the hotel. It was the function of the little house to preserve here, amid this great devastation of snow, an irregular V-shape of heavily encrusted grass, which crackled beneath the feet. One could imagine the great drifts piled against the windward side. When the party reached the comparative peace of this spot it was found that the Swede was still bellowing.

"Oh, I know what kind of a thing this is! I know you'll all pitch on me. I can't lick you all!"

Scully turned upon him panther-fashion. "You'll not have to whip all of us. You'll have to whip my son Johnnie. An' the man what troubles you durin' that time will have me to dale with."

The arrangements were swiftly made. The two men faced each other, obedient to the harsh commands of Scully, whose face, in the subtly luminous gloom, could be seen set in the austere impersonal lines that are pictured on the countenances of the Roman veterans. The Easterner's teeth were chattering, and he was hopping up and down like a mechanical toy. The cowboy stood rock-like.

The contestants had not stripped off any clothing. Each was in his ordinary attire. Their fists were up, and they eyed each other in a calm that had the elements of leonine cruelty in it.

During this pause, the Easterner's mind, like a film, took lasting impressions of three men—the iron-nerved master of the ceremony; the Swede, pale, motionless, terrible; and Johnnie, serene yet ferocious, brutish yet heroic. The entire prelude had in it a tragedy greater than the tragedy of action, and this aspect was accentuated by the long, mellow cry of the blizzard, as it sped the tumbling and wailing flakes into the black abyss of the south.

"Now!" said Scully.

The two combatants leaped forward and crashed together like bullocks. There was heard the cushioned sound of blows, and of a curse squeezing out from between the tight teeth of one.

As for the spectators, the Easterner's pent-up breath exploded from him with a pop of relief, absolute relief from the tension of the preliminaries. The cowboy bounded into the air with a yowl. Scully was immovable as from supreme amazement and fear at the fury of the fight which he himself had permitted and arranged.

For a time the encounter in the darkness was such a perplexity of flying arms that it presented no more detail than would a swiftly revolving wheel. Occasionally a face, as if illumined by a flash of light, would shine out, ghastly and marked with pink spots. A moment later, the men might have been known as shadows, if it were not for the involuntary utterance of oaths that came from them in whispers.

Suddenly a holocaust of warlike desire caught the cowboy, and he bolted forward with the speed of a broncho. "Go it, Johnnie! go it! Kill him! Kill him!"

Scully confronted him. "Kape back," he said; and by his glance the cowboy could tell that this man was Johnnie's father.

To the Easterner there was a monotony of unchangeable fighting that was an abomination. This confused mingling was eternal to his sense, which was concentrated in a longing for the end, the priceless end. Once the fighters lurched near him, and as he scrambled hastily backward he heard them breathe like men on the rack.

"Kill him, Johnnie! Kill him! Kill him! Kill him!" The cowboy's face was contorted like one of those agony masks in museums.

"Keep still," said Scully, icily.

Then there was a sudden loud grunt, incomplete, cut short, and Johnnie's body swung away from the Swede and fell with sickening heaviness to the grass. The cowboy was barely in time to prevent the mad Swede from flinging himself upon his prone adversary. "No, you don't," said the cowboy, interposing an arm. "Wait a second."

Scully was at his son's side. "Johnnie! Johnnie, me boy!" His voice had a quality of melancholy tenderness. "Johnnie! Can you go on with it?" He looked anxiously down into the bloody, pulpy face of his son.

There was a moment of silence, and then Johnnie answered in his ordinary voice, "Yes, I—it—yes."

Assisted by his father he struggled to his feet. "Wait a bit now till you git your wind," said the old man.

A few paces away the cowboy was lecturing the Swede. "No, you don't! Wait a second!"

The Easterner was plucking at Scully's sleeve. "Oh this is enough," he pleaded. "This is enough! Let it go as it stands. This is enough!"

"Bill," said Scully, "git out of the road." The cowboy stepped aside. "Now." The combatants were actuated by a new caution as they advanced toward collision. They glared at each other, and then the Swede aimed a lightning blow that carried with it his entire weight. Johnnie was evidently half stupid from weakness, but he miraculously dodged, and his fist sent the overbalanced Swede sprawling.

The cowboy, Scully, and the Easterner burst into a cheer that was like a chorus of triumphant soldiery, but before its conclusion the Swede had scuffled agilely to his feet and come in berserk abandon at his foe. There was another perplexity of flying arms, and Johnnie's body again swung away and fell, even as a bundle might fall from a roof. The Swede instantly staggered to a little wind-waved tree and leaned upon it, breathing like an engine, while his savage and flame-lit eyes roamed from face to face as the men bent over Johnnie. There was a splendor of isolation in his situation at this time which the Easterner felt once when, lifting his eyes from the man on the ground, he beheld that mysterious and lonely figure, waiting.

"Are you any good yet, Johnnie?" asked Scully in a broken voice.

The son gasped and opened his eyes languidly. After a moment he answered, "No—I ain't—any good—any—more." Then, from shame and bodily ill, he began to weep, the tears furrowing down through the bloodstains on his face. "He was too—too—too heavy for me."

Scully straightened and addressed the waiting figure. "Stranger," he said, evenly, "it's all up with our side." Then his voice changed into that vibrant huskiness which is commonly the tone of the most simple and deadly announcements. "Johnnie is whipped."

Without replying, the victor moved off on the route to the front door of the hotel.

The cowboy was formulating new and unspellable blasphemies. The Easterner was startled to find that they were out in a wind that seemed to come direct from the shadowed arctic floes. He heard again the wail of the snow as it was flung to its grave in the south. He knew now that all this time the cold had been sinking into him deeper and deeper, and he wondered that he had not perished. He felt indifferent to the condition of the vanquished man.

"Johnnie, can you walk?" asked Scully.

"Did I hurt—hurt him any?" asked the son.

"Can you walk, boy? Can you walk?"

Johnnie's voice was suddenly strong. There was a robust impatience in it. "I asked you whether I hurt him any!"

"Yes, yes, Johnnie," answered the cowboy, consolingly; "he's hurt a good deal."

They raised him from the ground, and as soon as he was on his feet he went tottering off, rebuffing all attempts at assistance. Then the party rounded the corner they were fairly blinded by the pelting of the snow. It burned their faces like fire. The cowboy carried Johnnie through the drift to the door. As they entered, some cards again rose from the floor and beat against the wall.

The Easterner rushed to the stove. He was so profoundly chilled that he almost dared to embrace the glowing iron. The Swede was not in the room. Johnnie sank into a chair and, folding his arms on his knees, buried his face in them. Scully, warming one foot and then the other at a rim of the stove, muttered to himself with Celtic mournfulness. The cowboy had removed his fur cap, and with a dazed and rueful air he was running one hand through his tousled locks. From overhead they could hear the creaking of boards, as the Swede tramped here and there in his room.

The sad quiet was broken by the sudden flinging open of a door that led toward the kitchen. It was instantly followed by an inrush of women. They precipitated themselves upon Johnnie amid a chorus of lamentation. Before they carried their prey off to the kitchen, there to be bathed and harangued with that mixture of sympathy and abuse which is a feat of their sex, the mother straightened herself and fixed old Scully with an eye of stern reproach. "Shame be upon you, Patrick Scully!" she cried. "Your own son, too. Shame be upon you!"

"There, now! Be quiet, now!" said the old man, weakly.

"Shame be upon you, Patrick Scully!" The girls, rallying to this slogan, sniffed disdainfully in the direction of those trembling accomplices, the cowboy and the Easterner. Presently they bore Johnnie away, and left the three men to dismal reflection.

VII

"I'd like to fight this here Dutchman myself," said the cowboy, breaking a long silence.

Scully wagged his head sadly. "No, that wouldn't do. It wouldn't be right. It wouldn't be right."

"Well, why wouldn't it?" argued the cowboy. "I don't see no harm in it."

"No," answered Scully, with mournful heroism. "It wouldn't be right. It was Johnnie's fight, and now we mustn't whip the man just because he whipped Johnnie."

"Yes, that's true enough," said the cowboy; "but—he better not get fresh with me, because I couldn't stand no more of it."

"You'll not say a word to him," commanded Scully, and even then they heard the tread of the Swede on the stairs. His entrance was made theatric. He swept the door back with a bang and swaggered to the middle of the room. No one looked at him. "Well," he cried, insolently, at Scully, "I s'pose you'll tell me now how much I owe you?"

The old man remained stolid. "You don't owe me nothin'."

"Huh!" said the Swede, "huh! Don't owe 'im nothin'."

The cowboy addressed the Swede. "Stranger, I don't see how you come to be so gay around here."

Old Scully was instantly alert. "Stop!" he shouted, holding his hand forth, fingers upward. "Bill, you shut up!"

The cowboy spat carelessly into the sawdust box. "I didn't say a word, did I?" he asked.

"Mr. Scully," called the Swede, "how much do I owe you?" It was seen that he was attired for departure, and that he had his valise in his hand.

"You don't owe me nothin'," repeated Scully in the same imperturbable way.

"Huh!" said the Swede. "I guess you're right. I guess if it was any way at all, you'd owe me somethin'. That's what I guess." He turned to the cowboy. "'Kill him! Kill him! Kill him!'" he mimicked, and then guffawed victoriously. "'Kill him!'" He was convulsed with ironical humor.

But he might have been jeering the dead. The three men were immovable and silent, staring with glassy eyes at the stove.

The Swede opened the door and passed into the storm, giving one derisive glance backward at the still group.

As soon as the door was closed, Scully and the cowboy leaped to their feet and began to curse. They trampled to and fro, waving their arms and smashing into the air with their fists. "Oh, but that was a hard minute!" wailed Scully. "That was a hard minute! Him there leerin' and scoffin'! One bang at his nose was worth forty dollars to me that minute! How did you stand it, Bill?"

"How did I stand it?" cried the cowboy in a quivering voice. "How did I stand it? Oh!"

The old man burst into sudden brogue. "I'd loike to take that Swade," he wailed, "and hould 'im down on a shtone flure and bate 'im to a jelly wid a shtick!"

The cowboy groaned in sympathy. "I'd like to git him by the neck and ha-ammer him"—he brought his hand down on a chair with a noise like a pistol shot—"hammer that there Dutchman until he couldn't tell himself from a dead coyote!"

"I'd bate 'im until he—"

"I'd show *him* some things—"

And then together they raised a yearning, fanatic cry—"Oh-o-oh! if we only could—"

"Yes! "

"Yes!"

"And then I'd—"

"O-o-oh!"

VIII

The Swede, tightly gripping his valise, tacked across the face of the storm as if he carried sails. He was following a line of little naked, grasping trees which, he knew, must mark the way of the road. His face, fresh from the pounding of Johnnie's fists, felt more pleasure than pain in the wind and the driving snow. A number of square shapes loomed upon him finally, and he knew them as the houses of the main body of the town. He found a street and made travel along it, leaning heavily upon the wind whenever, at a corner, a terrific blast caught him.

He might have been in a deserted village. We picture the world as thick with conquering and elate humanity, but here, with the bugles of the tempest pealing, it was hard to imagine a peopled earth. One viewed the existence of man then as a marvel, and conceded a glamor of wonder to these lice which were caused to cling to a whirling, fire-smitten, ice-locked, disease-stricken, spacelost bulb. The conceit of man was explained by this storm to be the very engine of life. One was a coxcomb not to die in it. However, the Swede found a saloon.

In front of it an indomitable red light was burning, and the snowflakes were made blood-color as they flew through the circumscribed territory of the lamp's shining. The Swede pushed open the door of the saloon and entered. A sanded expanse was before him, and at the end of it four men sat about a table drinking. Down one side of the room extended a radiant bar, and its guardian was leaning upon his elbows listening to the talk of the men at the table. The Swede dropped his valise upon the door and, smiling fraternally upon the barkeeper, said, "Gimme some whisky, will you?" The man placed a bottle, a whisky-glass, and a glass of ice-thick water upon the bar. The Swede poured himself an abnormal portion of whisky and drank it in three gulps. "Pretty bad night," remarked the bartender, indifferently. He was making the pretension of blindness which is usually a distinction of his class; but it could have been seen that he was furtively studying the half-erased bloodstains on the face of the Swede. "Bad night," he said again.

"Oh, it's good enough for me," replied the Swede, hardily, as he poured himself some more whisky. The barkeeper took his coin and maneuvered it through its reception by the highly nickelled cash machine. A bell rang; a card labelled "20 cts." had appeared.

"No," continued the Swede, "this isn't too bad weather. It's good enough for me."

"So?" murmured the barkeeper, languidly.

The copious drams made the Swede's eyes swim, and he breathed a trifle heavier. "Yes, I like this weather. I like it. It suits me." It was apparently his design to impart a deep significance to these words.

"So?" murmured the bartender again. He turned to gaze dreamily at the scroll-like birds and bird-like scrolls which had been drawn with soap upon the mirrors in back of the bar.

"Well, I guess I'll take another drink," said the Swede, presently. "Have something?"

"No, thanks; I'm not drinkin'," answered the bartender. Afterward he asked, "How did you hurt your face?"

The Swede immediately began to boast loudly. "Why, in a fight. I thumped the soul out of a man down here at Scully's hotel."

The interest of the four men at the table was at last aroused.

"Who was it?" said one.

"Johnnie Scully," blustered the Swede. "Son of the man what runs it. He will be pretty near dead for some weeks, I can tell you. I made a nice thing of him, I did. He couldn't get up. They carried him in the house. Have a drink?"

Instantly the men in some subtle way encased themselves in reserve. "No, thanks," said one. The group was of curious formation. Two were prominent local business men; one was the district attorney; and one was a professional gambler of the kind known as "square." But a scrutiny of the group would not have enabled an observer to pick the gambler from the men of more reputable pursuits. He was, in fact, a man so delicate in manner, when among people of fair class, and so judicious in his choice of victims, that in the strictly masculine part of the town's life he had come to be explicitly trusted and admired. People called him a thoroughbred. The fear and contempt with which his craft was regarded were undoubtedly the reason why his quiet dignity shone conspicuous above the quiet dignity of men who might be merely hatters, billiard-markers, or grocery clerks. Beyond an occasional unwary traveller who came by rail, this gambler was supposed to prey solely upon reckless and senile farmers, who, when flush with good crops, drove into town in all the pride and confidence of an absolutely invulnerable stupidity. Hearing at times in circuitous fashion of the despoilment of such a farmer, the important men of Romper invariably laughed in contempt of the victim, and if they thought of the wolf at all, it was with a kind of pride at the knowledge that he would never dare think of attacking their wisdom and courage. Besides, it was popular that this gambler had a real wife and two real children in a neat cottage in a suburb, where he led an exemplary home life; and when any one even suggested a discrepancy in his character, the crowd immediately vociferated descriptions of this virtuous family circle. Then men who led exemplary home lives, and men who did not lead exemplary home lives, all subsided in a bunch, remarking that there was nothing more to be said.

However, when a restriction was placed upon him—as, for instance, when a strong clique of members of the new Pollywog Club refused to permit him, even as a spectator, to appear in the rooms of the organization—the candor and gentleness with which he accepted the judgement disarmed many of his foes and made his friends more desperately partisan. He invariably distinguished between himself and a respectable Romper man so quickly and frankly that his manner actually appeared to be a continual broadcast compliment.

And one must not forget to declare the fundamental fact of his entire position in Romper. It is irrefutable that in all affairs outside his business, in all matters that occur eternally and commonly between man and man, this thieving card player was so generous, so just, so moral, that, in a contest, he could have put to flight the consciences of nine tenths of the citizens of Romper.

And so it happened that he was seated in this saloon with the two prominent local merchants and the district attorney.

The Swede continued to drink raw whisky, meanwhile babbling at the barkeeper and trying to induce him to indulge in potations. "Come on. Have a drink. Come on. What—no? Well, have a little one, then. By gawd, I've whipped a man tonight, and I want to celebrate. I whipped him good, too. Gentlemen," the Swede cried to the men at the table, "have a drink?"

"Ssh!" said the barkeeper.

The group at the table, although furtively attentive, had been pretending to be in deep talk, but now a man lifted his eyes toward the Swede and said, shortly, "Thanks. We don't want anymore."

At this reply the Swede ruffled out his chest like a rooster. "Well," he exploded, "it seems I can't get anybody to drink with me in this town. Seems so, don't it? Well!"

"Ssh!" said the barkeeper.

"Say," snarled the Swede, "don't you try to shut me up. I won't have it. I'm a gentleman, and I want people to drink with me. And I want 'em to drink with me now. *Now*—do you understand?" He rapped the bar with his knuckles.

Years of experience had calloused the bartender. He merely grew sulky. "I hear you," he answered.

"Well," cried the Swede, "listen hard then. See those men over there? Well, they're going to drink with me, and don't you forget it. Now you watch."

"Hi!" yelled the barkeeper, "this won't do!"

"Why won't it?" demanded the Swede. He stalked over to the table, and by chance laid his hand upon the shoulder of the gambler. "How about this?" he asked wrathfully. "I asked you to drink with me."

The gambler simply twisted his head and spoke over his shoulder. "My friend, I don't know you."

"Oh, hell!" answered the Swede, "come and have a drink."

"Now, my boy," advised the gambler, kindly, "take your hand off my shoulder and go 'way and mind your own business." He was a little, slim man, and it seemed strange to hear him use this tone of heroic patronage to the burly Swede. The other men at the table said nothing.

"What! You won't drink with me, you little dude? I'll make you, then! I'll make you!" The Swede had grasped the gambler frenziedly at the throat, and was dragging him from his chair. The other men sprang up. The barkeeper dashed around the corner of his bar. There was a great tumult, and then was seen a long blade in the hand of the gambler. It shot forward, and a human body, this citadel of virtue, wisdom, power, was pierced as easily as if it had been a melon. The Swede fell with a cry of supreme astonishment.

The prominent merchants and the district attorney must have at once tumbled out of the place backward. The bartender found himself hanging limply to the arm of a chair and gazing into the eyes of a murderer.

"Henry," said the latter, as he wiped his knife on one of the towels that hung beneath the bar rail, "you tell 'em where to find me. I'll be home, waiting for 'em." Then he vanished. A moment afterward the barkeeper was in the street dinning through the storm for help and, moreover, companionship.

The corpse of the Swede, alone in the saloon, had its eyes fixed upon a dreadful legend that dwelt atop of the cash machine: "This registers the amount of your purchase."

IX

Months later, the cowboy was frying pork over the stove of a little ranch near the Dakota line, when there was a quick thud of hoofs outside, and presently the Easterner entered with the letters and the papers.

"Well," said the Easterner at once, "the chap that killed the Swede has got three years. Wasn't much, was it?"

"He has? Three years?" The cowboy poised his pan of pork, while he ruminated upon the news. "Three years. That ain't much."

"No. It was a light sentence," replied the Easterner as he unbuckled his spurs. "Seems there was a good deal of sympathy for him in Romper."

"If the bartender had been any good," observed the cowboy, thoughtfully, "he would have gone in and cracked that there Dutchman on the head with a bottle in the beginnin' of it and stopped all this here murderin'."

"Yes, a thousand things might have happened," said the Easterner, tartly.

The cowboy returned his pan of pork to the fire, but his philosophy continued. "It's funny, ain't it? If he hadn't said Johnnie was cheatin' he'd be alive this minute. He was an awful fool. Game played for fun, too. Not for money. I believe he was crazy."

"I feel sorry for that gambler," said the Easterner.

"Oh, so do I," said the cowboy. "He don't deserve none of it for killin' who he did."

"The Swede might not have been killed if everything had been square."

"Might not have been killed?" exclaimed the cowboy. "Everythin' square? Why, when he said that Johnnie was cheatin' and acted like such a jackass? And then in the saloon he fairly walked up to git hurt?" With these arguments the cowboy browbeat the Easterner and reduced him to rage.

"You're a fool!" cried the Easterner, viciously. "You're a bigger jackass than the Swede by a million majority. Now let me tell you one thing. Let me tell you something. Listen! Johnnie *was* cheating!"

"'Johnnie,'" said the cowboy, blankly. There was a minute of silence, and then he said, robustly, "Why, no. The game was only for fun."

"Fun or not," said the Easterner, "Johnnie was cheating. I saw him. I know it. I saw him. And I refused to stand up and be a man. I let the Swede fight it out alone. And you—you were simply puffing around the place and wanting to fight. And then old Scully himself! We are all in it! This poor gambler isn't even a noun. He is kind of an adverb. Every sin is the result of a collaboration. We, five of us, have collaborated in the murder of this Swede. Usually there are from a dozen to forty women really involved in every murder, but in this case it seems to be only five men—you, I Johnnie, old Scully; and that fool of an unfortunate gambler came merely as a culmination, the apex of a human movement, and gets all the punishment."

The cowboy, injured and rebellious, cried out blindly into this fog of mysterious theory: "Well, I didn't do anythin', did I?"

Anderson

1876 September 13. Sherwood Anderson is born in Camden, Ohio.

1896 Quits high school and goes to Chicago seeking employment. After two years of working as a laborer, he enlists and goes to Cuba to serve in the Spanish-American War. Upon returning from Cuba, he goes back to Chicago, where he attends prep school and works in an advertising agency.

1905 Moves to Elyria, Ohio, where he manages a factory and sells roof paint, while writing poetry and prose in his spare time.

1912 Disillusioned with his life, Anderson walks out of the factory and returns to Chicago to pursue a full-time literary career. There he meets the likes of Floyd Dell, Carl Sandburg, and Theodore Dreiser, who encourage his work.

1916 *Windy McPherson's Son* is published, but receives little attention.

1919 *Winesburg, Ohio* is published. This loosely related collection of stories dealing with life in the Midwest brings Anderson great notoriety.

1921 Moves to New York and writes articles and stories for different periodicals. Travels to Europe, where he meets and is befriended by Gertrude Stein. Returns to New York in December, in time to pick up the first Dial Award for excellence in literature. *Triumph of the Egg* is published.

1922 Settles briefly in New Orleans, where he establishes the magazine *Double Dealer*. Befriends William Faulkner, and publishes his first works in the newly created magazine.

1925 Moves to Marion, Virginia, where he publishes both of the town's newspapers—one republican, one democratic. The novel *Dark Laughter* is published.

1941 March 8. While touring South America, he dies in Colon, Panama.

Sherwood Anderson

They pass us every day, a gray and driven throng, the common words that are the medium of Sherwood Anderson. In the thick ranks of the newspapers they go drab and indistinct as miners trooping by grim factory walls in latest dusk. Men's lips form them wherever in all the land talk is, but we mark their shapes no more than we mark those of the individual passengers in the subway press, the arm and overcoat jumble, each tired night at six. The objects symbolized by them lie in the range of vision of those who make each day the city trip to the office and workshop and back flatward again. They lie in the range of those who ride dully into country towns over dusty roadways, or work about their barns or their fields or inside farm cottages. But the walls of the city thoroughfares do not impinge on us, or on the men who talk, or on the backs who write. The earth and board sides and fences and plantations remain in a sullen murk. And the words that signify the things and their simple qualities remain in millions of voices dreary dead.

Storytellers have come with banner and hallo to lift them out of Malebolge, to burnish them, to write English, and have washed them to no more scintillance than has the tired crowd of Christmas shoppers in the Chicago loop. Dreiser himself sought to point and sharpen them, to set them together as squarely as dominoes are set together in the backrooms of German saloons. He merely succeeded in forming a surface like that of water-logged, splintery beams, unfit for any hardy service. It was only Brontosaurus rex lumbering through a mesozoic swamp. In American novels, the words remained the dreariest, most degraded of poor individuals. But out of these fallen creatures, Sherwood Anderson has made the pure poetry of his tales. He has taken the words surely, has set them firmly end to end, and underneath his hand there has come to be a surface as clean and fragrant as that of joyously made things in a fresh young country. The vocabulary of the simplest folk; words of a primer, a copy-book quotidianness, form a surface as hard as that of pungent fresh-planed boards of pine and oak. Into the ordered prose of Anderson the delicacy and sweetness of the growing corn, the grittiness and firmness of black earth sifted by the fingers, the broad-breasted power of great laboring horses, has wavered again. The writing pleases the eye. It pleases the nostrils. It is moist and adhesive to the touch, like milk.

No rare and precious and technical incrustations have stiffened it. The slang of the city proletariate has not whipped it into garish and raging color. Even in his pictures of life on the farms and in the towns of Ohio, Anderson is not colloquial. Very rarely some turn of language lifted from the speech of the Ohio country folk, gives a curious twist to the ordinary English. The language remains homely, sober, and spare. The simplest constructions abound. Few adjectives arrest the course of the sentence. At intervals, the succession of simple periods is broken by a compound sprawling its loose length. Qualifying clauses are unusual. Very occasionally, some of the plain massive silver and gold of the King James version shines when Biblical poetry is echoed in the balancing of phrases, in the full unhurried repetition of words in slightly varied order. But the words themselves are no longer those that daily sweep by us in dun and opaque stream. They no longer go bent and grimly in a fog. Contours are distinct as those of objects bathed in cool morning light. The words comport themselves with dignity. They are placed so quietly, so plumbly, so solidly, in order; they are arranged so nakedly, so four-squarely; stand so completely for what they are; ring so fully, that one perceives them bearing themselves as erectly and proudly as simple healthy folk can bear themselves. Aprons and overalls they still wear, for they are working words. But their garments became starched and fragrant again, when Anderson squared and edged his tools. They leave us freshened as gingham-clad girls driving past in a buggy do. If they are a little old and a little weary, they hold themselves like certain old folk who wear threadbare shawls and shiny black trousers, and still make their self-regard felt by their port.

It is the vague uncertain elusive music of folk in America that comes through this medium of words. Body of feeling in a groping struggling shoot of the Ohio countryside marshals the phrases, compels them into patterns, and makes the words pregnant with their real and transcendental meanings. In this writer, brother to all the dumb chaotic folk produced by two centuries of the pioneersman's life, the desire of the race is full a-cry. Sherwood Anderson was born among men who had sacrificed, that they might take root in virgin land, much of what the centuries had warmed to life in their forbears across the Atlantic. He grew in a corn-shipping town of post-Civil-War Ohio; grew among people who had forgotten the beauty laboriously accumulated in Europe; grew ignorant of the fact that beauty made by human toil existed anywhere on the globe. Around him, too, everything was quantity, not quality; everything urged to small, cold ambition. He lived the days lived by countless other smart little boys in this meager civilization; volunteered to fight Spain and typhoid in Cuba; spent the money gained in soldiering in acquiring a little education at a fresh-water college; worked in factories, in bicycle foundries; set out, driven by the universal goad, to become a successful business man; did become a successful business man. And still, in Anderson; in this creature sprung from out the raw American millions, desire for finer, larger life sings as it sings in every upspringing, aspiring stone of Chartres. Its low voice is louder in him than the hysterical American mouth with its fictitious tumult and assurance, its rhetorical trumpeting of the high state of women in Minneapolis, the efficiency and hygienic charms of clothing factories in Cleveland, the invigoration of the struggle for existence in New York. It will not down. It is too strong; it will not go to sleep in consenting in what happens to be powerful, or blind itself to the relationships of men and women the country over. Nor will it let itself be debouched into abdicating in favor of an interest centered entirely in children, or into the dream that possession of a house full of spark furniture and nickled faucets will suddenly make life flow sweet-colored and deep; nor ring bells of self-satisfaction to God for the reason that he has created a universe in which everyone or everyone's offspring can climb to the top of the human heap and become a millionaire. Cultures struggling for birth overcome the tribal fears in the man, make him tender, nervous, and musical with true feeling, quivering in readiness for motion toward the new life. Desire for new worlds, striving to connect with facts and

objects at every street corner fill him with tentative attitudes, tear at bonds, subside in pain, whisper promises of large movements and spaces. At the rear of his brain there murmurs always the liquid flow of worlds in progress in every living being. What Anderson veritably lives in Chicago and suffers and desires is known to him; what his muddy-streaming compatriots have done and still are doing to him; what his joys are, and what his pains. The man perceives the world and in perceiving it transcends it. A quiet stream, a deep black brook with a whispering trickle, faëry of starts and gushes carries life like a Niagara.

—from Port of New York *by Paul Rosenfeld*

Hands

Upon the half decayed veranda of a small frame house that stood near the edge of a ravine near the town of Winesburg, Ohio, a fat little old man walked nervously up and down. Across a long field that had been seeded for clover but that had produced only a dense crop of yellow mustard weeds, he could see the public highway along which went a wagon filled with berry pickers returning from the fields. The berry pickers, youths and maidens, laughed and shouted boisterously. A boy clad in a blue shirt leaped from the wagon and attempted to drag after him one of the maidens, who screamed and protested shrilly. The feet of the boy in the road kicked up a cloud of dust that floated across the face of the departing sun. Over the long field came a thin girlish voice. "Oh, you Wing Biddlebaum, comb your hair, it's falling into your eyes," commanded the voice to the man, who was bald and whose nervous little hands fiddled about the bare white forehead as though arranging a mass of tangled locks.

Wing Biddlebaum, forever frightened and beset by a ghostly band of doubts, did not think of himself as in any way a part of the life of the town where he had lived for twenty years. Among all the people of Winesburg but one had come close to him. With George Willard, son of Tom Willard, the proprietor of the New Willard House, he had formed something like a friendship. George Willard was the reporter on the *Winesburg Eagle* and sometimes in the evenings he walked out along the highway to Wing Biddlebaum's house. Now as the old man walked up and down on the veranda, his hands moving nervously about, he was hoping that George Willard would come and spend the evening with him. After the wagon containing the berry pickers had passed, he went across the field through the tall mustard weeds and climbing a rail fence peered anxiously along the road to the town. For a moment he stood thus, rubbing his hands together and looking up and down the road, and then, fear overcoming him, ran back to walk again upon the porch on his own house.

In the presence of George Willard, Wing Biddlebaum, who for twenty years had been the town mystery, lost something of his timidity, and his shadowy personality, submerged in a sea of doubts came forth to look at the world. With the young reporter at his side, he ventured in the light of day into Main Street or strode up and down on the rickety front porch of his own house, talking excitedly. The voice that had been low and trembling became shrill and loud. The bent figure straightened. With a kind of wriggle, like a fish returned to the brook by the fisherman, Biddlebaum the silent began to talk, striving to put into words the ideas that had been accumulated by his mind during long years of silence.

Wing Biddlebaum talked much with his hands. The slender expressive fingers, forever active, forever striving to conceal themselves in his pockets or behind his back, came forth and became the piston rods of his machinery of expression.

The story of Wing Biddlebaum is a story of hands. Their restless activity, like unto the beating of the wings of an imprisoned bird, had given him his name. Some obscure poet of the town had thought of it. The hands alarmed their owner. He wanted to keep them hidden away and looked with amazement at the quiet inexpressive hands of other men who worked beside him in the fields, or passed, driving sleepy teams on country roads.

When he talked to George Willard, Wing Biddlebaum closed his fists and beat with them upon a table or on the walls of his house. The action made him more comfortable. If the desire to talk came to him when the two were walking in the fields, he sought out a stump or the top board of a fence and with his hands pounding busily talked with renewed ease.

The story of Wing Biddlebaum's hands is worth a book in itself. Sympathetically set forth it would tap many strange, beautiful qualities in obscure men. It is a job for a poet. In Winesburg the hands had attracted attention merely because of their activity. With them Wing Biddlebaum had picked as high as a hundred and forty quarts of strawberries in a day. They became his distinguishing feature, the source of his fame. Also they made more grotesque an already grotesque and elusive individuality. Winesburg was proud of the hands of Wing Biddlebaum in the same spirit in which it was proud of Banker White's new stone house and Wesley Moyer's bay stallion, Tony Tip, that had won the two-fifteen trot at the fall races in Cleveland.

As for George Willard, he had many times wanted to ask about the hands. At times an almost overwhelming curiosity had taken hold of him. He felt that there must be a reason for their strange activity and their inclination to keep hidden away and only a growing respect for Wing Biddlebaum kept him from blurting out the questions that were often in his mind.

Once he had been on the point of asking. The two were walking in the fields on a summer afternoon and had stopped to sit upon a grassy bank. All afternoon Wing Biddlebaum had talked as one inspired. By a fence he had stopped and beating like a giant woodpecker upon the top board had shouted at George Willard, condemning his tendency to be too much influenced by the people about him. "You are destroying yourself," he cried. "You have the inclination to be alone and to dream and you are afraid of dreams. You want to be like others in town here. You hear them talk and you try to imitate them."

On the grassy bank Wing Biddlebaum had tried again to drive his point home. His voice became soft and reminiscent, and with a sigh of contentment he launched into a long rambling talk, speaking as one lost in a dream.

Out of the dream Wing Biddlebaum made a picture for George Willard. In the picture men lived again in a kind of pastoral golden age. Across a green open country came clean-limbed young men, some afoot, some mounted upon horses. In crowds the young men came to gather about the feet of an old man who sat beneath a tree in a tiny garden and who talked to them.

Wing Biddlebaum became wholly inspired. For once he forgot the hands. Slowly they stole forth and lay upon George Willard's shoulders. Something new and bold came into the voice that talked. "You must try to forget all you have learned," said the old man. "You must begin to dream. From this time on you a must shut your ears to the roaring of the voices."

Pausing in his speech, Wing Biddlebaum looked long and earnestly at George Willard. His eyes glowed. Again he raised the hands to caress the boy and then a look of horror swept over his face.

With a convulsive movement of his body, Wing Biddlebaum sprang to his feet and thrust his hands deep into his trousers pockets. Tears came to his eyes. "I must be getting along home. I can talk no more with you," he said nervously.

Without looking back, the old man had hurried down the hillside and across a meadow, leaving George Willard perplexed and frightened upon the grassy slope. With a shiver of dread the boy arose and went along the road toward town. "I'll not ask him about his hands," he thought, touched by the memory of the terror he had seen in the man's eyes. "There's something wrong, but I don't want to know what it is. His hands have something to do with his fear of me and of everyone."

And George Willard was right. Let us look briefly into the story of the hands. Perhaps our talking of them will arouse the poet who will tell the hidden wonder story of the influence for which the hands were but fluttering pennants of promise.

In his youth Wing Biddlebaum had been a schoolteacher in a town in Pennsylvania. He was not then known as Wing Biddlebaum, but went by the less euphonic name of Adolph Myers. As Adolph Myers he was much loved by the boys of his school.

Adolph Myers was meant by nature to be a teacher of youth. He was one of those rare, little-understood men who rule by a power so gentle that it passes as a lovable weakness. In their feeling for the boys under their charge such men are not unlike the finer sort of women in their love of men.

And yet that is but crudely stated. It needs the poet there. With the boys of his school, Adolph Myers had walked in the evening or had sat talking until dusk upon the schoolhouse steps lost in a kind of dream. Here and there went his hands, caressing the shoulders of the boys, playing about the tousled heads. As he talked his voice became soft and musical. There was a caress in that also. In a way the voice and the hands, the striking of the shoulders and the touching of the hair were a part of the schoolmaster's effort to carry a dream into the young minds. By the caress that was in his fingers he expressed himself. He was one of those men in whom the force that creates life is diffused, not centralized. Under the caress of his hands doubt and disbelief went out of the minds of the boys and they began also to dream.

And then the tragedy. A half-witted boy of the school became enamored of the young master. In his bed at night he imagined unspeakable things and in the morning went forth to tell his dreams as facts. Strange, hideous accusations fell from his loose-hung lips. Through the Pennsylvania town went a shiver. Hidden, shadowy doubts that had been in men's minds concerning Adolph Myers were galvanized into beliefs.

The tragedy did not linger. Trembling lads were jerked out of bed and questioned. "He put his arms about me," said one. "His fingers were always playing in my hair," said another.

One afternoon a man of the town, Henry Bradford, who kept a saloon, came to the schoolhouse door. Calling Adolph Myers into the school yard he began to beat him with his fists. As his hard knuckles beat down into the frightened face of the schoolmaster, his wrath became more and more terrible. Screaming with dismay, the children ran here and there like disturbed insects. "I'll teach you to put your hands on my boy, you beast," roared the saloon keeper, who, tired of beating the master, had begun to kick him about the yard.

Adolph Myers was driven from the Pennsylvania town in the night. With lanterns in their hands a dozen men came to the door of the house where he lived alone and commanded that he dress and come forth. It was raining and one of the men had a rope in his hands. They had intended to hang the schoolmaster, but something in his figure, so small, white, and pitiful, touched their hearts and they let him escape. As he ran away into the darkness they repented of their weakness and ran after him, swearing and throwing sticks and great balls of soft mud at the figure that screamed and ran faster and faster into the darkness.

For twenty years Adolph Myers had lived alone in Winesburg. He was but forty but looked sixty-five. The name of Biddlebaum he got from a box of goods seen at a freight station as he hurried through an eastern Ohio town. He had an aunt in Winesburg, a black-toothed old woman who raised chickens, and with her he lived until she died. He had been ill for a year after the experience in Pennsylvania, and after his recovery worked as a day laborer in the fields, going timidly about and striving to conceal his hands. Although he did not understand what had happened he felt that the hands must be to blame. Again and again the fathers of the boys had talked of the hands. "Keep your hands to yourself," the saloon keeper had roared, dancing with fury in the schoolhouse yard.

Upon the veranda of his house by the ravine, Wing Biddlebaum continued to walk up and down until the sun had disappeared and the road beyond the field was lost in the grey shadows. Going into his house he cut slices of bread and spread honey upon them. When the rumble of the evening train that took away the express cars loaded with the day's harvest of berries had passed and restored the silence of the summer night, he went again to walk upon the veranda. In the darkness he could not see the hands and they became quiet. Although he still hungered for the presence of the boy, who was the medium through which he expressed his love of man, the hunger became again a part of his loneliness and his waiting. Lighting a lamp, Wing Biddlebaum washed the few dishes soiled by his simple meal and, setting up a folding cot by the screen door that led to the porch, prepared to undress for the night. A few stray white bread crumbs lay on the cleanly washed floor by the table; putting the lamp upon a low stool he began to pick up the crumbs, carrying them to his mouth one by one with unbelievable rapidity, In the dense blotch of light beneath the table, the kneeling figure looked like a priest engaged in some service of his church. The nervous expressive fingers, flashing in and out of the light, might well have been mistaken for the fingers of the devotee going swiftly through decade after decade of his rosary.

The Untold Lie

Ray Pearson and Hal Winters were farm hands employed on a farm three miles north of Winesburg. On Saturday afternoons they came into town and wandered about through the streets with other fellows from the country.

Ray was a quiet, rather nervous man of perhaps fifty with a brown beard and shoulders rounded by too much and too hard labor. In his nature he was as unlike Hal Winters as two men can be unlike.

Ray was an altogether serious man and had a little sharp-featured wife who had also a sharp voice. The two, with half a dozen thin-legged children, lived in a tumbledown frame house beside a creek at the back end of the Wills farm where Ray was employed.

Hal Winters, his fellow employee, was a young fellow. He was not of the Ned Winters family, who were very respectable people in Winesburg, but was one of the three sons of the old man called Windpeter Winters who had a sawmill near Unionville, six miles away, and who was looked upon by everyone in Winesburg as a confirmed old reprobate.

People from the part of Northern Ohio in which Winesburg lies will remember old Windpeter by his unusual and tragic death. He got drunk one evening in town and started to drive home to Unionville along the railroad tracks. Henry Brattenburg, the butcher, who lived out that way, stopped him at the edge of the town and told him he was sure to meet the down train but Windpeter slashed at him with his whip and drove on. When the train struck and killed him and his two horses a farmer and his wife who were driving home along a nearby road saw the accident. They said that old Windpeter stood up on the seat of his wagon, raving and swearing at the onrushing locomotive, and that he fairly screamed with delight when the team, maddened by his incessant slashing at them, rushed straight ahead to certain death. Boys like young George Willard and Seth Richmond will remember the incident quite vividly because, although everyone in our town said that the old man would go straight to hell and that the community was better off without him, they had a secret conviction that he knew what he was doing and admired his foolish courage. Most boys have seasons of wishing they could die gloriously instead of just being grocery clerks and going on with their humdrum lives.

But this is not the story of Windpeter Winters nor yet of his son Hal who worked on the Wills farm with Ray Pearson. It is Ray's story. It will, however, be necessary to talk a little of young Hal so that you will get into the spirit of it.

Hal was a bad one. Everyone said that. There were three of the Winters boys in that family, John, Hal, and Edward, all broad-shouldered big fellows like old Windpeter himself and all fighters and woman-chasers and generally all-around bad ones.

Hal was the worst of the lot and always up to some devilment. He once stole a load of boards from his father's mill and sold them in Winesburg. With the money he bought himself a suit of cheap, flashy clothes. Then he got drunk and when his father came raving into town to find him, they met and fought with their fists on Main Street and were arrested and put into jail together.

Hal went to work on the Wills farm because there was a country schoolteacher out that way who had taken his fancy. He was only twenty-two then but had already been in two or three of what were spoken of in Winesburg as "women scrapes." Everyone who heard of his infatuation for the schoolteacher was sure it would turn out badly. "He'll only get her into trouble, you'll see," was the word that went around.

And so these two men, Ray and Hal, were at work in a field on a day in the late October. They were husking corn and occasionally something was said and they laughed. Then came silence. Ray, who was the more sensitive and always minded things more, had chapped hands and they hurt. He put them into his coat pockets and looked away across the fields. He was in a sad, distracted mood and was affected by the beauty of the country. If you knew the Winesburg country in the fall and how the low hills are all splashed with yellows and reds you would understand his feeling. He began to think of the time, long ago when he was a young fellow living with his father, then a baker in Winesburg, and how on such days he had wandered away to the woods to gather nuts, hunt rabbits, or just to loaf about and smoke his pipe. His marriage had come about through one of his days of wandering. He had induced a girl who waited on trade in his father's shop to go with him and something had happened. He was thinking of that afternoon and how it had affected his whole life when a spirit of protest awoke in him. He had forgotten about Hal and muttered words. "Tricked by Gad, that's what I was, tricked by life and made a fool of," he said in a low voice.

As though understanding his thoughts, Hal Winters spoke up. "Well, has it been worth while? What about it, eh? What about marriage and all that?" he asked and then laughed. Hal tried to keep on laughing but he too was in an earnest mood. He began to talk earnestly. "Has a fellow got to do it?" he asked. "Has he got to be harnessed up and driven through life like a horse?"

Hal didn't wait for an answer but sprang to his feet and began to walk back and forth between the corn shocks. He was getting more and more excited. Bending down suddenly he picked up an ear of the yellow corn and threw it at the fence. "I've got Nell Gunther in trouble," he said. "I'm telling you, but you keep your mouth shut."

Ray Pearson arose and stood staring. He was almost a foot shorter than Hal, and when the younger man came and put his two hands on the older man's shoulders they made a picture. There they stood in the big empty field with the quiet corn shocks standing in rows behind them and the red and yellow hills in the distance, and from being just two indifferent workmen they had become all alive to each other. Hal sensed it and because that was his way he laughed. "Well, old daddy," he said awkwardly, "come on, advise me. I've got Nell in trouble. Perhaps you've been in the same fix yourself. I know what everyone would say is the right thing to do, but what do you say? Shall I marry and settle down? Shall I put myself into the harness to be worn out like an old horse? You know me, Ray. There can't any-one break me but I can break myself. Shall I do it or shall I tell Nell to go to the devil? Come on, you tell me. Whatever you say, Ray, I'll do."

Ray couldn't answer. He shook Hal's hands loose and turning walked straight away toward the barn. He was a sensitive man and there were tears in his eyes. He knew there was only one thing to say to Hal Winters, son of old Windpeter Winters, only one thing that all his own training and all the beliefs of the people he knew would approve, but for his life he couldn't say what he knew he should say.

At half-past four that afternoon Ray was puttering about the barn-yard when his wife came up the lane along the creek and called him. After the talk with Hal he hadn't returned to the cornfield but worked about the barn. He had already done the evening chores and had seen Hal, dressed and ready for a roistering night in town, come out of the farmhouse and go into the road. Along the path to his own house he trudged behind his wife, looking at the ground and thinking. He couldn't make out what was wrong. Every time he raised his eyes and saw the beauty of the country in the failing light he wanted to do something he had never done before, shout or scream or hit his wife with his fists or something equally unexpected and terrifying. Along the path he went scratching his head and trying to make it out. He looked hard at his wife's back but she seemed all right.

She only wanted him to go into town for groceries and as soon as she had told him what she wanted began to scold. "You're always puttering," she said. "Now I want you to hustle. There isn't anything in the house for supper and you've got to get to town and back in a hurry."

Ray went into his own house and took an overcoat from a hook back of the door. It was torn about the pockets and the collar was shiny. His wife went into the bedroom and presently came out with a soiled cloth in one hand and three silver dollars in the other. Some-where in the house a child wept bitterly and a dog that had been sleeping by the stove arose and yawned. Again the wife scolded. "The children will cry and cry. Why are you always puttering?" she asked.

Ray went out of the house and climbed the fence into a field. It was just growing dark and the scene that lay before him was lovely. All the low hills were washed with color and even the little clusters of bushes in the corners by the fences were alive with beauty. The whole world seemed to Ray Pearson to have become alive with something just as he and Hal had suddenly become alive when they stood in the corn field staring into each other's eyes.

The beauty of the country about Winesburg was too much for Ray on that fall evening. That is all there was to it. He could not stand it. Of a sudden he forgot all about being a quiet old farm hand and throwing off the torn overcoat began to run across the field. As he ran he shouted a protest against his life, against all life, against everything that makes life ugly. "There was no promise made," he cried into the empty spaces that lay about him. "I didn't promise my Minnie anything and Hal hasn't made any promise to Nell. I know he hasn't. She went into the woods with him because she wanted to go. What he wanted she wanted. Why should I pay? Why should Hal pay? Why should anyone pay? I don't want Hal to become old and worn out. I'll tell him. I won't let it go on. I'll catch Hal before he gets to town and I'll tell him."

Ray ran clumsily and once he stumbled and fell down. "I must catch Hal and tell him," he kept thinking, and although his breath came in gasps he kept running harder and harder. As he ran he thought of things that hadn't come into his mind for years—how at the time he married he had planned to go west to his uncle in Portland, Oregon—how he hadn't wanted to be a farm hand, but had thought when he got out West he would go to sea and be a sailor or get a job on a ranch and ride a horse into Western towns, shouting and laughing and waking the people in the houses with his wild cries. Then as he ran he remembered his children and in fancy felt their hands clutching at him. All of his thoughts of himself were involved with the thoughts of Hal and he thought the children were clutching at the younger man also. "They are the accidents of life, Hal," he cried. "They are not mine or yours. I had nothing to do with them."

Darkness began to spread over the fields as Ray Pearson ran on and on. His breath came in little sobs. When he came to the fence at the edge of the road and confronted Hal Winters, all dressed up and smoking a pipe as he walked jauntily along, he could not have told what he thought or what he wanted.

Ray Pearson lost his nerve and this is really the end of the story of what happened to him. It was almost dark when he got to the fence and he put his hands on the top bar and stood staring. Hal Winters jumped a ditch and coming up close to Ray put his hands into his pockets and laughed. He seemed to have lost his own sense of what had happened in the corn field and when he put up a strong hand and took hold of the lapel of Ray's coat he shook the old man as he might have shaken a dog that had misbehaved.

"You came to tell me, eh?" he said. "Well, never mind telling me anything. I'm not a coward and I've already made up my mind." He laughed again and jumped back across the ditch. "Nell ain't no fool," he said. "She didn't ask me to marry her. I want to marry her. I want to settle down and have kids."

Ray Pearson also laughed. He felt like laughing at himself and all the world.

As the form of Hal Winters disappeared in the dusk that lay over the road that led to Winesburg, he turned and walked slowly back across the fields to where he had left his torn overcoat. As he went some memory of pleasant evenings spent with the thin-legged children in the tumble-down house by the creek must have come into his mind, for he muttered words. "It's just as well. Whatever I told him would have been a lie," he said softly, and then his form also disappeared into the darkness of the fields.

The Sad Horn Blowers

It had been a disastrous year in Will's family. The Appletons lived on one of the outlying streets of Bidwell, and Will's father was a house painter. In early February, when there was deep snow on the ground, and a cold bitter wind blew about the houses, Will's mother suddenly died. He was seventeen years old then, and rather a big fellow for his age.

The mother's death happened abruptly, without warning, as a sleepy man kills a fly with the hand in a warm room on a summer day. On one February day there she was coming in at the kitchen door of the Appletons' house, from hanging the wash out on the line in the back yard, and warming her long hands, covered with blue veins, by holding them over the kitchen stove—and then looking about at the children with that half-hidden, shy smile of hers—there she was like that, as the three children had always known her, and then, but a week later, she was cold in death and lying in her coffin in the place vaguely spoken of in the family as "the other room."

After that, and when summer came and the family was trying hard to adjust itself to the new conditions, there came another disaster. Up to the very moment when it happened it looked as though Tom Appleton the house painter was in for a prosperous season. The two boys, Fred and Will, were to be his assistants that year.

To be sure, Fred was only fifteen, but he was one to lend a quick alert hand at almost any undertaking. For example, when there was a job of paper hanging to be done, he was the fellow to spread on the paste, helped by an occasional sharp word from his father.

Down off his stepladder Tom Appleton hopped and ran to the long board where the paper was spread out. He liked this business of having two assistants about. Well, you see, one had the feeling of being at the head of something, of managing affairs. He grabbed the paste brush out of Fred's hand. "Don't spare the paste," he shouted. "Slap her on like this. Spread her out—so. Do be sure to catch all the edges."

It was all very warm, and comfortable, and nice, working at paper-hanging jobs in the houses on the March and April days. When it was cold or rainy outside, stoves were set up in the new houses being built, and in houses already inhabited the folks moved out of the rooms to be papered, spread newspapers on the floors over the carpets and put sheets over the furniture left in the rooms. Outside it rained or snowed, but inside it was warm and cozy.

To the Appletons it seemed, at the time, as though the death of the mother had drawn them closer together. Both Will and Fred felt it, perhaps Will the more consciously. The family was rather in the hole financially—the mother's funeral had cost a good deal of money, and Fred was being allowed to stay out of school. That pleased him. When they worked in a house where there were other children, they came home from school in the late afternoon and looked in through the door to where Fred was spreading paste over the sheets of wallpaper. He made a slapping sound with the brush, but did not look at them. Ah, go on, you kids, he thought. This was a man's business he was up to. Will and his father were on the stepladders, putting the sheets carefully into place on the ceilings and walls.

"Does she match down there?" the father asked sharply. "O.K., go ahead," Will replied. When the sheet was in place Fred ran and rolled out the laps with a little wooden roller. How jealous the kids of the house were. It would be a long time before any of them could stay out of school and do a man's work, as Fred was doing.

And then in the evening, walking homeward, it was nice, too. Will and Fred had been provided with suits of white overalls that were now covered with dried paste and spots of paint and looked really professional. They kept them on and drew their overcoats on over them. Their hands were stiff with paste, too. On Main Street the lights were lighted, and other men passing called to Tom Appleton. He was called Tony in the town. "Hello, Tony!" some storekeeper shouted. It was rather too bad, Will thought, that his father hadn't more dignity. He was too boyish. Young boys growing up and merging into manhood do not fancy fathers being too boyish. Tom Appleton played a cornet in the Bidwell Silver Cornet Band and didn't do the job very well—rather made a mess of it, when there was a bit of solo work to be done—but was so well liked by the other members of the band that no one said anything. And then he talked so grandly about music, and about the lip of a cornet player, that everyone thought he must be all right. "He has an education. I tell you what, Tony Appleton knows a lot. He's a smart one," the other members of the band were always saying to each other.

"Well, the devil! A man should grow up after a time, perhaps. When a man's wife had died but such a short time before, it was just as well to walk through Main Street with more dignity—for the time being, anyway."

Tom Appleton had a way of winking at men he passed in the street, as though to say, "Well, now I've got my kids with me, and we won't say anything, but didn't you and I have the very hell of a time last Wednesday night, eh? Mum's the word, old pal. Keep everything quiet. There are gay times ahead for you and me. We'll cut loose, you bet, when you and me are out together next time."

Will grew a little angry about something he couldn't exactly understand. His father stopped in front of Jake Mann's meat market. "You kids go along home. Tell Kate I am bringing a steak. I'll be right on your heels," he said.

He would get the steak and then he would go into Alf Geiger's saloon and get a good stiff drink of whisky. There would be no one now to bother about smelling it on his breath when he got home later. Not that his wife had ever said anything when he wanted a drink—but you know how a man feels when there's a woman in the house. "Why, hello, Bildad Smith, how's the old game leg? Come on, have a little nip with me. Were you on Main Street last band meeting night and did you hear us do that new gallop? It's a humdinger. Turkey White did that trombone solo simply grand."

Will and Fred had got beyond Main Street now, and Will took a small pipe with a curved stem out of his overcoat pocket and lighted it. "I'll bet I could hang a ceiling without Father there at all, if only someone would give me a chance," he said. Now that his father was no longer present to embarrass him with his lack of dignity, he felt comfortable and happy. Also, it was something to be able to smoke a pipe without discomfiture. When Mother was alive she was always kissing a fellow when he came home at night, and then one had to be mighty careful about smoking. Now it was different. One had become a man and one accepted manhood with its responsibilities. "Don't it make you sick at all?" Fred asked. "Huh, naw!" Will answered contemptuously.

The new disaster to the family came late in August, just when the fall work was all ahead, and the prospects good too. A. P. Wrigley, the jeweler, had just built a big new house and barn on a farm he had bought the year before. It was a mile out of town on the Turner Pike.

That would be a job to set the Appletons up for the winter. The house was to have three coats outside, with all the work inside, and the barn was to have two coats—and the two boys were to work with their father and were to have regular wages.

And just to think of the work to be done inside that house made Tom Appleton's mouth water. He talked of it all the time, and in the evenings liked to sit in a chair in the Appletons' front yard, get some neighbor over, and then go on about it. How he slung housepainter's lingo about! The doors and cupboards were to be grained in imitation of weathered oak, the front door was to be curly maple, and there was to be black walnut, too. Well, there wasn't another painter in the town could imitate all the various kinds of wood as Tom could. Just show him the wood, or tell him—you didn't have to show him anything. Name what you wanted—that was enough. To be sure, a man had to have the right tools, but give him the tools and then just go off and leave everything to him.

What the devil! When A. P. Wrigley gave him this new house to do, he showed he was a man who knew what he was doing.

As for the practical side of the matter, everyone in the family knew that the Wrigley job meant a safe winter. There wasn't any speculation, as when taking work on the contract plan. All work was to be paid for by the day, and the boys were to have their wages, too. It meant new suits for the boys, a new dress and maybe a hat for Kate, the house rent paid all winter, potatoes in the cellar. It meant safety—that was the truth.

In the evenings, sometimes, Tom got out his tools and looked at them. Brushes and graining tools were spread out on the kitchen table, and Kate and the boys gathered about. It was Fred's job to see that all brushes were kept clean and, one by one, Tom ran his fingers over them and then worked them back and forth over the palm of his hand. "This is a camel's hair," he said, picking a soft fine-haired brush up and handing it to Will. "I paid four dollars and eighty cents for that." Will also worked it back and forth over the palm of his hand, just as his father had done and then Kate picked it up and did the same thing. "It's as soft as the cat's back," she said. Will thought that rather silly. He looked forward to the day when he would have brushes, ladders and pots of his own, and could show them off before people, and through his mind went words he had picked up from his father's talk. One spoke of the "heel" and "toe" of a brush. The way to put on varnish was to "flow" it on. Will knew all the words of his trade now and didn't have to talk like one of the kind of muts who just does, now and then, a jack job of house painting.

On the fatal evening a surprise party was held for Mr. and Mrs. Bardshare, who lived just across the road from the Appletons on Piety Hill. That was a chance for Tom Appleton. In any such affair he liked to have a hand in the arrangements. "Come on now, we'll make her go with a bang. They'll be setting in the house after supper, and Bill Bardshare will be in his stocking feet, and Ma Bardshare washing the dishes. They won't be expecting nothing, and we'll slip up, all dressed in our Sunday clothes, and let out a whoop. I'll bring my cornet and let out a blast on that too. 'What in Sam Hill is that?' Say, I can just see Bill Bardshare jumping up and beginning to swear, thinking we're a gang of kids come to bother him, like Hallowe'en, or something like that. You just get the grub, and I'll make the coffee over to my house and bring it over hot. I'll get ahold of two big pots and make a whooping lot of it."

In the Appleton house all was in a flurry. Tom, Will and Fred were painting a barn, three miles out of town, but they knocked off work at four and Tom got the farmer's son to drive them to town. He himself had to wash up, take a bath in a tub in the woodshed, shave and everything—just like Sunday. He looked more like a boy than a man when he got all dogged up.

And then the family had to have supper, over and done with, a little after six, and Tom didn't dare go outside the house until dark. It wouldn't do to have the Bardshares see him so fixed up. It was their wedding anniversary, and they might suspect something. He kept trotting about the house, and occasionally looked out of the front window toward the Bardshare house. "You kid, you," Kate said, laughing. Sometimes she talked up to him like that, and after she said it he went upstairs, and getting out his cornet blew on it, so softly, you could hardly hear him downstairs. When he did that you couldn't tell how badly he played, as when the band was going it on Main Street and he had to carry a passage right through alone. He sat in the room upstairs thinking. When Kate laughed at him it was like having his wife back, alive. There was the same shy sarcastic gleam in her eyes.

Well, it was the first time he had been out anywhere since his wife had died, and there might be some people think it would be better if he stayed at home now—look better, that is. When he had shaved he had cut his chin, and the blood had come. After a time he went downstairs and stood before the looking glass, hung above the kitchen sink, and dabbed at the spot with the wet end of a towel.

Will and Fred stood about.

Will's mind was working—perhaps Kate's, too. "Was there—could it be?—well, at such a party—only older people invited—there were always two or three widow women thrown in for good measure, as it were."

Kate didn't want any woman fooling around her kitchen. She was twenty years old.

"And it was just as well not to have any monkeyshine talk about motherless children," such as Tom might indulge in. Even Fred thought that. There was a little wave of resentment against Tom in the house. It was a wave that didn't make much noise, just crept, as it were softly, up a low sandy beach.

"Widow women went to such places, and then of course, people were always going home in couples." Both Kate and Will had the same picture in mind. It was late at night and in fancy they were both peeking out at front upper windows of the Appleton house. There were all the people coming out at the front door of the Bardshare house, and Bill Bardshare was standing there and holding the door open. He had managed to sneak away during the evening, and got his Sunday clothes on all right.

And the couples were coming out. "There was that woman now, that widow, Mrs. Childers." She had been married twice, both husbands dead now, and she lived away over Maumee Pike way. "What makes a woman of her age want to act silly like that? It is the very devil how a woman can keep looking young and handsome after she has buried two men. There are some who say that, even when her last husband was alive—"

"But whether that's true or not, what makes her want to act and talk silly that way?" Now her face is turned to the light and she is saying to old Bill Bardshare, "Sleep light, sleep tight, sweet dreams to you tonight."

"It's only what one may expect when one's father lacks a sense of dignity. There is that old fool Tom now, hopping out of the Bardshare house like a kid, and running right up to Mrs. Childers. 'May I see you home?' he is saying, while all the others are laughing and smiling knowingly. It makes one's blood run cold to see such a thing."

"Well, fill up the pots. Let's get the old coffee pots started, Kate. The gang'll be creeping along up the street pretty soon now," Tom shouted self-consciously, skipping busily about and breaking the little circle of thoughts in the house.

What happened was that—just as darkness came and when all the people were in the front yard before the Appleton house—Tom went and got it into his head to try to carry his cornet and two big coffee pots at the same time. Why didn't he leave the coffee until later? There the people were in the dusk outside the house, and there was that kind of low whispering and tittering that always goes on at such a time—and then Tom stuck his head out at the door and shouted, "Let her go!"

And then he must have gone quite crazy, for he ran back into the kitchen and grabbed both of the big coffee pots, hanging on to his cornet at the same time. Of course he stumbled in the darkness in the road outside and fell, and of course all of that boiling hot coffee had to spill right over him.

It was terrible. The flood of boiling hot coffee made steam under his thick clothes, and there he lay screaming with the pain of it.

What a confusion! He just writhed and screamed, and the people ran round and round in the half darkness like crazy things. Was it some kind of joke the crazy fellow was up to at the last minute! Tom always was such a devil to think up things. "You should see him down at Alf Geiger's, sometimes on Saturday nights, imitating the way Joe Douglas got out on a limb, and then sawed it off between himself and the tree, and the look on Joe's face when the limb began to crack. It would make you laugh until you screamed to see him imitate that."

"But what now? My God!" There was Kate Appleton trying to tear her father's clothes off, and crying and whimpering, and young Will Appleton knocking people aside. "Say, the man's hurt! What's happened? My God! Run for the doctor, someone. He's burnt, something awful!"

Early in October Will Appleton sat in the smoking car of a day train that runs between Cleveland and Buffalo. His destination was Erie, Pennsylvania, and he had got on the passenger train at Ashtabula, Ohio. Just why his destination was Erie he couldn't very easily have explained. He was going there anyway, going to get a job in a factory or on the docks there. Perhaps it was just a quirk of the mind that had made him decide upon Erie. It wasn't as big as Cleveland or Buffalo or Toledo or Chicago, or any one of a lot of other cities to which he might have gone, looking for work.

At Ashtabula he came into the car and slid into a seat beside a little old man. His own clothes were wet and wrinkled, and his hair, eyebrows and ears were black with coal dust.

At the moment, there was in him a kind of bitter dislike of his native town, Bidwell. "Sakes alive, a man couldn't get any work there—not in the winter." After the accident to his father, and the spoiling of all the family plans, he had managed to find employment during September on the farms. He worked for a time with a threshing crew, and then got work cutting corn. It was all right. "A man made a dollar a day and board, and as he wore overalls all the time, he didn't wear out no clothes. Still and all, the time when a fellow could make any money in Bidwell was past now, and the burns on his father's body had gone pretty deep, and he might be laid up for months."

Will had just made up his mind one day, after he had tramped about all morning from farm to farm without finding work, and then he had gone home and told Kate. "Dang it all," he hadn't intended lighting out right away—had thought he would stay about for a week or two, maybe. Well, he would go up town in the evening, dressed up in his best clothes, and stand around. "Hello, Harry, what you going to do this winter? I thought I would run over to Erie, Pennsylvania. I got an offer in a factory over there. Well, so long—if I don't see you again."

Kate hadn't seemed to understand, had seemed in an almighty hurry about getting him off. It was a shame she couldn't have a little more heart. Still, Kate was all right—worried a good deal no doubt. After their talk she had just said, "Yes, I think that's best, you had better go," and had gone to change the bandages on Tom's legs and back. The father was sitting among pillows in a rocking chair in the front room.

Will went upstairs and put his things, overalls and a few shirts, into a bundle. Then he went downstairs and took a walk—went out along a road that led into the country, and stopped on a bridge. It was near a place where he and other kids used to come swimming on summer afternoons. A thought had come into his head. There was a young fellow worked in Pawsey's jewelry store came to see Kate sometimes on Sunday evenings and they went off to walk together. Did Kate want to get married? If she did, his going away now might be for good. He hadn't thought about that before. On that afternoon, and quite suddenly, all the world outside of Bidwell seemed huge and terrible to him and a few secret tears came into his eyes, but he managed to choke them back. For just a moment his mouth opened and closed queerly, like the mouth of a fish, when you take it out of the water and hold it in your hand.

When he returned to the house at suppertime things were better. He had left his bundle on a chair in the kitchen and Kate had wrapped it more carefully, and had put in a number of things he had forgotten. His father called him into the front room. "It's all right, Will. Every young fellow ought to take a whirl out in the world. I did it myself, at about your age," Tom had said, a little pompously.

Then supper was served, and there was apple pie. That was a luxury the Appletons had perhaps better not have indulged in at that time, but Will knew Kate had baked it during the afternoon—it might be as a way of showing him how she felt. Eating two large slices had rather set him up.

And then, before he realized how the time was slipping away, ten o'clock had come, and it was time for him to go. He was going to beat his way out of town on a freight train, and there was a local going toward Cleveland at ten o'clock. Fred had gone off to bed, and his father was asleep in the rocking chair in the front room. He had picked up his bundle, and Kate had put on her hat. "I'm going to see you off," she had said.

Will and Kate had walked in silence along the streets to where he was to wait, in the shadow of Whaley's Warehouse, until the freight came along. Later when he thought back over that evening he was glad that, although she was three years older, he was taller than Kate.

How vividly everything that happened later stayed in his mind. After the train came and he had crawled into an empty coal car, he sat hunched up in a corner. Overhead he could see the sky, and when the train stopped at towns there was always the chance the car in which he was concealed would be shoved into a siding, and left. The brakemen walked along the tracks beside the car shouting to each other and their lanterns made little splashes of light in the darkness.

"How black the sky!" After a time it began to rain. His suit would be in a pretty mess. After all a fellow couldn't come right out and ask his sister if she intended to marry. If Kate married, then his father would also marry again. It was all right for a young woman like Kate, but for a man of forty to think of marriage—the devil! Why didn't Tom Appleton have more dignity? After all, Fred was only a kid, and a new woman coming in to be his mother—that might be all right for a kid.

All during that night on the freight train Will had thought a good deal about marriage—rather vague thoughts—coming and going like birds flying in and out of a bush. It was all a matter—this business of man and woman—that did not touch him very closely—not yet. The matter of having a home—that was something else. A home was something at a fellow's back. When one went off to work all week at some farm, and at night maybe went into a strange room to sleep, there was always the Appleton house—floating, as it were, like a picture at the back of the mind—the Appleton house, and Kate moving about. She had been uptown and now had come home and was going up the stairs. Tom Appleton was fussing about in the kitchen. He liked a bite before he went off to bed for the night but presently he would go upstairs and into his own room. He liked to smoke his pipe before he slept and sometimes he got out his cornet and blew two or three soft sad notes.

At Cleveland Will had crawled off the freight train and had gone across the city in a streetcar. Workingmen were just going to the factories and he passed among them unnoticed. If his clothes were crumpled and soiled, their clothes weren't so fine. The workingmen were all silent, looking at the car floor, or out the car windows. Long rows of factories stood along the streets through which the car moved.

He had been lucky and had caught another freight out of a place called Collinswood at eight, but at Ashtabula had made up his mind it would be better to drop off the freight and take a passenger train. If he was to live in Erie it would be just as well to arrive, looking more like a gentleman and having paid his fare.

As he sat in the smoking car of the train he did not feel much like a gentleman. The coal dust had got into his hair and the rain had washed it in long dirty streaks down over his face. His clothes were badly soiled and wanted cleaning and brushing and the paper package, in which his overalls and shirts were tied, had become torn and dirty.

Outside the train window the sky was gray, and no doubt the night was going to turn cold. Perhaps there would be a cold rain.

It was an odd thing about the towns through which the train kept passing—all of the houses in all the towns looked cold and forbidding. "Dang it all." In Bidwell, before the night when his father got so badly burned being such a fool about old Bill Bardshare's party—all the houses had always seemed warm cozy places. When one was alone, one walked along the streets whistling. At night warm lights shone through the windows of the houses. "John Wyatt, the drayman, lives in that house. His wife has a wen on her neck. In that barn over there old Doctor Musgrave keeps his bony old white horse. The horse looks like the devil, but you bet he can go."

Will squirmed about on the car seat. The old man who sat beside him was small, almost as small as Fred, and he wore a queerlooking suit. The pants were brown, and the coat checked, gray and black. There was a small leather case on the floor at his feet.

Long before the man spoke Will knew what would happen. It was bound to turn out that such a fellow played a cornet. He was a man, old in years, but there was no dignity in him. Will remembered his father's marchings through the main street of Bidwell with the band. It was some great day, Fourth of July perhaps, and all the people were assembled and there was Tony Appleton, making a show of blowing his cornet at a great rate. Did all the people along the street know how badly he played, and was there a kind of conspiracy, that kept grown men from laughing at each other? In spite of the seriousness of his own situation a smile crept over Will's face.

The little man at his side smiled in return.

"Well," he began, not stopping for anything, but plunging headlong into a tale concerning some dissatisfaction he felt with life, "well, you see before you a man who is up against it, young fellow." The old man tried to laugh at his own words, but did not make much of a success of it. His lip trembled. "I got to go home like a dog, with my tail 'twixt my legs," he declared abruptly.

The old man balanced back and forth between two impulses. He had met a young man on a train, and hungered for companionship and one got oneself in with others by being jolly, a little gay perhaps. When one met a stranger on a train one told a story—"By the way, Mister, I heard a new one the other day—perhaps you haven't heard it? It's about the miner up in Alaska who hadn't seen a woman for years." One began in that way and then later perhaps spoke of oneself and one's affairs.

But the old man wanted to plunge at once into his own story. He talked, saying sad discouraged words, while his eyes kept smiling with a peculiar appealing little smile. "If the words uttered by my lips annoy or bore you, do not pay any attention to them. I am really a jolly fellow although I am an old man and not of much use any more," the eyes were saying. The eyes were pale blue and watery. How strange to see them set in the head of an old man. They belonged in the head of a lost dog. The smile was not really a smile. "Don't kick me, young fellow. If you can't give me anything to eat, scratch my head. At least show you are a fellow of good intentions. I've been kicked about quite enough." It was so very evident the eyes were speaking a language of their own.

Will found himself smiling sympathetically. It was true there was something doglike in the little old man and Will was pleased with himself for having so quickly caught the sense of him. "One who can see things with his eyes will perhaps get along all right in the world, after all," he thought. His thoughts wandered away from the old man. In Bidwell there was an old woman lived alone and owned a shepherd dog. Every summer she decided to cut away the dog's coat, and then—at the last moment and after she had in fact started the job—she changed her mind. Well, she grasped a long pair of scissors firmly in her hand and started on the dog's flanks. Her hand trembled a little. "Shall I go ahead, or shall I stop?" After two minutes she gave up the job. "It makes him look too ugly," she thought, justifying her timidity.

Later the hot days came, the dog went about with his tongue hanging out and again the old woman took the scissors in her hand. The dog stood patiently waiting but, when she had cut a long wide furrow through the thick hair of his back, she stopped again. In a sense, and to her way of looking at the matter, cutting away his splendid coat was like cutting away a part of himself. She couldn't go on. "Now there—that made him look worse than ever," she declared to herself. With a determined air she put the scissors away, and all summer the dog went about looking a little puzzled and ashamed.

Will kept smiling and thinking of the old woman's dog and then looked again at his companion of the train. The variegated suit the old man wore gave him something of the air of the half-sheared shepherd dog. Both had the same puzzled, ashamed air.

Now Will had begun using the old man for his own ends. There was something inside himself that wanted facing, he didn't want to face—not yet. Ever since he had left home, in fact ever since that day when he had come home from the country and had told Kate of his intention to set out into the world, he had been dodging something. If one thought of the little old man, and of the half-sheared dog, one did not have to think of oneself.

One thought of Bidwell on a summer afternoon. There was the old woman, who owned the dog, standing on the porch of her house, and the dog had run down to the gate. In the winter, when his coat had again fully grown, the dog would bark and make a great fuss about a boy passing in the street but now he started to bark and growl, and then stopped. "I look like the devil, and I'm attracting unnecessary attention to myself," the dog seemed to have decided suddenly. He ran furiously down to the gate, opened his mouth to bark, and then, quite abruptly, changed his mind and trotted back to the house with his tail between his legs.

Will kept smiling at his own thoughts. For the first time since he had left Bidwell he felt quite cheerful.

And now the old man was telling a story of himself and his life, but Will wasn't listening. Within the young man a crosscurrent of impulses had been set up and he was like one standing silently in the hallway of a house, and listening to two voices, talking at a distance. The voices came from two widely separated rooms of the house and one couldn't make up one's mind to which voice to listen.

To be sure, the old man was another cornet player like his father—he was a horn blower. That was his horn in the little worn leather case on the car floor.

And after he had reached middle age, and after his first wife had died, he had married again. He had a little property then and, in a foolish moment, went and made it all over to his second wife, who was fifteen years younger than himself. She took the money and bought a large house in the factory district of Erie, and then began taking in boarders.

There was the old man, feeling lost, of no account in his own house. It just came about. One had to think of the boarders—their wants had to be satisfied. His wife had two sons, almost fully grown now, both of whom worked in a factory.

Well, it was all right—everything on the square—the sons paid board all right. Their wants had to be thought of, too. He liked blowing his cornet a while in the evenings, before he went to bed, but it might disturb the others in the house. One got rather desperate going about saying nothing, keeping out of the way, and he had tried getting work in a factory himself, but they wouldn't have him. His gray hairs stood in his way, and so one night he had just got out, had gone to Cleveland, where he had hoped to get a job in a band, in a movie theatre perhaps. Anyway, it hadn't turned out, and now he was going back to Erie and to his wife. He had written and she had told him to come on home.

"They didn't turn me down back there in Cleveland because I'm old. It's because my lip is no good any more," he explained. His shrunken old lip trembled a little.

Will kept thinking of the old woman's dog. In spite of himself, and when the old man's lip trembled, his lip also trembled.

What was the matter with him?

He stood in the hallway of a house hearing two voices. Was he trying to close his ears to one of them? Did the second voice, the one he had been trying all day, and all the night before, not to hear, did that have something to do with the end of his life in the Appleton house at Bidwell? Was the voice trying to taunt him, trying to tell him that now he was a thing swinging in air, that there was no place to put down his feet? Was he afraid? Of what was he afraid? He had wanted so much to be a man, to stand on his own feet and now what was the matter with him? Was he afraid of manhood?

He was fighting desperately now. There were tears in the old man's eyes, and Will also began crying silently, and that was the one thing he felt he must not do.

The old man talked on and on, telling the tale of his troubles, but Will could not hear his words. The struggle within was becoming more and more definite. His mind clung to the life of his boyhood, to the life in the Appleton house in Bidwell.

There was Fred, standing in the field of his fancy now, with just the triumphant look in his eyes that came when other boys saw him doing a man's work. A whole series of pictures floated up before Will's mind. He and his father and Fred were painting a barn and two farmer boys had come along a road and stood looking at Fred, who was on a ladder, putting on paint. They shouted, but Fred wouldn't answer. There was a certain air Fred had—he slapped on the paint, and then turning his head, spat on the ground. Tom Appleton's eyes looked into Will's and there was a smile playing about the corners of the father's eyes and the son's eyes too. The father and his oldest son were like two men, two workmen, having a delicious little secret between them. They were both looking lovingly at Fred. "Bless him! He thinks he's a man already."

And now Tom Appleton was standing in the kitchen of his house, and his brushes were laid out on the kitchen table. Kate was rubbing a brush back and forth over the palm of her hand. "It's as soft as the cat's back," she was saying.

Something gripped at Will's throat. As in a dream, he saw his sister Kate walking off along the street on Sunday evening with that young fellow who clerked in the jewelry store. They were going to church. Her being with him meant—well, it perhaps meant the beginning of a new home—it meant the end of the Appleton home.

Will started to climb out of the seat beside the old man in the smoking car of the train. It had grown almost dark in the car. The old man was still talking, telling his tale over and over. "I might as well not have any home at all," he was saying. Was Will about to begin crying aloud on a train, in a strange place, before many strange men? He tried to speak, to make some commonplace remark, but his mouth only opened and closed like the mouth of a fish taken out of the water.

And now the train had run into a train shed, and it was quite dark. Will's hand clutched convulsively into the darkness and alighted upon the old man's shoulder.

Then suddenly, the train had stopped, and the two stood half embracing each other. The tears were quite evident in Will's eyes, when a brakeman lighted the overhead lamps in the car, but the luckiest thing in the world had happened. The old man, who had seen Will's tears, thought they were tears of sympathy for his own unfortunate position in life, and a look of gratitude came into his blue watery eyes. Well, this was something new in life for him, too. In one of the pauses, when he had first begun telling his tale, Will had said he was going to Erie to try to get work in some factory and now, as they got off the train, the old man clung to Will's arm. "You might as well come live at our house," he said. A look of hope flared up in the old man's eyes. If he could bring home with him, to his young wife, a new boarder, the gloom of his own home-coming would be somewhat lightened. "You come on. That's the best thing to do. You just come on with me to our house," he pleaded, clinging to Will.

Two weeks had passed and Will had, outwardly, and to the eyes of the people about him, settled into his new life as a factory hand at Erie, Pennsylvania.

Then suddenly, on a Saturday evening, the thing happened that he had unconsciously been expecting and dreading ever since the moment when he climbed aboard the freight train in the shadow of Whaley's Warehouse at Bidwell. A letter, containing great news, had come from Kate.

At the moment of their parting, and before he settled himself down out of sight in a corner of the empty coal car, on that night of his leaving, he had leaned out for a last look at his sister. She had been standing silently in the shadows of the warehouse but, just as the train was about to start, stepped toward him and a light from a distant street lamp fell on her face.

Well, the face did not jump toward Will, but remained dimly outlined in the uncertain light.

Did her lips open and close, as though in an effort to say something to him, or was that an effect produced by the distant, uncertain and wavering light? In the families of working people the dramatic and vital moments of life are passed over in silence. Even in the moments of death and birth, little is said. A child is born to a laborer's wife and he goes into the room. She is in bed with the little red bundle of new life beside her and her husband stands a moment, fumblingly, beside the bed. Neither he nor his wife can look directly into each other's eyes. "Take care of yourself, Ma. Have a good rest," he says, and hurries out of the room.

In the darkness by the warehouse at Bidwell Kate had taken two or three steps toward Will and then had stopped. There was a little strip of grass between the warehouse and the tracks, and she stood upon it. Was there a more final farewell trembling on her lips at the moment? A kind of dread had swept over Will, and no doubt Kate had felt the same thing. At the moment she had become altogether the mother, in the presence of her child, and the thing within that wanted utterance became submerged. There was a word to be said that she could not say. Her form seemed to sway a little in the darkness and, to Will's eyes, she became a slender indistinct thing. "Good-bye," he had whispered into the darkness, and perhaps her lips had formed the same words. Outwardly there had been only the silence, and in the silence she had stood as the train rumbled away.

And now, on the Saturday evening, Will had come home from the factory and had found Kate saying in the letter what she had been unable to say on the night of his departure. The factory closed at five on Saturday and he came home in his overalls and went to his room. He had found the letter on a little broken table under a spluttering oil lamp, by the front door, and had climbed the stairs carrying it in his hand. He read the letter anxiously, waiting as for a hand to come out of the blank wall of the room and strike.

His father was getting better. The deep burns that had taken such a long time to heal were really healing now and the doctor had said the danger of infection had passed. Kate had found a new and soothing remedy. One took slippery elm and let it lie in milk until it became soft. This applied to the burns enabled Tom to sleep better at night.

As for Fred, Kate and her father had decided he might as well go back to school. It was really too bad for a young boy to miss the chance to get an education, and anyway there was no work to be had. Perhaps he could get a job, helping in some store on Saturday afternoons.

A woman from the Woman's Relief Corps had had the nerve to come to the Appleton house and ask Kate if the family needed help. Well, Kate had managed to hold herself back and had been polite, but had the woman known what was in her mind her ears would have been itching for a month. The idea!

It had been fine of Will to send a postcard as soon as he had got to Erie and got a job. As for his sending money home—of course the family would be glad to have anything he could spare—but he wasn't to go depriving himself. "We've got good credit at the stores. We'll get along all right," Kate had said stoutly.

And then it was she had added the line, had said the thing she could not say that night when he was leaving. It concerned herself and her future plans. "That night when you were going away I wanted to tell you something, but I thought it was silly, talking too soon." After all though, Will might as well know she was planning to be married in the spring. What she wanted was for Fred to come and live with her and her husband. He could keep on going to school, and perhaps they could manage so that he could go to college. Someone in the family ought to have a decent education. Now that Will had made his start in life, there was no point in waiting longer before making her own.

Will sat, in his tiny room at the top of the huge frame house, owned now by the wife of the old cornet player of the train, and held the letter in his hand. The room was on the third floor, under the roof, in a wing of the house, and beside it was another small room, occupied by the old man himself. Will had taken the room because it was to be had at a low price and he could manage the room and his meals, get his washing done, send three dollars a week to Kate, and still have left a dollar a week to spend. One could get a little tobacco, and now and then see a movie.

"Ugh!" Will's lips made a little grunting noise as he read Kate's words. He was sitting in a chair, in his oily overalls, and where his fingers gripped the white sheets of the letter there was a little oily smudge. Also his hand trembled a little. He got up, poured water out of a pitcher into a white bowl, and began washing his face and hands.

When he had partly dressed, a visitor came. There was the shuffling sound of weary feet along a hallway, and the cornet player put his head timidly in at the door. The doglike appealing look Will had noted on the train was still in his eyes. Now he was planning something, a kind of gentle revolt against his wife's power in the house, and he wanted Will's moral support.

For a week he had been coming for talk to Will's room almost every evening. There were two things he wanted. In the evening sometimes, as he sat in his room, he wanted to blow upon his cornet, and he wanted a little money to jingle in his pockets.

And there was a sense in which Will, the newcomer in the house, was his property, did not belong to his wife. Often in the evenings he had talked to the weary and sleepy young workman, until Will's eyes had closed and he snored gently. The old man sat on the one chair in the room, and Will sat on the edge of the bed, while old lips told the tale of a lost youth, boasted a little. When Will's body had slumped down upon the bed the old man got to his feet and moved with cat-like steps about the room. One mustn't raise the voice too loudly after all. Had Will gone to sleep? The cornet player threw his shoulders back and bold words came, in a half-whisper, from his lips. To tell the truth, he had been a fool about the money he had made over to his wife and, if his wife had taken advantage of him, it wasn't her fault. For his present position in life he had no one to blame but himself. What from the very beginning he had most lacked was boldness. It was a man's duty to be a man and, for a long time, he had been thinking—well the boardinghouse no doubt made a profit and he should have his share. His wife was a good girl all right, but when one came right down to it, all women seemed to lack a sense of a man's position in life.

"I'll have to speak to her—yes sirree, I'm going to speak right up to her. I may have to be a little harsh, but it's my money runs this house, and I want my share of the profits. No foolishness now. Shell out, I tell you," the old man whispered, peering out of the corners of his blue, watery eyes at the sleeping form of the young man on the bed.

And now again the old man stood at the door of the room, looking anxiously in. A bell called insistently, announcing that the evening meal was ready to be served, and they went below, Will leading the way. At a long table in the dining room several men had already gathered, and there was the sound of more footsteps on the stairs.

Two long rows of young workmen eating silently. Saturday night and two long rows of young workmen eating in silence.

After the eating, and on this particular night, there would be a swift flight of all these young men down into the town, down into the lighted parts of the town.

Will sat at his place gripping the sides of his chair.

There were things men did on Saturday nights. Work was at an end for the week, and money jingled in pockets. Young workmen ate in silence and hurried away, one by one, down into the town.

Will's sister Kate was going to be married in the spring. Her walking about with the young clerk from the jewelry store, in the streets of Bidwell, had come to something.

Young workmen employed in factories in Erie, Pennsylvania, dressed themselves in their best clothes and walked about in the lighted streets of Erie on Saturday evenings. They went into parks. Some stood talking to girls, while others walked with girls through the streets. And there were still others who went into saloons and had drinks. Men stood talking together at a bar. "Dang that foreman of mine! I'll bust him in the jaw if he gives me any of his lip."

There was a young man from Bidwell, sitting at a table in a boardinghouse at Erie, Pennsylvania, and before him on a plate was a great pile of meat and potatoes. The room was not very well lighted. It was dark and gloomy, and there were black streaks on the gray wallpaper. Shadows played on the walls. On all sides of the young man sat other young men—eating silently, hurriedly.

Will got abruptly up from the table and started for the door that led into the street, but the others paid no attention to him. If he did not want to eat his meat and potatoes, it made no difference to them. The mistress of the house, the wife of the old cornet player, waited on table when the men ate, but now she had gone away to the kitchen. She was a silent grim-looking woman, dressed always in a black dress.

To the others in the room—except only the old cornet player—Will's going or staying meant nothing at all. He was a young workman, and at such places young workmen were always going and coming.

A man with broad shoulders and a black mustache, a little older than most of the others, did glance up from his business of eating. He nudged his neighbor, and then made a jerky movement with his thumb over his shoulder. "The new guy has hooked up quickly, eh?" he said, smiling. "He can't even wait to eat. Lordy, he's got an early date—some skirt waiting for him."

At his place, opposite where Will had been seated, the cornet player saw Will go, and his eyes followed, filled with alarm. He had counted on an evening of talk, of speaking to Will about his youth, boasting a little in his gentle hesitating way. Now Will had reached the door that led to the street, and in the old man's eyes tears began to gather. Again his lip trembled. Tears were always gathering in the man's eyes, and his lips trembled at the slightest provocation. It was no wonder he could no longer blow a cornet in a band.

And now Will was outside the house in the darkness and, for the cornet player, the evening was spoiled, the house a deserted, empty place. He had intended being very plain in his evening's talk with Will, and wanted particularly to speak of a new attitude he hoped to assume toward his wife in the matter of money. Talking the whole matter out with Will would give him new courage, make him bolder. Well, if his money had bought the house, that was now a boardinghouse, he should have some share in its profits. There must be profits. Why run a boardinghouse without profits? The woman he had married was no fool.

Even though a man was old, he needed a little money in his pockets. Well, an old man like himself has a friend, a young fellow, and now and then he wanted to be able to say to his friend, "Come on friend, let's have a glass of beer. I know a good place. Let's have a glass of beer and go to the movies. This is on me."

The cornet player could not eat his meat and potatoes. For a time he stared over the heads of the others, and then got up to go to his room. His wife followed into the little hallway at the foot of the stairs. "What's the matter, dearie—are you sick?" she asked.

"No," he answered, "I just didn't want any supper." He did not look at her, but tramped slowly and heavily up the stairs.

Will was walking hurriedly through streets but did not go down into the brightly lighted sections of town. The boardinghouse stood on a factory street and, turning northward, he crossed several railroad tracks and went toward the docks along the shore of Lake Erie. There was something to be settled with himself, something to be faced. Could he manage the matter?

He walked along, hurriedly at first, and then more slowly. It was getting into late October now, and there was a sharpness like frost in the air. The spaces between street lamps were long, and he plunged in and out of areas of darkness. Why was it that everything about him seemed suddenly strange and unreal? He had forgotten to bring his overcoat from Bidwell and would have to write Kate to send it.

Now he had almost reached the docks. Not only the night but his own body, the pavements under his feet and the stars far away in the sky—even the solid factory buildings he was now passing—seemed strange and unreal. It was almost as though one could thrust out an arm and push a hand through the walls, as one might push his hand into a fog or a cloud of smoke. All the people Will passed seemed strange and acted in a strange way. Dark figures surged toward him out of the darkness. By a factory wall there was a man standing—perfectly still, motionless. There was something almost unbelievable about the actions of such men and the strangeness of such hours as the one through which he was now passing. He walked within a few inches of the motionless man. Was it a man or a shadow on the wall? The life Will was now to lead alone had become a strange, a vast, terrifying thing. Perhaps all life was like that, a vastness and an emptiness.

He came out into a place where ships were made fast to a dock and stood for a time, facing the high wall-like side of a vessel. It looked dark and deserted. When he turned his head he became aware of a man and a woman passing along a roadway. Their feet made no sound in the thick dust of the roadway, and he could not see or hear them, but knew they were there. Some part of a woman's dress—something white—flashed faintly into view and the man's figure was a dark mass against the dark mass of the night.

"Oh, come on, don't be afraid," the man whispered, hoarsely. "There won't anything happen to you."

"Do shut up," a woman's voice answered, and there was a quick outburst of laughter. The figures fluttered away. "You don't know what you are talking about," the woman's voice said again.

Now that he had got Kate's letter, Will was no longer a boy. A boy is, quite naturally, and without his having anything to do with the matter, connected with something—and now that connection had been cut. He had been pushed out of the nest and that fact, the pushing of himself off the nest's rim, was something accomplished. The difficulty was that, while he was no longer a boy, he had not yet become a man. He was a thing swinging in space. There was no place to put down his feet.

He stood in the darkness under the shadow of the ship making queer little wriggling motions with his shoulders, that had become now almost the shoulders of a man. No need now to think of evenings at the Appleton house with Kate and Fred standing about, and his father, Tom Appleton, spreading his paint brushes on the kitchen table, no need of thinking of the sound of Kate's feet going up a stairway of the Appleton house, late at night when she had been out walking with her clerk. What was the good of trying to amuse oneself by thinking of a shepherd dog in an Ohio town, a dog made ridiculous by the trembling hand of a timid old woman?

One stood face to face with manhood now—one stood alone. If only one could get one's feet down upon something, could get over this feeling of falling through space, through a vast emptiness.

"Manhood"—the word had a queer sound in the head. What did it mean?

Will tried to think of himself as a man, doing a man's work in a factory. There was nothing in the factory where he was now employed upon which he could put down his feet. All day he stood at a machine and bored holes in pieces of iron. A boy brought to him the little, short, meaningless pieces of iron in a boxlike truck and, one by one, he picked them up and placed them under the point of a drill. He pulled a lever and the drill came down and bit into the piece of iron. A little, smokelike vapor arose, and then he squirted oil on the spot where the drill was working. Then the lever was thrown up again. The hole was drilled and now the meaningless pieces of iron was thrown into another boxlike truck. It had nothing to do with him. He had nothing to do with it.

At the noon hour, at the factory, one moved about a bit, stepped outside the factory door to stand for a moment in the sun. Inside, men were sitting along benches eating lunches out of dinner pails, and some had washed their hands while others had not bothered about such a trivial matter. They were eating in silence. A tall man spat on the floor and then drew his foot across the spot. Nights came, and one went home from the factory to eat, sitting with other silent men, and later a boastful old man came into one's room to talk. One lay on a bed and tried to listen, but presently fell asleep. Men were like the pieces of iron in which holes had been bored—one pitched them aside into a boxlike truck. One had nothing really to do with them. They had nothing to do with oneself. Life became a procession of days, and perhaps all life was just like that—just a procession of days.

"Manhood."

Did one go out of one place and into another? Were youth and manhood two houses in which one lived during different periods in life? It was evident something of importance must be about to happen to his sister Kate. First, she had been a young woman, having two brothers and a father, living with them in a house at Bidwell, Ohio.

And then a day was to come when she became something else. She married and went to live in another house and had a husband. Perhaps children would be born to her. It was evident that Kate had got hold of something, that her hands had reached out and had grasped something definite. Kate had swung herself off the rim of the home nest and, right away, her feet had landed on another limb of the tree of life—womanhood.

As he stood in the darkness something caught at Will's throat. He was fighting again, but what was he fighting? A fellow like himself did not move out of one house and into another. There was a house in which one lived, and then suddenly and unexpectedly, it fell apart. One stood on the rim of the nest and looked about, and a hand reached out from the warmth of the nest and pushed one off into space. There was no place for a fellow to put down his feet. He was one swinging in space.

What—a great fellow, nearly six feet tall now, and crying in the darkness, in the shadow of a ship, like a child! He walked, filled with determination, out of the darkness, along many streets of factories and came into a street of houses. He passed a store where groceries were sold and, looking in, saw by a clock on the wall that it was already ten o'clock. Two drunken men came out at the door of a house and stood on a little porch. One of them clung to a railing about the porch, and the other pulled at his arm. "Let me alone. It's settled. I want you to let me alone," grumbled the man clinging to the railing.

Will went to his boardinghouse and climbed the stairs wearily. The devil—one might face anything if one but knew what was to be faced!

He turned on a light and sat down in his room on the edge of the bed, and the old cornet player pounced upon him, pounced like a little animal lying under a bush along a path in a forest and waiting for food. He came into Will's room carrying his cornet, and there was an almost bold look in his eyes. Standing firmly on his old legs in the center of the room, he made a declaration. "I'm going to play it. I don't care what she says, I'm going to play it," he said.

He put the cornet to his lips and blew two or three notes—so softly that even Will, sitting so closely, could barely hear. Then his eyes wavered. "My lip's no good," he said. He thrust the cornet at Will. "You blow it," he said.

Will sat on the edge of the bed and smiled. There was a notion floating in his mind now. Was there something, a thought in which one could find comfort? There was now, before him, standing before him in the room, a man who was after all not a man. He was a child as Will was too, really, had always been such a child, would always be such a child. One need not be too afraid. Children were all about, everywhere. If one were a child and lost in a vast, empty space, one could at least talk to some other child. One could have conversations, understand perhaps something of the eternal childishness of oneself and others.

Will's thoughts were not very definite. He only felt suddenly warm and comfortable in the little room at the top of the boardinghouse.

And now the man was again explaining himself. He wanted to assert his manhood. "I stay up here," he explained, "and don't go down there, to sleep in the room with my wife because I don't want to. That's the only reason. I could if I wanted to. She has the bronchitis—but don't tell anyone. Women hate to have anyone told. She isn't so bad. I can do what I please."

He kept urging Will to put the cornet to his lips and blow. There was in him an intense eagerness. "You can't really make any music—you don't know how—but that don't make any difference," he said. "The thing to do is to make a noise, make a deuce of a racket, blow like the devil."

Again Will felt like crying but the sense of vastness and loneliness, that had been in him since he got aboard the train that night at Bidwell, had gone. "Well, I can't go on forever being a baby. Kate has a right to get married," he thought, putting the cornet to his lips. He blew two or three notes, softly.

"No, I tell you, no! That isn't the way! Blow on it! Don't be afraid! I tell you I want you to do it. Make a deuce of a racket! I tell you what, I own this house. We don't need to be afraid. We can do what we please. Go ahead! Make a deuce of a racket!" the old man kept pleading.

Joyce

1882 February 2. James Augustine Aloysius Joyce is born in Dublin, Ireland.

1904 Completes *Dubliners*. Leaves for Paris with Nora Barnacle. The following year their first child, Giorgio, is born in Trieste.

1907 Daughter Lucia is born. *Chamber Music*, a collection of poems, is published.

1912 Joyce travels to Dublin to fight for the publication of *Dubliners*; this would be his last trip to his native land.

1914 Through the influence of Ezra Pound, *Portrait of an Artist as a Young Man* is accepted for serial publication by the magazine *The Egoist*. *Dubliners* is published in June. Joyce begins work on *Ulysses* and completes the play *Exiles*.

1916 *Dubliners* and *Portrait* are published in New York.

1918 *Ulysses* begins to appear as a serial in *The Little Review*. A court order stops its ongoing publication in 1920 on the grounds of indecency.

1922 Amid bannings, burnings, and court actions, *Ulysses* is published in France. Joyce begins work on *Finnegan's Wake*.

1931 Joyce and Nora get married.

1939 *Finnegan's Wake* is published.

1941 January 13. After fleeing from war-torn France with his family, Joyce dies in Zurich from a perforated ulcer.

James Joyce

In the Victorian Age the young, virile and enterprising succumbed to the attraction of idealistic and materialistic agnosticisms. They despised parsons, heavy, cautious, dull-witted. They sang of the loss of faith with a brave attempt at lyric ecstasy. *Robert Elsmere* was a best seller. But no one reads *Robert Elsmere* now. So much that was new and exciting then is "weary, stale, flat and unprofitable."

The Way of All Flesh is a book with a certain permanent interest. Samuel Butler had the insight to see that Christian faith and morals form an integral whole. The easy cynicism at which Ernest in the end arrived is a constant creed, not a hotch-potch of Christian ideals and materialist politics. Nevertheless the Ernest Pontifexes, though not unknown in any age, are not very numerous today. Life is not smooth enough for them; two wars have undermined our sense of security.

James Joyce's novels, *A Portrait of the Artist as a Young Man,* and *Ulysses*, are also concerned with the loss of faith, but the gulf between Joyce and Butler lies deep. First of all there is the gulf between the Roman Catholic and the Protestant rebel. In *Ulysses:*

"You're not a believer, are you?" Haines asked. "I mean, a believer in the narrow sense of the word. Creation from nothing and miracles and a personal god."

"There's only one sense of the word, it seems to me." Stephen said. But there is also the gulf between the nineteenth and the twentieth century. Today for those who have believed in God and lost their belief there is nothing to believe in, nothing to love.

"Have you ever loved anyone?" Cranly asked. "I ask you if you ever felt love towards anyone or anything?"

Stephen walked on beside his friend, staring gloomily at the footpath. "I tried to love God," he said at length. "It seems now I failed. It is very difficult. I tried to unite my will with the will of God instant by instant. In that I did not always fail. I could perhaps do that still..."

Stephen Daedalus, who is Telemachus, who is Joyce, was brought up in a disorderly, improvident home. He was well educated at two Jesuit schools, but even in his early boyhood the restlessness that sprang from conflict between the disorder of his home and the order of his education led him into strange and sordid adventures. He repented. He became the devout model schoolboy. He was called, not only in the eyes of his superiors but in his own inner imagination, to complete self-dedication to the cause of God in the Society of Jesus. But when the time of decision came he rejected the call, not out of doubt as to his vocation, for the priesthood had been the ideal of his life, and he had no intellectual doubts, but because "The chill and order of the life repelled him." "A definite and irrevocable act of his threatened to end forever, in time and eternity, his freedom." His restlessness was "elusive of social or religious orders." *Non serviam*, I will not serve. And from that moment he knew that he would fall. "He felt the silent lapse of his soul, as it would be at some instant to come, falling, but yet not fallen, still unfallen, but about to fall."

He did fall. He lost his self-control. The picture of Stephen in the last chapters of *A Portrait*, and in *Ulysses* is the picture of an unbalanced mind, overshadowed by a great fear.

"I am sure he has an idée fixe," Haines said...Buck Milligan bent across the table gravely. "They drove his wits astray," he said, "by visions of hell. He will never capture the Attic note. The note of Swinburne, of all poets, the white death and the ruddy birth. That is his tragedy. He can never be a poet. The joy of creation..." "Eternal punishment," Haines said, nodding curtly. "I see. I tackled him this morning on belief. There was something on his mind, I saw."

What then did Joyce retain? Neither hope nor love, nor that faith which perfected in love holds fast to the object of faith and hope through all peril, but that faith which consists in orthodoxy of spiritual vision he still had. No other god, no other cause, no other ideal could fill the void in his heart where Christ was once.

"Et tu cum Jesu Galilaeo eras."

"And all hearts were touched and turned to her voice, shining like a young star, shining clearer as the voice intoned the proparoxyton and more faintly as the cadence died." "It is a curious thing, you know," Cranly said dispassionately, "how your mind is supersaturated with the religion in which you say you disbelieve."

But that mind was the mind of a deliberate artist, analyzing a situation and fashioning it into words. The man who spent ten years on his first full-length novel, seven years on his second, and seventeen on what was supposed to be his third, stands in the most startling contrast to such a man as D.H. Lawrence, writing as the spirit moved him, powerfully, passionately, sometimes carelessly. Joyce would call Lawrence a kinetic writer.

> The feelings excited by improper art are kinetic, desire or loathing. Desire urges us to possess, to go to something: loathing urges us to abandon, to go from something. The arts which excite them, pornographical or didactic, are therefore improper arts...The tragic emotion is static...Pity arrests the mind in the presence of whatsoever is grave and constant in human sufferings and unites it with the human sufferer. Terror is that which arrests the mind in the presence of whatsoever is grave and constant in human sufferings and unites it with the secret cause.

When we understand these two sentences, we begin to understand what Joyce is about. It is not propaganda, Catholic or anti-Catholic, nor is it any ordinary sense of the word autobiography. As the work proceeds Stephen diminishes in proportion to the size of the canvas. "The personality of the artist passes into the narration itself, flowing round and round the persons in the action like a vital sea." Stephen is the central figure of *A Portrait* ("lyrical"). In *Ulysses* (the "epical" novel) he will take second place. In *Finnegan's Wake* he has disappeared. He has become the rhythm and tempo of the book.

Mr. T.S. Eliot has told us that the more mature a poet's work is "the more distinct in him will be the mind that suffers and the mind that creates." In the strange case of James Joyce the mind that suffers endured the agonies of loss, while the mind that created remained essentially Catholic. The materials which go to make up *Ulysses* are clamped together in a Catholic framework of pity for human weakness and frailty, and terror of a judgment to come. The imagery is soaked in the language of the liturgy, of the breviary, of spiritual authors. Other elements are there, for the author has walked in many dark places. He lives in a coarse and cynical world, and vulgarity and cynicism are there. But these are in the picture. They are painted as they are. No illusory light is shed over them. There is nothing there which would excite desire in any normal person. There is much that would make the sensitive reader shudder, but in this world we are all called upon to suffer with the world and to share in the world's terror at the day of doom. In *Ulysses* "the prince of this world is judged." "The devils also believe, and tremble." They say "Alleluia, for the Lord God Omnipotent reigneth," though they do their best to say it backwards.

The mystery in Joyce is the continued vitality and orthodoxy of his vision, at least until the end of *Ulysses*. He succumbed to no heresy because he never stooped to justify himself. Stephen Daedalus said in *A Portrait of the Artist*: "I am not afraid to make a mistake, even a great mistake, a life-long mistake, and perhaps as long as eternity too." He said there, and again in *Ulysses*: "*Non-serviam*." This is all that Joyce could ever say, but in his rebellion he remained a witness to the creed he had rejected. In an obscure sense he did serve. Mr. Bethell is right when he call *Ulysses* "as nearly as possible a statement of experience from which all evaluation has been expelled." And yet Mr. Eliot was right when he called Joyce "the most ethically orthodox of the more eminent writers" of our time. There was no purpose in *Ulysses*, except to explain how and why there was nothing to say. But what values were implied were orthodox.

Finnegan's Wake revealed a sterility in this situation which was nothing like so obvious in the earlier books. The flaw in *Ulysses* as a work of art lies in the artificial association of Mr. Bloom's day in Dublin with the plot of the Odyssey. The classical and historical allusions are too much like an elaborate facade put up to conceal the negative nature of the theme. In *Finnegan's Wake*, as Dr. Leavis says "even in the best parts, we can never be unaware that the organization is eternal and mechanical." Joyce had explained why he had nothing to say, and he had acquired no new philosophy of his own. He was still interested in words and their possible mutations, so he strung them together on a string with some aid from Vico, Irish folk lore, and the river Laffrey. D.H. Lawrence called it:

> Nothing but old fags and cabbage stumps of quotations from the Bible and the rest, stewed in the juice of deliberate, journalistic dirty-mindedness—what old and hard-worked staleness, masquerading as the all new!

The comment is bitter, but is it not altogether unjust.

Yet even in this melancholy end Joyce remained an unwilling witness to the sterility of man when he has lost his creed, and cannot or will not either return to his starting point or find a valid alternative. The terrible verbal dexterity of his last work, a stream of consciousness, words without meaning, manipulated to "musical ends," deserves a comment from the very best of his early short stories, published in the volume called *Dubliners*. At the end of "The Dead" the protagonist says "Better pass boldly into that other world in the full glory of some passion, than fade and wither dismally with age." It is the awareness of "that other world,' of "the region where dwell the vast hosts of the dead,' that gives dignity to *Ulysses* and to *A Portrait of the Artist*, where at the very end the old man with "red rimmed horny eye" speaks of "the latter end of the world." The pity and the terror of *Ulysses* are the pity and terror of "The Dead".

—from "James Joyce" by George Every in The New Spirit *edited by E.W. Martin*

The Dead

Lily, the caretaker's daughter, was literally run off her feet. Hardly had she brought one gentleman into the little pantry behind the office on the ground floor and helped him off with his overcoat than the wheezy hall-door bell clanged again and she had to scamper along the bare hallway to let in another guest. It was well for her she had not to attend to the ladies also. But Miss Kate and Miss Julia had thought of that and had converted the bathroom upstairs into a ladies' dressing room. Miss Kate and Miss Julia were there, gossiping and laughing and fussing, walking after each other to the head of the stairs, peering down over the banisters and calling down to Lily to ask her who had come.

It was always a great affair, the Misses Morkan's annual dance. Everybody who knew them came to it, members of the family, old friends of the family, the members of Julia's choir, any of Kate's pupils that were grown up enough and even some of Mary Jane's pupils too. Never once had it fallen flat. For years and years it had gone off in splendid style as long as anyone could remember; ever since Kate and Julia, after the death of their brother Pat, had left the house in Stoney Batter and taken Mary Jane, their only niece, to live with them in the dark gaunt house on Usher's Island, the upper part of which they had rented from Mr Fulham, the cornfactor on the ground floor. That was a good thirty years ago if it was a day. Mary Jane, who was then a little girl in short clothes, was now the main prop of the household for she had the organ in Haddington Road. She had been through the Academy and gave a pupil's concert every year in the upper room of the Antient Concert Rooms. Many of her pupils belonged to better-class families on the Kingstown and Dalkey line. Old as they were, her aunts also did their share. Julia, though she was quite grey, was still the leading soprano in Adam and Eve's, and Kate, being too feeble to go about much, gave music lessons to beginners on the old square piano in the back room. Lily, the caretaker's daughter, did housemaid's work for them. Though their life was modest they believed in eating well; the best of everything: diamond-bone sirloins, three-shilling tea and the best bottled stout. But Lily seldom made a mistake in the orders so that she got on well with her three mistresses. They were fussy, that was all. But the only thing they would not stand was back answers.

Of course they had good reason to be fussy on such a night. And then it was long after ten o'clock and yet there was no sign of Gabriel and his wife. Besides they were dreadfully afraid that Freddy Malins might turn up screwed. They would not wish for worlds that any of Mary Jane's pupils should see him under the influence; and when he was like that it was sometimes very hard to manage him. Freddy Malins always came late but they wondered what could be keeping Gabriel: and that was what brought them every two minutes to the banisters to ask Lily had Gabriel or Freddy come.

—O, Mr. Conroy, said Lily to Gabriel when she opened the door for him, Miss Kate and Miss Julia thought you were never coming. Good-night, Mrs. Conroy.

—I'll engage they did, said Gabriel, but they forget that my wife here takes three mortal hours to dress herself.

He stood on the mat, scraping the snow from his goloshes, while Lily led his wife to the foot of the stairs and called out:

—Miss Kate, here's Mrs. Conroy.

Kate and Julia came toddling down the dark stairs at once. Both of them kissed Gabriel's wife, said she must be perished alive and asked was Gabriel with her.

—Here I am as right as the mail, Aunt Kate! Go on up. I'll follow, called out Gabriel from the dark.

He continued scraping his feet vigorously while the three women went upstairs, laughing, to the ladies' dressing room. A light fringe of snow lay like a cape on the shoulders of his overcoat and like toecaps on the toes of his goloshes; and, as the buttons of his overcoat slipped with a squeaking noise through the snow-stiffened frieze, a cold fragrant air from out-of-doors escaped from crevices and folds.

—Is it snowing again, Mr. Conroy? asked Lily.

She had preceded him into the pantry to help him off with his overcoat. Gabriel smiled at the three syllables she had given his surname and glanced at her. She was a slim, growing girl, pale in complexion and with hay-colored hair. The gas in the pantry made her look still paler. Gabriel had known her when she was a child and used to sit on the lowest step nursing a rag doll.

—Yes, Lily, he answered, and I think we're in for a night of it.

He looked up at the pantry ceiling, which was shaking with the stamping and shuffling of feet on the floor above, listened for a moment to the piano and then glanced at the girl, who was folding his overcoat carefully at the end of a shelf.

—Tell me, Lily, he said in a friendly tone, do you still go to school?

—O no, sir, she answered. I'm done schooling this year and more.

—O, then, said Gabriel gaily, I suppose we'll be going to your wedding one of these fine days with your young man, eh?

The girl glanced back at him over her shoulder and said with great bitterness:

—The men that is now is only all palaver and what they can get out of you.

Gabriel colored as if he felt he had made a mistake and, without looking at her, kicked off his goloshes and flicked actively with his muffler at his patent-leather shoes.

He was a stout tallish young man. The high color of his cheeks pushed upwards even to his forehead where it scattered itself in a few formless patches of pale red; and on his hairless face there scintillated restlessly the polished lenses and the bright gilt rims of the glasses which screened his delicate and restless eyes. His glossy black hair was parted in the middle and brushed in a long curve behind his ears where it curled slightly beneath the groove left by his hat.

When he had flicked luster into his shoes he stood up and pulled his waistcoat down more tightly on his plump body. Then he took a coin rapidly from his pocket.

—O Lily, he said, thrusting it into her hands, it's Christmas time, isn't it? Just...here's a little....

He walked rapidly towards the door.

—O no, sir! cried the girl, following him. Really, sir, I wouldn't take it.

—Christmas-time! Christmas-time! said Gabriel, almost trotting to the stairs and waving his hand to her in deprecation.

The girl, seeing that he had gained the stairs, called out after him:

—Well, thank you, sir.

He waited outside the drawing room door until the waltz should finish, listening to the skirts that swept against it and to the shuffling of feet. He was still discomposed by the girl's bitter and sudden retort. It had cast a gloom over him which he tried to dispel by arranging his cuffs and the bows of his tie. Then he took from his waistcoat pocket a little paper and glanced at the headings he had made for his speech. He was undecided about the lines from Robert Browning for he feared they would be above the heads of his hearers. Some quotation that they could recognize from Shakespeare or from the Melodies would be better. The indelicate clacking of the men's heels and the shuffling of their soles reminded him that their grade of culture differed from his. He would only make himself ridiculous by quoting poetry to them which they could not understand. They would think that he was airing his superior education. He would fail with them just as he had failed with the girl in the pantry. He had taken up a wrong tone. His whole speech was a mistake from first to last, an utter failure.

Just then his aunts and his wife came out of the ladies' dressing room. His aunts were two small plainly dressed old women. Aunt Julia was an inch or so taller. Her hair, drawn low over the tops of her ears, was grey; and grey also, with darker shadows, was her large flaccid face. Though she was stout in build and stood erect her slow eyes and parted lips gave her the appearance of a woman who did not know where she was or where she was going. Aunt Kate was more vivacious. Her face, healthier than her sister's, was all puckers and creases, like a shrivelled red apple, and her hair, braided in the same old-fashioned way, had not lost its ripe nut color.

They both kissed Gabriel frankly. He was their favorite nephew, the son of their dead elder sister, Ellen, who had married T. J. Conroy of the Port and Docks.

—Gretta tells me you're not going to take a cab back to Monkstown tonight, Gabriel, said Aunt Kate.

—No, said Gabriel, turning to his wife, we had quite enough of that last year, hadn't we. Don't you remember, Aunt Kate, what a cold Gretta got out of it? Cab windows rattling all the way, and the east wind blowing in after we passed Merrion. Very jolly it was. Gretta caught a dreadful cold.

Aunt Kate frowned severely and nodded her head at every word.

—Quite right, Gabriel, quite right, she said. You can't be too careful.

—But as for Gretta there, said Gabriel, she'd walk home in the snow if she were let.

Mrs. Conroy laughed.

—Don't mind him, Aunt Kate, she said. He's really an awful bother, what with green shades for Tom's eyes at night and making him do the dumbbells, and forcing Eva to eat the stirabout. The poor child! And she simply hates the sight of it!...O, but you'll never guess what he makes me wear now!

She broke out into a peal of laughter and glanced at her husband, whose admiring and happy eyes had been wandering from her dress to her face and hair. The two aunts laughed heartily too, for Gabriel's solicitude was a standing joke with them.

—Goloshes! said Mrs. Conroy. That's the latest. Whenever it's wet underfoot I must put on my galoshes. Tonight even he wanted me to put them on, but I wouldn't. The next thing he'll buy me will be a diving suit.

Gabriel laughed nervously and patted his tie reassuringly while Aunt Kate nearly doubled herself, so heartily did she enjoy the joke. The smile soon faded from Aunt Julia's face and her mirthless eyes were directed towards her nephew's face. After a pause she asked:

—And what are goloshes, Gabriel?

—Goloshes, Julia! exclaimed her sister. Goodness me, don't you know what goloshes are? You wear them over your. . . over your boots, Gretta, isn't it?

—Yes, said Mrs. Conroy. Guttapercha things. We both have a pair now. Gabriel says everyone wears them on the continent.

—O, on the continent, murmured Aunt Julia, nodding her head slowly.

Gabriel knitted his brows and said, as if he were slightly angered:

—It's nothing very wonderful but Gretta thinks it very funny because she says the word reminds her of Christy Minstrels.

—But tell me, Gabriel, said Aunt Kate, with brisk tact. Of course, you've seen about the room. Gretta was saying...

—O, the room is all right, replied Gabriel. I've taken one in the Gresham.

—To be sure, said Aunt Kate, by far the best thing to do. And the children, Gretta, you're not anxious about them?

—O, for one night, said Mrs. Conroy. Besides, Bessie will look after them.

—To be sure, said Aunt Kate again. What a comfort it is to have a girl like that, one you can depend on! There's that Lily, I'm sure I don't know what has come over her lately. She's not the girl she was at all.

Gabriel was about to ask his aunt some questions on this point but she broke off suddenly to gaze after her sister who had wandered down the stairs and was craning her neck over the banisters.

—Now, I ask you, she said, almost testily, where is Julia going? Julia! Julia! Where are you going?

Julia, who had gone halfway down one flight, came back and announced blandly:

—Here's Freddy.

At the same moment a clapping of hands and a final flourish of the pianist told that the waltz had ended. The drawing room door was opened from within and some couples came out. Aunt Kate drew Gabriel aside hurriedly and whispered into his ear:

—Slip down, Gabriel, like a good fellow and see if he's all right, and don't let him up if he's screwed. I'm sure he's screwed. I'm sure he is.

Gabriel went to the stairs and listened over the banisters. He could hear two persons talking in the pantry. Then he recognized Freddy Malin's laugh. He went down the stairs noisily.

—It's such a relief, said Aunt Kate to Mrs. Conroy, that Gabriel is here. I always feel easier in my mind when he's here....Julia, there's Miss Daly and Miss Power will take some refreshment. Thanks for your beautiful waltz, Miss Daly. It made lovely time.

A tall wizen-faced man, with a stiff grizzled moustache and swarthy skin, who was passing out with his partner said:

—And may we have some refreshment, too, Miss Morkan?

—Julia, said Aunt Kate summarily, and here's Mr. Browne and Miss Furlong. Take them in, Julia, with Miss Daly and Miss Power.

—I'm the man for the ladies, said Mr. Browne, pursing his lips until his moustache bristled and smiling in all his wrinkles. You know, Miss Morkan, the reason they are so fond of me is—

He did not finish his sentence, but, seeing that Aunt Kate was out of earshot, at once led the three young ladies into the back room. The middle of the room was occupied by two square tables placed end to end, and on these Aunt Julia and the caretaker were straightening and smoothing a large cloth. On the sideboard were arrayed dishes and plates, and glasses and bundles of knives and forks and spoons. The top of the closed square piano served also as a sideboard for viands and sweets. At a smaller sideboard in one corner two young men were standing, drinking hop-bitters.

Mr. Browne led his charges thither and invited them all, in jest, to some ladies' punch, hot, strong and sweet. As they said they never took anything strong he opened three bottles of lemonade for them. Then he asked one of the young men to move aside, and, taking hold of the decanter, filled out for himself a goodly measure of whisky. The young men eyed him respectfully while he took a trial sip.

—God help me, he said, smiling, it's the doctor's orders.

His wizened face broke into a broader smile, and the three young ladies laughed in musical echo to his pleasantry, swaying their bodies to and fro, with nervous jerks of their shoulders. The boldest said:

—O, now, Mr. Browne, I'm sure the doctor never ordered anything of the kind.

Mr. Browne took another sip of his whisky and said, with sidling mimicry:

—Well, you see, I'm like the famous Mrs. Cassidy, who is reported to have said: *Now, Mary Crimes, if I don't take it, make me take it, for I feel I want it.*

His hot face had leaned forward a little too confidentially and he had assumed a very low Dublin accent so that the young ladies, with one instinct, received his speech in silence. Miss Furlong, who was one of Mary Jane's pupils, asked Miss Daly what was the name of the pretty waltz she had played; and Mr. Browne, seeing that he was ignored, turned promptly to the two young men who were more appreciative.

A red-faced young woman, dressed in pansy, came into the room, excitedly clapping her hands and crying:

—Quadrilles! Quadrilles!

Close on her heels came Aunt Kate, crying:

—Two gentlemen and three ladies, Mary Jane!

—O, here's Mr. Bergin and Mr. Kerrigan, said Mary Jane. Mr. Kerrigan, will you take Miss Power? Miss Furlong, may I get you a partner, Mr. Bergin. O, that'll just do now.

—Three ladies, Mary Jane, said Aunt Kate.

The two young gentlemen asked the ladies if they might have the pleasure, and Mary Jane turned to Miss Daly.

—O, Miss Daly, you're really awfully good, after playing for the last two dances, but really we're so short of ladies tonight.

—I don't mind in the least, Miss Morkan.

—But I've a nice partner for you, Mr. Bartell D'Arcy, the tenor. I'll get him to sing later on. All Dublin is raving about him.

—Lovely voice, lovely voice! said Aunt Kate.

As the piano had twice begun the prelude to the first figure Mary Jane led her recruits quickly from the room. They had hardly gone when Aunt Julia wandered slowly into the room, looking behind her at something.

—What is the matter, Julia? asked Aunt Kate anxiously. Who is it? Julia, who was carrying in a column of table napkins, turned to her sister and said, simply, as if the question had surprised her:

—It's only Freddy, Kate, and Gabriel with him.

In fact right behind her Gabriel could be seen piloting Freddy Malins across the landing. The latter, a young man of about forty, was of Gabriel's size and build, with very round shoulders. His face was fleshy and pallid, touched with color only at the thick hanging lobes of his ears and at the wide wings of his nose. He had coarse features, a blunt nose, a convex and receding brow, tumid and protruded lips. His heavy-lidded eyes and the disorder of his scanty hair made him look sleepy. He was laughing heartily in a high key at a story which he had been telling Gabriel on the stairs and at the same time rubbing the knuckles of his left fist backwards and forwards into his left eye.

—Good-evening, Freddy, said Aunt Julia.

Freddy Malins bade the Misses Morkan good-evening in what seemed an offhand fashion by reason of the habitual catch in his voice and then, seeing that Mr. Browne was grinning at him from the sideboard, crossed the room on rather shaky legs and began to repeat in an undertone the story he had just told to Gabriel.

—He's not so bad, is he? said Aunt Kate to Gabriel.

Gabriel's brows were dark but he raised them quickly and answered:

—O no, hardly noticeable.

—Now, isn't he a terrible fellow! she said. And his poor mother made him take the pledge on New Year's Eve. But come on, Gabriel, into the drawing room.

Before leaving the room with Gabriel she signalled to Mr. Browne by frowning and shaking her forefinger in warning to and fro. Mr. Browne nodded in answer and, when she had gone, said to Freddy Malins:

—Now, then, Teddy, I'm going to fill you out a good glass of lemonade just to buck you up.

Freddy Malins, who was nearing the climax of his story, waved the offer aside impatiently but Mr. Browne, having first called Freddy Malin's attention to a disarray in his dress, filled out and handed him a full glass of lemonade. Freddy Malin's left hand accepted the glass mechanically, his right hand being engaged in the mechanical readjustment of his dress. Mr. Browne, whose face was once more wrinkling with mirth, poured out for himself a glass of whisky while Freddy Malins exploded, before he had well reached the climax of his story, in a kink of high-pitched bronchitic laughter and, setting down his untasted and overflowing glass, began to rub the knuckles of his left fist backwards and forwards into his left eye, repeating words of his last phrase as well as his fit of laughter would allow him.

Gabriel could not listen while Mary Jane was playing her Academy piece, full of runs and difficult passages, to the hushed drawing-room. He liked music but the piece she was playing had no melody for him and he doubted whether it had any melody for the other listeners, though they had begged Mary Jane to play something. Four young men, who had come from the refreshment room to stand in the doorway at the sound of the piano, had gone away quietly in couples after a few minutes. The only persons who seemed to follow the music were Mary Jane herself, her hands racing along the key-board or lifted from it at the pauses like those of a priestess in momentary imprecation, and Aunt Kate standing at her elbow to turn the page.

Gabriel's eyes, irritated by the floor, which glittered with beeswax under the heavy chandelier, wandered to the wall above the piano. A picture of the balcony scene in *Romeo and Juliet* hung there and beside it was a picture of the two murdered princes in the Tower which Aunt Julia had worked in red, blue and brown wools when she was a girl. Probably in the school they had gone to as girls that kind of work had been taught, for one year his mother had worked for him as a birthday present a waistcoat of purple tabinet, with little foxes' heads upon it, lined with brown satin and having round mulberry buttons. It was strange that his mother had had no musical talent though Aunt Kate used to call her the brains carrier of the Morkan family. Both she and Julia had always seemed a little proud of their serious and matronly sister. Her photograph stood before the pierglass. She held an open book on her knees and was pointing out something in it to Constantine who, dressed in a man-o'-war suit, lay at her feet. It was she who had chosen the names for her sons for she was very sensible of the dignity of family life. Thanks to her, Constantine was now senior curate in Balbriggan and, thanks to her, Gabriel himself had taken his degree in the Royal University. A shadow passed over his face as he remembered her sullen opposition to his marriage. Some slighting phrases she had used still rankled in his memory; she had once spoken of Gretta as being country cute and that was not true of Gretta at all. It was Gretta who had nursed her during all her last long illness in their house at Monkstown.

He knew that Mary Jane must be near the end of her piece for she was playing again the opening melody with runs of scales after every bar and while he waited for the end the resentment died down in his heart. The piece ended with a trill of octaves in the treble and a final deep octave in the bass. Great applause greeted Mary Jane as, blushing and rolling up her music nervously, she escaped from the room.

The most vigorous clapping came from the four young men in the doorway who had gone away to the refreshment room at the beginning of the piece but had come back when the piano had stopped.

Lancers were arranged. Gabriel found himself partnered with Miss Ivors. She was a frank-mannered talkative young lady, with a freckled face and prominent brown eyes. She did not wear a low-cut bodice and the large brooch which was fixed in the front of her collar bore on it an Irish device.

When they had taken their places she said abruptly:

—I have a crow to pluck with you.

—With me? said Gabriel.

She nodded her head gravely.

—What is it? asked Gabriel, smiling at her solemn manner.

—Who is G. C.? answered Miss Ivors, turning her eyes upon him.

Gabriel colored and was about to knit his brows, as if he did not understand, when she said bluntly:

—O, innocent Amy! I have found out that you write for *The Daily Express*. Now, aren't you ashamed of yourself?

—Why should I be ashamed of myself? asked Gabriel, blinking his eyes and trying to smile.

—Well, I'm ashamed of you, said Miss Ivors frankly. To say you'd write for a rag like that. I didn't think you were a West Briton.

A look of perplexity appeared on Gabriel's face. It was true that he wrote a literary column every Wednesday in *The Daily Express,* for which he was paid fifteen shillings. But that did not make him a West Briton surely. The books he received for review were almost more welcome than the paltry cheque. He loved to feel the covers and turn over the pages of newly printed books. Nearly every day when his teaching in the college was ended he used to wander down the quays to the second-hand booksellers, to Hickey's on Bachelor's Walk, to Webb's or Massey's on Aston's Quay, or to O'Clohissey's in the by-street. He did not know how to meet her charge. He wanted to say that literature was above politics. But they were friends of many years' standing and their careers had been parallel, first at the University and then as teachers: he could not risk a grandiose phrase with her. He continued blinking his eyes and trying to smile and murmured lamely that he saw nothing political in writing reviews of books.

When their turn to cross had come he was still perplexed and inattentive. Miss Ivors promptly took his hand in a warm grasp and said in a soft friendly tone:

—Of course, I was only joking. Come, we cross now.

When they were together again she spoke of the University question and Gabriel felt more at ease. A friend of hers had shown her his review of Browning's poems. That was how she had found out the secret: but she liked the review immensely. Then she said suddenly:

—O, Mr. Conroy, will you come for an excursion to the Aran Isles this summer? We're going to stay there a whole month. It will be splendid out in the Atlantic. You ought to come. Mr. Clancy is coming, and Mr. Kilkelly and Kathleen Kearney. It would be splendid for Gretta too if she'd come. She's from Connacht, isn't she?

—Her people are, said Gabriel shortly.

—But you will come, won't you? said Miss Ivors, laying her warm hand eagerly on his arm.

—The fact is, said Gabriel, I have already arranged to go—

—Go where? asked Miss Ivors.

—Well, you know, every year I go for a cycling tour with some fellows and so—

—But where? asked Miss Ivors.

—Well, we usually go to France or Belgium or perhaps Germany, said Gabriel awkwardly.

—And why do you go to France and Belgium, said Miss Ivors, instead of visiting your own land?

—Well, said Gabriel, it's partly to keep in touch with the languages and partly for a change.

—And haven't you your own language to keep in touch with—Irish? asked Miss Ivors.

—Well, said Gabriel, if it comes to that, you know, Irish is not my language.

Their neighbors had turned to listen to the cross-examination. Gabriel glanced right and left nervously and tried to keep his good humor under the ordeal which was making a blush invade his forehead.

—And haven't you your own land to visit, continued Miss Ivors, that you know nothing of, your own people, and your own country?

—O, to tell you the truth, retorted Gabriel suddenly, I'm sick of my own country, sick of it!

—Why? asked Miss Ivors.

Gabriel did not answer for his retort had heated him.

—Why? repeated Miss Ivors.

They had to go visiting together and, as he had not answered her, Miss Ivors said warmly:

—Of course, you've no answer.

Gabriel tried to cover his agitation by taking part in the dance with great energy. He avoided her eyes for he had seen a sour expression on her face. But when they met in the long chain he was surprised to feel his hand firmly pressed. She looked at him from under her brows for a moment quizzically until he smiled. Then, just as the chain was about to start again, she stood on tiptoe and whispered into his ear:

—West Briton!

When the lancers were over Gabriel went away to a remote corner of the room where Freddy Malins' mother was sitting. She was a stout feeble old woman with white hair. Her voice had a catch in it like her son's and she stuttered slightly. She had been told that Freddy had come and that he was nearly all right. Gabriel asked her whether she had had a good crossing. She lived with her married daughter in Glasgow and came to Dublin on a visit once a year. She answered placidly that she had had a beautiful crossing and that the captain had been most attentive to her. She spoke also of the beautiful house her daughter kept in Glasgow, and of all the nice friends they had there. While her tongue rambled on Gabriel tried to banish from his mind all memory of the unpleasant incident with Miss Ivors. Of course the girl or woman, or whatever she was, was an enthusiast but there was a time for all things. Perhaps he ought not to have answered her like that. But she had no right to call him a West Briton before people, even in joke. She had tried to make him ridiculous before people, heckling him and staring at him with her rabbit's eyes.

He saw his wife making her way towards him through the waltzing couples. When she reached him she said into his ear:

—Gabriel, Aunt Kate wants to know won't you carve the goose as usual. Miss Daly will carve the ham and I'll do the pudding.

—All right, said Gabriel.

—She's sending in the younger ones first as soon as this waltz is over so that we'll have the table to ourselves.

—Were you dancing? asked Gabriel.

—Of course I was. Didn't you see me? What words had you with Molly Ivors?

—No words. Why? Did she say so?

—Something like that. I'm trying to get that Mr. D'Arcy to sing. He's full of conceit, I think.

—There were no words, said Gabriel moodily, only she wanted me to go for a trip to the west of Ireland and I said I wouldn't.

His wife clasped her hands excitedly and gave a little jump.

—O, do go, Gabriel, she cried. I'd love to see Galway again.

—You can go if you like, said Gabriel coldly.

She looked at him for a moment, then turned to Mrs. Malins and said:

—There's a nice husband for you, Mrs. Malins.

While she was threading her way back across the room Mrs. Malins, without adverting to the interruption, went on to tell Gabriel what beautiful places there were in Scotland and beautiful scenery. Her son-in-law brought them every year to the lakes and they used to go fishing. Her son-in-law was a splendid fisher. One day he caught a fish, a beautiful big big fish, and the man in the hotel boiled it for their dinner.

Gabriel hardly heard what she said. Now that supper was coming near he began to think again about his speech and about the quotation. When he saw Freddy Malins coming across the room to visit his mother Gabriel left the chair free for him and retired into the embrasure of the window. The room had already cleared and from the back room came the clatter of plates and knives. Those who still remained in the drawing room seemed tired of dancing and were conversing quietly in little groups. Gabriel's warm trembling fingers tapped the cold pane of the window. How cool it must be outside! How pleasant it would be to walk out alone, first along by the river and then through the park! The snow would be lying on the branches of the trees and forming a bright cap on the top of the Wellington Monument. How much more pleasant it would be there than at the supper table!

He ran over the headings of his speech: Irish hospitality, sad memories, the Three Graces, Paris, the quotation from Browning. He repeated to himself a phrase he had written in his review: *One feels that one is listening to a thought-tormented music.* Miss Ivors had praised the review. Was she sincere? Had she really any life of her own behind all her propagandism? There had never been any ill-feeling between them until that night. It unnerved him to think that she would be at the supper-table, looking up at him while he spoke with her critical quizzing eyes. Perhaps she would not be sorry to see him fail in his speech. An idea came into his mind and gave him courage. He would say, alluding to Aunt Kate and Aunt Julia: *Ladies and Gentlemen, the generation which is now on the wane among us may have had its faults but for my part I think it had certain qualities of hospitality, of humor, of humanity, which the new and very serious and hypereducated generation that is growing up around us seems to me to lack.* Very good: that was one for Miss Ivors. What did he care that his aunts were only two ignorant old women?

A murmur in the room attracted his attention. Mr. Browne was advancing from the door, gallantly escorting Aunt Julia, who leaned upon his arm, smiling and hanging her head. An irregular musketry of applause escorted her also as far as the piano and then, as Mary Jane seated herself on the stool, and Aunt Julia, no longer smiling, half turned so as to pitch her voice fairly into the room, gradually ceased. Gabriel recognized the prelude. It was that of an old song of Aunt Julia's—*Arrayed for the Bridal.* Her voice, strong and clear in tone, attacked with great spirit the runs which embellish the air and though she sang very rapidly she did not miss even the smallest of the grace notes. To follow the voice, without looking at the singer's face, was to feel and share the excitement of swift and secure flight. Gabriel applauded loudly with all the others at the close of the song and loud applause was borne in from the invisible supper table. It sounded so genuine that a little color struggled into Aunt Julia's face as she bent to replace in the music-stand the old leather-bound songbook that had her initials on the cover. Freddy Malins, who had listened with his head perched sideways to hear her better, was still applauding when everyone else had ceased and talking animatedly to his mother who nodded her head gravely and slowly in acquiescence. At last, when he could clap no more, he stood up suddenly and hurried across the room to Aunt Julia whose hand he seized and held in both his hands, shaking it when words failed him or the catch in his voice proved too much for him.

—I was just telling my mother, he said, I never heard you sing so well, never. No, I never heard your voice so good as it is tonight. Now! Would you believe that now? That's the truth. Upon my word and honor that's the truth. I never heard your voice sound so fresh and so...so clear and fresh, never.

Aunt Julia smiled broadly and murmured something about compliments as she released her hand from his grasp. Mr. Browne extended his open hand towards her and said to those who were near him in the manner of a showman introducing a prodigy to an audience:

—Miss Julia Morkan, my latest discovery!

He was laughing very heartily at this himself when Freddy Malins turned to him and said:

—Well, Browne, if you're serious you might make a worse discovery. All I can say is I never heard her sing half so well as long as I am coming here. And that's the honest truth.

—Neither did I, said Mr. Browne. I think her voice has greatly improved.

Aunt Julia shrugged her shoulders and said with meek pride:

—Thirty years ago I hadn't a bad voice as voices go.

—I often told Julia, said Aunt Kate emphatically, that she was simply thrown away in that choir. But she never would be said by me.

She turned as if to appeal to the good sense of the others against a refractory child while Aunt Julia gazed in front of her, a vague smile of reminiscence playing on her face.

—No, continued Aunt Kate, she wouldn't be said or led by anyone, slaving there in that choir night and day, night and day. Six o'clock on Christmas morning! And all for what?

—Well, isn't it for the honor of God, Aunt Kate? asked Mary Jane, twisting round on the piano stool and smiling.

Aunt Kate turned fiercely on her niece and said:

—I know all about the honor of God, Mary Jane, but I think it's not at all honorable for the pope to turn out the women out of the choirs that have slaved there all their lives and put little whipper-snappers of boys over their heads. I suppose it is for the good of the Church if the pope does it. But it's not just, Mary Jane, and it's not right.

She had worked herself into a passion and would have continued in defense of her sister for it was a sore subject with her but Mary Jane, seeing that all the dancers had come back, intervened pacifically:

—Now, Aunt Kate, you're giving scandal to Mr. Browne who is of the other persuasion.

Aunt Kate turned to Mr. Browne, who was grinning at this allusion to his religion, and said hastily:

—O, I don't question the pope's being right. I'm only a stupid old woman and I wouldn't presume to do such a thing. But there's such a thing as common everyday politeness and gratitude. And if I were in Julia's place I'd tell that Father Healy straight up to his face...

—And besides, Aunt Kate, said Mary Jane, we really are all hungry and when we are hungry we are all very quarrelsome.

—And when we are thirsty we are also quarrelsome, added Mr. Browne.

—So that we had better go to supper, said Mary Jane, and finish the discussion afterwards.

On the landing outside the drawing room Gabriel found his wife and Mary Jane trying to persuade Miss Ivors to stay for supper. But Miss Ivors, who had put on her hat and was buttoning her cloak, would not stay. She did not feel in the least hungry and she had already overstayed her time.

—But only for ten minutes, Molly, said Mrs. Conroy. That won't delay you.

—To take a pick itself, said Mary Jane, after all your dancing.

—I really couldn't, said Miss Ivors.

—I am afraid you didn't enjoy yourself at all, said Mary Jane hopelessly.

—Ever so much, I assure you, said Miss Ivors, but you really must let me run off now.

—But how can you get home? asked Mrs. Conroy.

—O, it's only two steps up the quay.

Gabriel hesitated a moment and said:

—If you will allow me, Miss Ivors, I'll see you home if you really are obliged to go.

But Miss Ivors broke away from them.

—I won't hear of it, she cried. For goodness sake go in to your suppers and don't mind me. I'm quite well able to take care of myself.

—Well, you're the comical girl, Molly, said Mrs. Conroy frankly.

—*Beannacht libh,* cried Miss Ivors, with a laugh, as she ran down the staircase.

Mary Jane gazed after her, a moody puzzled expression on her face, while Mrs. Conroy leaned over the banisters to listen for the hall door. Gabriel asked himself was he the cause of her abrupt departure. But she did not seem to be in ill humor: she had gone away laughing. He stared blankly down the staircase.

At that moment Aunt Kate came toddling out of the supper room, almost wringing her hands in despair.

—Where is Gabriel? she cried. Where on earth is Gabriel? There's everyone waiting in there, stage to let, and nobody to carve the goose!

—Here I am, Aunt Kate! cried Gabriel, with sudden animation, ready to carve a flock of geese, if necessary.

A fat brown goose lay at one end of the table and at the other end, on a bed of creased paper strewn with sprigs of parsley, lay a great ham, stripped of its outer skin and peppered over with crust crumbs, a neat paper frill round its shin and beside this was a round of spiced beef. Between these rival ends ran parallel lines of side-dishes: two little minsters of jelly, red and yellow; a shallow dish full of blocks of blancmange and red jam, a large green leafshaped dish with a stalk-shaped handle, on which lay bunches of purple raisins and peeled almonds, a companion dish on which lay a solid rectangle of Smyrna figs, a dish of custard topped with grated nutmeg, a small bowl full of chocolates and sweets wrapped in gold and silver papers and a glass vase in which stood some tall celery stalks. In the center of the table there stood, as sentries to a fruit stand which upheld a pyramid of oranges and American apples, two squat old-fashioned decanters of cut glass, one containing port and the other dark sherry. On the closed square piano a pudding in a huge yellow dish lay in waiting and behind it were three squads of bottles of stout and ale and minerals, drawn up according to the colors of their uniforms, the first two black, with brown and red labels, the third and smallest squad white, with transverse green sashes.

Gabriel took his seat boldly at the head of the table and, having looked to the edge of the carver, plunged his fork firmly into the goose. He felt quite at ease now for he was an expert carver and liked nothing better than to find himself at the head of a well-laden table.

—Miss Furlong, what shall I send you? he asked. A wing or a slice of the breast?

—Just a small slice of the breast.

—Miss Higgins, what for you?

—O, anything at all, Mr. Conroy.

While Gabriel and Miss Daly exchanged plates of goose and plates of ham and spiced beef Lily went from guest to guest with a dish of hot floury potatoes wrapped in a white napkin. This was Mary Jane's idea and she had also suggested applesauce for the goose but Aunt Kate had said that plain roast goose without applesauce had always been good enough for her and she hoped she might never eat worse. Mary Jane waited on her pupils and saw that they got the best slices and Aunt Kate and Aunt Julia opened and carried across from the piano bottles of stout and ale for the gentlemen and bottles of minerals for the ladies. There was a great deal of confusion and laughter and noise, the noise of orders and counter-orders, of knives and forks, of corks and glass-stoppers. Gabriel began to carve second helpings as soon as he had finished the first round without serving himself. Everyone protested loudly so that he compromised by taking a long draught of stout for he had found the carving hot work. Mary Jane settled down quietly to her supper but Aunt Kate and Aunt Julia were still toddling round the table, walking on each other's heels, getting in each other's way and giving each other unheeded orders. Mr. Browne begged of them to sit down and eat their suppers and so did Gabriel but they said there was time enough so that, at last, Freddy Malins stood up and, capturing Aunt Kate, plumped her down on her chair amid general laughter.

When everyone had been well served Gabriel said, smiling:

—Now, if anyone wants a little more of what vulgar people call stuffing let him or her speak.

A chorus of voices invited him to begin his own supper and Lily came forward with three potatoes which she had reserved for him.

—Very well, said Gabriel amiably, as he took another preparatory draught, kindly forget my existence, ladies and gentlemen, for a few minutes.

He set to his supper and took no part in the conversation with which the table covered Lily's removal of the plates. The subject of talk was the opera company which was then at the Theatre Royal. Mr. Bartell D'Arcy, the tenor, a dark-complexioned young man with a smart moustache, praised very highly the leading contralto of the company but Miss Furlong thought she had a rather vulgar style of production. Freddy Malins said there was a negro chieftain singing in the second part of the Gaiety pantomime who had one of the finest tenor voices he had ever heard.

—Have you heard him? he asked Mr. Bartell D'Arcy across the table.

—No, answered Mr. Bartell D'Arcy carelessly.

—Because, Freddy Malins explained, now I'd be curious to hear your opinion of him. I think he has a grand voice.

—It takes Teddy to find out the really good things, said Mr. Browne familiarly to the table.

—And why couldn't he have a voice too? asked Freddy Malins sharply. Is it because he's only a black?

Nobody answered this question and Mary Jane led the table back to the legitimate opera. One of her pupils had given her a pass for *Mignon*. Of course it was very fine, she said, but it made her think of poor Georgina Burns. Mr. Browne could go back farther still, to the old Italian companies that used to come to Dublin—Tietjens, Ilma de Murzka, Campanini, the great Trebelli, Giuglini, Ravelli, Aramburo. Those were the days, he said, when there was something like singing to be heard in Dublin. He told too of how the top gallery of the old Royal used to be packed night after night, of how one night an Italian tenor had sung five encores to *Let Me Like a Soldier Fall*, introducing a high C every time, and of how the gallery boys would sometimes in their enthusiasm unyoke the horses from the carriage of some great *prima donna* and pull her themselves through the streets to her hotel. Why did they never play the grand old operas now, he asked, *Dinorah, Lucrezia Borgia?* Because they could not get the voices to sing them: that was why.

—O, well, said Mr. Bartell D'Arcy, I presume there are as good singers today as there were then.

—Where are they? asked Mr. Browne defiantly.

—In London, Paris, Milan, said Mr. Bartell D'Arcy warmly. I suppose Caruso, for example, is quite as good, if not better than any of the men you have mentioned.

—Maybe so, said Mr. Browne. But I may tell you I doubt it strongly.

—O, I'd give anything to hear Caruso sing, said Mary Jane.

—For me, said Aunt Kate, who had been picking a bone, there was only one tenor. To please me, I mean. But I suppose none of you ever heard of him.

—Who was he, Miss Morkan? asked Mr. Bartell D'Arcy politely.

—His name, said Aunt Kate, was Parkinson. I heard him when he was in his prime and I think he had then the purest tenor voice that was ever put into a man's throat.

—Strange, said Mr. Bartell D'Arcy. I never even heard of him.

—Yes, yes, Miss Morkan is right, said Mr. Browne. I remember hearing of old Parkinson but he's too far back for me.

—A beautiful pure sweet mellow English tenor, said Aunt Kate with enthusiasm.

Gabriel having finished, the huge pudding was transferred to the table. The clatter of forks and spoons began again. Gabriel's wife served out spoonfuls of the pudding and passed the plates down the table. Midway down they were held up by Mary Jane, who replenished them with raspberry or orange jelly or with blancmange and jam. The pudding was of Aunt Julia's making and she received praises for it from all quarters. She herself said that it was not quite brown enough.

—Well, I hope, Miss Morkan, said Mr. Browne, that I'm brown enough for you because, you know, I'm all brown.

All the gentlemen, except Gabriel, ate some of the pudding out of compliment to Aunt Julia. As Gabriel never ate sweets the celery had been left for him. Freddy Malins also took a stalk of celery and ate it with his pudding. He had been told that celery was a capital thing for the blood and he was just then under doctor's care. Mrs. Malins, who had been silent all through the supper, said that her son was going down to Mount Melleray in a week or so. The table then spoke of Mount Melleray, how bracing the air was down there, how hospitable the monks were and how they never asked for a penny-piece from their guests.

—And do you mean to say, asked Mr. Browne incredulously, that a chap can go down there and put up there as if it were a hotel and live on the fat of the land and then come away without paying a farthing?

—O, most people give some donation to the monastery when they leave, said Mary Jane.

—I wish we had an institution like that in our Church, said Mr. Browne candidly.

He was astonished to hear that the monks never spoke, got up at two in the morning and slept in their coffins. He asked what they did it for.

—That's the rule of the order, said Aunt Kate firmly.

—Yes, but why? asked Mr. Browne.

Aunt Kate repeated that it was the rule, that was all. Mr. Browne still seemed not to understand. Freddy Malins explained to him, as best he could, that the monks were trying to make up for the sins committed by all the sinners in the outside world. The explanation was not very clear for Mr. Browne grinned and said:

—I like that idea very much but wouldn't a comfortable spring bed do them as well as a coffin?

—The coffin, said Mary Jane, is to remind them of their last end.

As the subject had grown lugubrious it was buried in a silence of the table during which Mrs. Malins could be heard saying to her neighbor in an indistinct undertone:

—They are very good men, the monks, very pious men.

The raisins and almonds and figs and apples and oranges and chocolates and sweets were now passed about the table and Aunt Julia invited all the guests to have either port or sherry. At first Mr. Bartell D'Arcy refused to take either but one of his neighbors nudged him and whispered something to him upon which he allowed his glass to be filled. Gradually as the last glasses were being filled the conversation ceased. A pause followed, broken only by the noise of the wine and by unsettlings of chairs. The Misses Morkan, all three, looked down at the tablecloth. Someone coughed once or twice and then a few gentlemen patted the table gently as a signal for silence. The silence came and Gabriel pushed back his chair and stood up.

The patting at once grew louder in encouragement and then ceased altogether. Gabriel leaned his ten trembling fingers on the tablecloth and smiled nervously at the company. Meeting a row of upturned faces he raised his eyes to the chandelier. The piano was playing a waltz tune and he could hear the skirts sweeping against the drawing room door. People, perhaps, were standing in the snow on the quay outside, gazing up at the lighted windows and listening to the waltz music. The air was pure there. In the distance lay the park where the trees were weighted with snow. The Wellington Monument wore a gleaming cap of snow that flashed westward over the white field of Fifteen Acres.

He began:

—Ladies and Gentlemen.

—It has fallen to my lot this evening, as in years past, to perform a very pleasing task but a task for which I am afraid my poor powers as a speaker are all too inadequate.

—No, no! said Mr. Browne.

—But, however that may be, I can only ask you tonight to take the will for the deed and to lend me your attention for a few moments while I endeavor to express to you in words what my feelings are on this occasion.

—Ladies and Gentlemen. It is not the first time that we have gathered together under this hospitable roof, around this hospitable board. It is not the first time that we have been the recipients—or perhaps, I had better say, the victims—of the hospitality of certain good ladies.

He made a circle in the air with his arm and paused. Everyone laughed or smiled at Aunt Kate and Aunt Julia and Mary Jane who all turned crimson with pleasure. Gabriel went on more boldly:

—I feel more strongly with every recurring year that our country has no tradition which does it so much honor and which it should guard so jealously as that of its hospitality. It is a tradition that is unique as far as my experience goes (and I have visited not a few places abroad) among the modern nations. Some would say, perhaps, that with us it is rather a failing that anything to be boasted of. But granted even that, it is, to my mind, a princely failing, and one that I trust will long be cultivated among us. Of one thing, at least, I am sure. As long as this one roof shelters the good ladies aforesaid—and I wish from my heart it may do so for many and many a long year to come—the tradition of genuine warmhearted courteous Irish hospitality, which our forefathers have handed down to us and which we in turn must hand down to our descendants, is still alive among us.

A hearty murmur of assent ran round the table. It shot through Gabriel's mind that Miss Ivors was not there and that she had gone away discourteously: and he said with confidence in himself:

—Ladies and Gentlemen.

—A new generation is growing up in our midst, a generation actuated by new ideas and new principles. It is serious and enthusiastic for these new ideas and its enthusiasm, even when it is misdirected, is, I believe, in the main sincere. But we are living in a sceptical and, if I may use the phrase, a thought-tormented age: and sometimes I fear that this new generation, educated or hypereducated as it is, will lack those qualities of humanity, of hospitality, of kindly humor which belonged to an older day. Listening tonight to the names of all those great singers of the past it seemed to me, I must confess, that we were living in a less spacious age. Those days might, without exaggeration, be called spacious days: and if they are gone beyond recall let us hope, at least, that in gatherings such as this we shall still speak of them with pride and affection, still cherish in our hearts the memory of those dead and gone great ones whose fame the world will not willingly let die.

—Hear, hear! said Mr. Browne loudly.

—But yet, continued Gabriel, his voice falling into a softer inflection, there are always in gatherings such as this sadder thoughts that will recur to our minds: thoughts of the past, of youth, of changes, of absent faces that we miss here tonight. Our path through life is strewn with many such sad memories: and were we to brood upon them always we could not find the heart to go on bravely with our work among the living. We have all of us living duties and living affections which claim, and rightly claim, our strenuous endeavours.

—Therefore, I will not linger on the past. I will not let any gloomy moralizing intrude upon us here tonight. Here we are gathered together for a brief moment from the bustle and rush of our everyday routine. We are met here as friends, in the spirit of good fellowship, as colleagues, also to a certain extent, in the true spirit of *camaraderie,* and as the guests of—what shall I call them?—the Three Graces of the Dublin musical world.

The table burst into applause and laughter at this sally. Aunt Julia vainly asked each of her neighbors in turn to tell her what Gabriel had said.

—He says we are the Three Graces, Aunt Julia, said Mary Jane.

Aunt Julia did not understand but she looked up, smiling, at Gabriel, who continued in the same vein:

—Ladies and Gentlemen.

—I will not attempt to play tonight the part that Paris played on another occasion. I will not attempt to choose between them. The task would be an invidious one and one beyond my poor powers. For when I view them in turn, whether it be our chief hostess herself, whose good heart, whose too good heart, has become a byword with all who know her, or her sister, who seems to be gifted with perennial youth and whose singing must have been a surprise and a revelation to us all tonight, or, last but not least, when I consider our youngest hostess, talented, cheerful, hardworking and the best of nieces, I confess, Ladies and Gentlemen, that I do not know to which of them I should award the prize.

Gabriel glanced down at his aunts and, seeing the large smile on Aunt Julia's face and the tears which had risen to Aunt Kate's eyes, hastened to his close. He raised his glass of port gallantly, while every member of the company fingered a glass expectantly, and said loudly:

—Let us toast them all three together. Let us drink to their health, wealth, long life, happiness and prosperity and may they long continue to hold the proud and self-won position which they hold in their profession and the position of honor and affection which they hold in our hearts.

All the guests stood up, glass in hand, and, turning towards the three seated ladies, sang in unison, with Mr. Browne as leader:

For they are jolly gay fellows,
For they are jolly gay fellows,
For they are jolly gay fellows,
Which nobody can deny.

Aunt Kate was making frank use of her handkerchief and even Aunt Julia seemed moved. Freddy Malins beat time with his pudding-fork and the singers turned towards one another, as if in melodious conference, while they sang, with emphasis:

Unless he tells a lie,
Unless he tells a lie.

Then, turning once more towards their hostesses, they sang:

For they are jolly gay fellows,
For they are jolly gay fellows,
For they are jolly gay fellows,
Which nobody can deny.

The acclamation which followed was taken up beyond the door of the supper room by many of the other guests and renewed time after time, Freddy Malins acting as officer with his fork on high.

The piercing morning air came into the hall where they were standing so that Aunt Kate said:

—Close the door, somebody. Mrs. Malins will get her death of cold.

—Browne is out there, Aunt Kate, said Mary Jane.

—Browne is everywhere, said Aunt Kate, lowering her voice.

Mary Jane laughed at her tone.

—Really, she said archly, he is very attentive.

—He has been laid on here like the gas, said Aunt Kate in the same tone, all during the Christmas.

She laughed herself this time good-humoredly and then added quickly:

—But tell him to come in, Mary Jane, and close the door. I hope to goodness he didn't hear me.

At that moment the hall door was opened and Mr. Browne came in from the doorstep, laughing as if his heart would break. He was dressed in a long green overcoat with mock astrakhan cuffs and collar and wore on his head an oval fur cap. He pointed down the snow-covered quay from where the sound of shrill prolonged whistling was borne in.

—Teddy will have all the cabs in Dublin out, he said.

Gabriel advanced from the little pantry behind the office, struggling into his overcoat and, looking round the hall, said:

—Gretta not down yet?

—She's getting on her things, Gabriel, said Aunt Kate.

—Who's playing up there? asked Gabriel.

—Nobody. They're all gone.

—O no, Aunt Kate, said Mary Jane. Bartell D'Arcy and Miss O'Callaghan aren't gone yet.

—Someone is strumming at the piano, anyhow, said Gabriel.

Mary Jane glanced at Gabriel and Mr. Browne and said with a shiver:

—It makes me feel cold to look at you two gentlemen muffled up like that. I wouldn't like to face your journey home at this hour.

—I'd like nothing better this minute, said Mr. Browne stoutly, than a rattling fine walk in the country or a fast drive with a good spanking goer between the shafts.

—We used to have a very good horse and trap at home, said Aunt Julia sadly.

—The never-to-be-forgotten Johnny, said Mary Jane, laughing.

Aunt Kate and Gabriel laughed too.

—Why, what was wonderful about Johnny? asked Mr. Browne.

—The late lamented Patrick Morkan, our grandfather, that is, explained Gabriel, commonly known in his later years as the old gentleman, was a glue-boiler.

—O, now, Gabriel, said Aunt Kate, laughing, he had a starch mill.

—Well, glue or starch, said Gabriel, the old gentleman had a horse by the name of Johnny. And Johnny used to work in the old gentleman's mill, walking round and round in order to drive the mill. That was all very well; but now comes the tragic part about Johnny. One fine day the old gentleman thought he'd like to drive out with the quality to a military review in the park.

—The Lord have mercy on his soul, said Aunt Kate compassionately.

—Amen, said Gabriel. So the old gentleman, as I said, harnessed Johnny and put on his very best tall hat and his very best stock collar and drive out in grand style from his ancestral mansion somewhere near Back Lane, I think.

Everyone laughed, even Mrs. Malins, at Gabriel's manner and Aunt Kate said:

—O now, Gabriel, he didn't live in Back Lane, really. Only the mill was there.

—Out from the mansion of his forefathers, continued Gabriel, he drove with Johnny. And everything went on beautifully until Johnny came in sight of King Billy's statue: and whether he fell in love with the horse King Billy sits on or whether he thought he was back again in the mill, anyhow he began to walk round the statue.

Gabriel paced in a circle round the hall in his goloshes amid the laughter of the others.

—Round and round he went, said Gabriel, and the old gentleman, who was a very pompous old gentleman, was highly indignant. *Go on, sir! What do you mean, sir? Johnny! Johnny! Most extraordinary conduct! Can't understand the horse!*

The peals of laughter which followed Gabriel's imitation of the incident were interrupted by a resounding knock at the hall door. Mary Jane ran to open it and let in Freddy Malins. Freddy Malins, with his hat well back on his head and his shoulders humped with cold, was puffing and steaming after his exertions.

—I could only get one cab, he said.

—O, we'll find another along the quay, said Gabriel.

—Yes, said Aunt Kate. Better not keep Mrs. Malins standing in the draught.

Mrs. Malins was helped down the front steps by her son and Mr. Browne and, after many manoeuvres, hoisted into the cab. Freddy Malins clambered in after her and spent a long time settling her on the seat, Mr. Browne helping him with advice. At last she was settled comfortably and Freddy Malins invited Mr. Browne into the cab. There was a good deal of confused talk, and then Mr. Browne got into the cab. The cabman settled his rug over his knees, and bent down for the address. The confusion grew greater and the cabman was directed differently by Freddy Malins and Mr. Browne, each of whom had his head out through a window of the cab. The difficulty was to know where to drop Mr. Browne along the route and Aunt Kate, Aunt Julia and Mary Jane helped the discussion from the doorstep with cross-directions and contradictions and abundance of laughter. As for Freddy Malins he was speechless with laughter. He popped his head in and out of the window every moment, to the great danger of his hat, and told his mother how the discussion was progressing till at last Mr. Browne shouted to the bewildered cabman above the din of everybody's laughter:

—Do you know Trinity College?

—Yes, sir, said the cabman.

—Well, drive bang up against Trinity College gates, said Mr. Browne, and then we'll tell you where to go. You understand now?

—Yes, sir, said the cabman.

—Make like a bird for Trinity College.

—Right, sir, cried the cabman.

The horse was whipped up and the cab rattled off along the quay amid a chorus of laughter and adieus.

Gabriel had not gone to the door with the others. He was in a dark part of the hall gazing up the staircase. A woman was standing near the top of the first flight, in the shadow also. He could not see her face but he could see the terracotta and salmon pink panels of her skirt which the shadow made appear black and white. It was his wife. She was leaning on the banisters, listening to something. Gabriel was surprised at her stillness and strained his ear to listen also. But he could hear little save the noise of laughter and dispute on the front steps, a few chords struck on the piano and a few notes of a man's voice singing.

He stood still in the gloom of the hall, trying to catch the air that the voice was singing and gazing up at his wife.

There was grace and mystery in her attitude as if she were a symbol of something. He asked himself what is a woman standing on the stairs in the shadow, listening to distant music, a symbol of. If he were a painter he would paint her in that attitude. Her blue felt hat would show off the bronze of her hair against the darkness and the dark panels of her skirt would show off the light ones. *Distant Music* he would call the picture if he were a painter.

The hall-door was closed; and Aunt Kate, Aunt Julia and Mary Jane came down the hall, still laughing.

—Well, isn't Freddy terrible? said Mary Jane. He's really terrible.

Gabriel said nothing but pointed up the stairs towards where his wife was standing. Now that the hall door was closed the voice and the piano could be heard more clearly. Gabriel held up his hand for them to be silent. The song seemed to be in the old Irish tonality and the singer seemed uncertain both of his words and of his voice. The voice, made plaintive by distance and by the singer's hoarseness, faintly illuminated the cadence of the air with words expressing grief:

O, the rain falls on my heavy locks
And the dew wets my skin,
My babe lies cold...

—O, exclaimed Mary Jane. It's Bartell D'Arcy singing and he wouldn't sing all the night. O, I'll get him to sing a song before he goes.

—O do, Mary Jane, said Aunt Kate.

Mary Jane brushed past the others and ran to the staircase but before she reached it the singing stopped and the piano was closed abruptly.

—O, what a pity! she cried. Is he coming down, Gretta?

Gabriel heard his wife answer yes and saw her come down towards them. A few steps behind her were Mr. Bartell D'Arcy and Miss O'Callaghan.

—O, Mr. D'Arcy, cried Mary Jane, it's downright mean of you to break off like that when we were all in raptures listening to you.

—I have been at him all the evening, said Miss O'Callaghan, and Mrs. Conroy too and he told us he had a dreadful cold and couldn't sing.

—O, Mr. D'Arcy, said Aunt Kate, now that was a great fib to tell.

—Can't you see that I'm as hoarse as a crow? said Mr. D'Arcy roughly.

He went into the pantry hastily and put on his overcoat. The others, taken aback by his rude speech, could find nothing to say. Aunt Kate wrinkled her brows and made signs to the others to drop the subject. Mr. D'Arcy stood swathing his neck carefully and frowning.

—It's the weather, said Aunt Julia, after a pause.

—Yes, everybody has colds, said Aunt Kate readily, everybody.

—They say, said Mary Jane, we haven't had snow like it for thirty years; and I read this morning in the newspapers that the snow is general all over Ireland.

—I love the look of snow, said Aunt Julia sadly.

—So do I, said Miss O'Callaghan. I think Christmas is never really Christmas unless we have the snow on the ground.

—But poor Mr. D'Arcy doesn't like the snow, said Aunt Kate, smiling.

Mr. D'Arcy came from the pantry, full swathed and buttoned, and in a repentant tone told them the history of his cold. Everyone gave him advice and said it was a great pity and urged him to be very careful of his throat in the night air. Gabriel watched his wife who did not join in the conversation. She was standing right under the dusty fanlight and the flame of the gas lit up the rich bronze of her hair which he had seen her drying at the fire a few days before. She was in the same attitude and seemed unaware of the talk about her. At last she turned towards them and Gabriel saw that there was colour on her cheeks and that her eyes were shining. A sudden tide of joy went leaping out of his heart.

—Mr. D'Arcy, she said, what is the name of that song you were singing?

—It's called *The Lass of Aughrim,* said Mr. D'Arcy, but I couldn't remember it properly. Why? Do you know it?

—*The Lass of Aughrim,* she repeated. I couldn't think of the name.

—It's a very nice air, said Mary Jane. I'm sorry you were not in voice tonight.

—Now, Mary Jane, said Aunt Kate, don't annoy Mr. D'Arcy. I won't have him annoyed.

Seeing that all were ready to start she shepherded them to the door where good-night was said:

—Well, good-night, Aunt Kate, and thanks for the pleasant evening.

—Good-night, Gabriel. Good-night, Gretta!

—Good-night, Aunt Kate, and thanks ever so much. Good-night, Aunt Julia.

—O, good-night, Gretta, I didn't see you.

—Good-night, Mr. D'Arcy. Good-night, Miss O'Callaghan.

—Good-night, Miss Morkan.

—Good-night, again.

—Good-night, all. Safe home.

—Good-night. Good-night.

The morning was still dark. A dull yellow light brooded over the houses and the river; and the sky seemed to be descending. It was slushy underfoot; and only streaks and patches of snow lay on the roofs, on the parapets of the quay and on the area railings. The lamps were still burning redly in the murky air and, across the river, the palace of the Four Courts stood out menacingly against the heavy sky.

She was walking on before him with Mr. Bartell D'Arcy, her shoes in a brown parcel tucked under one arm and her hands holding her skirt up from the slush. She had no longer any grace of attitude but Gabriel's eyes were still bright with happiness. The blood went bounding along his veins; and the thoughts went rioting through his brain, proud, joyful, tender, valorous.

She was walking on before him so lightly and so erect that he longed to run after her noiselessly, catch her by the shoulders and say something foolish and affectionate into her ear. She seemed to him so frail that he longed to defend her against something and then to be alone with her. Moments of their secret life together burst like stars upon his memory. A heliotrope envelope was lying beside his breakfast cup and he was caressing it with his hand. Birds were twittering in the ivy and the sunny web of the curtain was shimmering along the floor: he could not eat for happiness. They were standing on the crowded platform and he was placing a ticket inside the warm palm of her glove. He was standing with her in the cold, looking in through a grated window at a man making bottles in a roaring furnace. It was very cold. Her face, fragrant in the cold air, was quite close to his; and suddenly she called out to the man at the furnace:

—Is the fire hot, sir?

But the man could not hear her with the noise of the furnace. It was just as well. He might have answered rudely.

A wave of yet more tender joy escaped from his heart and went coursing in warm flood along his arteries. Like the tender fires of stars moments of their life together, that no one knew of or would ever know of, broke upon and illumined his memory. He longed to recall to her those moments, to make her forget the years of their dull existence together and remember only their moments of ecstasy. For the years, he felt, had not quenched his soul or hers. Their children, his writing, her household cares had not quenched all their soul's tender fire. In one letter that he had written to her then he had said: *Why is it that words like these seem to me so dull and cold? Is it because there is no word tender enough to be your name?*

Like distant music these words that he had written years before were borne towards him from the past. He longed to be alone with her. When the others had gone away, when he and she were in their room in the hotel, then they would be alone together. He would call her softly:

—Gretta!

Perhaps she would not hear at once: she would be undressing. Then something in his voice would strike her. She would turn and look at him....

At the corner of Winetavern Street they met a cab. He was glad of its rattling noise as it saved him from conversation. She was looking out of the window and seemed tired. The others spoke only a few words, pointing out some building or street. The horse galloped along wearily under the murky morning sky, dragging his old rattling box after his heels, and Gabriel was again in a cab with her, galloping to catch the boat, galloping to their honeymoon.

As the cab drove across O'Connell Bridge Miss O'Callaghan said:

—They say you never cross O'Connell Bridge without seeing a white horse.

—I see a white man this time, said Gabriel.

—Where? asked Mr. Bartell D'Arcy.

Gabriel pointed to the statue, on which lay patches of snow. Then he nodded familiarly to it and waved his hand.

—Good-night, Dan, he said gaily.

When the cab drew up before the hotel Gabriel jumped out and, in spite of Mr. Bartell D'Arcy's protest, paid the driver. He gave the man a shilling over his fare. The man saluted and said:

—A prosperous New Year to you, sir.

—The same to you, said Gabriel cordially.

She leaned for a moment on his arm in getting out of the cab and while standing at the curbstone, bidding the others good-night. She leaned lightly on his arm, as lightly as when she had danced with him a few hours before. He had felt proud and happy then, happy that she was his, proud of her grace and wifely carriage. But now, after the kindling again of so many memories, the first touch of her body, musical and strange and perfumed, sent through him a keen pang of lust. Under cover of her silence he pressed her arm closely to his side; and, as they stood at the hotel door, he felt that they had escaped from their lives and duties, escaped from home and friends and run away together with wild and radiant hearts to a new adventure.

An old man was dozing in a great hooded chair in the hall. He lit a candle in the office and went before them to the stairs. They followed him in silence, their feet falling in soft thuds on the thickly carpeted stairs. She mounted the stairs behind the porter, her head bowed in the ascent, her frail shoulders curved as with a burden, her skirt girt tightly about her. He could have flung his arms about her hips and held her still for his arms were trembling with desire to seize her and only the stress of his nails against the palms of his hands held the wild impulse of his body in check. The porter halted on the stairs to settle his guttering candle. They halted too on the steps below him. In the silence Gabriel could hear the falling of the molten wax into the tray and the thumping of his own heart against his ribs.

The porter led them along a corridor and opened a door. Then he set his unstable candle down on a toilet table and asked at what hour they were to be called in the morning.

—Eight, said Gabriel.

The porter pointed to the tap of the electric light and began a muttered apology but Gabriel cut him short.

—We don't want any light. We have light enough from the street. And I say, he added, pointing to the candle, you might remove that handsome article, like a good man. The porter took up his candle again, but slowly for he was surprised by such a novel idea. Then he mumbled good-night and went out. Gabriel shot the lock to.

A ghostly light from the street lamp lay in a long shaft from one window to the door. Gabriel threw his overcoat and hat on a couch and crossed the room towards the window. He looked down into the street in order that his emotion might calm a little. Then he turned and leaned against a chest of drawers with his back to the light. She had taken off her hat and cloak and was standing before a large swinging mirror, unhooking her waist. Gabriel paused for a few moments, watching her, and then said:

—Gretta!

She turned away from the mirror slowly and walked along the shaft of light towards him. Her face looked so serious and weary that the words would not pass Gabriel's lips. No, it was not the moment yet.

—You looked tired, he said.

—I am a little, she answered.

—You don't feel ill or weak?

—No, tired: that's all.

She went on to the window and stood there, looking out. Gabriel waited again and then, fearing that diffidence was about to conquer him, he said abruptly:

—By the way, Gretta!

—What is it?

—You know that poor fellow Malins? he said quickly.

—Yes. What about him?

—Well, poor fellow, he's a decent sort of chap after all, continued Gabriel in a false voice. He gave me back that sovereign I lent him and I didn't expect it really. It's a pity he wouldn't keep away from that Browne, because he's not a bad fellow at heart.

He was trembling now with annoyance. Why did she seem so abstracted? He did not know how he could begin. Was she annoyed, too, about something? If she would only turn to him or come to him of her own accord! To take her as she was would be brutal. No, he must see some ardor in her eyes first. He longed to be master of her strange mood.

—When did you lend him the pound? she asked, after a pause.

Gabriel strove to restrain himself from breaking out into brutal language about the sottish Malins and his pound. He longed to cry to her from his soul, to crush her body against his, to overmaster her. But he said:

—O, at Christmas, when he opened that little Christmas card shop in Henry Street.

He was in such a fever of rage and desire that he did not hear her come from the window. She stood before him for an instant, looking at him strangely. Then, suddenly raising herself on tiptoe and resting her hands lightly on his shoulders, she kissed him.

—You are a very generous person, Gabriel, she said.

Gabriel, trembling with delight at her sudden kiss and at the quaintness of her phrase, put his hands on her hair and began smoothing it back, scarcely touching it with his fingers. The washing had made it fine and brilliant. His heart was brimming over with happiness. Just when he was wishing for it she had come to him of her own accord. Perhaps her thoughts had been running with his. Perhaps she had felt the impetuous desire that was in him and then the yielding mood had come upon her. Now that she had fallen to him so easily he wondered why he had been so diffident.

He stood, holding her head between his hands. Then, slipping one arm swiftly about her body and drawing her towards him, he said softly:

—Gretta dear, what are you thinking about?

She did not answer nor yield wholly to his arm. He said again, softly:

—Tell me what it is, Gretta. I think I know what is the matter. Do I know?

She did not answer at once. Then she said in an outburst of tears:

—O, I am thinking about that song, *The Lass of Aughrim.*

She broke loose from him and ran to the bed and, throwing her arms across the bed rail, hid her face. Gabriel stood stock-still for a moment in astonishment and then followed her. As he passed in the way of the chevalglass he caught sight of himself in full length, his broad, well-filled shirt-front, the face whose expression always puzzled him when he saw it in a mirror and his glimmering gilt-rimmed eyeglasses. He halted a few paces from her and said:

—What about the song? Why does that make you cry?

She raised her head from her arms and dried her eyes with the back of her hand like a child. A kinder note than he had intended went into his voice.

—Why, Gretta? he asked.

—I am thinking about a person long ago who used to sing that song.

—And who was the person long ago? asked Gabriel, smiling.

—It was a person I used to know in Galway when I was living with my grandmother, she said.

The smile passed away from Gabriel's face. A dull anger began to gather again at the back of his mind and the dull fires of his lust began to glow angrily in his veins.

—Someone you were in love with? he asked ironically.

—It was a young boy I used to know, she answered, named Michael Furey. He used to sing that song, *The Lass of Aughrim.* He was very delicate.

Gabriel was silent. He did not wish her to think that he was interested in this delicate boy.

—I can see him so plainly, she said after a moment. Such eyes as he had: big dark eyes! And such an expression in them—an expression!

—O then, you were in love with him? said Gabriel.

—I used to go out walking with him, she said, when I was in Galway.

A thought flew across Gabriel's mind.

—Perhaps that was why you wanted to go to Galway with that Ivors girl? he said coldly.

She looked at him and asked in surprise:

—What for?

Her eyes made Gabriel feel awkward. He shrugged his shoulders and said:

—How do I know? To see him perhaps.

She looked away from him along the shaft of light towards the window in silence.

—He is dead, she said at length. He died when he was only seventeen. Isn't it a terrible thing to die so young as that?

—What was he? asked Gabriel, still ironically.

—He was in the gasworks, she said.

Gabriel felt humiliated by the failure of his irony and by the evocation of this figure from the dead, a boy in the gasworks. While he had been full of memories of their secret life together, full of tenderness and joy and desire, she had been comparing him in her mind with another. A shameful consciousness of his own person assailed him. He saw himself as a ludicrous figure, acting as a pennyboy for his aunts, a nervous well-meaning sentimentalist, orating to vulgarians and idealizing his own clownish lusts, the pitiable fatuous fellow he had caught a glimpse of in the mirror. Instinctively he turned his back more to the light lest she might see the shame that burned upon his forehead.

He tried to keep up his tone of cold interrogation but his voice when he spoke was humble and indifferent.

—I suppose you were in love with this Michael Furey, Gretta, he said.

—I was great with him at that time, she said.

Her voice was veiled and sad. Gabriel, feeling now how vain it would be to try to lead her whither he had purposed, caressed one of her hands and said, also sadly:

—And what did he die of so young, Gretta? Consumption, was it?

—I think he died for me, she answered.

A vague terror seized Gabriel at this answer as if, at that hour when he had hoped to triumph, some impalpable and vindictive being was coming against him, gathering forces against him in its vague world. But he shook himself free of it with an effort of reason and continued to caress her hand. He did not question her again for he felt that she would tell him of herself. Her hand was warm and moist: it did not respond to his touch but he continued to caress it just as he had caressed her first letter to him that spring morning.

—It was in the winter, she said, about the beginning of the winter when I was going to leave my grandmother's and come up here to the convent. And he was ill at the time in his lodgings in Galway and wouldn't be let out and his people in Oughterard were written to. He was in decline, they said, or something like that. I never knew rightly.

She paused for a moment and sighed.

—Poor fellow, she said. He was very fond of me and he was such a gentle boy. We used to go out together, walking, you know, Gabriel, like the way they do in the country. He was going to study singing only for his health. He had a very good voice, poor Michael Furey.

—Well; and then? asked Gabriel.

—And then when it came to the time for me to leave Galway and come up to the convent he was much worse and I wouldn't be let see him so I wrote a letter saying I was going up to Dublin and would be back in the summer and hoping he would be better then.

She paused for a moment to get her voice under control and then went on:

—Then the night before I left I was in my grandmother's house in Nun's Island, packing up, and I heard gravel thrown up against the window. The window was so wet I couldn't see so I ran downstairs as I was and slipped out the back into the garden and there was the poor fellow at the end of the garden, shivering.

—And did you not tell him to go back? asked Gabriel.

—I implored him to go home at once and told him he would get his death in the rain. But he said he did not want to live. I can see his eyes as well as well! He was standing at the end of the wall where there was a tree.

—And did he go home? asked Gabriel.

—Yes, he went home. And when I was only a week in the convent he died and he was buried in Oughterard where his people came from. O, the day I heard that, that he was dead!

She stopped, choking with sobs, and, overcome by emotion, flung herself face downward on the bed, sobbing in the quilt. Gabriel held her hand for a moment longer, irresolutely, and then, shy of intruding on her grief, let it fall gently and walked quietly to the window.

She was fast asleep.

Gabriel, leaning on his elbow, looked for a few moments unresentfully on her tangled hair and half-open mouth, listening to her deep-drawn breath. So she had had that romance in her life: a man had died for her sake. It hardly pained him now to think how poor a part he, her husband, had played in her life. He watched her while she slept as though he and she had never lived together as man and wife. His curious eyes rested long upon her face and on her hair: and, as he thought of what she must have been then, in that time of her first girlish beauty, a strange friendly pity for her entered his soul. He did not like to say even to himself that her face was no longer beautiful but he knew that it was no longer the face for which Michael Furey had braved death.

Perhaps she had not told him all the story. His eyes moved to the chair over which she had thrown some of her clothes. A petticoat string dangled to the floor. One boot stood upright, its limp upper fallen down: the fellow of it lay upon its side. He wondered at his riot of emotions of an hour before. From what had it proceeded? From his aunt's supper, from his own foolish speech, from the wine and dancing, the merrymaking when saying good-night in the hall, the pleasure of the walk along the river in the snow. Poor Aunt Julia! She, too, would soon be a shade with the shade of Patrick Morkan and his horse. He had caught that haggard look upon her face for a moment when she was singing *Arrayed for the Bridal.* Soon, perhaps, he would be sitting in that same drawing room, dressed in black, his silk hat on his knees. The blinds would be drawn down and Aunt Kate would be sitting beside him, crying and blowing her nose and telling him how Julia had died. He would cast about in his mind for some words that might console her, and would find only lame and useless ones. Yes, yes: that would happen very soon.

The air of the room chilled his shoulders. He stretched himself cautiously along under the sheets and lay down beside his wife. One by one they were all becoming shades.

Better pass boldly into that other world, in the full glory of some passion, than fade and wither dismally with age. He thought of how she who lay beside him had locked in her heart for so many years that image of her lover's eyes when he had told her that he did not wish to live.

Generous tears filled Gabriel's eyes. He had never felt like that himself towards any woman but he knew that such a feeling must be love. The tears gathered more thickly in his eyes and in the partial darkness he imagined he saw the form of a young man standing under a dripping tree. Other forms were near. His soul had approached that region where dwell the vast hosts of the dead. He was conscious of, but could not apprehend, their wayward and flickering existence. His own identity was fading out into a grey impalpable world: the solid world itself which these dead had one time reared and lived in was dissolving and dwindling.

A few light taps upon the pane made him turn to the window. It had begun to snow again. He watched sleepily the flakes, silver and dark, falling obliquely against the lamplight. The time had come for him to set out on his journey westward. Yes, the newspapers were right: snow was general all over Ireland. It was falling on every part of the dark central plain, on the treeless hills, falling softly upon the Bog of Allen and, farther westward, softly falling into the dark mutinous Shannon waves. It was falling, too, upon every part of the lonely churchyard on the hill where Michael Furey lay buried. It lay thickly drifted on the crooked crosses and headstones, on the spears of the little gate, on the barren thorns. His soul swooned slowly as he heard the snow falling faintly through the universe and faintly falling, like the descent of their last end, upon all the living and the dead.

Mansfield

1888	October 4. Kathleen Beauchamp, the third daughter of banker Harold Beauchamp, is born in Wellington, New Zealand.
1903-06	Studies at Queen's College in London. Returns home at her father's request after three years.
1907	Three stories are published in *The Native Companion*, a Melbourne monthly.
1908-09	Returns to England and is granted a 100 pound a year allowance by her father. Marries George Bowden, a young musician, only to leave him a few days later. Flees to Germany where she bears a child (of which Bowden is not the father), and returns to England in 1910.
1910-11	Stories which were published in *The New Age* under the name Katherine Mansfield appear in her first collection, *In a German Pension.*
1912	Meets critic John Middleton Murry; they live together but are unable to marry until Bowden grants her a divorce in 1918.
1915-16	Suffering from depression, Mansfield is visited by her younger brother, Leslie, who is on his way to the front. Shortly after, Leslie dies in the action of World War I, leaving his sister devastated. This tragedy inspires *The Aloe*, which is later revised and published as *Prelude* in 1918.
1917-20	Declining in health, she seeks the milder climate of France. *Bliss and Other Stories* is published in England and the United States; this is followed by *The Garden Party and Other Stories* in 1922.
1923	Suffering from tuberculosis, her search for a cure ends at Fontainebleau, France, where she dies on January 9. *The Dove's Nest and Other Stories* is published posthumously.

Katherine Mansfield

Katherine Mansfield was born Kathleen Beauchamp, in New Zealand, in 1888. At the age of thirteen, her father considered it essential that Kathleen be sent to complete her education in London, where she entered Queen's College, in Harley Street. There, as in her own home, she was a solitary and a dreamer. Sometimes she wrote. Her journal and letters are striking, in their seriousness and their acute sense of the beauty of the world. She edited the school magazine, and wrote a good deal of verse which has been preserved, fluent and graceful. In one form or another, music or poetry or storytelling, she was impelled to give expression to the peculiar note which life sounded for her, and which, in Katherine Mansfield's belief, did not sound just thus for anyone else.

But the time came when her father came over to bring her back to New Zealand. The Beauchamps had returned to the city, and occupied a large house in Wellington. Her father had become a man of mark in commerce, banking, and public activities: soon he would be Sir Harold Beauchamp. He quite realized that his daughter wished to write; he was fond of her, and thought her gentle and delicate, but weak, rather unreal, aloof from the world and life. Here in the Antipodes she would think only of London, imagining the crowds coming out of the theaters, longing for the company of people with whom she could talk about poetry and books and feelings. Sustained by her resolve to become an artist, Katherine Mansfield had an inner strength which enabled her to preserve her balance, and a power of persuasion which enabled her to convince her father and obtain an allowance from him. In July 1908 he allowed her to leave New Zealand, and she left never to return. She settled in London and made Wilde her master. With the naïveté of methodical youth, she extracted from reading him a dangerous doctrine concerning the artist's duty of experience. She wanted to sacrifice her person to enrich her art. The day was to come when she regretted it: "But it hadn't all been experience. There is waste—destruction too."

In this way she lived an absurd romance. It was her belief that she would marry a man with no prejudices, who would not only protect her but respect her right to live as an untrammelled artist. She found a music teacher who apparently accepted this strange agreement, married him, found him absurd, and left him after a few days. A period of extreme loneliness and depression followed: "I felt rather like a frightened child lost in a funeral procession." Her health was poor; she had no real home, and sought vainly for a possible refuge. Her mother came to London to see her, but they did not understand each other. She was now expecting a child, not her husband's, and she had to go abroad to hide her condition and the coming birth. She was sent to a village in Germany, where she wrote a whole series of short stories and sketches, which made up her first book, *In a German Pension*.

When she wrote these stories, she was delighted to have them printed in a weekly paper, the *New Age*. She returned to London, lived alone, and worked. One day she received a letter from a young writer, John Middleton Murry, asking her to contribute to a small literary review published at Oxford. She met him, and found an enthusiastic and fluent young undergraduate. They met frequently, and before long were planning to publish a new review, to be called *Rhythm*. She said that she was not quite in sympathy with the *New Age*: "They have a conviction that I can only write satire. And I'm not a very satirical person—really. I believe in something. Let's call it truth. It's a very big thing. We have to discover it. That's what the artist is for—to become true by discovering truth. Truth is so important that when you discover a tiny bit of it, you forget all about everything else—and all about yourself."

She suggested that Murry should rent a room in the small flat where she was living. He agreed, and for a long time they carried on separate lives, though living thus side by side. In the end he married her. He hesitated before doing so, because he was poor, while she received a little money from her family. Neither of them earned anything appreciable. *Rhythm* died, as nearly all young reviews die. Katherine Mansfield had published some of her stories there, and did not know where she could place her work. Editors did not seem to understand the interest of the manuscripts she submitted, and perhaps they were not altogether wrong. What she wrote at this time was good, but a little too good; it lacked just that ring of truth which she longed above all things to capture. She had not yet discovered, or rather rediscovered, the fountainhead of her strongest impressions, which lay in her New Zealand childhood. But it was still near enough for her to be able to free herself from them and recreate them in her writings.

When the War broke out, Katherine Mansfield's young brother arrived from New Zealand to enlist. He was certainly the one person she loved above all others. He brought back all their childhood memories. Her brother had told her he was sure of coming home from the war. In him, it seems, this war was a mysterious but absolute certainty. "It's so curious—my absolute confidence that I'll come back." He went, and was immediately killed. This was the great agony of his sister's life. She left the real world for good, and gave herself over entirely to the refashioning of that tiny world of the past which, in memory, and blending with the image of her brother, became a place of enchantment.

She was also beginning to suffer from the illness that in the end killed her, tuberculosis of the lungs, and she left England for Bandol, in the South of France. Her husband accompanied her, but had soon to return to England; in any case, she wanted solitude for the sake of the work which was to occupy her last year, work of similar quality and kind as that of Proust, the capture of memory, the search for time past. The finest works of art, it may be, require this total detachment, this death before death.

When Katherine Mansfield published the first of her new stories, very few critics discerned the unique character of what lay before them. Like so many people in the postwar years, they confused strangeness with beauty. They preferred Dostoevsky to Chekhov, and Katherine Mansfield seemed to them too simple. Fortunately she had admirers of taste and influence, such as D.H. Lawrence, Sydney Schiff (that excellent novelist "Stephen Hudson" and a friend of Proust), the young novelist William Gerhardi, and Lady Ottoline Morrell. Still better, the public, which is generally receptive to a quality of naturalness, discovered her with delight.

Her first collections of stories, *Bliss* and *The Garden Party*, now began to show signs of real "selling" success.

Katherine Mansfield's artistic method is not that of those English novelists who take up a story at the moment of the hero's birth and slowly conduct it through a consecutive series of incidents towards a final catastrophe or into the luminous deltas of contentment. What Katherine Mansfield does is to select a family, a setting, and there make a deep cut into time, describing the impressions of the people during the brief chosen moment, and telling us nothing about them except through their own thoughts and remarks at that moment. From the opening lines, she makes them speak, and mentions them by name, without making any effort to instruct us about them. We come to know her heroes rather as we know our fellow passengers in a railway carriage, or our neighbors in a restaurant: that is to say, by building them up from their conversation.

Nor is Katherine Mansfield's method that of the French novelists, such as that of François Mauriac in *Genitrix* or *La Fin de La Nuit*, which likewise make an incision in time. The French novelists, like the French tragedians, choose for such a process a moment of crisis, whereas one particular feature of Katherine Mansfield's art is that, for the theme of her composition she chooses an ordinary day, a day marked only by some small family event—a garden party, a child's journey with her grandmother, an episode after a bereavement. It is precisely the intensity of this commonplace day which quickens our emotion or our sense of wonder, just as is done by those artists who can convey a sense of all the beauty of the world by painting a plate of fruit and a white table cloth.

Crisis it may be, for everything is a crisis in life, but a crisis in miniature. That a painting need not be large to be great has been proved by Chardin, Vuillard, and many others. That a short story can contain and suggest as much truth about the world as a long novel, had been shown by Chekhov and Mérimeé, whom Katherine Mansfield held in passionate admiration. But it is doubtful whether Chekhov himself would have dared to build up anything on a foundation so fragile as that of *Prelude*. Amongst his stories, *An Ordinary Story* is a crisis in the sense of the French tragedies; *Three Years* is a short novel, and Chekhov says more than once how he regrets it cannot be longer. But here Katherine Mansfield parts company with her master. "Chekhov made a mistake," she says, "in thinking that if he had had more time he would have written more fully, described the rain, and the midwife and the doctor having tea. The truth is one can only get so much into a story; there is always a sacrifice. One has to leave out what one knows and longs to use. Why? I haven't any idea, but there it is. It's always a kind of race to get in as much as one can before it disappears."

—*from* Prophets and Poets *by Andre Maurois (translated by Hamish Miles)*

Germans at Meat

Bread soup was placed upon the table, "Ah," said the Herr Rat, leaning upon the table as he peered into the tureen, "that is what I need. My 'magen' has not been in order for several days. Bread soup, and just the right consistency. I am a good cook myself"—he turned to me.

"How interesting," I said, attempting to infuse just the right amount of enthusiasm into my voice.

"Oh yes—when one is not married it is necessary. As for me, I have had all I wanted from women without marriage." He tucked his napkin into his collar and blew upon his soup as he spoke. "Now at nine o'clock I make myself an English breakfast, but not much. Four slices of bread, two eggs, two slices of cold ham, one plate of soup, two cups of tea—that is nothing to you."

He asserted the fact so vehemently that I had not the courage to refute it.

All eyes were suddenly turned upon me. I felt I was bearing the burden of the nation's preposterous breakfast—I who drank a cup of coffee while buttoning my blouse in the morning.

"Nothing at all," cried Herr Hoffmann from Berlin. "Ach, when I was in England in the morning I used to eat."

He turned up his eyes and his moustache, wiping the soup drippings from his coat and waistcoat.

"Do they really eat so much?" asked Fraulein Stiegelauer. "Soup and baker's bread and pig's flesh, and tea and coffee and stewed fruit, and honey and eggs, and cold fish and kidneys, and hot fish and liver. All the ladies eat, too, especially the ladies?"

"Certainly. I myself have noticed it, when I was living in a hotel in Leicester Square," cried the Herr Rat. "It was a good hotel, but they could not make tea—now—"

"Ah, that's one thing I *can* do," said I, laughing brightly. "I can make very good tea. The great secret is to warm the teapot."

"Warm the teapot," interrupted the Herr Rat, pushing away his soup plate. "What do you warm the teapot for? Ha! ha! that's very good! One does not eat the teapot, I suppose?"

He fixed his cold blue eyes upon me with an expression which suggested a thousand premeditated invasions.

"So that is the great secret of your English tea? All you do is to warm the teapot."

I wanted to say that was only the preliminary canter, but could not translate it, and so was silent.

The servant brought in veal, with sauerkraut and potatoes.

"I eat sauerkraut with great pleasure," said the Traveller from North Germany, "but now I have eaten so much of it that I cannot retain it. I am immediately forced to—"

"A beautiful day," I cried, turning to Fraulein Stiegelauer. "Did you get up early?"

"At five o'clock I walked for ten minutes in the wet grass. Again in bed. At halfpast five I fell asleep, and woke at seven, when I made an 'overbody' washing! Again in bed. At eight o'clock I had a cold-water poultice, and at half-past eight I drank a cup of mint tea. At nine I drank some malt coffee, and began my 'cure.' Pass me the sauerkraut, please. You do not eat it?"

"No, thank you. I still find it a little strong."

"Is it true," asked the Widow, picking her teeth with a hairpin as she spoke, "that you are a vegetarian?"

"Why, yes; I have not eaten meat for three years."

"Im—possible! Have you any family?"

"No."

"There now, you see, that's what you're coming to! Who ever heard of having children upon vegetables? It is not possible. But you never have large families in England now; I suppose you are too busy with your suffragetting. Now I have had nine children, and they are all alive, thank God. Fine, healthy babies—though after the first one was born I had to—"

"How *wonderful*!" I cried.

"Wonderful," said the Widow contemptuously, replacing the hairpin in the knob which was balanced on the top of her head. "Not at all! A friend of mine had four at the same time. Her husband was so pleased he gave a supper party and had them placed on the table. Of course she was very proud."

"Germany," boomed the Traveller, biting round a potato which he had speared with his knife, "is the home of the Family."

Followed an appreciative silence.

The dishes were changed for beef, red currants and spinach. They wiped their forks upon black bread and started again.

"How long are you remaining here?" asked the Herr Rat.

"I do not know exactly. I must be back in London in September."

"Of course you will visit München?"

"I am afraid I shall not have time. You see, it is important not to break into my 'cure.'"

"But you *must* go to München. You have not seen Germany if you have not been to München. All the Exhibitions, all the Art and Soul life of Germany are in München. There is the Wagner Festival in August, and Mozart and a Japanese collection of pictures—and there is the beer! You do not know what good beer is until you have been to München. Why, I see fine ladies every afternoon, but fine ladies, I tell you, drinking glasses so high." He measured a good washstand pitcher in height, and I smiled.

"If I drink a great deal of München beer I sweat so," said Herr Hoffmann. "When I am here, in the fields or before my baths, I sweat, but I enjoy it; but in the town it is not at all the same thing."

Prompted by the thought, he wiped his neck and face with his dinner napkin and carefully cleaned his ears.

A glass dish of stewed apricots was placed upon the table.

"Ah, fruit!" said Fraulein Stiegelauer, "that is so necessary to health. The doctor told me this morning that the more fruit I could eat the better."

She very obviously followed the advice.

Said the Traveller: "I suppose you are frightened of an invasion, too, eh? Oh, that's good. I've been reading all about your English play in a newspaper. Did you see it?"

"Yes." I sat upright. "I assure you we are not afraid."

"Well, then, you ought to be," said the Herr Rat. "You have got no army at all—a few little boys with their veins full of nicotine poisoning."

"Don't be afraid," Herr Hoffmann said. "We don't want England. If we did we would have had her long ago. We really do not want you."

He waved his spoon airily, looking across at me as though I were a little child whom he would keep or dismiss as he pleased.

"We certainly do not want Germany," I said.

"This morning I took a half bath. Then this afternoon I must take a knee bath and an arm bath," volunteered the Herr Rat; "then I do my exercises for an hour, and my work is over. A glass of wine and a couple of rolls with some sardines—"

They were handed cherry cake with whipped cream.

"What is your husband's favorite meat?" asked the Widow.

"I really do not know," I answered.

"You really do not know? How long have you been married?"

"Three years."

"But you cannot be in earnest! You would not have kept house as his wife for a week without knowing that fact."

"I really never asked him; he is not at all particular about his food."

A pause. They all looked at me, shaking their heads, their mouths full of cherry stones.

"No wonder there is a repetition in England of that dreadful state of things in Paris," said the Widow, folding her dinner napkin. "How can a woman expect to keep her husband if she does not know his favorite food after three years?"

"Mahlzeit!"

"Mahlzeit!"

I closed the door after me.

The Child-Who-Was-Tired

She was just beginning to walk along a little white road with tall black trees on either side, a little road that led to nowhere, and where nobody walked at all, when a hand gripped her shoulder, shook her, slapped her ear.

"Oh, oh, don't stop me," cried the Child-Who-Was-Tired. "Let me go."

"Get up, you good-for-nothing brat," said a voice; "get up and light the oven or I'll shake every bone out of your body."

With an immense effort she opened her eyes, and saw the Frau standing by, the baby bundled under one arm. The three other children who shared the same bed with the Child-Who-Was-Tired, accustomed to brawls, slept on peacefully. In a corner of the room the Man was fastening his braces.

"What do you mean by sleeping like this the whole night through—like a sack of potatoes? You've let the baby wet his bed twice."

She did not answer, but tied her petticoat string, and buttoned on her plaid frock with cold, shaking fingers.

"There, that's enough. Take the baby into the kitchen with you, and heat that cold coffee on the spirit lamp for the master, and give him the loaf of black bread out of the table drawer. Don't guzzle it yourself or I'll know."

The Frau staggered across the room, flung herself on to her bed, drawing the pink bolster round her shoulders.

It was almost dark in the kitchen. She laid the baby on the wooden settle, covering him with a shawl, then poured the coffee from the earthenware jug into the saucepan, and set it on the spirit lamp to boil.

"I'm sleepy," nodded the Child-Who-Was-Tired, kneeling on the floor and splitting the damp pine logs into little chips. "That's why I'm not awake."

The oven took a long time to light. Perhaps it was cold, like herself, and sleepy....

Perhaps it had been dreaming of a little white road with black trees on either side, a little road that led to nowhere.

Then the door was pulled violently open and the Man strode in.

"Here, what are you doing, sitting on the floor?" he shouted. "Give me my coffee. I've got to be off. Ugh! You haven't even washed over the table."

She sprang to her feet, poured his coffee into an enamel cup, and gave him bread and a knife, then, taking a wash rag from the sink, smeared over the black linoleumed table.

"Swine of a day—swine's life," mumbled the Man, sitting by the table and staring out of the window at the bruised sky, which seemed to bulge heavily over the dull land. He stuffed his mouth with bread and then swilled it down with the coffee.

The Child drew a pail of water, turned up her sleeves, frowning the while at her arms, as if to scold them for being so thin, so much like little stunted twigs, and began to mop over the floor.

"Stop sousing about the water while I'm here," grumbled the man. "Stop the baby snivelling; it's been going on like that all night."

The Child gathered the baby into her lap and sat rocking him.

"Ts—ts—ts," she said. "He's cutting his eye teeth, that's what makes him cry so. *And* dribble—I never seen a baby dribble like this one." She wiped his mouth and nose with a corner of her skirt. "Some babies get their teeth without you knowing it," she went on, "and some take on this way all the time. I once heard of a baby that died, and they found all its teeth in its stomach."

The Man got up, unhooked his cloak from the back of the door, and flung it round him.

"There's another coming," said he.

"What—a tooth!" exclaimed the Child, startled for the first time that morning out of her dreadful heaviness, and thrusting her finger into the baby's mouth.

"No," he said grimly, "another baby. Now, get on with your work; it's time the others got up for school." She stood a moment quite silently, hearing his heavy steps on the stone passage, then the gravel walk, and finally the slam of the front gate.

"Another baby! Hasn't she finished having them *yet*?" thought the Child. "Two babies getting eye teeth—two babies to get up for in the night—two babies to carry about and wash their little piggy clothes!" She looked with horror at the one in her arms, who, seeming to understand the contemptuous loathing of her tired glance, doubled his fists, stiffened his body, and began violently screaming.

"Ts—ts—ts." She laid him on the settle and went back to her floor-washing. He never ceased crying for a moment, but she got quite used to it and kept time with her broom. Oh, how tired she was! Oh, the heavy broom handle and the burning spot just at the back of her neck that ached so, and a funny little fluttering feeling just at the back of her waistband, as though something were going to break.

The clock struck six. She set the pan of milk in the oven, and went into the next room to wake and dress the three children. Anton and Hans lay together in attitudes of mutual amity which certainly never existed out of their sleeping hours. Lena was curled up, her knees under her chin, only a straight, standing-up pigtail of hair showing above the bolster.

"Get up," cried the Child, speaking in a voice of immense authority, pulling off the bedclothes and giving the boys sundry pokes and digs. "I've been calling you this last half-hour. It's late, and I'll tell on you if you don't get dressed this minute."

Anton awoke sufficiently to turn over and kick Hans on a tender part, whereupon Hans pulled Lena's pigtail until she shrieked for her mother.

"Oh, do be quiet," whispered the Child. "Oh, do get up and dress. You know what will happen. There—I'll help you."

But the warning came too late. The Frau got out of bed, walked in a determined fashion into the kitchen, returning with a bundle of twigs in her hand fastened together with a strong cord. One by one she laid the children across her knee and severely beat them, expending a final burst of energy on the Child-Who-Was-Tired, then returned to bed, with a comfortable sense of her maternal duties in good working order for the day. Very subdued, the three allowed themselves to be dressed and washed by the Child, who even laced the boys' boots, having found through experience that if left to themselves they hopped about for at least five minutes to find a comfortable ledge for their foot, and then spat on their hands and broke the bootlaces.

While she gave them their breakfast they became uproarious, and the baby would not cease crying. When she filled the tin kettle with milk, tied on the rubber teat, and, first moistening it herself, tried with little coaxing words to make him drink, he threw the bottle on to the floor and trembled all over.

"Eye teeth!" shouted Hans, hitting Anton over the head with his empty cup; "he's getting the evil-eye teeth, I should say."

"Smarty!" retorted Lena, poking out her tongue at him, and then, when he promptly did the same, crying at the top of her voice, "Mother, Hans is making faces at me!"

"That's right," said Hans; "go on howling, and when you're in bed tonight I'll wait till you're asleep, and then I'll creep over and take a little tiny piece of your arm and twist and twist it until—" He leant over the table making the most horrible faces at Lena, not noticing that Anton was standing behind his chair until the little boy bent over and spat on his brother's shaven head.

"Oh, weh! oh, weh!"

The Child-Who-Was-Tired pushed and pulled them apart, muffled them into their coats, and drove them out of the house.

"Hurry, hurry! the second bell's rung," she urged, knowing perfectly well she was telling a story, and rather exulting in the fact. She washed up the breakfast things, then went down to the cellar to look out the potatoes and beetroot.

Such a funny, cold place the coal cellar! With potatoes banked on one corner, beetroot in an old candle box, two tubs of sauerkraut, and a twisted mass of dahlia roots—that looked as real as though they were fighting one another, thought the Child.

She gathered the potatoes into her skirt, choosing big ones with few eyes because they were easier to peel, and bending over the dull heap in the silent cellar, she began to nod.

"Here, you, what are you doing down there?" cried the Frau, from the top of the stairs. "The baby's fallen off the settle, and got a bump as big as an egg over his eye. Come up here, and I'll teach you!"

"It wasn't me—it wasn't me!" screamed the Child, beaten from one side of the hall to the other, so that the potatoes and beetroot rolled out of her skirt.

The Frau seemed to be as big as a giant, and there was a certain heaviness in all her movements that was terrifying to anyone so small.

"Sit in the corner, and peel and wash the vegetables, and keep the baby quiet while I do the washing."

Whimpering she obeyed, but as to keeping the baby quiet, that was impossible.

His face was hot, little beads of sweat stood all over his head, and he stiffened his body and cried. She held him on her knees, with a pan of cold water beside her for the cleaned vegetables and the ducks' bucket for the peelings.

"Ts—ts—ts!" she crooned, scraping and boring; "there's going to be another soon, and you can't both keep on crying. Why don't you go to sleep, baby? I would, if I were you. I'll tell you a dream. Once upon a time there was a little white road—"

She shook back her head, a great lump ached in her throat and then the tears ran down her face on to the vegetables.

"That's no good," said the Child, shaking them away. "Just stop crying until I've finished this, baby, and I'll walk you up and down."

But by that time she had to peg out the washing for the Frau. A wind had sprung up. Standing on tiptoe in the yard, she almost felt she would be blown away. There was a bad smell coming from the ducks' coop, which was half full of manure water, but away in the meadow she saw the grass blowing like little green hairs. And she remembered having heard of a child who had once played for a whole day in just such a meadow with real sausages and beer for her dinner—and not a little bit of tiredness. Who had told her that story? She could not remember, and yet it was so plain.

The wet clothes flapped in her face as she pegged them; danced and jigged on the line, bulged out and twisted. She walked back to the house with lagging steps, looking longingly at the grass in the meadow.

"What must I do now, please?" she said.

"Make the beds and hang the baby's mattress out of the window, then get the wagon and take him for a little walk along the road. In front of the house, mind—where I can see you. Don't stand there, gaping! Then come in when I call you and help me cut up the salad."

When she had made the beds the Child stood and looked at them. Gently she stroked the pillow with her hand, and then, just for one moment, let her head rest there. Again the smarting lump in her throat, the stupid tears that fell and kept on falling as she dressed the baby and dragged the little wagon up and down the road.

A man passed, driving a bullock wagon. He wore a long, queer feather in his hat, and whistled as he passed. Two girls with bundles on their shoulders came walking out of the village—one wore a red handkerchief about her head and one a blue. They were laughing and holding each other by the hand. Then the sun pushed by a heavy fold of grey cloud and spread a warm yellow light over everything.

"Perhaps," thought the Child-Who-Was-Tired, "if I walked far enough up this road I might come to a little white one, with tall black trees on either side—a little road—"

"Salad, salad!" cried the Frau's voice from the house.

Soon the children came home from school, dinner was eaten, the Man took the Frau's share of pudding as well as his own, and the three children seemed to smear themselves all over with whatever they ate. Then more dish-washing and more cleaning and baby-minding. So the afternoon dragged coldly through.

Old Frau Gerathwohl came in with a fresh piece of pig's flesh for the Frau, and the Child listened to them gossiping together.

"Frau Manda went on her 'journey to Rome' last night, and brought back a daughter. How are you feeling?"

"I was sick twice this morning," said the Frau. "My insides are all twisted up with having children too quickly."

"I see you've got a new help," commented old Mother Gerathwohl.

"Oh, dear Lord"—the Frau lowered her voice—"don't you know her? She's the free-born one—daughter of the waitress at the railway station. They found her mother trying to squeeze her head in the wash-hand jug, and the child's half silly."

"Ts—ts—ts!" whispered the free-born one to the baby.

As the day drew in the Child-Who-Was-Tired did not know how to fight her sleepiness any longer. She was afraid to sit down or stand still. As she sat at supper the Man and the Frau seemed to swell to an immense size as she watched them, and then become smaller than dolls, with little voices that seemed to come from outside the window. Looking at the baby, it suddenly had two heads, and then no head. Even his crying made her feel worse. When she thought of the nearness of bedtime she shook all over with excited joy. But as eight o'clock approached there was the sound of wheels on the road, and presently in came a party of friends to spend the evening.

Then it was:

"Put on the coffee."

"Bring me the sugar tin."

"Carry the chairs out of the bedroom."

"Set the table."

And, finally, the Frau sent her into the next room to keep the baby quiet.

There was a little piece of candle burning in the enamel bracket. As she walked up and down she saw her great big shadow on the wall like a grown-up person with a grown-up baby. Whatever would it look like when she carried two babies so!

"Ts—ts—ts! Once upon a time she was walking along a little white road, with oh! such great big black trees on either side."

"Here, you!" called the Frau's voice, "bring me my new jacket from behind the door." And as she took it into the warm room one of the women said, "She looks like an owl. Such children are seldom right in their heads."

"Why don't you keep that baby quiet?" said the Man, who had just drunk enough beer to make him feel very brave and master of his house.

"If you don't keep that baby quiet you'll know why later on."

They burst out laughing as she stumbled back into the bedroom.

"I don't believe Holy Mary could keep him quiet," she murmured. "Did Jesus cry like this when He was little? If I was not so tired perhaps I could do it; but the baby just knows that I want to go to sleep. And there is going to be another one."

She flung the baby on the bed, and stood looking at him with terror.

From the next room there came the jingle of glasses and the warm sound of laughter.

And she suddenly had a beautiful marvelous idea.

She laughed for the first time that day, and clapped her hands.

"Ts—ts—ts!" she said, "lie there, silly one; you *will* go to sleep. You'll not cry any more or wake up in the night. Funny, little ugly baby."

He opened his eyes, and shrieked loudly at the sight of the Child-Who-Was-Tired. From the next room she heard the Frau call out to her.

"One moment—he is almost asleep," she cried.

And then gently, smiling, on tiptoe, she brought the pink bolster from the Frau's bed and covered the baby's face with it, pressed with all her might as he struggled, "like a duck with its head off, wriggling," she thought.

She heaved a long sigh, then fell back on to the floor, and was walking along a little white road with tall black trees on either side, a little road that led to nowhere, and where nobody walked at all—nobody at all.

The Daughters of the Late Colonel

I

The week after was one of the busiest weeks of their lives. Even when they went to bed it was only their bodies that lay down and rested; their minds went on, thinking things out, talking things over, wondering, deciding, trying to remember where...

Constantia lay like a statue, her hands by her sides, her feet just overlapping each other, the sheet up to her chin. She stared at the ceiling.

"Do you think father would mind if we gave his top-hat to the porter?"

"The porter?" snapped Josephine. "Why ever the porter? What a very extraordinary idea!"

"Because," said Constantia slowly, "he must often have to go to funerals. And I noticed at—at the cemetery that he only had a bowler." She paused. "I thought then how very much he'd appreciate a top hat. We ought to give him a present, too. He was always very nice to father."

"But," cried Josephine, flouncing on her pillow and staring across the dark at Constantia, "father's head!" And suddenly, for one awful moment, she nearly giggled. Not, of course, that she felt in the least like giggling. It must have been habit. Years ago, when they had stayed awake at night talking, their beds had simply heaved. And now the porter's head, disappearing, popped out, like a candle, under father's hat.... The giggle mounted, mounted; she clenched her hands; she fought it down; she frowned fiercely at the dark and said "Remember" terribly sternly.

"We can decide tomorrow," she sighed.

Constantia had noticed nothing; she sighed.

"Do you think we ought to have our dressing gowns dyed as well?"

"Black?" almost shrieked Josephine.

"Well, what else?" said Constantia. "I was thinking—it doesn't seem quite sincere, in a way, to wear black out of doors and when we're fully dressed, and then when we're at home—"

"But nobody sees us," said Josephine. She gave the bedclothes such a twitch that both her feet became uncovered, and she had to creep up the pillows to get them well under again.

"Kate does," said Constantia. "And the postman very well might."

Josephine thought of her dark-red slippers, which matched her dressing gown, and of Constantia's favorite indefinite green ones which went with hers. Black! Two black dressing gowns and two pairs of black woolly slippers, creeping off to the bathroom like black cats.

"I don't think it's absolutely necessary," said she.

Silence. Then Constantia said, "We shall have to post the papers with the notice in them tomorrow to catch the Ceylon mail.... How many letters have we had up till now?"

"Twenty-three."

Josephine had replied to them all, and twenty-three times when she came to "We miss our dear father *so* much" she had broken down and had to use her handkerchief, and on some of them even to soak up a very light blue tear with an edge of blotting paper. Strange! She couldn't have put it on—but twenty-three times. Even now, though, when she said over to herself sadly. "We miss our dear father *so* much" she could have cried if she'd wanted to.

"Have you got enough stamps?" came from Constantia.

"Oh, how can I tell?" said Josephine crossly. "What's the good of asking me that now?"

"I was just wondering," said Constantia mildly.

Silence again. There came a little rustle, a scurry, a hop.

"A mouse," said Constantia.

"It can't be a mouse because there aren't any crumbs," said Josephine.

"But it doesn't know there aren't," said Constantia.

A spasm of pity squeezed her heart. Poor little thing! She wished she'd left a tiny piece of biscuit on the dressing table. It was awful to think of it not finding anything. What would it do?

"I can't think how they manage to live at all," she said slowly.

"Who?" demanded Josephine.

And Constantia said more loudly than she meant to, "Mice."

Josephine was furious. "Oh, what nonsense, Con!" she said. "What have mice got to do with it? You're asleep."

"I don't think I am," said Constantia. She shut her eyes to make sure. She was.

Josephine arched her spine, pulled up her knees, folded her arms so that her fists came under her ears, and pressed her cheek hard against the pillow.

II

Another thing which complicated matters was they had Nurse Andrews staying on with them that week. It was their own fault; they had asked her. It was Josephine's idea. On the morning—well, on the last morning, when the doctor had gone, Josephine had said to Constantia, "Don't you think it would be rather nice if we asked Nurse Andrews to stay on for a week as our guest?"

"Very nice," said Constantia.

"I thought," went on Josephine quickly, "I should just say this afternoon, after I've paid her, 'My sister and I would be very pleased, after all you've done for us, Nurse Andrews, if you would stay on for a week as our guest.' I'd have to put that in about being our guest in case—"

"Oh, but she could hardly expect to be paid!" cried Constantia.

"One never knows," said Josephine sagely.

Nurse Andrews had, of course, jumped at the idea. But it was a bother. It meant they had to have regular sit-down meals at the proper times, whereas if they'd been alone they could just have asked Kate if she wouldn't have minded bringing them a tray wherever they were. And meal times now that the strain was over were rather a trial.

Nurse Andrews was simply fearful about butter. Really they couldn't help feeling that about butter, at least, she took advantage of their kindness. And she had that maddening habit of asking for just an inch more bread to finish what she had on her plate, and then, at the last mouthful, absent-mindedly—of course it wasn't absent-mindedly—taking another helping. Josephine got very red when this happened, and she fastened her small, bead-like eyes on the tablecloth as if she saw a minute strange insect creeping through the web of it. But Constantia's long, pale face lengthened and set, and she gazed away—away—far over the desert, to where that line of camels unwound like a thread of wool....

"When I was with Lady Tukes," said Nurse Andrews, "she had such a dainty little contrayvance for the buttah. It was a silvah Cupid balanced on the—on the bordah of a glass dish, holding a tayny fork. And when you wanted some buttah you simply pressed his foot and he bent down and speared you a piece. It was quite a gayme."

Josephine could hardly bear that. But "I think those things are very extravagant" was all she said.

"But whey?" asked Nurse Andrews, beaming through her eyeglasses. "No one, surely, would take more buttah than one wanted—would one?"

"Ring, Con," cried Josephine. She couldn't trust herself to reply.

And proud young Kate, the enchanted princess, came in to see what the old tabbies wanted now. She snatched away their plates of mock something or other and slapped down a white, terrified blancmange.

"Jam, please, Kate," said Josephine kindly.

Kate knelt and burst open the sideboard, lifted the lid of the jam-pot, saw it was empty, put it on the table, and stalked off.

"I'm afraid," said Nurse Andrews a moment later, "there isn't any."

"Oh, what a bother!" said Josephine. She bit her lip. "What had we better do?"

Constantia looked dubious. "We can't disturb Kate again," she said softly.

Nurse Andrews waited, smiling at them both. Her eyes wandered, spying at everything behind her eyeglasses. Constantia in despair went back to her camels. Josephine frowned heavily—concentrated. If it hadn't been for this idiotic woman she and Con would, of course, have eaten their blancmange without. Suddenly the idea came.

"I know," she said. "Marmalade. There's some marmalade in the sideboard. Get it, Con."

"I hope," laughed Nurse Andrews, and her laugh was like a spoon tinkling against a medicine-glass—"I hope it's not very bittah marmalayde."

III

But, after all, it was not long now, and then she'd be gone for good. And there was no getting over the fact that she had been very kind to father. She had nursed him day and night at the end. Indeed, both Constantia and Josephine felt privately she had rather overdone the not leaving him at the very last. For when they had gone in to say good-bye Nurse Andrews had sat beside his bed the whole time, holding his wrist and pretending to look at her watch. It couldn't have been necessary. It was so tactless, too. Supposing father had wanted to say something—something private to them. Not that he had. Oh, far from it! He lay there, purple, a dark, angry purple in the face, and never even looked at them when they came in. Then, as they were standing there, wondering what to do, he had suddenly opened one eye. Oh, what a difference it would have made, what a difference to their memory of him, how much easier to tell people about it, if he had only opened both! But no—one eye only. It glared at them a moment and then...went out.

IV

It had made it very awkward for them when Mr. Farolles, of St. John's, called the same afternoon.

"The end was quite peaceful, I trust?" were the first words he said as he glided towards them through the dark drawing room.

"Quite," said Josephine faintly. They both hung their heads. Both of them felt certain that eye wasn't at all a peaceful eye.

"Won't you sit down?" said Josephine.

"Thank you, Miss Pinner," said Mr. Farolles gratefully. He folded his coattails and began to lower himself into father's armchair, but just as he touched it he almost sprang up and slid into the next chair instead.

He coughed. Josephine clasped her hands; Constantia looked vague.

"I want you to feel, Miss Pinner," said Mr. Farolles, "and you, Miss Constantia, that I'm trying to be helpful. I want to be helpful to you both, if you will let me. These are the times," said Mr. Farolles, very simply and earnestly, "when God means us to be helpful to one another."

"Thank you very much, Mr. Farolles," said Josephine and Constantia.

"Not at all," said Mr. Farolles gently. He drew his kid gloves through his fingers and leaned forward. "And if either of you would like a little Communion, either or both of you, here *and* now, you have only to tell me. A little Communion is often very help—a great comfort," he added tenderly.

But the idea of a little Communion terrified them. What! In the drawing room by themselves—with no—no altar or anything! The piano would he much too high, thought Constantia, and Mr. Farolles could not possibly lean over it with the chalice. And Kate would be sure to come bursting in and interrupt them, thought Josephine. And supposing the bell rang in the middle? It might be somebody important—about their mourning. Would they get up reverently and go out, or would they have to wait...in torture?

"Perhaps you will send round a note by your good Kate if you would care for it later," said Mr. Farolles.

"Oh yes, thank you very much!" they both said.

Mr. Farolles got up and took his black straw hat from the round table.

"And about the funeral," he said softly. "I may arrange that—as your dear father's old friend and yours, Miss Pinner—and Miss Constantia?"

Josephine and Constantia got up too.

"I should like it to be quite simple," said Josephine firmly, "and not too expensive. At the same time, I should like—"

"A good one that will last," thought dreamy Constantia, as if Josephine were buying a nightgown. But of course Josephine didn't say that. "One suitable to our father's position." She was very nervous.

"I'll run round to our good friend Mr. Knight," said Mr. Farolles soothingly. "I will ask him to come and see you. I am sure you will find him very helpful indeed."

V

Well, at any rate, all that part of it was over, though neither of them could possibly believe that father was never coming back. Josephine had had a moment of absolute terror at the cemetery, while the coffin was lowered, to think that she and Constantia had done this thing without asking his permission. What would father say when he found out? For he was bound to find out sooner or later. He always did. "Buried. You two girls had me *buried*!" She heard his stick thumping. Oh, what would they say? What possible excuse could they make? It sounded such an appallingly heartless thing to do. Such a wicked advantage to take of a person because he happened to be helpless at the moment. The other people seemed to treat it all as a matter of course. They were strangers; they couldn't be expected to understand that father was the very last person for such a thing to happen to. No, the entire blame for it all would fall on her and Constantia. And the expense, she thought, stepping into the tight-buttoned cab. When she had to show him the bills. What would he say then?

She heard him absolutely roaring, "And do you expect me to pay for this gimcrack excursion of yours?"

"Oh," groaned poor Josephine aloud, "we shouldn't have done it, Con!"

And Constantia, pale as a lemon in all that blackness, said in a frightened whisper, "Done what, Jug?"

"Let them bu-bury father like that," said Josephine, breaking down and crying into her new, queer-smelling mourning handkerchief.

"But what else could we have done?" asked Constantia wonderingly. "We couldn't have kept him, Jug—we couldn't have kept him unburied. At any rate, not in a flat that size."

Josephine blew her nose; the cab was dreadfully stuffy.

"I don't know," she said forlornly. "It is all so dreadful. I feel we ought to have tried to, just for a time at least. To make perfectly sure. One thing's certain"—and her tears sprang out again—"father will never forgive us for this—never!"

VI

Father would never forgive them. That was what they felt more than ever when, two mornings later, they went into his room to go through his things. They had discussed it quite calmly. It was even down on Josephine's list of things to be done. *Go through father's things and settle about them.* But that was a very different matter from saying after breakfast:

"Well, are you ready, Con?"

"Yes, Jug—when you are."

"Then I think we'd better get it over."

It was dark in the hall. It had been a rule for years never to disturb father in the morning, whatever happened. And now they were going to open the door without knocking even.... Constantia's eyes were enormous at the idea; Josephine felt weak in the knees.

"You—you go first," she gasped, pushing Constantia.

But Constantia said, as she always had said on those occasions, "No, Jug, that's not fair. You're eldest."

Josephine was just going to say—what at other times she wouldn't have owned to for the world—what she kept for her very last weapon, "But you're tallest," when they noticed that the kitchen door was open, and there stood Kate....

"Very stiff," said Josephine, grasping the door handle and doing her best to turn it. As if anything ever deceived Kate!

It couldn't be helped. That girl was...Then the door was shut behind them, but—but they weren't in father's room at all. They might have suddenly walked through the wall by mistake into a different flat altogether. Was the door just behind them? They were too frightened to look. Josephine knew that if it was it was holding itself tight shut; Constantia felt that, like the doors in dreams, it hadn't any handle at all. It was the coldness which made it so awful. Or the whiteness—which? Everything was covered. The blinds were down, a cloth hung over the mirror, a sheet hid the bed; a huge fan of white paper filled the fireplace. Constantia timidly put out her hand; she almost expected a snowflake to fall. Josephine felt a queer tingling in her nose, as if her nose was freezing. Then a cab klop-klopped over the cobbles below, and the quiet seemed to shake into little pieces.

"I had better pull up a blind," said Josephine bravely.

"Yes, it might be a good idea," whispered Constantia.

They only gave the blind a touch, but it flew up and the cord flew after, rolling round the blindstick, and the little tassel tapped as if trying to get free. That was too much for Constantia.

"Don't you think—don't you think we might put it off for another day?" she whispered.

"Why?" snapped Josephine, feeling, as usual, much better now that she knew for certain that Constantia was terrified. "It's got to be done. But I do wish you wouldn't whisper, Con."

"I didn't know I was whispering," whispered Constantia.

"And why do you keep on staring at the bed?" said Josephine, raising her voice almost defiantly. "There's nothing *on* the bed."

"Oh, Jug, don't say so!" said poor Connie. "At any rate, not so loudly."

Josephine felt herself that she had gone too far. She took a wide swerve over to the chest of drawers, put out her hand, but quickly drew it back again.

"Connie!" she gasped, and she wheeled round and leaned with her back against the chest of drawers.

"Oh, Jug—what?"

Josephine could only glare. She had the most extraordinary feeling that she had just escaped something simply awful. But how could she explain to Constantia that father was in the chest of drawers? He was in the top drawer with his handkerchiefs and neckties, or in the next with his shirts and pajamas, or in the lowest of all with his suits. He was watching there, hidden away—just behind the door handle—ready to spring.

She pulled a funny old-fashioned face at Constantia, just as she used to in the old days when she was going to cry.

"I can't open," she nearly wailed.

"No, don't, Jug," whispered Constantia earnestly. "It's much better not to. Don't let's open anything. At any rate, not for a long time."

"But—but it seems so weak," said Josephine, breaking down.

"But why not be weak for once, Jud?" argued Constantia, whispering quite fiercely. "If it is weak." And her pale stare flew from the locked writing table—so safe—to the huge glittering wardrobe, and she began to breathe in a queer, panting way. "Why shouldn't we be weak for once in our lives, Jug? It's quite excusable. Let's be weak—be weak, Jug. It's much nicer to be weak than to be strong."

And then she did one of those amazingly bold things that she'd done about twice before in their lives; she marched over to the wardrobe, turned the key, and took it out of the lock. Took it out of the lock and held it up to Josephine, showing Josephine by her extraordinary smile that she knew what she'd done, she'd risked deliberately father being in there among his overcoats.

If the huge wardrobe had lurched forward, had crashed down on Constantia, Josephine wouldn't have been surprised. On the contrary, she would have thought it the only suitable thing to happen. But nothing happened. Only the room seemed quieter than ever, and bigger flakes of cold air fell on Josephine's shoulders and knees. She began to shiver.

"Come, Jug," said Constantia, still with that awful callous smile, and Josephine followed just as she had that last time, when Constantia had pushed Benny into the round pond.

VII

But the strain told on them when they were back in the dining-room. They sat down, very shaky, and looked at each other.

"I don't feel I can settle to anything," said Josephine "until I've had something. Do you think we could ask Kate for two cups of hot water?"

"I really don't see why we shouldn't," said Constantia carefully. She was quite normal again. "I won't ring. I'll go to the kitchen door and ask her."

"Yes, do," said Josephine, sinking down into a chair. "Tell her, just two cups, Con, nothing else—on a tray."

"She needn't even put the jug on, need she?" said Constantia, as though Kate might very well complain if the jug had been there.

"Oh no, certainly not! The jug's not at all necessary. She can pour it direct out of the kettle," cried Josephine, feeling that would be a labor-saving indeed.

Their cold lips quivered at the greenish brims. Josephine curved her small red hands round the cup; Constantia sat up and blew on the wavy stream, making it flutter from one side to the other.

"Speaking of Benny," said Josephine.

And though Benny hadn't been mentioned Constantia immediately looked as though he had.

"He'll expect us to send him something of father's, of course. But it's so difficult to know what to send to Ceylon."

"You mean things get unstuck so on the voyage," murmured Constantia.

"No, lost," said Josephine sharply. "You know there's no post. Only runners."

Both paused to watch a black man in white linen drawers running through the pale fields for dear life, with a large brown-paper parcel in his hands. Josephine's black man was tiny; he scurried along glistening like an ant. But there was something blind and tireless about Constantia's tall, thin fellow, which made him, she decided, a very unpleasant person indeed.... On the veranda, dressed all in white and wearing a cork helmet, stood Benny. His right hand shook up and down, as father's did when he was impatient. And behind him, not in the least interested, sat Hilda, the unknown sister-in-law. She swung in a cane rocker and flicked over the leaves of the *Tatler*.

"I think his watch would be the most suitable present," said Josephine.

Constantia looked up; she seemed surprised.

"Oh, would you trust a gold watch to a native?"

"But of course I'd disguise it," said Josephine. "No one would know it was a watch." She liked the idea of having to make a parcel such a curious shape that no one could possibly guess what it was. She even thought for a moment of hiding the watch in a narrow cardboard corset box that she'd kept by her for a long time, waiting for it to come in for something. It was such beautiful firm cardboard. But, no, it wouldn't be appropriate for this occasion. It had lettering on it: *Medium Women's 28. Extra Firm Busks*. It would be almost too much of a surprise for Benny to open that and find father's watch inside.

"And of course it isn't as though it would be going—ticking, I mean," said Constantia, who was still thinking of the native love of jewelery. "At least," she added, "it would be very strange if after all that time it was."

VIII

Josephine made no reply. She had flown off on one of her tangents. She had suddenly thought of Cyril. Wasn't it more usual for the only grandson to have the watch? And then dear Cyril was so appreciative, and a gold watch meant so much to a young man. Benny, in all probability, had quite got out of the habit of watches; men so seldom wore waistcoats in those hot climates. Whereas Cyril in London wore them from year's end to year's end. And it would be so nice for her and Constantia, when he came to tea, to know it was there. "I see you've got on grandfather's watch, Cyril." It would be somehow so satisfactory.

Dear boy! What a blow his sweet, sympathetic little note had been! Of course they quite understood; but it was most unfortunate.

"It would have been such a point, having him," said Josephine.

"And he would have enjoyed it so," said Constantia, not thinking what she was saying.

However, as soon as he got back he was coming to tea with his aunties. Cyril to tea was one of their rare treats.

"Now, Cyril, you mustn't be frightened of our cakes. Your Auntie Con and I bought them at Buszard's this morning. We know what a man's appetite is. So don't be ashamed of making a good tea."

Josephine cut recklessly into the rich dark cake that stood for her winter gloves or the soling and heeling of Constantia's only respectable shoes. But Cyril was most unmanlike in appetite.

"I say, Aunt Josephine, I simply can't. I've only just had lunch, you know."

"Oh, Cyril, that can't be true! It's after four," cried Josephine. Constantia sat with her knife poised over the chocolate roll.

"It is, all the same," said Cyril. "I had to meet a man at Victoria, and he kept me hanging about till...there was only time to get lunch and to come on here. And he gave me—phew"—Cyril put his hand to his forehead—"a terrific blow-out," he said.

It was disappointing—today of all days. But still he couldn't be expected to know.

"But you'll have a meringue, won't you, Cyril?" said Aunt Josephine. "These meringues were bought specially for you. Your dear father was so fond of them. We were sure you are, too."

"I am, Aunt Josephine," cried Cyril ardently. "Do you mind if I take half to begin with?"

"Not at all, dear boy; but we mustn't let you off with that."

"Is your dear father still so fond of meringues?" asked Auntie Con gently. She winced faintly as she broke through the shell of hers.

"Well, I don't quite know, Auntie Con," said Cyril breezily.

At that they both looked up.

"Don't know?" almost snapped Josephine. "Don't know a thing like that about your own father, Cyril?"

"Surely," said Aunty Con softly.

Cyril tried to laugh it off. "Oh, well," he said, "it's such a long time since—" He faltered. He stopped. Their faces were too much for him.

"Even *so*," said Josephine.

And Auntie Con looked.

Cyril put down his teacup. "Wait a bit," he cried. "Wait a bit, Aunt Josephine. What am I thinking of?"

He looked up. They were beginning to brighten. Cyril slapped his knee.

"Of course," he said, "it was meringues. How could I have forgotten? Yes, Aunt Josephine, you're perfectly right. Father's most frightfully keen on meringues."

They didn't only beam. Aunt Josephine went scarlet with pleasure; Auntie Con gave a deep, deep sigh.

"And now, Cyril, you must come and see father," said Josephine. "He knows you were coming today."

"Right," said Cyril, very firmly and heartily. He got up from his chair; suddenly he glanced at the clock.

"I say, Auntie Con, isn't your clock a bit slow? I've got to meet a man at—at Paddington just after five. I'm afraid I shan't be able to stay very long with grandfather."

"Oh, he won't expect you to stay *very* long!" said Aunt Josephine.

Constantia was still gazing at the clock. She couldn't make up her mind if it was fast or slow. It was one or the other, she felt almost certain of that. At any rate, it had been.

Cyril still lingered. "Aren't you coming along, Auntie Con?"

"Of course," said Josephine, "we shall all go. Come on, Con."

IX

They knocked at the door, and Cyril followed his aunts into grandfather's hot, sweetish room.

"Come on," said Grandfather Pinner. "Don't hang about. What is it? What've you been up to?"

He was sitting in front of a roaring fire, clasping his stick. He had a thick rug over his knees. On his lap there lay a beautiful pale yellow silk handkerchief.

"It's Cyril, father," said Josephine shyly. And she took Cyril's hand and led him forward.

"Good afternoon, grandfather," said Cyril, trying to take his hand out of Aunt Josephine's. Grandfather Pinner shot his eyes at Cyril in the way he was famous for. Where was Auntie Con? She stood on the other side of Aunt Josephine; her long arms hung down in front of her; her hands were clasped. She never took her eyes off grandfather.

"Well," said Grandfather Pinner, beginning to thump, "what have you got to tell me?"

What had he, what had he got to tell him? Cyril felt himself smiling like a perfect imbecile. The room was stifling, too.

But Aunt Josephine came to his rescue. She cried brightly, "Cyril says his father is still very fond of meringues, father dear."

"Eh?" said Grandfather Pinner, curving his hand like a purple meringue-shell over one ear.

Josephine repeated, "Cyril says his father is still very fond of meringues."

"Can't hear," said old Colonel Pinner. And he waved Josephine away with his stick, then pointed with his stick to Cyril. "Tell me what she's trying to say," he said.

(My God!) "Must I?" said Cyril, blushing and staring at Aunt Josephine.

"Do, dear," she smiled. "It will please him so much."

"Come on, out with it!" cried Colonel Pinner testily, beginning to thump again.

And Cyril leaned forward and yelled, "Father's still very fond of meringues."

At that Grandfather Pinner jumped as though he had been shot.

"Don't shout!" he cried. "What's the matter with the boy? *Meringues*! What about 'em?"

"Oh, Aunt Josephine, must we go on?" groaned Cyril desperately.

"It's quite all right, dear boy," said Aunt Josephine, as though he and she were at the dentist's together. "He'll understand in a minute." And she whispered to Cyril, "He's getting a bit deaf, you know." Then she leaned forward and really bawled at Grandfather Pinner, "Cyril only wanted to tell you, father dear, that *his* father is still very fond of meringues."

Colonel Pinner heard that time, heard and brooded, looking Cyril up and down.

"What an esstrordinary thing!" said old Grandfather Pinner. "What an esstrordinary thing to come all this way here to tell me!"

And Cyril felt it *was*.

"Yes, I shall send Cyril the watch," said Josephine.

"That would be very nice," said Constantia. "I seem to remember last time he came there was some little trouble about the time."

X

They were interrupted by Kate bursting through the door in her usual fashion, as though she had discovered some secret panel in the wall.

"Fried or boiled?" asked the bold voice.

Fried or boiled? Josephine and Constantia were quite bewildered for the moment. They could hardly take it in.

"Fried or boiled what, Kate?" asked Josephine, trying to begin to concentrate.

Kate gave a loud sniff. "Fish."

"Well, why didn't you say so immediately?" Josephine reproached her gently. "How could you expect us to understand, Kate? There are a great many things in this world, you know, which are fried or boiled." And after such a display of courage she said quite brightly to Constantia, "Which do you prefer, Con?"

"I think it might be nice to have it fried," said Constantia. "On the other hand, of course boiled fish is very nice. I think I prefer both equally well...Unless you...In that case—"

"I shall fry it," said Kate, and she bounced back leaving their door open and slamming the door of her kitchen.

Josephine gazed at Constantia; she raised her pale eyebrows until they rippled away into her pale hair. She got up. She said in a very lofty, imposing way, "Do you mind following me into the drawing-room, Constantia? I've something of great importance to discuss with you."

For it was always to the drawing room they retired when they wanted to talk over Kate.

Josephine closed the door meaningly. "Sit down, Constantia," she said, still very grand. She might have been receiving Constantia for the first time. And Con looked round vaguely for a chair, as though she felt indeed quite a stranger.

"Now the question is," said Josephine, bending forward, "whether we shall keep her or not."

"That is the question," agreed Constantia.

"And this time," said Josephine firmly, "we must come to a definite decision."

Constantia looked for a moment as though she might begin going over all the other times, but she pulled herself together and said, "Yes, Jug."

"You see, Con," explained Josephine, "everything is so changed now." Constantia looked up quickly. "I mean," went on Josephine, "we're not dependent on Kate as we were." And she blushed faintly. "There's not father to cook for."

"That is perfectly true," agreed Constantia. "Father certainly doesn't want any cooking now, whatever else—"

Josephine broke in sharply, "You're not sleepy, are you, Con?"

"Sleepy, Jug?" Constantia was wide-eyed.

"Well, concentrate more," said Josephine sharply, and she returned to the subject. "What it comes to is, if we did"—and this she barely breathed, glancing at the door—"give Kate notice"—she raised her voice again—"we could manage our own food."

"Why not?" cried Constantia. She couldn't help smiling. The idea was so exciting. She clasped her hands. "What should we live on, Jug?"

"Oh, eggs in various forms!" said Jug, lofty again. "And, besides, there are all the cooked foods."

"But I've always heard," said Constantia, "they are considered so very expensive."

"Not if one buys them in moderation," said Josephine. But she tore herself away from this fascinating bypath and dragged Constantia after her.

"What we've got to decide now, however, is whether we really do trust Kate or not."

Constantia leaned back. Her flat little laugh flew from her lips.

"Isn't it curious, Jug," said she, "that just on this one subject I've never been able to quite make up my mind?"

XI

She never had. The whole difficulty was to prove anything. How did one prove things, how could one? Suppose Kate had stood in front of her and deliberately made a face. Mightn't she very well have been in pain? Wasn't it impossible, at any rate, to ask Kate if she was making a face at her? If Kate answered "No"—and of course she would say "No"—what a position! How undignified! Then again Constantia suspected, she was almost certain that Kate went to her chest of drawers when she and Josephine were out, not to take things but to spy. Many times she had come back to find her amethyst cross in the most unlikely places, under her lace ties or on top of her evening Bertha. More than once she had laid a trap for Kate. She had arranged things in a special order and then called Josephine to witness.

"You see, Jug?"

"Quite, Con."

"Now we shall be able to tell."

But, oh dear, when she did go to look, she was as far off from a proof as ever! If anything was displaced, it might so very well have happened as she closed the drawer; a jolt might have done it so easily.

"You come, Jug, and decide. I really can't. It's too difficult."

But after a pause and a long glare Josephine would sigh, "Now you've put the doubt into my mind, Con, I'm sure I can't tell myself."

"Well, we can't postpone it again," said Josesephine. "If we postpone it this time—"

XII

But at that moment in the street below a barrel organ struck up. Josephine and Constantia sprang to their feet together.

"Run, Con," said Josephine. "Run quickly. There's sixpence on the—"

Then they remembered. It didn't matter. They would never have to stop the organ grinder again. Never again would she and Constantia be told to make that monkey take his noise somewhere else. Never would sound that loud, strange bellow when father thought they were not hurrying enough. The organ grinder might play there all day and the stick would not thump.

It never will thump again,
It never will thump again,

played the barrel organ.

What was Constantia thinking? She had such a strange smile; she looked different. She couldn't be going to cry.

"Jug, Jug," said Constantia softly, pressing her hands together. "Do you know what day it is? It's Saturday. It's a week today, a whole week."

A week since father died,
A week since father died,

cried the barrel organ. And Josephine, too, forgot to be practical and sensible; she smiled faintly, strangely. On the Indian carpet there fell a square of sunlight, pale red; it came and went and came—and stayed, deepened—until it shone almost golden.

"The sun's out," said Josephine, as though it really mattered.

A perfect fountain of bubbling notes shook from the barrel organ, round, bright notes, carelessly scattered.

Constantia lifted her big, cold hands as if to catch them, and then her hands fell again. She walked over to the mantelpiece to her favorite Buddha. And the stone and gilt image, whose smile always gave her such a queer feeling, almost a pain and yet a pleasant pain, seemed today to be more than smiling. He knew something; he had a secret. "I know something that you don't know," said her Buddha. Oh, what was it, what could it be? And yet she had always felt there was...something.

The sunlight pressed through the windows, thieved its way in, flashed its light over the furniture and the photographs. Josephine watched it. When it came to mother's photograph, the enlargement over the piano, it lingered as though puzzled to find so little remained of mother, except the earrings shaped like tiny pagodas and a black feather boa. Why did the photographs of dead people always fade so? wondered Josephine. As soon as a person was dead their photograph died too. But, of course, this one of mother was very old. It was thirty-five years old. Josephine remembered standing on a chair and pointing out that feather boa to Constantia and telling her that it was a snake that had killed their mother in Ceylon.... Would everything have been different if mother hadn't died? She didn't see why. Aunt Florence had lived with them until they had left school, and they had moved three times and had their yearly holiday and...and there'd been changes of servants, of course.

Some little sparrows, young sparrows they sounded, chirped on the window-ledge. Yeep—eyeep—yeep. But Josephine felt they were not sparrows, not on the window-ledge. It was inside her, that queer little crying noise. Yeep—eyeep—yeep. Ah, what was it crying, so weak and forlorn?

If mother had lived, might they have married?

But there had been nobody for them to marry. There had been father's Anglo-Indian friends before he quarrelled with them. But after that she and Constantia never met a single man except clergymen. How did one meet men? Or even if they'd met them, how could they have got to know men well enough to be more than strangers? One read of people having adventures, being followed, and so on. But nobody had ever followed Constantia and her. Oh yes, there had been one year at Eastbourne a mysterious man at their boardinghouse who had put a note on the jug of hot water outside their bedroom door! But by the time Connie had found it the steam had made the writing too faint to read; they couldn't even make out to which of them it was addressed. And he had left next day. And that was all. The rest had been looking after father, and at the same time keeping out of father's way. But now? But now? The thieving sun touched Josephine gently. She lifted her face. She was drawn over to the window by gentle beams....

Until the barrel organ stopped playing Constantia stayed before the Buddha, wondering, but not as usual, not vaguely. This time her wonder was like longing. She remembered the times she had come in here, crept out of bed in her nightgown when the moon was full, and lain on the floor with her arms outstretched, as though she was crucified. Why? The big, pale moon had made her do it. The horrible dancing figures on the carved screen had leered at her and she hadn't minded. She remembered too how, whenever they were at the seaside, she had gone off by herself and got as close to the sea as she could, and sung something, something she had made up, while she gazed all over that restless water. There had been this other life, running out, bringing things home in bags, getting things on approval, discussing them with Jug, and taking them back to get more things on approval, and arranging father's trays and trying not to annoy father. But it all seemed to have happened in a kind of tunnel. It wasn't real. It was only when she came out of the tunnel into the moonlight or by the sea or into a thunderstorm that she really felt herself. What did it mean? What was it she was always wanting? What did it all lead to? Now? Now?

She turned away from the Buddha with one of her vague gestures. She went over to where Josephine was standing. She wanted to say something to Josephine, something frightfully important, about—about the future and what...

"Don't you think perhaps—" she began.

But Josephine interrupted her. "I was wondering if now" she murmured. They stopped; they waited for each other.

"Go on, Con," said Josephine.

"No, no, Jug; after you," said Constantia.

"No, say what you were going to say. You began," said Josephine.

"I...I'd rather hear what you were going to say first," said Constantia.

"Don't be absurd, Con."

"Really, Jug."

"Connie!"

"Oh, *Jug*!"

A pause. Then Constantia said faintly, "I can't say what I was going to say, Jug, because I've forgotten what it was...that I was going to say."

Josephine was silent for a moment. She stared at a big cloud where the sun had been. Then she replied shortly, "I've forgotten too."

Index to Volumes I and II